A PROPER *Scoundrel*

OTHER BOOKS AND AUDIOBOOKS
BY ESTHER HATCH

Roses of Feldstone

A Proper Scandal

A Proper Charade

All Hearts Come Home for Christmas (contributor)

A PROPER *Scoundrel*

a novel

from award-winning author

Esther Hatch

Covenant Communications, Inc.

For Greg

Thanks for making me laugh for the first few years of marriage. I've heard all your jokes now, so please stop telling them.

(Also, thanks for writing that for me when I couldn't think of the proper way to immortalize our love. You still make me laugh, and I'm still sorry I gave you mono.)

Cover image: *Handsome Aristocratic Man Holding Hat While Standing in Suit* © LightField Studios / Shutterstock.com
Interior image: Lily Flowers Hand-drawn Illustration © Nataleana / iStock.com

Cover and interior design by Kimberly Kay copyright © 2021 by Covenant Communications, Inc.

Published by Covenant Communications, Inc.
American Fork, Utah

Printed in the United States of America
First Printing: May 2021

27 26 25 24 23 22 21 10 9 8 7 6 5 4 3 2 1

ISBN: 978-1-52441-698-0

ACKNOWLEDGMENTS

THIS BOOK DIDN'T COME EASILY, but it did come with a lot of help along the way. Thank you to all of my friends and family who read portions of this book as well as those who read all of it at various points of completion: Paula Anderson, Alice Patron, Laura Rupper, Audrey Mangum, Kasey Stockton, Mindy Strunk, Anneka Walker, Julie Donaldson, Deborah Hathaway, Mandy Biesinger, Joanna Barker, Megan Walker, Sally Britton, Heidi Maxfield, Karin Smith, McCall Shoff, Lisa Kendrick, April Young, Kim Dubois, Clarissa Kae, Greg Hatch, and Loretta Porter.

Also, a big thanks to the Facebook group Writing Sprints; so often I relied on you to get me working when I needed to. Clarissa Kae and Melanie Jacobson have been motivating sprint partners as well, rising to the call of Zoom sprints when everything was shutting down because of the pandemic (Remember Covid-19? Is it over yet? I hope so.) and I still needed some author interaction.

So many of you gave me great ideas; some I used, and some I wished I could have used. I loved hearing them all the same. Thank you for making this story better, and for believing in it even when I had my doubts.

Thank you to my immediate as well as extended family members; my writing has now become a part of our lives, and it isn't always easy, but I'm grateful for the love and support I get from all of you. I could not continue without it.

Thank you to my amazing team at Covenant. No one needs an editor more than I do, and Ashley Gebert does a fantastic job making my stories shine. Kim Miller and my previous design teams—thanks for amazing covers. I know for a fact the quality of those designs have sold many books. I'll try to keep writing books that are as beautiful on the inside as they are on the outside. And to my publicist, Amy Parker, thank you for sharing my books with the world as well as answering my weird panic questions during releases.

I also need to thank Shakespeare for providing a quote for all my previous books. Benedick had some amazing ones I could have used for Lord Bryant. But in the end, this one needed to start with a psalm.

Thank you, Heavenly Father, for turning me to the path of writing and for letting me see each book as the miracle it is.

And thank you, Lord Bryant. You started out as a creepy old man and a plot device, but finally, when I realized there needed to be more to you (oh, and that you were hot), you exploded on the page in a way no other character ever has. It has been an honor to tell your story.

PRAISE FOR ESTHER HATCH

A Proper Scoundrel

"I found *A Proper Scoundrel* by Esther Hatch to be everything the book description said and more. This book is the perfect example of a romantic historical Christian novel. *A Proper Scoundrel* has all of the elements needed to make this book a number one winner. Esther Hatch has given us characters that are impossible not to like, a plot that keeps moving forward, and she has a really good fix on the events and times of the day. To tell you more would reveal too much of the story that you must read for yourself and enjoy. I highly recommend *A Proper Scoundrel* to fans of historical romances."

—Readers' Favorite Five Star Review

"I have read and loved every one of Esther Hatch's novels, so of course I looked forward to *A Proper Scoundrel.* But oh my goodness, it exceeded every one of my expectations! Diana is smart and admirable and stuck in a bind . . . Everton is wounded and noble and surprising in every way as he (somewhat unwillingly) comes to Diana's aid. Together, they're perfection. Between the witty banter, the breathtaking romance, and a plot that kept me turning pages, *A Proper Scoundrel* is Esther Hatch's best book yet!"

—Melissa Tagg, *Christy Award* winning author of *Now and Then and Always*

"Esther Hatch's wonderful writing shines once again in *A Proper Scoundrel.* Readers will adore Diana, fall in love with Lord Bryant, and be swept away by this enchanting romance."

—Joanna Barker, *Otherwise Engaged*

"With Lord Bryant's dark past and Diana Barton's hope for the future, Esther Hatch has gifted historical romance enthusiasts a love story that is heartwarming, beautifully written, and extremely satisfying. Diana's quick wit and Lord Bryant's dry sense of humor are delightfully pitted against each other, making their romance entertaining, and keeps us turning the pages to find out what happens next. The attention to historical detail blends perfectly with this clever work of fiction, engaging readers of the genre and inviting them back to the early days of railroad empires. Esther Hatch is known for writing heroines meeting the challenges of their era head on, and this novel is no exception. She's also known for writing the perfect kiss in her books. Spoilers: She's done it again."

—Sally Britton, best-selling author of the Inglewood Series

"Stick out your pinky finger and flip the pages for a properly delightful romance! I could not put it down. It was the sweetest of romances for my favorite scoundrel.

Miss Diana Barton is tired of men trying to propose marriage while she's working on railroad business. Her solution? Ruin her reputation and who better than with the rakish Baron Bryant. But Lord Bryant is not at all what she expected and maybe there's more to his story than meets the eye. Although, what meets the eye is pretty nice too! #wink

Just the right amount of swoon for a sweet romance. Author Esther Hatch does an amazing job of building up the tension and bringing the two leads together in a satisfying and endearing way. I loved the business-minded, capable, strong heroine! This book exceeded all my high expectations."

—Samantha Hastings, *The Invention of Sophie Carter*

A Proper Charade

"The irony of the situation and the humorous scenes are entertaining."

—Historical Novel Society

"Chock full of dreamy heroes, touching stories, and delightful humor, Ms. Hatch's books remind us why we read romance in the first place."

—Jennifer Moore, *Whitney Award* winning author

A Proper Scandal

"*A Proper Scandal* is funny, sweet, and romantic and it has a large twist that I never saw coming. I really enjoy Esther Hatch's writing style. I love her characters; even the side characters are interesting and well developed."

—Timeless Novels

"Another winner from author Esther Hatch! She knows how to write a captivating story, and I was thoroughly entertained all the way through. I loved Grace and Nate and the hilarious predicaments they got themselves into. I laughed out loud several times, and just enjoyed being immersed in the beautiful writing. A lovely historical romance that I highly recommend."

—Joanna Barker, *Otherwise Engaged*

The Roses of Feldstone

"*The Roses of Feldstone* is the perfect blend of charm, wit, and romance. Rose and William will draw you in from the first page until the very last word. All the way around, a lovely read."

—Heather B. Moore, *USA Today* best-selling author

"Esther Hatch writes swoony romance with laugh-out-loud dialogue and unforgettable characters. Once you read one of her books, you will want to read them all!"

—Anneka Walker, *The Masked Baron*

"Weeping may endure for a night, but joy cometh in the morning."
—Psalm 30:5

CHAPTER 1

There were two types of men who walked through the door of Diana Barton's office on Rochester Street—legitimate men of business and those who utterly wasted her time. Mr. Broadcreek was one of the latter and the worst of the lot.

Diana Barton's eyes slid to the pocket watch she kept in her partially opened desk drawer. Running both her brother Nate's and the Richardsons' railroad companies would have been much easier if word hadn't gotten out that an unmarried young woman was now the owner of Richardson Rail. Diana would have pushed Mr. Broadcreek out of her office an hour ago if it weren't for the fact that he had more members of Parliament as investors than any other man in the railroad business.

Or women in the railroad business, for that matter. But as far as Diana knew, she was currently the only one of those, and as of yet, she had exactly zero members of Parliament under her thumb. An unfortunate oversight when every new line needed an act of Parliament to be passed before the first railroad tie could be laid.

"My last line was finished two weeks ahead of schedule," Mr. Broadcreek bragged, his mustache rolling about the top of his mouth like a brown caterpillar as he spoke. He scooted his chair closer to her desk and leaned forward. Diana leaned back. Mr. Broadcreek's mouth belonged as far away from hers as possible. At least he hadn't proposed again. She was running out of ways to politely say no.

She still had an hour to get her payment into the ballast office. She would suffer Mr. Broadcreek's ramblings for only five more minutes. Then she would make him leave, even if she had to resort to a fit of the vapors. He had already been rambling for an hour and twenty minutes. Surely he couldn't go on much longer.

As if to prove her wrong, Mr. Broadcreek's mouth continued to operate undeterred. "So you see, Miss Barton, I know you felt my assessment of Richardson Rail was undervalued when I offered to buy it from Mrs. Richardson, but I truly felt my expertise and experience would add greatly to its value. Not to mention, after a few well-placed questions, I discovered you didn't pay any more for it than I had offered. You cannot still hold that against me when you did the exact thing yourself."

Diana gritted her teeth. She would have to fire Mrs. Richardson's solicitor. Nate's solicitor would never have divulged such secrets to anyone, let alone Mr. Broadcreek. "That is hardly the same. Mrs. Richardson and I are friends. When Mr. Richardson passed away, I promised I would help in any way possible."

His caterpillar mustache bunched to one side of his mouth. "By swindling her out of her railroad company and running it into the ground? How is that helpful?"

Diana grasped both sides of her chair. It was the first time he admitted that the price he had offered Charlotte for Richardson Rail was scandalously low, but she couldn't count that as a win while he defamed her ability to run the company.

"Mr. Broadcreek, one thing you can count on is that I won't be running Richardson Rail into the ground. Another thing you can count on is that Mrs. Richardson will not be swindled by me. Once I finish our current line and receive an act of Parliament to build another, Richardson Rail will be worth double what you offered to pay for it. She may no longer be an owner of Richardson Rail, but she still has a monetary interest in the company." Any profits Diana gained would be shared with Mrs. Richardson when Diana sold a much more valuable company. It would be enough for Charlotte to live comfortably on with her three children for the rest of her life.

Mr. Broadcreek coughed. "That is a lot for a young lady like yourself to accomplish alone. I could help you. It isn't as though I don't know my way around the railroad business."

Diana knew what he would want in exchange for his help—marriage. This was an even cheaper option for obtaining a railroad company than buying it for less than its value. But a middle-aged bachelor with only Diana's railroad company on his mind was the last type of man she would choose to marry. Only the husband could sign for a married woman after the vows were said, even if the company would technically belong to both of them. Mr. Broadcreek would never honor her agreement with Charlotte, which would most definitely make a swindler out of Diana.

"I've been running Richardson Rail for nearly a month now, and most of Barton Rail for several months before that. I'm quite certain I can manage."

"Are you positive?" Mr. Broadcreek pulled out a pocket watch and pursed his lips together. "Didn't you need to place an order for ballast today?"

Diana's heart stopped. Her eyes flew to her own watch, safe in the drawer, but it had only been a few minutes since she last checked. She still had an hour—plenty of time as long as Mr. Broadcreek left soon. "I do. In fact, I'm afraid I'm going to have to cut our conversation short so Mrs. Oliver and I can do that now."

Diana stood, and Mr. Broadcreek, ever the gentleman in all the ways that didn't matter, followed suit. Diana walked to the coatrack by the front of her office and reached for her cloak. Mrs. Oliver was tidying up her desk in order to leave for the day. Mr. Broadcreek put his meaty hands out to help Diana with her cloak, but she pretended not to notice.

He lowered his hands. "London Ballast & Company closed an hour ago."

Diana pulled her bonnet off the rack with more force than necessary. He couldn't be right. The ballast office closed at six. Mr. Broadcreek had wasted hours of her time on multiple occasions, but she had never let it impact a deadline. She simply stayed later until she got everything done. When all of London was watching and waiting for her to fail, there was no room for error. "I believe you must have the time wrong. It is not yet five o'clock."

"It isn't the time that is your problem; it is the day."

Mr. Broadcreek was making no sense.

Mrs. Oliver came up beside Diana and reached for her coat. "Thursday?"

Mr. Broadcreek kept his eyes on Diana even though Mrs. Oliver had asked the question. "Tomorrow is St. Andrew's Day."

St. Andrew's Day? What did it matter if it was? "St. Andrew's Day is a Scottish holiday. It should have nothing to do with my ballast."

Mr. Broadcreek's grin was growing broader with every word. "This is the reason a husband would be an asset to you, Miss Barton, especially one who does business with London Ballast. The owner, Mr. Boyd, is Scottish and proud. He always closes the shop early the day before St. Andrew's."

It couldn't be true. She never left things to the last minute, but each day, more and more men had come to her office and wasted her time. Deadlines were getting harder to meet, but she would never actually miss one.

"That cannot be right."

"Go check for yourself." Mr. Broadcreek put an arm out. "I would be happy to escort you."

And have him gloat over her humiliation if he was correct? Never. Her reputation as a businesswoman would be shot if she couldn't complete the line on schedule. Without an upstanding business record, would Parliament even grant her an act to build another line? Despite the chill in the office, a bead of sweat formed at the back of her neck.

"No, Mrs. Oliver will accompany me as always. Perhaps you are wrong."

"For your sake, I hope I am," Mr. Broadcreek said, but his eyes gleamed as he said it.

Diana opened the door and motioned for him to leave—something she should have done over an hour ago. She shut the door behind him and bent over, taking deep breaths through her nose.

"Would it be so bad if the order was late?" Mrs. Oliver asked, hastily putting on her coat.

Diana pressed her hands to her temples. "I could rush the shipping."

"So it wouldn't be so bad." Mrs. Oliver plopped her bonnet over her graying hair.

"We don't have the capital to pay for rushed shipping on an order that large. I used most of what I earned from Barton Rail to buy Richardson Rail. And the Richardson Rail budget is slim until we get that line up and running."

"Well then," Mrs. Oliver tied the knot of her bonnet under her chin, "hopefully Mr. Broadcreek is wrong."

Diana peered through the front window. He was gone. "We will talk on the way. If they really are closed, we will need to come up with a plan to raise a substantial amount of money by Monday."

They had not gone a block before Mr. Keaton with his hair freshly combed and a flower in his buttonhole stepped in front of them.

Diana didn't acknowledge him. Quickly pivoting, she didn't even slow her step. She had declined his company on her walk home three times this week, and she didn't have the time to decline him again. Mrs. Oliver muttered an apology under her breath and then caught up to Diana.

With each step toward the ballast office, Diana's stomach tightened. Blast every single one of those men. If they wanted a rail company so badly, they should learn to work and build one. That was what Nate had done.

Unfortunately, there weren't many men like her brother around London.

Mrs. Oliver's steps matched her own. "You could always ask Mr. Barton for some money."

"There is no time for that. He is in Baimbury, and we would need the capital in just a few days." Ask her brother Nate? Never. He was finally living his dream of bringing their estate in Baimbury back to productivity. It was Diana's turn to shoulder the burdens in London. If she made the slightest reference to having troubles, Nate would be on the first train back to London.

Besides, then she would have to tell him she had bought Richardson Rail, and he might think running both companies would be too much for her. It wasn't. Nate and Mr. Richardson had both done an excellent job growing them. It was up to her to simply keep them running. She could do that.

Nate had never had to deal with women chasing him simply because he owned a railroad company.

"It may be time to ask Mr. Barton to return." Mrs. Oliver matched her pace, even though she was triple Diana's age. What would Diana do without Mrs. Oliver? She wanted the rail line to succeed almost as much as Diana did. She pushed down the niggle of worry that Mrs. Oliver was right. London wasn't set up for women to run businesses, at least not without a man to protect them. "We could use him to intimidate all those fools who keep coming into the office."

"Not yet. I'm not going to send for him to come back just yet."

"Then you might just need to pick one of the men coming into the office and allow him to court you. It would turn off most of the others. You would finally have the time you need to get everything done."

Pick one of those pretentious men? Even if she started a courtship with one of them, the rest wouldn't be easily persuaded to leave her alone. Not unless he was a fearsome man, and what would she do with a fearsome man once she was done with him?

Diana quickened her pace. The payment for the ballast was heavy in her reticule, and it bounced against her leg with each step. She prayed the purse would be empty on their way home.

Rain slashed down, filling the streets of London with muddy rivulets and puddles. Diana pulled her bonnet low over her face and sprang from her hired carriage. The last of her jewelry—the emerald necklace she had managed to save even when Nate was selling off everything he could get his hands on to start his railroad business—was gone. It had been her grandmother's, but if it meant the ballast would be delivered on time, the sacrifice was worth it. People were more important than jewels, and Charlotte was counting on her.

"Rather late for a young lady to be out on the street alone." Diana jerked her head up and landed awkwardly on the side of her foot from the puddle she had been hopping over. She would know that mustache anywhere. No amount of rain could alter or disguise it.

Mr. Broadcreek.

Diana had spent the past three days fixing the problem he had so happily witnessed. It was late, the sun was already set, she was wet, and she simply wanted to drop into bed.

"Mr. Broadcreek, what are you doing here?"

"I was hoping to escort you home."

The door to Mrs. Richardson's house—Diana's home for the past three months—was exactly ten feet away. "I believe I can manage that myself."

"Handling things yourself isn't always the best option though. Not when you have someone willing to help."

"Nate is in Baimbury; the estate and his wife need him there. I'm perfectly capable of handling this on my own. If I weren't, Nate wouldn't have left me in charge."

Mr. Broadcreek smoothed down his mustache and stepped forward. "I didn't mean your brother."

Something snapped deep inside Diana's chest. It was bad enough that men were coming to her office. This was her home for at least as long as Mrs. Richardson needed her.

"Do you mean like a suitor?"

Mr. Broadcreek paused, his body frozen. "I could mean that."

She could see the hunger in his eyes. After weeks of wearing her down, he thought he was finally going to win.

Impossible.

Diana smiled. "I have one of those."

Mr. Broadcreek's brow furrowed. If he asked any questions, she would have no answers for him. She needed to be out of his presence immediately, but the door to Mrs. Richardson's home would be barred. She would have to knock before being let in, and she refused to spend another moment in Mr. Broadcreek's presence.

"And you are right—he has been very helpful. In fact, I have one more thing I need to speak with him about tonight." Diana spun around and hopped back onto the step of the carriage. The driver looked at her in surprise, but with a glance at Mr. Broadcreek, he gave her a subtle nod.

"Miss Barton," Mr. Broadcreek called out from behind her, "you cannot possibly be visiting with a man after dark. It would absolutely ruin your reputation." Diana didn't pause; she flung herself into the carriage. Better to ruin her reputation than Richardson Rail. "No man in London will want you." Mr. Broadcreek's voice was low with warning.

No man in London would want her if her reputation was ruined? She sat down on the upholstered seat, and the driver came behind her to shut the door. Rain still pounded on the carriage, but at least she was away from the noise of Mr. Broadcreek. She leaned back and rested her head on the wall of the carriage. A sort of calm washed over her. The mere idea of not a single man wanting her stilled something inside her. Mr. Broadcreek had thought to issue a warning, but instead, he had offered her a slice of hope.

A ruined reputation wasn't the end of the world. The men she had met in London so far were all ridiculously pushy. She would like to marry someday. She couldn't look at Nate and Grace and not want the same happiness for herself. The carriage pulled forward into the night. She rubbed her temples and took a deep, steadying breath. When she wanted to marry, she would simply return to Baimbury. She didn't need to marry for wealth or status. She could find a nice man and settle down far from London once this railroad business was behind her.

A few streets and one turn later, the driver stopped the carriage. "Where are we going, miss?" he called over the rain. How was it that this middle-aged carriage driver was more considerate than any of the gentlemen of her acquaintance? He had waited until Mr. Broadcreek was well away from her to even ask where she was going, and now he sat in the pouring rain awaiting her answer.

She needed a man who would ruin her reputation and not want her railroad in return—one who wouldn't force a marriage on her or take their charade seriously.

A name had been floating in her mind ever since she had declared herself in a courtship. The two of them had only met twice. He may not even remember who she was. But he was impossible to forget. Her hand shook, but she rubbed it down the side of her dress. He was simply a man like any other in London. Surely she could handle one man if the alternative was multiple men every day.

She called an address to the driver. Raindrops pounded, but the hackney didn't move. Had he not heard her through the window? She leaned forward to call out again, but before she could, he answered, "Yes, miss."

Based on the pause, even he must know whose home address she had given him. As the carriage jerked forward, she pinched her nose and breathed deeply. Her dress was a disaster, her bonnet ruined, and she hadn't slept well for days.

This was not at all how she had expected to see Lord Bryant again.

CHAPTER 2

A KNOCK ON THE DOOR of Everton's study at this hour never boded well. His servants knew better than to disturb him during his brandy time. And he had no family. Everton's parents were dead, his mother and father both taken by the same disease not long after arranging his disastrous marriage. Always separated in life, it was odd they died within days of each other.

Rachel had been gone four years. Not that she would have ever knocked on his door, even if she were still alive. Their marriage had only lasted a year, only six months of which she had suffered living under the same roof as him. A long line of unhappy marriages was immortalized in portraits in the corridor just outside his study. He hadn't had time to commission one of him and Rachel, which meant the Baron Bryant portraits would end with his. As they should. Enough misery had taken place in this home to last several more generations, but hopefully when his cousin took residence, all of that would change.

Everton stared at the amber liquid in his glass, contemplating whether or not to answer. He poured himself a brandy every night, but he never drank it. He had spent over a year drinking, but all it had given him was a headache each morning. Two years had passed since he had touched anything but the weakest of wines. It was a waste to pour a glass each night only to watch it, but he didn't stop. Waste was something he was accustomed to, and something about the opaque nature of the liquid numbed him just by looking at it.

He may as well answer the knock, otherwise Nelson would stand outside his door waiting silently for the devil knows how long.

"What is it, Nelson?" Everton asked without hiding the growl that enveloped his voice. With no one to talk to, his voice became gravellier with each evening he didn't go out.

"Lord Bryant, you've a guest." His butler's voice was calm and collected, not that Nelson's demeanor ever revealed anything about who had the audacity to invade Everton's solitude. Nelson's voice had been calm and collected months ago, on the day Prime Minister Robert Peel had come for a social call.

Outside his window, a flash of lightning brightened the sky. He ran through the possibilities of who would brave a storm in the darkness. Most likely it was a second or third cousin who had lost his shirt at the tables. He never should have helped out his devil cousin last year; it was as if he were advertising his willingness to bail out anyone who shared a drop of blood with him. Fortunately for Everton, there weren't many people left alive who shared his blood.

He would have to make an example of the poor fellow outside. Otherwise, word would get out that he was willing to entertain during his liquor-watching time. "Who is it?"

Nelson cracked open the door. "It is a young lady, sir. A soaking wet one."

"At this hour? What does she want?"

Nelson furrowed his brows, a strong reaction for him. "I didn't think to ask. I'll return shortly."

Nelson hadn't thought to ask? A rare slip for his butler. Everton ran his hand down his face. Who would brave a night like this for a social call? Lady Emily? There was no possibility her father would allow her out of her home at this hour. A few other names came to mind, but most of them were unlikely. Whoever she was, and whatever this woman wanted, it wouldn't be respectable. The prospect may have amused him a few years ago, but now, and truthfully even then, he simply wanted to be alone.

Nelson had left the door slightly ajar, so he didn't knock when he returned but instead slipped inside the study without opening the door all the way.

Everton waited a moment for him to speak, but Nelson only stood there. "Well," Everton said, "what does she want?"

Nelson tugged on his neckcloth—a motion Everton had never seen him do—and cleared his throat.

"Out with it." At no time had Everton needed to ask Nelson twice for anything. What was wrong with him tonight? "If it is another wretch claiming to have borne a child of mine, we both know that isn't true."

"That's not it," Nelson said with a shake of his head and a glance sideways. He leaned forward and lowered his voice. "But I am afraid you aren't far off. You are thirty-one." He furrowed his brows. "Perhaps it is time you stopped all this nonsense."

As if he could. That *nonsense* was the only thing that helped him feel alive, useful, and anything other than a complete leech on Society. His age had nothing to do with it.

"Just tell me what she wants."

"She has come for . . ." Nelson cleared his throat again.

"For what?"

"A. . . a man, sir. One to . . ." He shifted. "Ruin her. Apparently, your reputation has preceded you."

A man to ruin her? Had Mrs. Cuthbert sent her? Mrs. Cuthbert should have known better. He was occupied with Lady Emily at the moment. Mrs. Cuthbert had arranged it herself. "Please tell me you didn't bring her to the drawing room. Transactions like these should not be performed at night. Send her away."

Nelson shifted uncomfortably. "I didn't send her to the drawing room."

"Thank the heavens you had the sense for that. What was her name? I can arrange to meet her in town if she is desperate, I suppose, but the timing—did she say it was urgent?"

The door to his office swung open, and a soaking-wet, dark-haired woman stepped inside. Her dress clung to her legs and arms, and her drenched bonnet drooped over half her face. What the devil?

Nelson pulled on his neckcloth a second time. "She wouldn't go to the drawing room, sir. She thought you might not see her if she went there."

She was deuced right—he wouldn't have. The woman was dripping on his Parisian rug.

"Lord Bryant," she said in a voice slightly familiar and out of breath. Her bonnet still hung forward on her face, shrouding her in shadows. Her hand lay still on his study door as if she were afraid she would be pushed out and it would be slammed closed. A fair assumption. Where had he heard her voice before? He met an excessive number of women in London. Her shape was decent. More than decent. Tall and slender with well-made but unembellished clothing. She didn't seem like the type of woman who would need his help.

She could be here to actually be ruined. It wouldn't be the first time, but it would be the first time a lady found him in his study. It had taken him two years of refusing visits before cards stopped coming to his home. Disturbing Lord Bryant at his home was an offense not easily overcome. Someone should have told that to this chit.

"It seems you have an advantage over me," Everton said.

She released the door and swiped her bonnet off her face with the back of her forearm. It fell back and dangled behind her by the strings, making her look like a willful child. Her eyes widened at his open shirt and disheveled hair, but how had she expected to find him at this late hour? Sitting home alone in his blacks? Despite the general dampness of her clothing and face, she was young and fresh and brought with her a light that didn't belong in his home. "Miss Diana Barton," she said. "We have met on a few occasions."

Nate Barton's sister? His eyes narrowed. Why would she need to associate with a rogue like himself? The few times he had seen her, she had been a perfectly presentable young lady.

"So we have. And yet, none of those situations led me to believe I would one day find you dripping late at night in my study. Did Mrs. Cuthbert give you my address? She shouldn't have."

Miss Barton's bold countenance was broken by a few unmeasured blinks. Up until he had mentioned Mrs. Cuthbert, she had stood her ground, her chin jutting out as if she belonged in a man's home on such a night as this.

"Are you speaking of Mrs. Lucinda Cuthbert? I hardly know her," she scoffed. In *his* study. "Besides, I didn't need anyone's help to find you. Everyone knows where the Baron Bryant lives."

So Mrs. Cuthbert hadn't sent her. That changed things. "So, deep into the night—on your own—you decided to come to my home and charge into my study?"

That blasted chin finally lowered a slight margin, and a delicate blush rose up her neck. "I wouldn't classify the time as *deep into the night*."

"But it is much too late to be here."

"I didn't see another way to ask. I am out of time and a letter seemed . . ."

He raised an eyebrow. Miss Barton and her flashing copper eyes were proving to be a welcome distraction. "Inappropriate?" he asked.

She shook her head, the movement causing a dark, damp lock of hair to slide along her neck. "Unlikely to produce the desired outcome."

"Which is . . . ?" He hadn't stood at her arrival, and his leg was starting to twitch. He pushed it down with his hand. His mother wasn't here to be disappointed in him, and Miss Barton hadn't come because he was known to act like a gentleman.

"As your butler said, I've come to ruin my reputation—bad enough that no man in London will want me. Or at the very least, that they will all leave me to work in peace."

Work? What type of work required a ruined reputation and a desire for men to leave her alone?

"You've likely already ruined whatever reputation you have by coming here."

Miss Barton shook her head. "No, that won't be enough. I need to be thoroughly ruined. And not just for tonight. What I need is some sort of ongoing ruination for the next two months."

Thoroughly ruined? His twitching leg went still. Nelson shifted uncomfortably but knew better than to speak. Miss Barton held her ground like a Greek statue. What exactly was she asking? Did she understand how she sounded? Any other man in his position would have dismissed his butler and taken advantage of her on the spot. It would be so simple to snuff out that light she had no business bringing into a home where only darkness belonged.

He cleared his throat. "And if I don't agree, what will you do?" The last thing he needed was the guilt of knowing another young woman's life was ruined because of him. "Find a more willing man to visit this evening?"

She shook her head once again, and the same wayward tendril bounced against her pale skin. "No, I'm quite convinced you are the only man who is suitable for what I have in mind."

He slid his chair away from his desk and stood. The ground swayed beneath him for a moment, but it steadied. He needed more sleep. Good sleep. How long had it been since he'd had a full night of rest?

Years.

He stepped around his desk and crossed to the middle of the room, close enough that he could see the fire in Miss Barton's eyes. They were similar in color to his brandy, familiar and deep because of it. It was as if he had been staring into them long before she had arrived. "Miss Barton, your timing is unfortunate." He gave her a smile. Brick walls would only encourage a woman like Miss Barton, who traipsed through London and stormed his study. Despite her bold claims of wanting to be ruined, she held herself aloft like a lady. He could scare away most proper young ladies with honeyed words and phrases. And when those didn't work, a simple touch would do the trick. The idea of Lord Bryant, the rake, was often enticing but only while he remained a vague threat. "You see . . ." He stepped forward, bringing himself well within an arm's reach of her. "I only ruin young ladies before dinner." His arm lifted, his forefinger pointed toward her throat, ready to caress that delicate curl of hair. He stopped himself and pulled his hand back. "You will have to come back tomorrow."

Instead of backing away, one of her feet slid forward, and her hand went to her waist. Her lips curled into a smile. "I am busy during the day."

"And I am busy during the night. It seems this ongoing ruination you have planned for us simply isn't in the cards. Our schedules won't permit it."

Miss Barton's chest rose and fell, and a small crease folded between her dark, sweeping eyebrows. "I wouldn't take up much of your time, just a meeting here and there to cause a bit of a scandal. Heaven knows you have had plenty of those."

"Not with the sister of a man I respect and who manages to tolerate me. Your brother only just started allowing me to invest with him, and the return on that investment has been phenomenal. I'll not put it at risk."

She popped out one of her shapely hips and raised an eyebrow, the furrow long gone. "Nate doesn't really tolerate you."

"He takes my money." Which was really all that mattered. He didn't want to form an attachment to the man. He needed no one's respect.

Miss Barton smiled, and if he thought she looked confident before, her full smile changed her into a woman with no fear. "*I* take your money, Lord Bryant." She leaned forward. "I've been running the investment side of the business for six months. If Nate knew I was allowing you to invest with us, he would put a stop to it."

Everton cocked his head to one side. *That* was an interesting tidbit. Miss Barton was full of surprises this evening. But even still, she didn't belong here. No woman did. Perhaps it was time he surprised her. His eyes met her insistent ones. Her hand flew back to the interior handle of the door, her elbow locked straight as if announcing her intentions to stay. If she was so determined, there was only one thing to do.

He leaned back so he could see all of her. Slowly and deliberately, he took in her figure. Even wet, and with a multitude of skirts to hide her shape, he still knew all the right places to pause in his assessment to cause a slow rise of a blush on her cheeks. It was one of his very few skills, and he was quite proud of it. Nothing in Miss Barton's demeanor suggested she actually wanted to be ruined. Despite coming to visit him unchaperoned, she was a young lady of moral uprightness if ever he saw one.

Which meant there was a very simple way to make her leave.

"You may leave, Nelson. I can hardly expect to ruin a lady with you around."

Miss Barton swallowed softly, the delicate movement bringing his eyes once again to her throat. How long had it been since his fingers had brushed a throat like that? Longer than it had been since he had slept well, of that much he was certain. The two weren't exactly unrelated.

"No," she said, her chin rising again. Her eyes did not leave his own. "Nelson, stay." Instead of shrinking or dashing out of the door, she stood taller and stepped closer to him.

He smiled. Miss Barton would be a challenge. He had a sudden desire to listen to her plan. He could use a diversion. But his situation with Lady Emily was tenuous at best, and he couldn't be seen showing interest in another woman.

Not yet.

He took a small step, closing the distance between the two of them. "He is my servant. Do you actually think he will listen to you over me?"

Nelson stood at attention. "I'll stay, miss."

Blast Nelson, the traitor. Everton would threaten to relieve him of his position, but Nelson would know he was bluffing.

His late-night intruder flashed Nelson a brilliant smile, the sad remains of which she turned to him. The small, unlikely spike of energy he felt as he gazed at her throat was gone, replaced by exhaustion deep in his bones. He wouldn't allow this woman, who gave broader smiles to his butler than to him, remain in his home another moment.

"Whatever it is you had planned, I don't agree to it."

Her eyes flashed back and forth between his, as if she could tell he was truly withdrawing. "I simply need you to come into my office a few times over the next two months and scare away the men that are constantly there." Her words came out in a rush.

"No."

"But they are ruining my business."

Protecting Miss Barton was her brother's responsibility. Everton had a responsibility to Lady Emily now, and he couldn't put that in jeopardy. Not for a woman who could take care of herself. "You have acted rashly by coming alone to my house at this time of night. If it is ruination you want, you have got it. You won't recover from this. If at some future point you wish to catch a husband, you should have left yourself plausible deniability at the very least. The *ton* can think the worst of you, but a husband never should. There is no way a well-known scoundrel like myself would allow a woman of the most delectable shape, so apparent in your wet clothing, to escape his house untouched. And truthfully, if you stay much longer, I will happily live up to my reputation."

For a moment, she stood her ground. A strange sensation opened in his chest—longing. His breath shortened as he waited for her verdict. By the heavens, if she stayed . . .

It happened then. All her pomp and determination melted away. One mention of actually being touched by him and she was suddenly darting her eyes to the door. He sighed and stepped away from the light this young lady had brought with her. He had no idea what had possessed her to think he would help, but at last, he had convinced her to leave. "Nelson, show the young lady out."

Nelson nodded, and this time, Miss Barton followed. She took two steps before changing her mind and spinning back around.

"It doesn't have to be for the full two months. Come once or twice; I could make that work if that is all you are willing to do."

Would the woman not leave? A burst of resentment flared in his chest. Didn't she know what kind of place this was? His home was not meant for a genteel woman like her. This was where gentle spirits came to die.

He rushed forward and placed a hand at the back of her neck, his thumb pressed against her throat. His touch was light, but her reaction was instantaneous. She flinched but didn't step away. Nelson stepped forward, but Everton gave him a look that made him retreat.

Miss Barton's throat jostled with a swallow, and her breathing quickened through a clenched jaw. She was determined enough to stand her ground even with his hand upon her.

A delicate young lady that despised his touch but allowed it. Bile rose to his throat, and the room started spinning again.

He pulled his hand away from her soft skin as if he had been burned. "Get out."

"But . . ."

"I will hear no more reasons from you. You came into my house uninvited, and you have been asked to leave multiple times. If you don't leave now, I will call for a constable."

With a shaky nod, she finally agreed. Nelson gave her a smile, placed a gentle hand to her back, and showed her out of the room. She didn't flinch when Nelson touched her. If anything, Everton noticed relief on her striking features.

He turned his back to the two of them and plodded back to his desk. He took each step carefully; he wouldn't stumble while Miss Barton was watching. He reached the side of his desk and heard the study door shut. He immediately put a hand out to steady himself. After a few moments of deep breathing, he slid into his seat and shoved the brandy back in front of him. The drink would give him no answers on this night. But at least he had been diverted for a moment. It was a painful moment, but sometimes any diversion was better than the empty life he lived at present. Perhaps one day, when Miss Barton was happily married, he would thank her for the strange visit.

If only to see the look of horror on her poor sap of a husband's face.

Diana pulled away from the elderly butler and stepped over the threshold of Lord Bryant's home, back into the darkness of the pounding rain. If she never returned, it would be too soon. Her legs still shook from her encounter with Lord Bryant. "I can manage returning to my carriage on my own," she assured the servant. The butler glanced up at the sky and back at her in indecision. She took one more deep breath and, summoning the last of her courage, sent the poor man a smile. It served its purpose. With one last regretful look, he slowly swung the door closed. A second later, the latch clanked into place. Diana spun and immediately slid to the ground, her back dragging along the rough stone exterior of Lord Bryant's home. Her dress was already a disaster. A few minutes in the rain couldn't make it any worse.

Lord Bryant was not going to help her. She didn't know what had possessed her into thinking he would. Her anger at Mr. Broadcreek accounted for most of her foolishness. She was never late to send in an order. Never. Her desperation accounted for the rest of it. Any sane woman would write to Nate and ask him to return, but Nate had done enough for their family. It was time for him to live his own life. And it was time for Diana to stand on her own two feet and do what she could for their business.

Diana wiped a hand across her brow before her fingers found the small pin on her chest. The simple gold knot calmed her. It was a silly daily prize, created by Mr. Richardson to keep Nate interested in the railroad, even after his heart was turning back toward Baimbury. Each day the three of them would argue about who had accomplished the most that day, and the winner would wear the pin home. If either Nate or Mr. Richardson had still been here, it would have been pinned on one of their chests. Nate would have dealt with Mr. Broadcreek immediately while Mr. Richardson put the order in.

Now there was no one to compete with. That tiny pin was heavy against her chest. It was her prize to take every single day no matter what disasters she created. What kind of prize was that?

She sighed. There was nothing left to do but return home to Mrs. Richardson's house. The boys would be asleep, and Mrs. Richardson would be waiting up for her. She didn't sleep until Diana made it home each night. Diana's hands shook as she wiped several raindrops away from her eyes.

The emerald she had sold would pay for the rushed order of ballast. Mr. Broadcreek would not see her flustered or set back. But what would the man do next to thwart her? If Lord Bryant would have simply agreed to her plan, his name alone would have kept Mr. Broadcreek away.

What was so wrong with Diana that Lord Bryant, who had several scandals a year, wouldn't stoop to having one with her? Her stomach hardened, and she squeezed her eyes shut. How foolish must she have looked to him? At least she hadn't broken down in tears. It had been months since she had seen him. She had hoped he wouldn't prove to be quite so devastatingly handsome in his own home in less formal clothing. With no jacket and the top buttons of his shirt undone, he had seemed perhaps more human but definitely not less handsome. Men like that shouldn't be allowed to also be rich and titled. Or if they were, they should be required to help any young lady who was desperately in need.

Her hands finally stopped shaking, and she stood up. If Lord Bryant wasn't willing to help her, she would have to figure something else out. Business could not continue as it was. She had no more jewelry to sell, and if anything else went wrong, she wouldn't be able to get Parliament to grant her an act to build another railroad line. Without that act, Richardson Rail would be worth less than she paid for it, Charlotte Richardson would be left destitute, and Diana would have bankrupted a previously successful railroad company.

Nate would have to come back to London and pick up the broken pieces of both companies. He had already cleaned up the mess their estate was in when he inherited. Heaven help her if he had to clean up her mess as well.

She wasn't about to let Charlotte Richardson and herself down simply because Lord Bryant refused to help her. She had made two grave mistakes. Her first mistake had been to come here, and her second was to ask Lord Bryant's permission. She kicked the stones of his hulking London estate. There was nothing she could do about her first mistake. She was here, with no way to turn back time and save herself from the humiliation of begging Lord Bryant for help.

But her mistake in asking his permission? That was a mistake she could learn from. She took a deep breath and walked to the hired carriage. Her shoes were already damaged badly enough that she didn't bother to avoid puddles as she went. She wouldn't resort to asking Nate to leave home. Not yet. Lord Bryant ruined numerous women every year—enough that there was a distinct possibility he could ruin one more without ever finding out about it.

And if he did?

She would have to deal with that when the time came.

CHAPTER 3

"How many pounds would you be interested in investing?" Diana eyed Mr. Winston from across her desk. He seemed sincere, but then again, so had Mr. Yates, and he had spent three weeks coming into the office and taking up her time only to decline investment after she declined a ride in Hyde Park. She had learned a few things about running off false investors since her experience with Mr. Yates, though, especially in the last three weeks since she had been using Lord Bryant's name as a shield. Work was finally running smoothly. Her main problem now was deducing which men were actual investors and which were after the railroad.

She cocked her head to one side. Mr. Winston was young enough to be interested in marriage, but some of her investors were young as well. She couldn't use Lord Bryant's name until she knew for certain what kind of man Mr. Winston was. The last thing she wanted was for a serious contact to believe her foolish enough to fall for the silver-tongued Lord Bryant. She would have to deny her relationship with him if they did. Which—after all—was the truth.

"Is there a limit?" Mr. Winston asked.

"There is, but it is rather a large one."

"For today, I would like to invest five hundred pounds." Mr. Winston swallowed and ran a hand up and down his leg. His clothes were well kept but not expensive. Five hundred pounds would be a large sum to a man like him. It should be flattering, really, that a man would part with so much money just for a chance to woo her. She would give him the money back and more, though, once the line was completed. She wouldn't feel burdened by it. His eyes searched hers. "Would that be an acceptable amount?"

Five hundred pounds was acceptable. It wasn't the smallest investment she had taken, but neither was it anywhere near the largest. Despite Mr. Winston's kind eyes and his refreshingly hesitant demeanor, she wanted to know exactly whom she was dealing with before she answered. She reached into her desk drawer and pulled out a list of questions as well as a blank sheet of paper for Mr. Winston. "Would you please write the answers to these questions?"

Mr. Winston nodded, and Diana watched each stroke of his pen, waiting for the moment he reached the last inquiry.

He set down the pen halfway through. "If I become an investor, will I be able to meet the owner?"

Meet the owner? Diana leaned back in her seat. Didn't he know? She had pegged him for a hopeful suitor almost from the moment he walked into her office.

"The owner is available to talk to investors if there is a need."

Mr. Winston nodded, slid his hands once more down his legs, less hesitantly this time. If anything, he was invigorated by her answer.

He renewed filling out his form, the scratches of the pen tapping a furious beat. "I would very much like to meet the owner."

Diana pursed her lips. The man seemed to know there was a new owner of Richardson Rail. He may have even known it was a woman. Based on his excitement to meet the owner, he must have known it was a single woman. Why did he not expect it to be her? He must have thought her too young. It wasn't as if she was a child; she was twenty-two years old for heaven's sake.

Which, admittedly, was quite young.

But still, did she seem so incompetent to him? Or was she misjudging him somehow? Did he not know at all?

"It would depend on her schedule."

He didn't look up in interest at her use of the feminine pronoun but kept scratching away. It was one thing to be pursued because of her ownership in the company but quite another to be completely looked over as incapable.

"I could come back anytime she was available."

She bit her tongue for a moment, but the pain did nothing to diffuse the steady fume rising in her chest. "No need, Mr. Winston. You are speaking to her now."

His pen paused, and his head jerked up as if pulled by a puppeteer holding strings above him.

"I am?"

"Yes." His shock was not surprising, but it didn't help the buzz of anger stirring in her chest. She had helped Nate for months before taking over parts of his business, and before buying Richardson Rail, she had operated solely on her own for weeks. She was capable.

Mr. Winston's eyes roamed the room around them. "Mr. Richardson passed away not long ago. How is it that you are the owner?"

"I bought it from Mrs. Richardson. It was a bit much for her to handle while in mourning."

"I was sorry to hear of his passing." His demeanor changed. His head bowed, and he wouldn't look her in the eye. "His marriage to Mrs. Richardson was a happy one?"

Other than Nate and Grace, it had been one of the happiest she had ever seen. She glanced at Mr. Richardson's old desk. Mrs. Oliver sat there now. The few months that she, Nate, and Mr. Richardson had worked here together had been some of the happiest of her life. "It was."

"How is she faring now?"

How was she faring? That was a difficult question to answer and not a topic she wished to discuss with a stranger. She wished she knew herself. For the past month, Charlotte hadn't had to deal with any railroad issues, but at home, she was still listless. "She is taking comfort in her children."

He nodded and picked up his pen again. At last, he reached the question she had been waiting for. He answered without pause.

Unmarried.

With all of his questions about the owner of the company, and almost none about the business, that answer was the final nail in Mr. Winston's coffin. She reached into her desk and pulled out her charcoal drawing of Lord Bryant. She hadn't managed to get his perfect Roman nose just right, but other than that, she was quite proud of her depiction of him. She placed the frame on her desk, brushed an imaginary speck of dust from it, and sighed heavily.

Mr. Winston paused in the middle of signing his name. "Is that your father?"

Diana stifled a groan. She wished she had a talent for watercolor or the time for an oil painting. It was hard to depict youth in charcoal. Perhaps she should get a small portrait of him commissioned. She used this one enough that it might be worth it.

"No, it is not my father." Diana gave her best simpering look and gently stroked Lord Bryant's cheek. Time to dive in and be done with Mr. Winston. She leaned forward conspiratorially. "If I tell you a secret, will you promise not to tell anyone?"

Mr. Winston's brows furrowed as the men's often did at this point. He was not here to invest, although he had done a much better job of pretending than most. He had made it all the way to the paperwork. Most men couldn't manage more than a few stilted questions before she needed to pull out her artwork.

"Lord Bryant and I are to be married. It hasn't been announced yet, so you must keep this solely to yourself."

"Lord Bryant? The baron?"

"Yes, do you know him?" She widened her eyes and blinked in what she hoped was an enthralled fashion.

"He asked you to marry him?" She could see the unspoken question in his eyes. Lord Bryant wasn't the marrying type. It had been the one hitch in her plan, but there were ways around Lord Bryant's reputation.

"Well, not in so many words, but he did say he would send any man who looked at me more than twice on a boat to New South Wales. So surely a proposal won't be far off."

Mr. Winston pulled on his cravat. She hated acting like a lovesick schoolgirl in her office. This was her place of work. But if she wanted to get any actual work done, this is what she had to do. And in the three weeks since she had started using the drawing and story, she had seen a significant drop in the number of unmarried men coming in to "invest."

Thankfully, not all of them were keeping her secret.

"Miss Barton, I don't know how to put this delicately, but are you quite certain about that man's intentions? I have heard—"

"Do not repeat rumors to me, Mr. Winston. If you do, I will have to ask you to leave and never return. I cannot abide a man who talks negatively about the man I love."

She pushed the word *love* through her teeth. Why was that one so hard to say?

"Even still . . . I feel it is my duty . . ." Mr. Winston paused, perhaps taking in her clenched fists and jaw. She didn't have time for this today.

"I would be wary of how you finish that sentence, Mr. Winston."

Mr. Winston stood, picked up his paperwork, narrowed his eyes at the framed portrait, and then cleared his throat. "I've just remembered one more thing I need to look over at home before I decide to invest."

Diana stood and smiled. "Of course. If there is anything you aren't certain about, I would suggest determining that now. Once the money is invested, it will have to stay invested at least until our next line is completed. That is when the true benefit will pay out. I always advise my investors to look over any upcoming expenses or plans before deciding for certain."

His eyes shifted to the door. "Yes, that is it. I did just remember some upcoming plans. I will look them over and—perhaps—be back in a week."

"That sounds wise."

He nodded and backed away from her desk, holding his sheet of paper in both hands. He reached the door and pulled it open in a mad rush.

"You will remember to keep my secret," Diana called after him. "Lord Bryant hates to have my name bandied about town almost as much as he hates men who come here with less-than-serious intentions to invest."

"I don't bandy names about," he said stiffly, but she could tell her portrait had done the trick. Mr. Winston wouldn't be back. He gave her a stiff nod and helped himself out the door.

The door shut behind him with the clang of the bell, and Diana sighed. Perhaps it was time to stop taking investments altogether. Once this line was complete and income started coming in, between her funds and Nate's, they should be able to keep both companies running.

But only just.

And she didn't want to only keep the companies running—she wanted to build more lines. She still needed to raise at least twenty thousand pounds to prove to Parliament that the company was solvent. Without those funds, she wouldn't be granted the act of Parliament to build another line.

For once, the office was empty other than herself and Mrs. Oliver, just as Nate had thought it would always be when he left for Baimbury. Their Barton lines had been—and still were—running smoothly. Diana had been helping Mrs. Richardson with her company when he'd left, but Nate had been confident that the two of them had everything under control.

She rubbed her hand along her desk—Nate's old desk. Things were so very different now than they were when she first started. Working day in and day out with Nate and Mr. Richardson had been one of the most rewarding experiences of her life. The two had both started in the railroad business at the same time, and it had made sense to keep an office together, even with their separate companies. Nate particularly liked having someone in the office as it gave him the freedom to observe the lines whenever they came close enough to London for him to visit and even work with the navvies from time to time.

But then Mr. Richardson took ill and passed away. What a strange world where a man could be healthy and strong one minute, then gone only days later. The office was never the same after that. All of them could feel it. When Grace's pregnancy proved difficult, Diana hadn't had to tell Nate twice to return to Baimbury and leave things to her. He had never truly belonged in London. Now it was her turn to help the family. And as long as Nate didn't hear that she had bought Richardson Rail, she felt fairly certain he would stay home and finally get the chance to live out his dreams of restoring the estate to productivity.

But still, she missed those first days of laughter. Mrs. Oliver wasn't nearly as engaging as Nate and Mr. Richardson had been.

Three more months. She just needed three more months. Once she had an act of Parliament passed for another Richardson Rail line to be built, the value of the company would be double what Mr. Broadcreek had originally offered to pay for it. She could sell both the railroad companies and return to Bainbridge with Nate and Grace. Life could finally go back to normal.

She pulled out the last paper she had been working on—an order for more track. It was presumptive to order it now. This would be for the line she hadn't even started yet, the one she still needed an act for. But if she ordered now before the rush of orders came in when Parliament was in session and passing acts to build new lines, she would save about a fifth of the costs. It was a gamble . . .

The bell over the doorway rang, announcing someone's arrival. Diana didn't look up. Now that she had finally gotten rid of Mr. Winston, Mrs. Oliver could deal with whomever had just walked through the door. She needed to finish filling out her order form.

"How can I help you, sir?" Mrs Oliver asked.

It couldn't have been Mr. Winston or another returning investor, as Mrs. Oliver was excellent with names.

The man cleared his throat, but Diana refused to look up. Just a few more specifications to enter and—

"That is a very nice likeness. Wherever did you get it?"

Diana's pen froze in her hand. She would recognize Lord Bryant's masculine drawl anywhere. It rolled over her shoulders and slammed into her chest like sticky, sweet honey. A little bit of charm was pleasant, but his was purposely overpowering. Her head shot up, and her hand flashed to the portrait, slamming it facedown on the desk. Why hadn't she remembered to return it to the drawer?

She stood and gave Lord Bryant a slight bow. Gone were the haunted eyes from her late-night visit. His clothes were impeccable, his emerald-green striped waistcoat matched his brilliant, flashing eyes. But were they flashing in humor or in anger? She couldn't tell. "Lord Bryant, how pleasant to see you. Have you come to speak of your investments?"

"Investments?" Lord Bryant shook his head, one of his thick brows arched perfectly. "Speak of investments with the woman to whom I am utterly devoted?" He clicked his tongue. "Don't be ridiculous. I had much more diverting activities planned."

That sounded like humor.

Perhaps?

A gasp escaped Mrs. Oliver, and Diana coughed to cover the fact that she had nothing to say in response. Her throat was dry. She had known this day would come, but she had hoped to have more time. Much more time. Lord Bryant held one hand inside his waistcoat. A lazy bend at one knee seemed to encapsulate his nonchalance and power. With not much more than a flick of his wrist, he could put an end to both Barton Rail and Richardson Rail. All she wanted to do was help her family and Charlotte Richardson, and what had seemed like an intelligent idea mere minutes ago was—under the baron's unscrupulous eye—quickly becoming the most impudent and ridiculous scheme she had ever concocted.

"*This* is the beau you have been telling everyone about?" Mrs. Oliver asked. Diana stood from her desk and brushed her hands down her skirts the way she did whenever an important investor came to the office. Perhaps she should have told Mrs. Oliver the truth.

A muscle moved in Lord Bryant's cheek. That wasn't humor. "It seems I am." At his home, his eyes had been guarded and weary. In the daylight, with his hair styled to perfection and his eyes lazily perusing her office, Lord Bryant seemed much more alive. He strolled over to Mrs. Oliver's smaller desk and gave her a flourishing bow. "And you must be Miss . . ."

At sixty-seven years old, Mrs. Oliver positively simpered, her hand coming to her cheek as if to cool it.

"This is my assistant, *Mrs.* Oliver," Diana informed him.

"You can call me Miss. My husband won't mind. We have been married long enough for him to—"

"Mrs. Oliver." Diana didn't hide the rebuke in her voice.

"Oh dear, I suppose I forget myself. How can I help you, Lord Bryant?"

Lord Bryant turned to look at Diana, and in that moment, he transformed. As a young girl, Diana had had a favorite hunting dog. He had been sold just before her father died like many other things of value. But that dog had loved Diana. His eyes would light up in devotion every time she visited him, most likely because she usually came bearing scraps from breakfast. No matter the reason, he couldn't contain his excitement when he saw her coming.

That was how Lord Bryant was looking at her. Completely, utterly smitten, from the hesitancy in his stance to the wide guilelessness of his lash-framed eyes. Lord Bryant was *skilled.*

If only he would have agreed to her plan, he could have played his part perfectly. As it was, those loving looks set Diana on edge. She glanced toward the door, but she wouldn't be reduced to running out of her own office. He noticed her gaze and almost imperceptibly quirked one corner of his mouth. He was enjoying her discomfort far too much. She straightened her shoulders. Even if she was in the wrong here, she wouldn't give him the satisfaction of seeing her squirm. He gave a deep, lovesick sigh before turning to Mrs. Oliver. "I have come to speak with Miss Barton alone. Is there a place where we could have some privacy?"

Mrs. Oliver's other hand flew to her cheek, and her wide eyes found Diana's. A smile as broad as a river crossed her face. Mrs. Oliver was reacting to Lord Bryant's shenanigans like a parched woman being offered a glass of pure spring water. Diana bit the inside of her cheek. This was her own fault. She was the one who had been telling every other man that came into the office that she was expecting a proposal any day. Mrs. Oliver was only too eager to allow the privacy for that much-awaited event to occur.

Predictably, Mrs. Oliver nodded. "Of course." Mrs. Oliver looked frantically about the room. "In fact, we are nearly out of . . . candles. It is fortunate you came—I don't like to leave Miss Barton here on her own. I'll just pop out and buy some. I will be back within five minutes."

Diana shook her head back and forth but stopped when Lord Bryant turned his head to look at her. Taking a deep breath, she reminded herself that she was calm and collected and not at all intimidated by Lord Bryant. Certainly he was a baron and a well-known rake, but somewhere deep inside, she had always thought him to be a gentleman as well.

That gentleman could very well have been a man of her own making though. Her silly eighteen-year-old heart had most likely measured his good looks and assumed they must be matched by a goodness in his heart.

Hopefully there was a grain of truth in her foolishness, for now, she absolutely knew better. More often than not, it was the handsome men one had to watch out for.

Lord Bryant gave Mrs. Oliver a wink. Did good men wink at matronly ladies? "Why don't you make that ten minutes, *Miss* Oliver. Much has happened since I have last seen Miss Barton. She is always so busy here at the office; she doesn't make time to inform me of anything." Mrs. Oliver sighed with a silly half grin on her face and nodded in agreement with him. "I want to make certain she feels the full effect of my disappointment in her."

Mrs. Oliver bounced away from her desk like a fifteen-year-old. A woman her age should be immune to Bryant's charms. How had she suddenly turned into a schoolgirl with just a few words?

"We have enough candles for a few days," Diana said. "Surely they can wait."

"Nonsense." Mrs. Oliver was already putting on her hat. "When we have someone here to watch over you, we should take advantage of the opportunity." She drew out every syllable of her last few words.

Diana would murder her.

Only after Mrs. Oliver gave her the candles, of course. They really were running low.

Mrs. Oliver scurried out of the office, and then it was simply Lord Bryant and Diana.

Alone.

He came toward her in a steady stroll, each long, slim leg stepping forward with a promise of retribution. One didn't go about using Baron Bryant for one's own personal gain. Not without some sort of repercussion.

She could grovel and apologize, but the image of him turning her down in his study without even bothering to hear her out flashed into her mind. No, she had made this choice for a reason. Lord Bryant was the perfect excuse to send would-be suitors away. Her scheme had worked flawlessly. Two weeks ago, she would never have had the time to finish this order. She would have still been trying to dispose of Mr. Winston. Now she was protected by just a hint of a relationship to Lord Bryant.

She wouldn't give it up simply because the man didn't agree to it.

Diana cleared her throat. "Well, now that you have rid us of my chaperone, what did you have in mind? Didn't you say something diverting? I haven't seen you in three weeks, my . . ." Here was that word again. "My love. Diverting is exactly what I was hoping for."

Lord Bryant's head tipped to one side, a wicked grin curling the side of one lip. She straightened and smiled back. She wouldn't cower before Lord Bryant. Yes, she had been using his name without his consent, but he had deserved it.

Surely, somehow, he had deserved it.

"Ah, Diana." He said her Christian name almost like a sigh. A well-practiced art form for Lord Bryant for certain. She ignored the small burst of thrilling lightness that flared in her stomach. Diana wouldn't melt like Mrs. Oliver had. "Your attempt to distract me is appreciated, but I must know—why do you have a portrait of me on your desk?"

She didn't break eye contact. "So that when I miss you, I might look at it." She didn't mention the use of her Christian name as she could hardly rebuke him for it. Not after what she had done.

"And do you miss me often?"

She ran her fingers over the wooden frame she had placed the portrait in. "Nearly every day. Although lately it's been a bit less." The day before, she hadn't had to pull it out once.

He took the portrait from her desk. In the process, his fingers grazed the tops of hers before she pulled away. Not too quickly of course. She didn't want him to think she could be scared off by a simple touch of the hand. As a result of her forbearance, the warmth of his gloved hand lingered on her fingers even after she pulled them to her side. Lord Bryant tipped his head to one side as his eyes roamed the little charcoal drawing. "The nose isn't quite right. Mine is much more regal."

Diana held back a laugh. Of course he would see that. "Yes, well, with a nose as regal as yours, can you fault the artist?" Her eyes instinctively went to his strong Roman nose, so perfect in its symmetry. "It is hard to capture."

A small laugh escaped Lord Bryant's mouth, and for a moment, his haughty facade seemed to fade. His smooth face brandished a few lines on each side of his eyes. As handsome as he was while playing the devil's own servant, she preferred that flash of normalcy. But it was gone before she could do much more than take note of it.

Lord Bryant set the portrait back on her desk and strolled over to the one table in the room. He ran his finger along the outside edge while examining the topography maps laid out on it. Everything he touched seemed to light up brightly, then dim as he walked away. She wouldn't forget where his hands had been in her office.

"Would you please stop touching things?"

His eyebrows furrowed, and he pulled his hand away from the table. Placing his hands behind his back, he cleared his throat. "Are you aware that I am in the middle of a delicate situation with a lady at the moment?"

"You mean besides me?"

He pursed his lips together as if to argue the point but then gave up. "Yes, besides you."

Who was she? And what exactly constituted *delicate*? "I was not."

"I'm going to have to ask you to stop connecting your name with mine. Lady Emily is a frightened young woman in general, and I don't need rumors of another scandal scaring her off."

The soft way he said *Lady Emily* grated on her ears. "It seems to me your past scandals would be enough to do that for you. I don't see why one more will hurt you."

"Trust me, it won't hurt me," he scoffed. "Society is always harshest toward women."

Lord Bryant reflecting on the difficulty of women's lots in life? How quaint of him. "And yet you still manage to scandalize at least three a year."

He sauntered from the table back to her desk, this time coming around to her side. "Oh, come now, not every year. Last year there were surely only two."

She stood her ground, even though her immediate reaction was to want to step back, out of the sphere of his influence.

He sat on the corner of her desk with his long legs hanging over the side in a very un-baron-like manner, crossed his arms in front of himself, and waited for her reply. Blast. One more surface in her office that would remind her of his visit every time she looked at it. And her desk too. She spent hours here every day. Diana narrowed her eyes. She was no longer an impressionable young woman. She owned what was certain to become one of the most profitable businesses in London and nearly half of another. Lord Bryant would not get the best of her.

"Perfect—you can make up your deficit with me."

"I refuse to damage your reputation, Miss Barton. That is final."

Why was he being so stubborn about this? "And yet you are in the middle of damaging the reputation of Lady Emily. In what realm of possibilities is my reputation of more import than hers?"

"I am the one who decides whose reputation needs sullying. This could ruin your possibility of getting married. And I would rather not come to blows with your brother a second time."

He and Nate had come to blows? Why in heavens? Oh, of course.

Grace.

"Nonsense." Diana shrugged. "Every one of the ladies you scandalized ended up getting married. At least the ones I've heard of."

"But not necessarily to someone of their equal."

"You seem to be under the impression that I am a diamond of the first water. I am simply Miss Diana Barton, and I have managed to damage what reputation I did have by buying a railroad company."

"Every woman is a diamond of the first water." Still sitting on her desk, he leaned forward, bringing his sculpted face and very Roman nose only inches from her own. "Every woman. You won't be sullied by me."

Diana sucked in a quick breath. His words contradicted the way his eyes paused at her lips. Lord Bryant was a dangerous man, but she wouldn't fall for his charming words. Not even when they were paired with his fine brow, now raised in seeming concern for her situation.

"I have much bigger problems than my reputation, Lord Bryant," she said, straightening in her chair. "Every day a barrage of men passes through this office under the pretense of being interested in investing when, in truth, all they are looking for is an easy path to railroad ownership. I don't have time to deal with all of them." Mr. Broadcreek's leering face flashed into her mind. He was getting bolder in his actions toward her. And yet she couldn't outright disdain him, not with the friends he had in Parliament. "While I would like to possibly marry one day, it is at the moment the farthest thing from my mind. When the time comes, I will most likely find a gentleman far outside of London who doesn't care a fig about what Society has to say about me." Hopefully a man like that existed. At the moment, it was hard to imagine not being wanted. Men were practically hounding her now. "At least allow me to keep your portrait, and do not deny the rumors."

He snatched up her portrait of him and examined it. She wished she were a better artist. Every flaw seemed to jump out at her as he carefully perused her charcoal. "I will be taking this," he said finally. "And if I hear another word about the two of us, I will be back."

Sliding off her desk, he turned and walked away from her. If he walked out that door, everything she had worked for over the past few months could come to naught. No railroad act, no profit to share with Charlotte.

She raised her chin. "I can always draw another."

Lord Bryant stopped. He lowered his head and examined the portrait again, then turned around. "You drew this?"

"Yes."

"From memory?"

Oh dear. The charcoal wasn't perfect, but that had nothing to do with her memory. Lord Bryant's face had haunted her memories ever since meeting him at Nate's wedding. Blast her childhood fancies. Was it her fault that no men of note ever visited Baimbury?

"Yes," she admitted. "And I will draw another. I cannot handle all these men on my own. I understand that you are in the middle of an affair with a much more important woman than I, but I promise you this: she doesn't need you as much as I do."

"And I can promise you this." He returned to her desk and leaned forward on it once again. "She does."

"Two months, Lord Bryant. All I need from you is two months."

"You cannot have it. Not right now. You will find another solution. Lady Emily will not."

He strode to the door. This time she would not stop him.

Why couldn't Lord Bryant just allow her even the slightest of victories? With just a few simple acts, he could drive away most of her false investors. Perhaps it would not be quite enough to stop Mr. Broadcreek, but if most of the other men were removed from the picture, she could at least have a bit of time to focus on her work.

A carriage pulled to a stop outside the office. The gold trim and coat of arms were unmistakable—Mr. Broadcreek. Any second now, he would descend from his carriage as if he were some sort of sultan. He was the epitome of pride and misplaced power. She cursed under her breath. He had been away from London for a few weeks, and she had been waiting for him to come to her office ever since he had returned. Even with all the other men not coming, Mr. Broadcreek alone had the power to influence investors' opinions of her company. She had to convince him of her affair with Lord Bryant.

Lord Bryant was halfway out the door, but he stopped at her muttered curse. He turned to look at her and then back at the carriage. The door opened, and Mr. Broadcreek descended the steps of his carriage.

"Is that heavily mustached man here to do you harm?"

Diana had only a split second to make her decision. Mr. Broadcreek didn't seem likely to cause her physical harm. He'd had many chances to do so, and thus far, he had only damaged her business. If Lord Bryant meant physical harm, then no, Mr. Broadcreek wasn't here for that. And Lord Bryant most likely cared very little about what happened to her business. There was only one thing to do.

Her hand flew to her chest. "Mrs. Oliver is gone. Please do not leave me alone with him." She blinked her eyes rapidly in hopes of looking innocent and frightened.

Lord Bryant's eyes narrowed. He wasn't fooled by her pretending. She glanced back outside as Mr. Broadcreek finished descending the steps of his carriage.

Lord Bryant stepped fully back into the office and shut the door behind him. "So he is the reason you have asked for my protection?"

"He and many, many others like him. But of all of them, Mr. Broadcreek has the most power to do my business harm."

Lord Bryant muttered a curse. He must at least know of Mr. Broadcreek. "You have no reputation, you say."

Diana shook her head. "None."

"My position with Lady Emily is precarious. I will not help you if you set foot in a drawing room or a ballroom where people of note will be present. I may go so far as to pretend not to know you. But here in this office, with the likes of Mr. Broadcreek outside, I will. Do you agree to those terms?"

She stood from her desk. People of note? He didn't consider her a person of note? She bit the inside of her cheek. Now was not the time to argue about what the baron thought of her. When was the last time she set foot in a drawing room, let alone a ballroom? "Of course I agree."

He strode to her desk and placed his portrait back on it, facing out. "And you are certain you want the sliver of a reputation you have to be destroyed?"

"Yes, yes." Diana walked around to where he stood in front of her desk. Lord Bryant was actually going to help her. The weight of weeks of uncertainty slipped off her chest. "He is almost to the door—what should we do? I could smile and laugh with you a bit, or you could stare at me adoringly or—"

"I know a bit of Mr. Broadcreek, even if we haven't been introduced. Convincing him will take more than simpering looks." He stepped so close to her that his legs touched the outside of her full skirt. "I may need to handle you a bit."

"Of course. Whatever you feel needs to be done."

"Whatever?" His eyes were on her mouth once again.

"Yes." Her answer spilled from her lips in a barely audible puff of air.

His hands were about her waist in a flash, and he pulled her to him. Her body was suddenly flush with warmth. Had she made a terrible mistake? Invited a fox into her personal den of snakes? An unpredictable gleam shone in his eyes. The bell behind them rang, announcing that Mr. Broadcreek had arrived in the office. Diana sucked in a breath, but it was stopped by Lord Bryant's mouth covering her own. His hands slid up her back, and her mind went completely blank.

She was being kissed by a man. Not just any man, but Lord Bryant. Arguably the most desired man in all of London.

She had never been kissed before. What exactly was a woman supposed to do in circumstances such as these?

Nothing, apparently. Lord Bryant seemed to be taking complete control of the situation. His mouth moved in the most interesting way. First kissing her top lip, a soft brush she barely felt, then her bottom, and finally both. Her hands hung limp at her sides as her mind tried to process precisely what was happening. But limp arms were evidently not how kissing was done. Lord Bryant tightened his grip on her with one of his hands at her waist, while the other lifted her arm and slid up to her wrist, placing it at his neck.

Apparently Lord Bryant wanted her to at least pretend to participate.

She hadn't managed to take over a railroad company in less than six months because she was a slow learner. She lifted her other arm and intertwined her fingers at the back of his neck.

Lord Bryant gave a subtle nod of approval, then slowly and persuasively went to work convincing Mr. Broadcreek that the two of them were involved with one another.

Very involved.

A low cough and a cleared throat sounded from the other side of the room, but rather than this discouraging Lord Bryant, a smile rose on his lips. A smile that she felt. If Diana had still been eighteen, this kiss would have been the fulfillment of all her dreams.

At twenty-two—her fingertips brushed the bottom of Lord Bryant's hair—it was causing all types of commotion behind her eyelids, flashes of light she didn't understand, but it wasn't a fulfillment of a dream. There was no love behind Lord Bryant's actions. He was acting. The way his hand slid up her back and rested between her shoulder blades was only for the benefit of Mr. Broadcreek. Well, she could act as well as he. She followed his lead and allowed herself to make the most of the few things she had caught on to. The office blurred away, and eighteen-year-old Diana rose to the surface. She smiled against Lord Bryant's lips. This was the most fun she had had since taking over the Richardsons' business. She pushed her fingers into Lord Bryant's hair and pulled him firmly against her.

After all, with the unconventional life she was living here in London, it could be years before a man deigned to kiss her again.

CHAPTER 4

In the history of Everton's many scandals, he had only resorted to kissing two ladies. They had both been stiff and obviously uncomfortable with the situation.

Miss Barton had stiffened but for only a moment. He had thought to scare her while convincing that blackguard, Mr. Broadcreek, to leave her alone. But Miss Barton didn't seem to scare easily.

At the moment, her lips were kissing the corner of his mouth in a way he found quite distracting. Somewhere between the time his lips first met hers and now, she had taken over his kiss and made it her own. Her fingers curled into his hair, and she pulled him to her.

She pulled *him* to her.

Something snapped inside him, and he tightened his arms, crushing her into his chest. Every nerve was on edge as he waited for her to pull away or to stiffen in shock and disgust, but instead, she sighed into him. She smelled of ink and paper, not roses like other women. When had paper become a heady scent?

Precisely two minutes ago.

The bell above the door clanged a second time, announcing what Everton assumed was the departure of Mr. Broadcreek. He loosened his hands at Miss Barton's waist and immediately took a step back. He had thought to discourage her, to make her see that she was in over her head with a man like him, but he had gone overboard and lost control in the very moment he shouldn't have. He didn't bother opening his eyes as he fully expected to be slapped and would rather not see it coming.

After a moment, he cracked one eye open. Miss Barton was back at her desk.

As if nothing had happened.

Miss Barton slid the paper she had been reading to the side and concentrated on the one that had been below it. Surely the woman wasn't so unaffected by him.

He strode to her chair and lifted her by her hands until she was standing close to him once again. Paper and ink flooded his nose.

"That rascal could come back at any moment. You can't look as though kissing me had no influence on you whatsoever."

Miss Barton's eyes slid to the window. He couldn't see it, but he hadn't heard the carriage pull away yet. Her dark, copper eyes found their way back to his, that chin of hers lifting as haughtily as ever.

Lord Bryant tilted his head. "I hope this little episode hasn't made you want to change your mind. It is a little late now. If you can't handle being kissed by me, you shouldn't have invited me to cause a scandal with you."

"No, I don't want to change my mind."

"Good." He grinned at her, paying close attention to her pleasantly swollen lips. His glance didn't escape her notice, and a slight blush rose in her neck. A small fragment in the back of his mind relaxed. She wasn't so unaffected after all. "I find I like ruining your reputation just fine."

Miss Barton took a deep breath and ran her fingers up the pen in her hand. "I'm glad you find it no trouble."

"No trouble at all."

"But if we are ever put in a similar situation, where we need to display affection in front of one of my would-be suitors . . ." She paused, and for the first time since he had set foot in her office, she looked unsure.

"Try to do it less convincingly?" he asked. "I'm afraid that, my dear, isn't in my power."

"No, that wasn't what I was going to say."

He leaned forward. He never seemed to guess correctly what would come out of her mouth next. "What were you going to say?"

She cleared her throat and swallowed, making the hollows of her neck more pronounced. "Only that you should feel free to mess up my hair a little."

A laugh rose from deep within his chest. A scandal with Miss Barton was going to be more diverting than he had thought. "I won't forget," he said. And he meant it. Already he was imagining his fingers curled into the nape of her neck. "Do you think anyone else will come today?"

Her fingers paused on the pen. "It wouldn't be a surprise if they did. I usually get multiple men coming each afternoon, but the number has slowed down significantly."

"Because of my portrait there?"

"Yes."

"Well, in that case, I will most certainly be taking it with me when I go." If he had to choose between a portrait sending men away or doing it himself, he would do it himself. He hadn't felt this alive in ages, and even if Miss Barton had been nearly unaffected by his kiss, at least she hadn't been revolted by him.

"I'm not sure we have come to an understanding on what exactly I would like you to do for me."

"Of course we have." He winked at her. "I get to kiss you anytime a man walks through that door."

Miss Barton immediately looked down and smoothed her hand over a stack of papers. "No, some of the men who walk through that door actually do have business with me. I can't have you swooping me into your arms every time someone walks in here." She cleared her throat. "Although, I do appreciate that you were able to perform that function today."

She appreciated it. The corner of his lip lifted. Everton could get used to being appreciated by Miss Barton. As long as Lady Emily's family didn't catch wind of his time in Miss Barton's office, he could get very used to it. "What else would you like me to do for you, then?"

"Hopefully, with your help, it will only be men of business walking through the door. In two months, there will be a vote on whether or not to grant Richardson Rail an act of Parliament so we can begin construction on another rail line. Business was going well until word got out that I owned the company. As everyone knows, a single woman in possession of a railroad company must be in want of a husband."

Miss Barton paused, as if waiting for Everton to react to her last sentence. He furrowed his eyebrows. What exactly did she mean? It was a rather large leap to believe everyone would think she was in want of a husband. In general, most women were, but he didn't understand why owning a railroad changed things.

She sighed, shook her head, and continued. "I have a railroad line to complete and an act of Parliament to obtain in less than two months, and ever since I bought Mr. Richardson's line from his wife, the suitors have been insufferable."

"They want your business."

"Yes."

Of course they wanted the railroad. In the past two years, Lord Bryant had made more money on railroad lines than any of his other investments. If Miss Barton owned Richardson Rail, she was a very wealthy woman indeed.

"Why do you need me for only those two months? You will still own a rail company, and if you are granted permission to build, your company will be even more enticing."

"I don't plan to own anything after that. Mrs. Richardson only sold me the company because she was overwhelmed with losing her husband and now raising their three children, who are lost without their father. At first she hired me to work for her, but even bringing the paperwork for her to sign each evening became too much. Mr. Broadcreek offered to buy the company for roughly half of what it is worth, and she nearly sold it. Fortunately, she came to me to discuss the sale before going through with it."

"Where was your brother during all of this?"

"He was here for Mr. Richardson's funeral, of course, but his wife needed him in Baimbury. So after making certain I could manage the paperwork for Mrs. Richardson, he went back home."

"And how did you come to own it?"

"Mrs. Richardson sold it to me for what money I could come up with at the time—which was not much more than what Mr. Broadcreek had offered her—with the understanding that we would sell at the end of two months. I would get my money back plus twenty-five percent of the increased value."

"But if you marry before then—"

"My husband will take control of the business. None of the men coming through that door would fulfill the agreement I have with Mrs. Richardson. I will have swindled a woman I care deeply about and hurt the wife of a man I greatly respected."

"Why don't you just tell these men no?"

Miss Barton's shoulders drooped. "I have, and I do, but Lord Bryant—" She threw her hands up in the air. "They waste so much of my time. Mrs. Richardson didn't sell me this business so I could dally about with men in the office. If we are going to complete the paperwork and raise the funds we need to build another rail line in two months, I have a crushing amount of work to do each day."

Everton nodded thoughtfully. Her plan wasn't a bad one. If he weren't working like the devil to keep Lady Emily from succumbing to her father's wishes, helping Diana would be simple enough. Distracting even. Any distraction was a good one. "What, exactly, would you have me do?"

"Stay at the office a while. Add credence to my claim that we are seriously involved, perhaps on the brink of marriage."

Marriage? Everton blinked twice, placed his hand on Miss Barton's desk, and leaned in. "I'm sorry." He shook his head to clear it. "I thought for a moment you said *marriage*."

"Yes, I want to make certain the men coming here feel thwarted. They need to think your intent is serious."

He lowered his brows. "No one would believe I would marry you."

Her face paled slightly, and she sat straighter in her seat. Perhaps he should have worded that better, but he had made it quite clear to all of London he would never marry again. She should have known better than to spread that particular rumor.

"As long as they believe *I* believe it, that should at least deter some of them. So if you kindly refrain from making disparaging remarks like the previous one, I believe we can still make this work."

"It wasn't meant to be a disparaging remark, only a statement of fact. I've been married once, and I have made it no secret I will never marry again."

He waited for it—the look that would find its way to almost every young woman's eyes when he made that statement.

Determination.

Young women would try to change his mind. Older women would calculate which sweet young girl would be the one to convert him to the idea of marriage. Nothing was more intriguing than a titled man of his fortune and age vowing never to marry.

But the look didn't come. Miss Barton simply nodded. "Should we draw up a contract? How often are you willing to spend an afternoon in my office?"

A contract? Definitely not. "I will sign no contract. I'll do my best to help you, but it will have to be in my spare time. I'll come when I am able, and you will need to accept that the arrangement is—at the very least—better than a drawing of me on your desk and a few poorly crafted lies."

She tapped the edge of her pen on the corner of the paper in front of her. "It isn't perfect, but it will do." She stood from her desk and offered him her hand. His instinct was to kiss it, but her knuckles were turned to the outside. He chuckled. She was waiting for him to shake her hand.

From a kiss to a handshake. He took her hand, and she pumped it up and down.

Dealing with Miss Barton was going to be interesting at the very least.

CHAPTER 5

Diana stood outside the Richardsons' doorway and smoothed down her dress. She had been living here since a few days after Mr. Richardson passed away, but it still didn't feel like home. For the first time in weeks, Diana was able to arrive in the early evening instead of late at night. Mrs. Oliver had returned soon after Diana and Lord Bryant had reached an agreement, and the rest of the evening had been filled with work. Not a single suitor or investor graced her door after he left.

Diana had had a few good ideas in her lifetime, but she was beginning to think her scandal with Lord Bryant was one of the best.

Diana pushed on the front door and stepped into her temporary home. Mrs. Jenkins, the housekeeper, was halfway up the stairs but turned at the sound of the door opening. Her shoulders relaxed, and her lined face settled into a smile. "Miss Barton, thank goodness you are home."

Diana peered up the stairway. "Is everyone all right?"

Mrs. Jenkins shrugged. "Everyone is as usual. They could certainly use some of your cheer to brighten their day."

Diana took a deep breath and followed Mrs. Jenkins upstairs toward the nursery. Cheer. She grabbed her skirts and forced a bounce in her step. It had been a long day but not as long as most. She could muster up a bit more spirit for tea with the Richardson family.

In the first few weeks after moving into the Richardsons' home, she and Charlotte had taken tea in the drawing room whenever Diana had arrived home in time. But they had never lasted through more than half a cup before one of the children wanted their mother. Since they always ended up there anyway, now they skipped that first unnecessary step and took tea in the nursery.

At least this evening she had gotten here before the children's bedtime. Not that bedtime meant they would be asleep. Even when she came home well into the night, she would find Charlotte in the bedroom just off the nursery, curled up in a bed much too small for her with a young child.

No sounds came from the nursery as they neared it. Only the sound of their footsteps echoed through the corridor. If Diana didn't know better, she would never guess that three young children were behind the door in front of them. Mrs. Jenkins opened the door to a scene Diana was all too familiar with: Charlotte on her rocking chair, her baby girl in her lap, the other two boys sitting at her feet. No one was playing or reading or even speaking. They were surviving because that was all Charlotte could muster, and her children followed her lead.

The two boys turned at the sound of Diana's entrance, and Tommy jumped to his feet. "Miss Diana!" He ran to her side. "We haven't seen you for ages and ages."

"It has only been a few weeks, but it feels like ages to me as well. It was a good day at the office, and I was able to sneak away early."

"A good day at the office?" Charlotte asked, her eyes showing a spark of interest. "Are investments coming in all right?"

Diana hadn't told her of Mr. Broadcreek's visit three weeks ago or the late shipment, but Charlotte was astute enough to know when Diana was worried. The lines of Charlotte's eyes softened. Diana needed to be better at pretending. The last thing Charlotte needed was to be worried about the railroad business. She had enough to deal with at home.

"They are coming along well."

"Have those men started to leave you alone?"

Diana bent over and pulled Drue into her arms. "Believe it or not, they have."

"And you are certain none of them caught your fancy?"

"Very certain." Diana had mentioned the problem of men showing up at the office to Charlotte when it had first started happening. At the time, she hadn't realized how persistent some of the men would be, nor quite how many there would be. No matter how many times she had explained to her friend that she wasn't interested in any man who came to pursue her solely for the purpose of gaining a railroad, Charlotte had held out hope that there would be some diamond hiding among them. "Even if one of them did prove to be half decent, we both know I couldn't marry until the company was sold. I'll not have a man taking control of the company."

"But if you trusted him . . ."

Diana laughed and spun around once with Drue still in her arms, making him laugh as well. The very sound seemed to brighten the room. "You married a very good man, Charlotte. Not all men are like him. As soon as Richardson Rail is sold, these men will be gone."

"But when the company is sold, you will be wealthy, and you will still have your share in your brother's business. Your riches will always be a part of your appeal whether they are tied to a company or not."

Diana took a deep breath. Charlotte was right. But once the company was sold and Charlotte was taken care of, things would be far less complicated. The decision of whether or not to trust a man would affect only Diana. There would be no risk to this little family. They had seen enough tragedy.

Diana knelt by Tommy. "Should we read a story?"

Tommy and Drue both nodded.

Diana popped Drue onto her hip and took Tommy by the hand. She led them to the small bookcase that sat against the wall. Together, they picked out a large stack of books. She sat down at the miniature table and opened the first one. As her words filled the nursery, Charlotte sighed and relaxed into a slow rhythm of rocking her baby girl.

In half an hour, Diana and the boys made it through the books they had chosen. Tommy and Drue's eyes were starting to look heavy.

"Would you like me to help the boys get dressed for bed?" Diana asked.

Charlotte shook her head and put a finger to her lips. She stood from her chair with Emma in her arms and gently walked to the children's adjoining bedchamber. Diana ruffled the two boys' hair, dark like their father's, and waited for Charlotte to return.

"Boys," Charlotte said, "Mrs. Jenkins is going to help you prepare for bed tonight. I'm going to have some tea downstairs with Miss Barton." After a few complaints, which Charlotte miraculously ignored, Mrs. Jenkins returned to prepare them for bed.

Diana followed Charlotte into the drawing room, where Mrs. Jenkins had already laid out the tea things. Charlotte must have spoken with Mrs. Jenkins while Diana had been engrossed in stories with the boys.

"Tell me what is different," Charlotte said. "Why were you able to manage such a good day at the office? I can tell by looking at you that something has changed."

How much should she tell Charlotte? She certainly could not tell her that she ran to Lord Bryant in the middle of the night after Mr. Broadcreek delayed her ballast. Nor could she reveal she had been fabricating a relationship with

Lord Bryant for the past three weeks. And she would definitely not tell Charlotte that she had kissed Lord Bryant in her office this afternoon.

"I've enlisted some help."

"You've hired someone?" Charlotte smiled. She had been trying to convince Diana to hire more help since she sold the company to her, but it wasn't easy for Diana to find someone she could trust. Diana wasn't ready to take the risk of having a man in the office, nor had she had any luck finding another woman besides Mrs. Oliver to work with her.

"No, not exactly."

"Has Nate returned?"

"No."

"Then who is helping?"

Diana ran a finger along the edge of her teacup. How many of the events of the past weeks should she tell Charlotte? The lines of her eyes were still softened. Diana hated to deepen them. "What do you know of Lord Bryant?"

"Lord Bryant the baron?"

"Is there another Lord Bryant?"

"Not that I know of. But . . ."

Diana could see the wheels turning in her friend's head. Charlotte raised an eyebrow. "How exactly is Lord Bryant helping you?"

Diana shrugged as if having a baron's help was an everyday occurrence. "Honestly, he isn't doing much." Diana blinked hard to get rid of the image of him pulling her to him just before leaning down and . . . "Just having my name connected with his is enough to keep many of the railroad-grabbing men away."

"Your name?"

"Yes," Diana said.

"Your name connected with Lord Bryant's." Charlotte's wrinkles were starting to come back. Perhaps Diana shouldn't have said anything.

Diana grabbed her teacup and put it to her mouth. If she finished her tea quickly, this conversation could end faster. "Yes."

"You do know what kind of man he is . . ."

Did she? What kind of man was Lord Bryant? She could still feel the pressure of his hands on her back. Oddly enough, that sensation had stayed with her more than the touch of his lips—Lord Bryant pulling her to him, as if she belonged to him. A ridiculous thought. She belonged to no one. Nor would she ever. She might marry someday, but she would always remain her own person.

Diana took a large sip of tea. "What kind of man is he?"

"The worst kind. And if your name is bandied about with his, it will do you no favors socially. No one will believe his intentions are honorable. The man was married once, and he has sworn to never marry again."

"I had heard."

She hadn't heard much, though. Even last summer, when she had bumped into him at a picnic soon after arriving in London, she hadn't wanted to pry, not with the other women there. Sitting across from her was the man she had dreamt about for over a year. But seeing him in the flesh, paying particular attention to three of the women there, she knew he was someone left better to her imagination than discovering who he was in real life.

Not long after that, she began to hear stories about him. He was a scoundrel and a rake.

He had ruined multiple women.

But with all the scandal and gossip, she had still never heard his wife's name. It was almost as if the woman hadn't existed.

Charlotte took a sip of tea and set her cup down, leaning forward. "Why, last year, a marquess threatened to call Lord Bryant out if he didn't marry his daughter, and he still didn't. He left the country for three months rather than face the father in a duel or marry his daughter. In the meantime, the poor woman married a farmer." Charlotte leaned forward. "If he wouldn't agree to marry the daughter of a marquess, he won't be saddled with anyone."

"I have heard him say as much."

"And yet you will accept help from him when you know he won't marry? What kind of help is he offering?"

"Are you implying that the only help I could get from a man is marriage?" That was almost exactly the rumor Diana had been spreading, but still . . .

"I'm not implying that. I'm only struggling to understand what else he could do to help."

"He could invest; he could hire guards to protect the office. The man is as rich as the queen. He could do any number of things that have nothing to do with marriage."

Even as she said the words, Diana wondered why she hadn't thought of those things when she ran to Lord Bryant's home in the middle of the night. Why hadn't she thought to ask for his protection or for more of his money? He had already invested heavily, but he could easily double or even triple the amount he had given her. With all the investments taken care of, she could, in essence, lock the office doors and get her work done in peace.

But she hadn't asked for his money. She had asked him for the one thing he had given so many other women so easily.

A ruined reputation.

Heavens above, did she still carry some strange torch for the man? She should know better. She had two families counting on her now. She couldn't get caught up in her foolish dreams of three years ago.

She touched a finger to her lips. Her traitorous mouth already had.

"Did he hire you guards or invest an exorbitant amount of money?"

"No."

"Then what has he done to help?"

Diana ducked her head and reached for another sugar cube with Charlotte's tongs. Her tea was too sweet already, but she needed something to do with her hands.

"Diana?"

"Oh, um . . ." She grabbed her spoon and stirred her sugar into the tea. "He has offered to spend time at the office a few times a week or so."

"Why would he do that?"

"To intimidate the men who have hoped to pursue me."

"And why would he do that?"

Diana's spoon froze. Why would Lord Bryant—arguably one of the most selfish men in London—do that? He had made it quite obvious that he didn't want to. She set her spoon down and took another sip of tea. Her eyes widened at the sweetness of it, but she swallowed. As long as Lord Bryant helped her reach the goal of getting the railroad line act to pass, she didn't have to understand him. "Perhaps he enjoys intimidating people."

"You know," Charlotte said, "he would never take a relationship between the two of you seriously."

Diana smiled and nodded. "I know. We have no relationship. Do not worry."

"Mrs. Oliver will be with you whenever he comes?"

Mrs. Oliver had quite easily been persuaded to leave as soon as he had arrived. She supposed that Mrs. Oliver wouldn't leave the two of them alone for long. Besides, for some strange reason, she didn't feel fear with Lord Bryant. She wouldn't put it past him to kiss her again—her heart sped up a bit at the thought—but he wouldn't do her any real harm. In a strange way, he was protecting her.

"Mrs. Oliver will make certain nothing untoward happens. And I trust Lord Bryant more than I trust the other men who come to the office."

Charlotte frowned. "Why?"

Diana shrugged. "Because he wants nothing from me, I suppose."

A twinge of regret pricked the back of her neck. It was ridiculous—she wouldn't allow the paltry nag of disappointment to weigh her down. Diana smiled at Charlotte broader than she needed to. Diana had chosen the perfect man for her task, and it was a comfort, not a disadvantage, that he saw nothing desirable in her.

She hoped she wouldn't have to remind herself of that very often.

CHAPTER 6

Mrs. Cuthbert poured Everton's tea slowly. The clock on her drawing room mantle ticked off the seconds, and still the tea only trickled into his cup. It had only taken Mrs. Cuthbert three days to catch wind of Everton's visit to Miss Barton. She always managed to find out everything about everyone. She was the one who had alerted him to the fact that Miss Barton was using his name without permission. A widow with grown children, she had plenty of time on her hands. Enough to meddle in the lives of other people and certainly enough to pour her tea slowly when she wanted to. It was as if he could see her mind racing, and the speed of her thoughts was slowing her hand.

"So, you have agreed to help Miss Barton."

"Yes." There wasn't much else he could say since it was the truth. Mrs. Cuthbert deserved to know the truth. It could, after all, affect their plans.

"I like Miss Barton." Mrs. Cuthbert finally stopped pouring and set the teapot down on an intricate and very colorful doily. Mrs. Cuthbert had spent a few years embroidering and knitting for hours on end after her children had left home and her husband had died. Only after helping a young friend of her daughter's marry the man of her choice did she quit needlework and turn that flurry of activity into more meddling pursuits. She was a woman who couldn't remain still, which made her slow, steady movements this afternoon disquieting. "She knows her own mind. I'm happy you are helping her, but have you considered how this might affect things with Lady Emily?"

"Of course I have considered it. I wouldn't have agreed in the first place, except a gentleman, who has no right to claim that title, was on his way into Miss Barton's office. She was alone, and I saw no other choice than to help her."

"And how exactly did you *help* her?"

A slow smile rose to his lips. "I kissed her."

Lord Bryant didn't like the way Mrs. Cuthbert's hand froze over the sugar tongs.

"You kissed a young woman who was alone in her office?"

At this rate, he would never get his tea. He reached over and dropped a cube of sugar into his cup with his fingers. "Not completely alone. Most of the time, another man was there."

"Miss Barton isn't like the young ladies I send to you, Lord Bryant. She isn't in love with someone else, nor does she have a family trying to control her life."

"She has a brother and a friend who have left her alone to try to run two companies while they are off comforting wives and mourning husbands."

"That is true, but they wouldn't have done that had she not been up to the challenge."

He tipped his head to one side. She could have a point. He took a sip from his cup. "If she had been up to the challenge, she wouldn't have asked me for help."

"And so you kissed her. Yes, I understand. But are you certain that she understands?"

Mrs. Cuthbert didn't elaborate, but he knew what she meant. Did Miss Barton understand that he could kiss her without feeling any sense of obligation toward her? "Yes, I explained my situation to her well enough. She knows I will never marry, and she is the one who asked for assistance."

His hostess narrowed her eyes, but he stood his ground. Miss Barton was a businesswoman and a shrewd one. She understood their terms. Not only that, Miss Barton hadn't been fazed by his kiss. She got right back to work as if nothing had happened. A fact that would possibly put Mrs. Cuthbert's mind at ease.

Not that he would ever admit to it.

With a sip of tea, Mrs. Cuthbert continued her interrogations. "Even if that is true, I'm still not sure how you are going to make this work with Lady Emily. Her father has already put off her engagement for two weeks because I have told him you might actually be serious about his daughter. If he hears of this scandal with Miss Barton, that will be the end of that. Lady Emily will be married off to Lord Silverstone within three weeks. It is a terrible match for her; he is three times her age."

Everton was well aware of the disparity of age between the two. Lord Silverstone was much too old for the quiet, seventeen-year-old Lady Emily. Lord Bryant didn't know Lord Silverstone personally, but if a fifty-year-old man wanted to remarry, he should have the decency to find a woman older than his children.

"It has been three days, and my involvement with Miss Barton hasn't reached the ears of anyone of consequence. I don't think too many in Lord and Lady Falburton's circle will hear of it. Besides, enough rumors about me float about town that I'm not certain anyone will take this one seriously." Parents should care more about their own children's happiness than he did. But unfortunately for Lady Emily, that simply wasn't the case. "Any concerns should be soothed by this confounded ball you have talked me into hosting at the request of Lady Falburton." Everton shook his head. He hadn't hosted a ball in . . . Well, he had never hosted a ball. If that didn't convince Lord Falburton that he was serious about Lady Emily, there was nothing else he could do.

"I'm still so very pleased about that."

Of course she was. Mrs. Cuthbert loved nothing more than to meddle where she wasn't needed. That meddling had quite possibly saved his life, though, so he put up with her. Hosting a ball, however, was one of her worst ideas by far. "And I am very displeased."

"No one has been in your house in town for ages."

"Exactly. Now people will start sending cards again. Do you know how long it will take me to retrain all of London to understand that I don't want to be bothered?"

"We have gone over this a thousand times. With your past, there wasn't much else we could do to prove to Lord Falburton that your intentions were honorable toward his daughter. And now that you are committed to *assisting* Miss Barton as well . . ." Mrs. Cuthbert took another sip of tea. "You should be grateful I came up with the idea of a ball."

"One of the few things I have discovered about Lady Emily is her love for music. That should make the ball a bit less painful for her." The only other interest of hers that he had discovered were rocks, and although he didn't mind speaking of stones and fossils now and again, he doubted they would find a social function involving that particular passion of hers.

Mrs. Cuthbert pursed her lips together. "Do you think her situation is causing her stress?"

"I think most situations cause Lady Emily stress, including choosing which torte she would like me to fetch when we are in company."

"We shan't tell her of Miss Barton, then. We don't need to add to her worries." Mrs. Cuthbert stroked the top of a crocheted cat, her movements once again languid and unhurried. Never a good sign. "If news reaches her father, we shall have to move to a different plan."

Everton didn't like the sound of that. "What, exactly, did you have in mind?"

"Keep in mind there isn't much more we *can* do after hosting a ball. Before long, Lord Falburton will be asking you for an engagement."

Everton narrowed his eyes. This was where his scandals became either quite entertaining or quite uncomfortable. They usually had a man ready and waiting to swoop in and save the lady's reputation, but Lady Emily Falburton was too young and had no gentleman in mind for herself.

Mrs. Cuthbert set her teacup down and placed both hands in her lap. She took a deep breath. "What would you think about settling down?"

Everton closed his eyes against the magnitude of colors suddenly swirling in the room. An icy hardness took hold of his throat. When he opened his eyes, the room stilled. Mrs. Cuthbert rubbed her fingers in her lap, the only indication that she was nervous. Had he heard her correctly?

"Pardon me? I'm quite certain I misheard you."

Mrs. Cuthbert swallowed. "We have been telling Lord and Lady Falburton you are serious about their daughter, and at some point, we will need to stop—"

Everton stood. Mrs. Cuthbert knew better than to ask him that. Suggesting a marriage to Lady Emily? She was too much like Rachel. Any of the other women he scandalized would have been a better choice. Even Miss Paynter, whom he'd purused last year, would have been better. She was quiet as well, but at least she could stand up for herself.

"Mrs. Cuthbert, matrimony is out of the question." His tone was icy. "It is the whole reason you chose me for these games you play. One more suggestion like that and you will have to find yourself another gentleman with whom you can manipulate Society."

"She is such a sweet and good young woman, though; she would be no trouble to you."

"Like Rachel was no trouble?" He clenched the ring on his pinkie until he felt the thin gold bend under his pressure. He dropped his hand, and his shoulders sagged. One more beautiful thing ruined by his touch.

"Ah, she is rather similar to Lady Bryant, isn't she?" Mrs. Cuthbert grimaced. "I shouldn't have mentioned the idea. I wasn't thinking." Mrs. Cuthbert stood and reached for his hand. "I'm sure you are right. She would be a disaster for you, but perhaps someone else—"

Everton pulled his hand away. "Not another word." A cold sweat formed at the back of his neck. He couldn't be in this room another instant. Not with the thought of marrying Lady Emily in his mind. He knew what that marriage would be, and he wouldn't be responsible for another young life devastated because of him. He scrambled out of the drawing room, leaving Mrs. Cuthbert without a word of farewell. They were good enough friends that she would forgive him. Without waiting for his hat, he stumbled out the front door. Hands on his knees and gulping for air, he scanned the busy street for anything that would distract him.

Carriages. His eyes caught hold of the first one that passed him, and he numbered it. One. Another came from the other direction. Two.

Three, four, five. It wasn't working. Flashes of walking into Rachel's bedroom during the first few months of their marriage passed over his eyes. The months when he thought he would be able to make her happy. He reached for the brick wall behind him. What a fool he had been. Three months of being oblivious to the fact that Rachel had despised his touch. But discovering the fact hadn't helped matters for him. The harder he tried with her and the more he showed he cared, the more she shrank into her shell. He couldn't reach her with kindness, and he couldn't reach her with gentleness. So he stopped and waited for her to come to him.

She never did.

Then he made the worst mistake of his life.

He thought, perhaps, if she knew he was waiting for her, she would come. So he told her. He told her whether or not she came into his room was her choice. Oh, he had his reasons. What if she thought he no longer desired her? What if she didn't know he was waiting for her? It was ridiculous to spend two months waiting for your wife to do something without ever letting her know what you expected of her.

Her face had gone white, and she had nodded. Like she always did. Like she had at their wedding with her parents looking over her shoulder. Rachel always did what was expected of her whether she wanted to or not.

But she couldn't make herself open the door between them. He had listened for her footsteps near the door every night. Sometimes she had paced in front of the door. Once he had even heard the key slide into the lock on her side. But she never opened it, and neither of them slept well after that. Even with a door and a wall between them, he could hear her fretting late into the night.

And then one morning after he had finally fallen asleep, he had awoken to find her gone with not even a note to explain where.

He had never seen her alive again.

Months later, her blasted parents came apologizing.

To *him.*

He had made Rachel's life one of perdition, causing her so much pain that she ran away in the middle of winter. When she came down with a fever in the cottage of her old nurse, she hadn't even sent word to him.

He could have helped.

He had the resources that might have saved her.

But she had died rather than contact him. He had snuffed out a young and innocent life. And her parents had apologized to him about it. Everton threw his head against the brick wall behind him and bit down on his forefinger.

They'd apologized because he was a baron and Rachel hadn't provided him with an heir.

Everton closed his eyes. He needed something to count. He pulled his hand out of his mouth and rubbed his temples until he no longer felt light-headed. He opened his eyes and focused again on the carriages. Starting over, he counted sixteen of them.

He pushed off the brick wall and started walking in the direction of his carriage. Mrs. Cuthbert should have known better. She had seen him at his worst. Did she want him to return to that? The blithering idiot stuck in the drink and unable to leave his house? If she turned into another one of those prattling women who expected him to marry, he didn't know what he would do.

Move to Scotland.

A footman scurried to assist him. He must have been watching the whole time, wondering at what point he should call for help. "Send for my carriage," Everton growled. He would come back for his hat later. Or not at all—he had plenty of other hats at home. Right now he needed something to keep his mind off Mrs. Cuthbert's suggestion. He could go home and be alone with an untouched brandy cup. But his hands still shook, and he didn't trust himself not to drink it. He needed to go somewhere else, somewhere he could be distracted. Or even better, somewhere he could distract someone, but not someone quiet and submissive like Lady Emily or Rachel. Not someone who made him feel like half a man. He needed to be near someone who knew exactly what kind of a cad he was.

It was time to pay Miss Barton a second visit.

CHAPTER 7

WITH NO CONTRACT IN PLACE for when Lord Bryant would come, she had spent the last three days on edge, constantly looking for a carriage outside. It wasn't that she was looking forward to his visit so much as she wished she had some way of knowing when it would come. At least then she could relax while she worked.

Thanks to him, though, she had finally been able to work. The first day after his visit, she had a decent number of men come to her office, but most of them had visited before. All of them eventually got around to asking if the rumors of her and Lord Bryant were true.

She always responded the same way: "Rumors often are."

It had been enough, even without his portrait on her desk.

The sound of a carriage stopping outside her office pricked her ears, but she didn't look up. She had stopped looking up the day before. It made her feel too hopeful. Why was she hoping Lord Bryant would come by, anyway? He was certain to distract her from her work in more ways than one. The carriage was probably stopping at one of the nearby shops.

The jingle of the bell told her otherwise. Mrs. Oliver's sharp intake of breath should have been all the hint Diana needed. She finished writing out the sentence she was working on before allowing herself to look up.

It was Lord Bryant. He stood leaning against the frame of the door, looking much too relaxed for a man whose name was currently being bandied about with two different women.

"Did you miss me?" he asked when her eyes met his.

His question, after days of missing him or, at the very least, looking for him, made her laugh. "No salutations? Just questions as soon as you walk in the door?"

His eyes fell to her lips. "What type of salutation would you like? Should I ask Miss Oliver to get more candles?" Lord Bryant was being flippant, which was not unusual for him, but there was a hard edge to his smile. One she didn't trust.

"We don't need candles," Mrs. Oliver said. Perhaps she had come to her senses and would be a better office chaperone. That was more than half the reason Diana had hired her. Then Mrs. Oliver smiled in such a way that Diana felt certain her chaperone had not—in fact—come to her senses. "But we could use more coal." Mrs. Oliver's voice was bouncing and flighty. Diana stifled a groan. She had never heard anyone sound so happy about the prospect of buying coal.

"It is quite warm outside." Diana waved a hand. "We don't need coal."

"Which is why we are nearly out of it. Winter will be here before you know it." Mrs. Oliver stood. "I had better get some just in case. Then you can have a word with Miss Barton in private, Lord Bryant."

"No." Diana didn't shout, but neither did she speak calmly. The last thing she needed was for her assistant to try to orchestrate a proposal every time Lord Bryant came into the office. "Lord Bryant will be visiting more often. And I would much rather you stayed. We would hate to start rumors."

"We would?" Lord Bryant raised an eyebrow. She glared at him. Mrs. Oliver didn't know Diana had begged Lord Bryant to do just that. And she would rather keep it that way. Lord Bryant's mouth formed an exaggerated O, and he nodded solemnly. "Miss Barton is correct, of course. Rumors would be devastating to my stellar reputation."

It was hard to maintain a businesslike demeanor with him in her office. They were playing far too many games. Even with that hard look in his eye, Lord Bryant couldn't act in a serious manner. "Yes, Mrs. Oliver, please stay and protect Lord Bryant's reputation for him."

Mrs. Oliver sighed and sat back down in her chair.

Lord Bryant pushed himself off the doorframe. "It is settled then. Miss Oliver, you may stay, at least for today. But in exchange, Diana, you must answer my question. Did you miss me?"

Mrs. Oliver sniggered. "She's been looking up every time a carriage drives by for the last three days."

Diana sunk lower in her seat. She would have to fire Mrs. Oliver. There was no other option. But she couldn't. Diana couldn't spend all day in an office alone. "I have not," Diana said.

"You haven't looked up every time a carriage passed by or you haven't missed me?"

"I didn't look up every time a carriage passed by." Diana scrunched her face together. "I know that for a fact. The last day and a half, I made certain not to."

"Ah," he said, striding toward her like a cat stalking its prey. He hadn't brought a hat with him, and his typically over-styled hair was mussed slightly. Where exactly had he come from? He placed a hand on the exact spot of her desk that he had sat on before kissing her the last time he was here. His emerald eyes sparked with amusement. "So you did miss me."

She raised her chin. "You took your portrait, so of course I did. I had nothing to display when I needed it."

"My portrait that you drew from memory?"

She swallowed her blush. "Yes, that one."

"That is where his portrait went," Mrs. Oliver said. "I was wondering. She used to pull it out of her desk multiple times a day. She would even stroke it."

Diana stood from her desk fast enough that the chair nearly fell over behind her. She grabbed the back of it to steady both it and herself. Mrs. Oliver was much too happy to tell Lord Bryant all of her most incriminating actions of the past few weeks.

"And you should have heard the sweet things she told those men about what you have done for her. Did you really lay your cloak over a puddle so she could cross it?"

Lord Bryant gave Diana a coy look. "That does sound like something I would do. I am generally known for my chivalry."

Mrs. Oliver clapped her hands. Heavens above, did Mrs. Oliver live in a hole? Lord Bryant, chivalrous? Hearing the stories she had told investors come from Mrs. Oliver's lips made them seem even more ridiculous. How had any of them believed her?

"What happened to the cloak?" Mrs. Oliver said. "It must have been quite ruined. And oh, the time you threatened a man's livelihood if he so much as looked at her the wrong way. I tell you, Lord Bryant, by the time you actually did show up, I was starting to wonder if such a man could exist. Not to mention that drawing she had of you. Could a man be as handsome as that? But then you walked through the door, and it turned out the drawing didn't do you justice—not at all."

If whatever hole Mrs. Oliver had been living in could open up and swallow Diana, she would welcome it. "Lord Bryant and I have already discussed his portrait. We are all in agreement that it wasn't well done."

Lord Bryant spoke up. "Oh, come, Diana, I never said it wasn't well done."

Now it was her turn to be incredulous. "I'm quite certain you did."

"I only said the nose wasn't quite right."

That sounded a lot like a criticism to her.

"Is that why you took it away?" Mrs. Oliver asked. "I'm sure she misses it. She used to pull it out all the time, especially when she was speaking of you. There was even a day last week where a particularly handsome young man came in. But she wouldn't give him the time of day. She pulled out your portrait and—"

Oh no, she knew where this was going. That was not her proudest moment. She had listed Lord Bryant's features one by one in praise. It hadn't been hard for her; there were many praiseworthy features to list. But the last thing she wanted was for Mrs. Oliver to repeat them. "Perhaps we need that coal after all." Diana reached into a drawer, pulled out a shilling, crossed the room, and pressed it into Mrs. Oliver's hand.

Mrs. Oliver sputtered a bit, but Diana ignored her, pressing her hand at the small of Mrs. Oliver's back and gently guiding her to the door.

Lord Bryant stopped them just before they reached the door. "Ah, Miss Oliver, I shall miss your company. Sometime I hope we will have the chance to catch up on what Diana has been doing during my absence. That last story sounds particularly interesting." The wicked smile in his voice seemed to capture the air around him.

"I work," Diana said before giving Mrs. Oliver a chance to embarrass her further. She pulled the door open with a yank. "That is truly all I do."

Mrs. Oliver nodded a farewell to Lord Bryant and gave Diana a none-too-subtle wink. "I'll take my time getting the coal. I've heard the next borough over has quality products. I may make my way there."

"Perfect," Diana and Lord Bryant said in unison, although Diana suspected it was for very different reasons. She wasn't certain she wanted to know what Lord Bryant's were. Mrs. Oliver glanced back and forth between the two of them and smiled broadly. The spring in Mrs. Oliver's step belied her advancing age. Apparently Lord Bryant made every woman feel like a younger version of herself.

Diana shook her head and turned to face her tormentor.

He was half sitting on the outside of her desk, this time with his arms folded and that arrogantly superior smirk on his perfectly sculpted face. Was it too much to hope that today he would be civil?

He tilted his head to one side and raised both his dark eyebrows. "You stroked my picture?"

Apparently it was.

"Only when men were here." She turned her head to the side and tried to mimic his unaffected smile. "The few times I forgot, they were inclined to believe you were my father."

A muscle in Lord Bryant's jaw clenched, but otherwise he remained smiling. Diana took the small movement as a victory.

"Well, you are quite young, I suppose," he said with a shrug. "What part of my portrait did you stroke? My cheek?" His eyes darted to her lips, and there could be no doubt in Diana's mind that he was reliving their kiss. At least she wasn't the only one. If she wasn't picturing him sitting on her desk just like he was now, she was remembering that kiss, his hands pulling her possessively to him. "Or perhaps my mouth?"

Diana pursed her lips together. She wouldn't give him the pleasure of using them for his imagination. Nor would she give him the upper hand. She wasn't exactly sure what kind of game she and Lord Bryant were playing, but showing embarrassment or answering with a dull answer would certainly make her the loser. She put a fist to her hip. "Your nose."

Lord Bryant's eyes widened, and he coughed into his hand. Almost a laugh, but not quite. A laugh from Lord Bryant would certainly gain her a point. "My nose?"

"Yes."

"But my nose wasn't even correct in that portrait. It had an unbecoming bump."

"Perhaps that is why I liked it so much. You might be better looking if your nose had a bump."

He stood and advanced around her desk, catlike and smooth. "I'll have you know three women commented on the perfection of my nose this week alone."

Oh, Lord Bryant was good. Diana stood her ground, safely behind her chair. She raised an eyebrow. "But are you sure they were compliments? Too much perfection can be off-putting," Diana lied through her teeth. She couldn't think of any other disparagement to give him. How could someone fault Lord Bryant's looks, other than by saying they were too brilliant? "A man should be a bit rough around the edges." Another clench in his jaw. She was enjoying this too much. "And surely three women didn't comment on your nose."

He pulled his lips to one side and furrowed his eyebrows as if he were solemnly thinking. "You know, I believe you are right. Now that I think of it, it was four women."

Diana swallowed a scoff in a sound that mimicked Lord Bryant's earlier cough. She wouldn't hand him any points by laughing. Instead, she nodded knowingly. "Ah, yes. That sounds much more likely. With a nose like yours, I can't imagine you getting fewer than four comments a week."

He frowned, but his eyes still had that playful light in them. "It is a hard lot in life to have such a perfect nose, but it is my lot, and I bear it as well as I know how. Take care and do not fall in love with me because of it, although if you have already resorted to stroking its likeness, I believe it may be too late."

Diana snorted.

"Most women do, you know."

"Stroke your nose?" She closed her eyes, trying to shake that image out of her mind. When she was with Lord Bryant, it was easy to forget that he had this kind of rapport with dozens of young ladies. He had a way of gazing at her as if she were the most interesting person in England.

"No, of course not. You are the only woman who has admitted to that. But most women tend to fall in love with me."

"Because of your nose?"

"I can't see what else it would be." His lips turned down slightly. "The adoration comes so quickly I can't fathom any other reason."

"You don't think it has anything to do with your title, income, or position in Society?"

For the briefest moment, Lord Bryant's devilish gleam seemed to dim, but it was back before she was certain. "I don't think most women think of those things—not like they do a perfect nose."

They couldn't spend the rest of the afternoon speaking of his nose. She wasn't that adept at lying. She gestured around the room. "As you can see, I am not most women."

Lord Bryant stepped closer to her, moving from a distance of pleasant conversation to something much more intimate. Her hands tightened on the chair. "I'm starting to see that. But I would hazard a guess that even you are not immune to my position, title, and looks."

Diana bit the insides of her cheeks. The man was infuriating. It was as if the only thing that mattered to him was his ability to attract women—but not for who he was as a person and not for anything permanent. It was as if he knew he would only have superficial relationships, and he was happy to leave it at that. Of course he was. Most rakes were. She needed to stop thinking of him as the dashing person she had seen at Nate's wedding and remember exactly what type of man he was. "I admit, when I first met you at Nate's wedding, I did find you attractive. But I'm not a young, impressionable eighteen-year-old anymore."

"And how old are you now, Grandmother?"

Diana lifted her chin. "I'm twenty-two, but more to the point, I am running two businesses and making a lot of people—including you—quite rich."

"I already was rich."

"Richer, then."

He nodded as if that answer was acceptable.

"So," Lord Bryant said, "seeing as you are so wise and—dare I say—old . . ." He smiled at that. He must still think of her as a baby. "No matter how charming I am, nor how perfect my nose is, you won't fall in love with me?"

"Correct."

"Ah, Miss Barton. You are just the distraction I need. That makes this much more fun." Lord Bryant was already unseemly close to her, but he bent forward until his face was only inches from her own. Lifting his hand, he placed a gloved finger under her chin. "I find this chin of yours quite distracting. It is always lifted, which makes that delicate throat of yours much too accessible."

Diana fought the impulse to lower her chin, instead keeping it raised. "Accessible to what? Strangling?" A dark glint sparked in his eye, and a half-curled smile appeared on his lips. She had been right. "You have thought of strangling me?"

He chuckled but not in a surprised way. He removed his hand from her face and placed it behind his back, then took one step away from her. "No, Diana. Strangling is not at all what I had in mind," he said with his eyes still at her throat. She swallowed and turned to sit down at her desk. She had work to do, and she would need to do it whether Lord Bryant was here or not.

Lord Bryant took his seat on the inside corner of her desk. Diana kept her head lowered over her work, but from the corner of her eye, she saw him pick up a pen from her desk and hold it softly between two fingers. He then waved it up and down in a slow, smooth movement. The pen became like a string waving in the air. How did he do that? No matter, she wouldn't give him the pleasure of asking.

Work. She needed to work. What was the good of imploring Lord Bryant to help her if it didn't actually equate to getting more work done? He set the pen down and hopped off her desk. Finally, a bit of space between them. Lord Bryant strode to the door. Was he leaving already? He couldn't handle more than a minute of being ignored?

That sounded accurate.

She watched Lord Bryant through her lowered eyelashes as, instead of leaving, he removed his jacket. Underneath his plain, black jacket was a deep-green velvet waistcoat. Lighter green vines were embroidered on it, drawing attention to his narrow waist and broad chest. Her pen froze in her hand—not that she had actually been writing anything, but now the pretense was gone. He hung the jacket on the coatrack by the door before his hand went to his cravat.

She gave up the charade and looked up. "Are you undressing in my place of business?"

His black cravat stayed mostly in place, but with only a few tugs, it would follow his jacket and end up on her coatrack. "I'm only making myself comfortable. I haven't had the best morning."

"How comfortable are you planning on making yourself?"

"Only about as comfortable as I was when you visited me in my study."

Oh dear. Although he was fully clothed at that time, his open neck and the V of his chest was an image she wouldn't soon forget. She didn't need a reminder of it. "Please leave your cravat in place. How would you get home with a ruined cravat?"

"In my carriage."

"But your footman . . ."

"If my footman was shocked by a hastily tied cravat, he wouldn't be my footman."

Diana pushed away the images of what exactly he could mean by that. "Still, if you wouldn't mind leaving it on, it would make it easier for me to do my work without worrying that a legitimate investor would come in and get the wrong idea."

"That is your only worry about me removing my cravat?" His hand hovered dangerously above the intricate knot. "I seemed to notice your eye often drawn to my neck the last time you saw me without one."

"Lord Bryant, I was hardly myself that night—"

With a flick of his wrist, the cravat was undone and lying flat against his chest. He gave one side a slow, steady pull, and the material slid off his shoulder and into his hand. Diana did not look at his neck. She wouldn't. Lord Bryant hung his cravat on the coatrack and, before she had a chance to complain further, quickly undid and rolled up his shirtsleeves.

Avoiding his neck meant she was stuck looking at his forearms. This was only his second time visiting her office, and he had managed to half undress. What exactly had she gotten herself into?

"It is nice to feel so comfortable in front of a woman. Usually I would have to remain respectable for fear that the sight of me in such a casual state would make her instantly taken with my physique. I can't tell you what a comfort it is to know that you are completely immune to my charms." He lifted one eyebrow slowly and then, as if that weren't bad enough, the other.

The man was completely ridiculous, no matter how well-formed his arms.

"I am immune." Her face was slightly warm, and her pulse elevated, but as skilled as Lord Bryant was, even he couldn't be a mind reader. "So you may stop all this silly nonsense. It isn't going to work."

"These types of things usually do work."

They worked on loads of women, Diana reminded herself. They wouldn't work on her. She was smarter than that. She set her pen down. At this point, it was useless to pretend to work. But she wouldn't allow Lord Bryant to think that was because she was fascinated by him. Lord Bryant was supremely confident—it would do him good to show him that not all women fell for his tricks.

"For someone who spends so much time wooing women, I would think you would know better than to mention previous conquests. It hardly makes one feel noteworthy."

He strode forward, away from the coatrack but closer to her. She could still feel the warmth from his fingers on her chin, but it wouldn't do to tell him that.

"A mere twenty-two years of experience has made you an expert on the ways of the heart, has it? I am inclined to disagree."

As if Lord Bryant knew anything about her twenty-two years. She wasn't a London lady, hoping to catch the most eligible unwed gentleman in town. Lord Bryant may know how to impress almost any woman with a heartbeat and a pair of working eyes, but even he couldn't be irresistible to every single individual of her sex. There was more to a man than fine arms and a perfect nose.

"I don't believe your years of philandering have made you any more of an expert."

He reached her desk, placed both hands on it, and leaned down until his face was level with hers. Once again, he raised an eyebrow. Couldn't those things stay still? "Again, I would have to disagree."

Diana gathered a few papers and stacked them neatly together. There was nothing else to tidy on her desk, so she faced Lord Bryant again. His eyes were the exact shade of his waistcoat, and they were only inches from her own. "You may have fascinated a few women with these types of activities, but no woman will love you because of them. You will never touch a woman's heart. Not truly. That simply isn't how women work."

Lord Bryant swallowed, then pushed off her desk and stood straight. His eyes closed for a moment as if he were in pain, but when they opened again, she couldn't see any hurt, only determination. He pushed his sleeves up higher on his arms, then strode back to her desk, once again half leaning on the corner. He spun a delicate gold signet ring on his pinkie finger. It was thinner than most men's rings. Had it been his wife's?

"What makes this so interesting is that I'm not actually trying to make you fall in love with me. You know as well as I do that all this pretense stops if either of us truly forms an interest in the other party. That being said, if I had wanted to make a woman fall in love with me, truly—" He pivoted on her desk, his eyes now watching the street through the window. "What should I have done?"

Diana stilled. He wasn't laughing or being a shameless flirt. He almost seemed in earnest. Lord Bryant in earnest was something for which she was not prepared. She much preferred him jesting and removing clothing. At least then she could sigh and throw her eyes to the ceiling. She blinked hard and slid a small mountain of paperwork to the outside of her desk. "Well." She cleared her throat. "If said women were anything like me, you could have started by underlining all the expenses related to the current Barton line. Once they are marked, add them all together."

He turned and eyed the paperwork with a half grimace. "This doesn't seem like a task for a gentleman."

"You asked my opinion, and I gave it."

"I'd much rather trace a kiss or two along the inside of your wrist."

Diana forcefully kept her wrists facing down. She wouldn't look at them or give him the satisfaction of letting him see her interest. She had never even considered the inside of her wrist to be a place of seduction, and now suddenly she could think of no other spot on her body. It was as if all her nerves were focused on those two joints. The veins that ran through them felt as though they were on fire. She grabbed her pen and the closest paper she could find on her desk. She needed to get back to work. "And that, Lord Bryant, is exactly why I will never fall in love with you."

Lord Bryant laughed and slid off the desk into a standing position. "Thank the heavens for that." A small part of Diana withered at his comment. Of course she didn't want to fall in love with him, but would it have hurt him so much to appear offended by her declaration? He sauntered behind her and put a hand on the desk on either side of her, making his arms impossible to ignore. When he spoke, his voice was in her ear. "However, my dear Diana, your bold statement feels quite a bit like a challenge, and I do love a challenge."

"But not enough to help me with my paperwork?"

"Helping you with your paperwork would actually feel more like losing the challenge. You've already trapped me into this charade with that portrait; that is one point to you. My doing paperwork would most definitely be another point to you. It is my turn to win some points."

"So we *are* playing a game."

"It would seem so."

"And for points?"

"Yes."

"How will we know when one of us has won?"

The bell above the door clanged. Mrs. Oliver walked through the door, looking as pleased as punch to see Lord Bryant hovering over Diana in his shirtsleeves. He pushed off her desk and away from her. Under his breath, he whispered, "When I win, I will be sure to let you know."

Lord Bryant spent the next twenty minutes ignoring her and making Mrs. Oliver blush like a sunset. Instead of a farewell, he strode by her desk and touched a finger to her chin, and then he was gone.

Now that he had visited, she had no reason to look for him out the window.

And yet, every few moments, she did.

CHAPTER 8

EVERTON HAD NEARLY FORGOTTEN WHAT his ballroom looked like, especially all lit up. The last time it had been in use, his mother had hosted a ball especially for the purpose of introducing him to Rachel. Rachel had been vibrant with a shy innocence that immediately appealed to him. Of all the people his parents could have picked for him, he was surprised they had chosen so well. Here was a woman he felt he could have a happy marriage with. He had been confident, young, and foolish.

Tonight he had the opportunity to change another young, quiet woman's fate. Here was a chance to show Lord Silverstone that, despite the blessing of Lady Emily's parents, he should know better than to marry her. If a young man like Everton could be charmed by her, she should be charming enough for anyone.

Lady Emily had no need to settle for an arranged marriage.

If only she would talk.

At the moment, Lady Emily wasn't doing herself any favors. She sat in the corner of the ballroom, surrounded by some of the older matrons who had given up dancing. Unlike Miss Barton, Lady Emily's chin was always down, her eyes always lowered. Her pale-blonde hair was stacked expertly atop her head, and her gown was one of the more revealing her family had dressed her in. Every effort they made for the poor girl only made it worse. If they allowed her to wear something plainer with a top that was—well—more of a top, she might actually get up the nerve to speak to some of the attendees.

He shook his head and plastered a half smile on his face. The crowd made way for him as he strode across the ballroom.

"Lady Emily," he said when he reached her side. Her fan covered her chest, fluttering nearly as much as her eyes did at his salutation. "It took me much too long to find you. What are you doing hiding away like this?"

Another flutter from the fan as he waited patiently, and just as her mouth was about to open, an older woman to his left answered for her. "We have been discussing the latest fashions. Haven't we, my dear?"

Lady Emily's eyes widened. Everton had watched her for a good ten minutes before coming over. That woman hadn't once bothered to talk to her. If they had been speaking of fashions, it must have been quite some time ago. Her parents needed to send her with a companion to these functions if they insisted on immediately finding their own friends and leaving her to fend for herself—something she wasn't capable of, at least not yet.

"Has your dance card been filled yet? If not, I would like to take your next open set."

Lady Emily shook her head no but still wouldn't speak up enough to say which of the next dances would be his.

"Is your next set free?"

A subtle nod.

"Then I shall claim it."

The plump lady who had supposedly been speaking of fashions with Lady Emily slid on her chair to be closer to the two of them. "My daughter is also free for the next set if Lady Emily would rather be excused."

The woman next to the plump matron furrowed her eyebrows. "But I thought your daughter was dancing—" A sharp elbow jab from her friend cut her off.

"I have hosted this ball with the express purpose of dancing with Lady Emily. No other woman will do."

The woman huffed, and Lady Emily blushed. He put his arm out to her, and she reluctantly took it. He couldn't imagine why she would want to sit next to these women, but he had a feeling the low lighting in that corner had something to do with it.

At this point, he would typically remark on a woman's appearance or make a disparaging remark about one of the overdressed gentlemen hoping to catch any young woman of fortune's eye, but after several weeks spent in Lady Emily's company, he had learned that she was most comfortable with silence.

Silence was not one of his strong points, but he hated to frighten the poor girl, so he kept his observation of Mr. Rushland's orange-flowered vest to himself.

It only took one turn about the room for the current set to finish, and Everton led Lady Emily to the outer edge of the dancers to await their set. He had yet to dance with the shy Lady Emily, as most of their interactions had been at card parties and house calls.

The music for a Schottische started. Her fan finally dropped from her hand to her wrist, and Everton quickly looked away so she wouldn't notice his reaction. Not only had her family forced her into a ballgown with a low bodice, but they had placed the most ridiculous chartreuse bow at the center of her bosom. The next time he had a chance to speak with Lady Emily's mother, he would have some choice words for her.

Lady Emily started out the dance timidly. But within the first few bars of music, something changed in her. Her steps lifted higher, and when he pushed her out and then back into him, she actually smiled.

A smile.

A smile he could work with. He tightened his grip on her hand and, as a test, added an extra hop to their turn. It didn't faze her, and on her following turn, she repeated the same hop. Her chin was finally raised, and her pale-blue eyes sparked with excitement.

He pulled her close as they performed a series of steps with her in his arms. "I didn't know you could dance so well."

"I don't often get the chance."

Her voice was a bit breathless, but he caught every word. Lady Emily was quite a different person when she was dancing.

"You don't think that has anything to do with you hiding in the corner?"

She lowered her head, and without thinking, he put his finger under her chin to lift it. Her eyes immediately dulled, and he pulled his hand away as if he had been burned. Or to be more accurate, as if his touch would burn her.

"I don't know anyone here," she said, still not looking at him. She was the daughter of an earl. It shouldn't be difficult for her to get to know people in this room.

"Would you like me to introduce you to a few of the women I know? Perhaps that would help. The Duchess of Harrington is here. She is one of the few very good women in London. Her son is a bit tedious, but he opted not to come, so there is no concern about speaking to him."

"Perhaps." Lady Emily didn't sound interested. Most women he knew would be delighted to be introduced to a duchess.

"Don't you want to meet people?"

"I'm not sure I like people."

"But you like dancing."

"Yes, I do like dancing and music, but I don't like balls."

This was more insight into his conquest than he'd had since she had whispered over tea that she was interested in geology. He had the sudden desire to agree with her. Dancing could be entertaining—a hand at a woman's waist, a chance to move to well-played music. Really, it was the people at balls that disturbed him. But there wasn't a way to be rid of them or else he would, for Lady Emily's sake. He leaned forward, careful not to come too close to her pale-blonde curls. Distance seemed to be a key to keeping her comfortable. "Close your eyes."

Her eyes flashed up to his. "Pardon me?"

"Close your eyes. I will watch the crowds. You are a good enough dancer that you can follow me with your eyes closed. Allow yourself to simply dance and enjoy the music. Don't worry about people."

The corner of her mouth rose slightly, and she nodded in agreement. Her eyes fluttered closed, and Everton tightened his grip on her hand and waist, making certain each turn and step would be clear to her.

At first, Lady Emily was stiff and unsure, but after two turns without incident, she relaxed and started to move more freely with him. They finished that dance and the next one of the set in the same manner—never speaking, only dancing. When the strains of music stopped and Lady Emily finally opened her eyes, he could tell it was with great reluctance.

"The next set is the supper dance. Would you like to continue?" Dancing two sets with the same woman wouldn't be the most scandalous thing he had ever done.

"I wish I could, but Mama has promised the supper dance to Lord Silverstone."

"Is that why he left you alone in a corner up until now?" He held his arm out to her, and she took it, her touch barely there, as if a butterfly had landed on his arm.

"Perhaps. We haven't actually talked much. I cannot claim to understand his reasons."

If Lord Silverstone was as talkative as Lady Emily, the two of them would have a silent home indeed. Lady Emily's eyes had started to wander to the darkened corners. It wouldn't do for her to sneak back to one of those. Even if Everton were successful in stopping her marriage to Lord Silverstone, she was going to have a hard time finding a man she cared for if she was always hiding in corners.

Everton cleared his throat, which brought her attention back to him. "I must say, I was pleased with one aspect of Lord Silverstone when being introduced to him."

Lady Emily waited for him to continue, but he wouldn't until she spoke again. "What was pleasing about him?" she finally asked.

Everton grinned. "He had hair. If your parents are going to marry you off to a widower three times your age, at least he has hair."

Lady Emily sighed, his lame attempt at humor lost on her. "I wish I could go back to last year, when all that was expected of me was to sit at home, reading and practicing the pianoforte."

"Well, if we create a big enough scandal, perhaps you can do just that. Should I not hand you off to him?" Where was Lord Silverstone? When Everton had first met Rachel and discovered they were soon to be wed, he had tried to seek her out at each of the few events they had attended together. Didn't Lord Silverstone want to get to know his bride-to-be? He scanned the ballroom. Lady Falburton was in a large group of overly trimmed women. Even Lady Emily's chartreuse bow wouldn't be out of place amongst that set. He shuddered, not looking forward to the questions such a group of women like that would regale him with. Even though he hated the idea of it, he would rather pass Lady Emily off directly to Lord Silverstone than enter those shark-infested waters.

His eyes finally landed on Lord Silverstone on the other side of the ballroom. He was deep in conversation with three other men. One of the men stood over the others, commanding attention with his broad smile.

Blast.

Lord Yolten. When had he arrived? And how had he ended up with an invitation? Mrs. Cuthbert must have sent him an invitation. She should know better. And if he was here . . .

Certainly enough, Lady Yolten, with her broad mouth and presence that, despite her small stature, seemed to encompass those around her, stood in a small group of women. His weeks with her had been good ones. One of the ladies next to her said something in Lady Yolten's ear. Lady Yolten put a hand to the other lady's elbow and threw her head back with a laugh. Despite the distance and the rumblings of the crowd, he could hear the way she took pleasure in a laugh. The chime of it rang through his mind if not his ears.

Everton blinked and brought his attention back to the lady at his side. Not all women could be as full of life as Lady Yolten. That didn't mean they didn't deserve to gain what they wanted out of life. He smiled at Lady Emily.

He couldn't hand her to Lord Silverstone now, not with Lord Yolten standing right next to him. He would have to acknowledge Lord Yolten, and for all he knew, Lord Yolten would treat him like some kind of friend. There was nothing more awkward than publicly facing a man whose wife he had dallied about with. Even if it was before they were married.

"Why don't we dance again and drive Lord Silverstone off in a huff?"

Lady Emily chewed on her lip and sighed. "I should like to dance with him. Just once."

Everton waited for her to elaborate on her reasonings, but she never seemed to offer up more than what was asked. "Why?" he prodded.

"I don't know what my parents have told him about me, but I'm certain it wasn't accurate. If he is disappointed in me, we can end this whole fiasco tonight."

It wasn't the best of plans. In many ways, Lady Emily was probably exactly the type of wife that kind of man was looking for. She was quiet and unassuming. Silverstone would probably see her as someone easy to control and manipulate to do his bidding.

Lady Emily would slowly lose herself with a man like that when she hadn't been given a chance to find herself in the first place.

But if she desired a dance with Lord Silverstone, Everton wasn't going to stop her. She had enough people telling her what to do. He wasn't about to ignore the first thing she had admitted to wanting. "I'll escort you to your mother. I refuse to hand you off to him." Not only because Lord Yolten was in his circle of friends. He couldn't watch Lady Emily put her butterfly touch on a man who bartered for a young wife at that age.

She simply nodded.

After a few quick words to Lady Emily's mother and a few long ones to her frilled companions, Everton strode away from them. His main goal was accomplished for the evening. He had danced only with Lady Emily. After tonight, he suspected a few more gentlemen would notice her. But she was a hard one to figure out. By all rights, men should already be flocking about her. She simply managed to find the most unlikely hiding places. Even if a man came with the express purpose of pursuing her, he would have to find her first.

He shook his head. Lady Emily was so different from the other women he had had scandals with. They all knew what they wanted. Lady Emily wanted to stay home and not face the reality of her future. She didn't want to marry, nor did she want to be out among people. There wasn't much he could do to procure that for her. But at least he could stop a marriage with the man who was now addressing Lady Emily's mother. Lord Silverstone didn't even look at Lady Emily. What kind of man bartered with parents over a wife without even trying to involve her in the process?

He cursed under his breath. At one point in time, he had been just that sort of man. He had never thought to ask Rachel how she felt about the two of them marrying. He had assumed she had come to the same conclusions as he: they would marry because their parents expected it, and they would make the best of that marriage.

A gentle tap on his shoulder brought him out of his musings.

"Pardon me, Lord Bryant." It was a servant, one of the temporary ones he'd hired to help with the ball. "There is a gentleman and two ladies here to see you."

"Here to see me?" He scoured the ballroom. Who would be wanting to speak with him?

"They aren't in the ballroom, sir. They have been shown to the drawing room."

The drawing room? He was supposed to meet these three people in his drawing room whilst in the middle of hosting a ball? Who in the world would think of such a thing? Dark-brown hair and scathing eyes flashed into his mind.

"Was one of the ladies young with dark-brown hair?"

"Yes, sir. She had a rather strange message for me to send you."

"What kind of message?"

"Something about your nose."

He clenched his jaw. Miss Barton. Why in the world would she be here? This was his one stipulation—they couldn't meet in ballrooms or anywhere remotely social. Miss Barton was constantly cropping up in his life when she shouldn't be. First, unchaperoned at his home late at night, and now in the midst of a ball. Why couldn't she follow simple instructions? Not everyone respected Everton, and he was fine with that. He didn't deserve or want respect. But he was used to people listening to him, even if for no other reason than that they were intimidated by his position in Society.

For whatever reason, Miss Barton wasn't intimidated by him. That had to stop tonight or who knew where she would turn up next. It was bad enough having Lady Yolten and Lady Emily in the same room. Now he had to deal with a third woman? Perhaps Nelson was right, and it was time he gave up on all this nonsense. Soon he wouldn't be able to go anywhere.

He followed the reticent servant to the drawing room. So help him, if Miss Barton was haughtily raising her chin when he got to that room . . .

"What exactly did she say about my nose?" he asked.

"I didn't really understand it, sir."

Everton took a deep breath, trying to calm himself. "Just tell me what she said."

"She said if you didn't come, she would improve your nose for you." The servant shook his head. "I didn't understand her, though. Nothing is wrong with your nose."

Everton wished, for the fifteenth time, that everyone was out of his home. He wanted nothing more than to tear off his cravat and stamp on it. "Frankly, I don't understand her either, but after today, I'll make certain she understands me."

CHAPTER 9

Diana did her best to appear calm. She and Lord Bryant were in a supposed relationship together. It wouldn't do to look worried or unsure of herself. She kept her head lifted and her shoulders back as she waited for Lord Bryant to walk through the drawing room door. Mrs. Oliver looked as pleased as punch. She was as certain of Lord Bryant's love for Diana as she was that the sun would rise tomorrow morning. Mr. Broadcreek looked as he always did: as if he had just swallowed vinegar. Loathsome man.

Blast Mr. Broadcreek and his interfering ways.

He had known about this ball when he had so persistently asked her to accompany him to Lord Bryant's home. He wasn't even clever enough to cover up his knowledge once they had arrived.

As soon as Lord Bryant's home—lit up like a chandelier—had come into view, he had turned to her with a smile on his face. "Weren't you invited?" Mr. Broadcreek asked. "If Lord Bryant was truly interested in you, as you seem to believe he is, one would think you would have been invited to a ball that he was hosting. And word has it he is hosting it at the request of a certain titled young lady."

Diana's pride hadn't allowed her to answer truthfully. "Lord Bryant understands my need to work. He knows I wouldn't take time away for something so frivolous."

"So you weren't invited?"

"Of course Lord Bryant invited her," Mrs. Oliver had chimed in. "Our Miss Barton doesn't enjoy these types of things is all. She would rather be in the office, and Lord Bryant understands that."

Mrs. Oliver's words stung, despite their truth. She *would* rather be in the office, and yet . . . Diana pushed her feelings aside and nodded, grateful that

Mrs. Oliver had so much faith in Lord Bryant and could save Diana from outright lying to Mr. Broadcreek.

"Well, should we go in?" Diana had asked.

The look on Mr. Broadcreek's face when she called his bluff was almost worth the discomfort she felt sitting on Lord Bryant's settee. It helped that Mr. Broadcreek looked at least as uncomfortable as she did.

Mr. Broadcreek leaned forward in his chair. "Are you certain we should stay?"

Diana smiled. Making Mr. Broadcreek shift in his seat was an added bonus she hadn't expected in this charade. "I was under the impression that you had something of utmost importance to ask Lord Bryant."

"I do . . ." He pulled on his sleeves and cleared his throat. "It just seems, under the circumstances, it might be best if we came another time."

"Under the circumstances? You mean the ball? If you knew about the ball and I knew about the ball . . . why did we come all this way only to leave when a ball we both knew was happening is happening?"

Mr. Broadcreek furrowed his brows, but he didn't remove himself from his seat.

As much as Diana enjoyed watching Mr. Broadcreek squirm, her pride came with a heavy price tag. Any moment now Lord Bryant would walk through that door, having just excused himself from his own ball.

A ball. The one place she had promised him she would never go.

Still, it wasn't as if they were socializing. They were in the drawing room. Lady Emily wouldn't even know they had been here. Nor would Diana get a chance to see her. What type of woman inspired Lord Bryant to host a ball?

The door opened, and Diana gripped the sides of her heavy practical skirt. A servant motioned with his hand, and Lord Bryant stomped into the room. All eyes turned to him, a situation the baron must be used to. He commanded the attention of any room he entered. He stopped as soon as he saw who was there. First his eyes flashed to Diana, scanning her face, then pausing at her throat. Diana sucked in a breath and silently prayed that he would stop looking at her like she was a lamb thrown into a lion's den. The den of a hungry, majestic lion with eyes that sparked like fire. Her breath released in a rush when he finally cast his attention on Mrs. Oliver. He gave her a slight nod, and then his eyes narrowed as they took in Mr. Broadcreek. With some sort of silent agreement, all of them waited for the servant to leave and shut the door before speaking.

"Diana," Lord Bryant said with a hand to his waist. "What are you doing here?"

He was using her Christian name at least. That was a good sign. If he was about to kick her outside, pretending to never know her, he wouldn't have called her by name. What should she call him? Calling him Lord Bryant didn't seem right since he had addressed her so intimately.

"Darling," she tried. His eyebrow rose. Perhaps not that. She stood and walked behind the settee. It seemed a good idea to put something between her and Lord Bryant. "Do you know Mr. Broadcreek? He wanted to meet you."

Lord Bryant barely gave Mr. Broadcreek a nod. "Mr. Broadcreek and I know of each other even if we haven't met. And that is a situation I'm not trying to change. There is no reason for you to come find me here, especially not tonight."

"Lord Bryant," Mr. Broadcreek started, but he was immediately silenced by a glare.

"Mr. Broadcreek, I have no desire to speak to you. You have dragged two young ladies to seek me out, late into the night, under the false pretenses that I would have any interest in meeting you. I have no desire to associate with you."

"But, Lord Bryant, are you aware of what Miss Barton is saying about you?" Mr. Broadcreek's neck was turning a deep red and the hollows under his eyes a dark shade of purple. Lord Bryant, on the other hand, appeared to be in complete control of his composure.

The stare Lord Bryant gave Mr. Broadcreek was icy and cold. "If I say I am not, are you going to repeat unfounded rumors about a gentlewoman here in my drawing room?"

"Well . . ."

"Mr. Broadcreek, leave."

Mr. Broadcreek sputtered. "How can they be called unfounded when I personally—"

"Mr. Broadcreek." Lord Bryant's elegant frame was still, like a cat ready to pounce. "Now."

"Should I go too?" Mrs. Oliver jumped up from her chair. "Would you like to speak to Diana alone?"

Mrs. Oliver would be the death of her.

"What could he possibly have to speak with her about?" Mr. Broadcreek's sputtering finally formed words. "Everyone knows Lord Bryant has an aversion to marriage. To think that he would stoop so low as to actually be honorable with Miss Barton, a working woman who spends all of her time with men. You shouldn't leave a young lady alone with such a man, Mrs. Oliver."

"Oh, posh." Mrs. Oliver hit Mr. Broadcreek with her glove. "Love knows nothing of Society and position. They are practically engaged. I'm not going to begrudge them a few minutes alone."

Diana leaned forward against the settee. The last thing in the world she wanted was to be left alone with Lord Bryant right now. His jaw was still clenched in that way it was when he was angry. No, it wouldn't be a good idea to be left alone with him now at all.

"I'm sorry we troubled you, dear." A quirk of his jaw. Also not the right word. "We will be going. If you have need to speak with me, please come to the office tomorrow."

Mr. Broadcreek motioned for her to leave before him. Diana stepped around the settee toward the door.

Lord Bryant slid in front of her path. "Since you have come so far, I don't think you should leave without having a private word with me."

Diana took another step toward the door. "Now is perhaps not the best time for a conversation."

"Then perhaps I won't say anything at all." Lord Bryant's eyes narrowed toward Mr. Broadcreek, and his jaw clenched again. Could it be too much to hope that Lord Bryant was upset with Mr. Broadcreek and not her? "Mr. Broadcreek has obviously come here because he doesn't believe the rumors about us are true, and I see no better way to prove him wrong." Lord Bryant's hand went to her waist. "Or we could prove him wrong while he is still in the room. Which would you prefer?"

A dangerous glint sparked in Lord Bryant's eyes. His fingertips dug into her waist, beckoning her closer. She didn't know what Lord Bryant looked like when he was bluffing, but if she were a betting woman, she didn't think this was it.

He was at least a little bit upset with her.

Diana turned to Mr. Broadcreek. "You had better leave."

"But . . ." Mr. Broadcreek said.

"You led her here." Lord Bryant didn't take his eyes off Diana's, even as he growled at Mr. Broadcreek. "You cannot complain of the outcome."

"Oh, come," Mrs. Oliver said, grabbing Mr. Broadcreek by the elbow. "Let them be for a few minutes. We will be back to collect Diana in five minutes—not a moment more."

Mr. Broadcreek took a step toward the door, then stopped, then took another step toward the door.

"Miss Barton." Mr. Broadcreek wrenched his arm away from Mrs. Oliver when they reached the door. He turned around and pulled on the hem of his jacket. "Are you certain you will be all right alone with him?"

Now Mr. Broadcreek was worried about her reputation after dragging her all the way across town well into the night? The man was shameless.

"I will be quite safe. Lord Bryant only looks dangerous. Inside he is soft like a skein of yarn. Aren't you, my treasure?" She really needed to figure out what to call him.

"Like a room full of yarn," he said in that hard way of his.

Diana threw a smile at Mr. Broadcreek. He looked back and forth between Diana and Lord Bryant, his eyes pausing where Lord Bryant still held her at the waist. Diana had never seen him more hesitant. It was almost worth the baron's wrath.

Lord Bryant indicated with a lift of his head that Mr. Broadcreek should vacate the room. After only half a breath's hesitation, he turned and left. The door clicked closed, and Lord Bryant immediately dropped his hand from her waist.

"So . . ." Diana looked over the space between them. "You won't be carrying out your threats?"

Lord Bryant threw his hands up in the air. "What are you doing here, Diana? It has been barely a week since we came to an agreement, and already you are breaking it. You cannot be here. Why won't you comply with the one single thing I asked of you?"

"I wasn't planning to come here. Mr. Broadcreek insisted on needing to ask you something. He waited all afternoon and into the evening for you to come into the office. When you never did, he demanded I take him to you."

"Why do you do what that man says? He isn't even a good man."

"Oh, and you are a saint."

"It doesn't matter what I am, and you don't listen to me anyway."

"Mr. Broadcreek is an influential man. I have that vote coming up, and he knows people in the House of Lords."

For the first time this evening, Lord Bryant raised his voice. "I'm *in* the House of Lords."

Diana took a deep breath. It was doing neither of them good to speak so harshly to one another, and she was the one in the wrong. "I'm sorry, Lord Bryant. This was a breach of trust. I should never have come here. Mr. Broadcreek is an infuriating, busnacking ratbag."

Lord Bryant blinked. "What did you say?"

"Shall I repeat it? Mr. Broadcreek is a vazey, stinking ratbag." The man had kept her from hours upon hours of work. He had forced her to get help from Lord Bryant, and now he had interrupted Lord Bryant's evening with Lady Emily.

The muscle in Lord Bryant's cheek relaxed. He placed his fingers on his forehead, his thumb on his cheek, and massaged the skin above his eyes. "Miss Barton, I don't know what I'm going to do with you."

Diana wrinkled her nose. "I hope you will bear with me a little longer. A few months are all I need."

"I cannot believe that your brother left you alone to wreak havoc on London. Didn't he know what kind of trouble you would get yourself into?"

"Believe it or not, up until six months ago, I hadn't gotten myself into any trouble at all."

"I find that hard to believe."

It was true. Her life in Baimbury had been calm and restful. She and her mother enjoyed quiet evenings at home and never had any cause to upset peers of the realm. But they hadn't been much help to Nate either. He had borne the burden of saving the family on his own for far too long. Now he needed his time of rest with Grace in Baimbury. Diana simply needed to keep Lord Bryant happy so he would continue to help her.

"How is Lady Emily?"

His shoulders sagged. "Quiet as always."

His eyes flitted to the doorway, concern written all over his face. What type of woman had Lord Bryant so worried? "I've heard that most men like their women to be quiet. I suppose that is one more strike against me, as if being a businesswoman weren't bad enough."

"Oh, don't worry about that, Miss Barton. I'm certain that when you decide you want to marry, you will be able to browbeat some young, unsuspecting gentleman into matrimony quite easily."

Diana smiled up at him. "Do you really think so? A gentleman, even?"

Something changed in Lord Bryant. His face softened. "I'm certain of it. Not all men want quiet women."

Lord Bryant did though, didn't he? Otherwise, he wouldn't be so worried about his relationship with Lady Emily. The way he was looking at Diana now made her wonder. She swallowed and stepped toward the door. Lord Bryant looked at every woman that way. She wouldn't fall for his roguish charm.

"I think our five minutes are finished if that is all you wanted to speak to me about."

To her disappointment, Lord Bryant nodded and held his hand toward the door. It looked as though he wouldn't be carrying out his threats of kissing her after all. And why should he? No one was here to see it.

She reached for the doorknob, but his hand came from behind her and covered her own. A shock ran up her arm at his touch, and she hastily pulled her hand away.

Had he felt that?

She snuck a glance at him through lowered lashes. His face was unreadable. Of course he hadn't. This was a man who had multiple scandals a year. An accidental touch of the hand wouldn't make his nerves catch fire.

He was standing directly behind her, his arm extended above her shoulder. Her back was nearly pressed into him. He leaned forward and placed his mouth next to her ear. "Next time you feel the need to show your love through pet names, don't."

Diana frowned. What was she to do then? "You expect me to call you Lord Bryant in front of Mr. Broadcreek?" Her voice sounded small. She still hadn't recovered from the touch of his hand, and his nearness wasn't helping matters.

"If you were in love with me, I would think you would call me Everton."

Of course she would.

Lord Bryant tugged on the knob and opened the door. She ducked out of the room and found Mrs. Oliver and Mr. Broadcreek waiting with a maid by the front door. She turned back and almost bumped into Lord Bryant. Flushing, she raised her eyes to his steely green ones. "Once again, I'm sorry to have disturbed your evening."

"It is always a pleasure to see you, Diana. It's only unfortunate I cannot steal you away for a dance."

Now that Mr. Broadcreek was behind her, he was back to his charming ways. If she hadn't known better, she would have taken one look at his openly appreciative eyes and thought he was being sincere.

Everton stood in the drawing room doorway. Diana Barton reached for Mrs. Oliver's hand and, without casting a second glance at Mr. Broadcreek, made her way to the door. The servant who had led him here waited to let them outside. Mr. Broadcreek turned his head to glare at Everton, eyes narrowed, before following the two women.

He needed to head back into the ballroom. It was nearly time for supper. Lady Emily would have to sit by Lord Silverstone, and he should be there in case she ran into any trouble.

He couldn't force himself back into that room, though. Not yet. He needed a moment to regroup. He glanced down at his fingers and rubbed them together. What exactly had that been? He wasn't some young buck in his first Season, blushing at the chance to brush fingers with a beautiful young woman. He had kissed Miss Barton. He had kissed many women, to be precise. He had been married for Pete's sake.

He shook his head. He needed to get more sleep. That could be the only explanation. Even if he had been a man young enough to tempt that firebrand, he wouldn't have wanted to. A man should be comfortable around his wife.

Miss Barton had only managed to make him uncomfortable and on edge.

He was halfway back to the ballroom when he suddenly reached for a wall to steady himself. He glanced around the corridor, but no one was nearby. Closing his eyes, he reached deep down inside himself to make certain his heart was calm.

It was.

For the first time in four years, he had thought about marriage, and it hadn't turned him into a blubbering mess. He clenched his fingers together again, remembering the feel of Miss Barton's hand beneath his own. What in the world was happening to him?

CHAPTER 10

Diana shook her hand to relieve the cramp between her fingers. This was the fourth letter she had written to her investors, and she still had to write six more. She needed the final guarantees of investments to include in her petition to Parliament.

"Mrs. Oliver, do you have the address for Mr. Galbraith in Rochester?"

"It is on your desk, miss, just to the left of your envelopes. It's on the same list as all of your other investors."

Of course it was. She rubbed her face and stood to stretch out her back. Running a railroad business wasn't difficult so much as it was time-consuming, thought-consuming, and just life-consuming. No wonder Nate had wanted to be with Grace in Baimbury. If they had stayed in London, he wouldn't have had much time to see her at all. He would be at the office late every night just as Diana was.

She turned to face Mrs. Oliver, shook her arms, and, throwing propriety out the window, kicked her legs up one at a time. Hardly anyone came to the office anymore. Even Lord Bryant hadn't shown up in over a week, though he was in her thoughts every day. He might never come again since she had broken their agreement and arrived at his home on the one night he had decided to host a ball. No one was likely to walk in, and she dearly missed exercising her limbs. She kicked up higher. "Won't you join me, Mrs. Oliver? Your legs must be as stiff as mine from sitting all day."

Diana squatted down and stood back up with a jump. The bell chimed, announcing a visitor. Diana landed hard on her right foot and twisted just in time to see Lord Bryant enter the room. Her first instinct was to cover up what she had been doing, but it was Lord Bryant. She didn't need to pretend to be a lady with Lord Bryant. At least he hadn't arrived in time to see her kick her legs into the air high enough to show plenty of petticoat.

Lord Bryant removed his hat and placed it on the coatrack with a half smile. "What exactly did I interrupt?"

"Exercises," Diana answered. "Sitting at a desk all day is an unfortunate endeavor for anyone. I was just asking Mrs. Oliver to join me."

Mrs. Oliver stood up. "I would rather get my exercise on the street. If you don't mind, Miss Barton, I will go for a short walk."

Lord Bryant placed his coat on the coatrack underneath his hat, then, unfortunately, stopped undressing. "Please, Mrs. Oliver, stay. Today I will be behaving myself."

It seemed to Diana that Mrs. Oliver's sole purpose in the office was for times when a gentleman was *not* going to behave himself, but Diana didn't argue the point. Her face still heated up when she thought about how he had stormed into the drawing room. All because she couldn't allow Mr. Broadcreek to gain the upper hand in his attempt to control her.

She eyed her desk, not quite ready to sit down again. "I'm sorry about the other evening."

He shook his head. "Not as sorry as I am."

She took two steps closer to Lord Bryant and leaned forward. Mrs. Oliver was pretending to be busy working at her desk, and her hearing had never been stellar. "There wasn't any trouble, was there? With Lady Emily? She didn't discover our visit?"

"No, she didn't discover your visit." His face grew hard. "But I'm dreadfully sorry Mr. Broadcreek dragged you across town. That man has no propriety."

"No, he does not."

Lord Bryant played with the gloves in his hands. If Diana didn't know any better, she would think he was nervous. But that would be ridiculous. What did Lord Bryant have to be nervous about?

"Everything is fine with your investments with us?" she asked. "You don't need to pull out any funds, do you?"

"Pull out funds now? My investments with Barton Rail have been most considerably worthwhile. Don't be ridiculous."

Diana sighed. One less thing to worry about. She took a step back, giving both of them a bit more space.

"What can I help you with, Lord Bryant?" Diana asked. Mrs. Oliver snickered into her elbow. Did she sound too formal? "I mean, besides, um . . . seeing each other again, which we have done."

Lord Bryant raised his eyebrow, and Mrs. Oliver guffawed. This was ridiculous. Why would neither of them help her out of this awkward conversation?

She wanted Lord Bryant to come to the office now and again, but she didn't know what to do with him once he got here.

"What are you working on today besides the exercises?"

Diana heaved a sigh and rolled her head from one shoulder to the other. If Lord Bryant had come earlier in the day, she would have been ready with witty answers to all of his questions, but now she was simply too tired.

"I've a few more letters to write, and I need to put in orders for more ballast. I'm three weeks early putting in that next order, but I won't let what happened last month happen again."

Lord Bryant stepped forward, as if interested in what she was saying. "What happened last month?"

"I didn't get my order to the post on time. It almost put us back two weeks on one of the Barton lines."

"When was this?"

"Just before I came to your home."

Lord Bryant glanced over to Mrs. Oliver, who was busy copying numbers into a ledger. A charade, for certain. She was listening to every word they spoke loud enough for her to hear. Mrs. Oliver lived for Lord Bryant's visits.

"Ah, I had always assumed Mr. Broadcreek had something to do with that."

"Yes, well he did. He wouldn't leave my office until it was too late to make it to the ballast office."

Lord Bryant cursed under his breath. "Does Mr. Broadcreek have nothing better to do with his evenings than accost you?"

"He has—thankfully—yet to accost me. But he does seem to end up here later in the day than most men. He has his own rail lines to worry about during business hours."

"I will make a note to come later in the day, then."

Mrs. Oliver sighed happily over her pretend work. She didn't know that Diana had asked specifically for Lord Bryant to help her with Mr. Broadcreek.

Diana wouldn't have minded kicking her legs up a few more times before returning to her chair, but with Lord Bryant here, that wasn't a possibility. She regretfully returned to her seat.

Lord Bryant took his usual position on the inside corner of her desk.

"If you deign to come at all," Diana said under her breath so Mrs. Oliver wouldn't hear. "I thought our agreement was for you to come a few times a week."

Lord Bryant leaned forward. "And I thought you were to stay out of ballrooms."

Blast. "It is worth noting that I did not actually enter the ballroom."

"Ah, heaven forbid Miss Barton do anything wrong."

Diana started her fifth letter of the day. Lord Bryant leaned forward, watching her. She set her pen down and pushed the letter to the side. If she was going to have an audience, filling out payroll forms seemed to be a less distractible task. She reached for the stack of papers her man of business had dropped off yesterday.

"What are you doing?"

"Looking over payroll."

"How many men do you employ?"

"Just over two hundred with the two companies and three lines."

"That looks difficult."

"It isn't difficult." She needed to sign a few places and make certain the funds were available for the managers of each line to pay the navvies working on the line. "But it does require a certain degree of concentration."

"As I said, difficult." Lord Bryant shuffled closer to her, his head craned to one side in an attempt to follow what she was doing.

"Would you like a chair?"

"Do you have one?" He sounded almost excited.

"Yes, in the back room there is a chair you can use." She had to get him off her desk. She could never concentrate with a pair of legs dangling just to her left. She pointed to the storage room.

"Ah, the back room? It isn't dark in there, is it?"

"It is a bit dark, but you should be able to find the chair easily enough."

Mrs. Oliver suddenly came to life, dropping her pen. "Diana, it truly is a bit dark in there. You should help him."

Lord Bryant's eyes sparked. "Thank you, Mrs. Oliver. I'm glad you understand me."

"I'm happy to help you, Lord Bryant. Miss Barton spends too much time at that desk. She should take breaks now and again."

"Especially when I come here expressly to see her. It does make courting difficult."

Diana dropped both her hands onto her desk and rose. She didn't mind the chance to stand up again. But she almost sat back down when Lord Bryant's face beamed back at her.

Agreeing to go to the back room with him was a loss. She had allowed him to win a point.

"If Lord Bryant is afraid of a dark room, I suppose I can help him."

"Thank you." Lord Bryant wasn't hurt by her assessment of his bravery. If anything, he seemed pleased by it. "And thank you, Mrs. Oliver, I will enjoy the few moments I have with Diana's full attention."

Mrs. Oliver smiled. Her assistant was very proud of herself. Never mind. Diana could spare a few seconds while she showed Lord Bryant to the chair.

"Follow me." She led Lord Bryant to the storage room on the back wall between her and Mrs. Oliver's desks. She opened the door, and a shot of light illuminated rows of boxes along with a spare chair and her old desk near the back of the room. "There it is." Diana pointed with her head.

"All the way at the back?"

"Yes, all the way at the back." Surely he wasn't actually afraid of the dark? He was testing her, as always, and as always, she was falling for it. She stepped inside the room with him, and their bodies shadowed most of the light that had come through the doorway, making the room even darker. There wasn't much room to move about, thanks to the many boxes. She had meant to go through them at some point, but she simply hadn't had the time.

Lord Bryant strode over to the chair and picked it up easily. Halfway back to her, the door slammed shut behind them, and she was engulfed in darkness.

"Mrs. Oliver?" Diana stepped backward to the door. "Mrs. Oliver, are you out there?"

"Yes, dear." Mrs. Oliver's voice was faint. She must be at the opposite side of the room. "I'm headed out to buy more candles. I'll be back before you know it."

Diana pushed on the door handle, but the door wouldn't budge. "Mrs. Oliver, the door is locked," she called out. But the only answer she got was the sound of the outer door opening and shutting. Her insufferable employee was gone. An unlikely gust of wind inside her office may have caused the door to swing shut, but only the key hanging from Mrs. Oliver's chatelaine could have locked them inside. Curse Mrs. Oliver and her silly desire to *help*.

She couldn't see. Her eyes were still not adjusted to the darkness, but Lord Bryant's footsteps neared her. "Diana?" His voice was steady and not at all afraid. Fear was not what had prompted him to ask her to join him. Of course it wasn't. Had he planned this with Mrs. Oliver? When would he have had the chance?

"I'm right here." She reached her hand out in front of her only to find Lord Bryant's hands outstretched and looking for her. Her fingers brushed his, and she hastily pulled them away. She couldn't allow a repeat of the feeling she'd had in Lord Bryant's drawing room. Not here. Not in the dark.

"Mrs. Oliver has locked us in."

A low laugh filled the darkness. This was no win for Diana—it was only a win for Mrs. Oliver and, based on the delight in Lord Bryant's laugh, a win for him as well. It might be time to let Mrs. Oliver in on what kind of man Lord Bryant really was: a notorious rake. And now Diana was trapped in her storage room with him. Diana had spent the first twenty-two years without having ever been alone with a man, and yet, since starting this scandal, she had found herself alone with Lord Bryant on multiple occasions. This time, however, they were alone in the dark, and there was no escape. At least not for five minutes.

Which of them would regret this the most remained to be seen.

"Have I told you how much I like Mrs. Oliver?" Lord Bryant asked. "She is excellent at her work."

"I'm not certain she will have work after this fiasco."

Lord Bryant's laugh again echoed through the dark room. The small amount of light that spilled through the edges of the door made it possible to barely make out Lord Bryant's silhouette.

"If she loses her position with you, I will be certain to hire her."

"Please don't tell her that. She is incorrigible enough as it is."

Lord Bryant's footsteps shuffled closer. "I won't tell her." His voice was a whisper, which somehow seemed fitting for the dark. His ears must have been on alert as well.

Diana gritted her teeth. "You won't be able to if she no longer works here."

"Are you certain it is locked?"

"Would you like to try for yourself?"

"I would."

Diana scooted to the side, feeling adrift in the darkness. If she had grabbed his hand instead of shying away from it, she would at least know for certain where Lord Bryant was. She wasn't adrift for long, though. There wasn't quite enough room for Lord Bryant to pass her without the two of them touching. His hand went to her shoulder as he slid past. She was grounded for a moment, but a breath later, his hand was gone, and she could hear him pushing on the door.

"It looks as though, once again, you are correct. We are very much locked in. Now what are we to do with this gift Mrs. Oliver has so thoughtfully given us?"

All of Diana's senses—save her sight—heightened. No unwanted suitors were here for them to impress, so there was no reason for them to . . . well . . . do anything really. They could simply wait for Mrs. Oliver to return.

Somehow she doubted that Lord Bryant would come to the same conclusion.

CHAPTER 11

Everton would certainly have to find some way to get Mrs. Oliver a raise. He couldn't remember the last time his senses had been so on edge. Where, exactly, was Miss Barton? Still somewhere to his left, as he could just make out the outline of her gown against the floor.

"What should we do while we wait for her to return?" Diana asked. Her voice was a bit higher than normal. He was making her nervous. He hadn't known that was possible. Diana always seemed so certain of herself. Now he was doubly grateful to Mrs. Oliver. A chance to discomfort Diana Barton? He was a lucky man indeed.

"I have one or two ideas."

Diana gave him a derisive laugh. "Why did I even ask you?"

Ah, that was even better. He wanted to ruffle her edges a bit, like she had done to him. He didn't want to scare her. Even though he couldn't see her, he was certain she was standing straight with her chin lifted in irritation. He could remind her that she was the one who had asked for a relationship like this one. He had only done what was asked of him.

Somehow he didn't think now was the time.

"I suppose," he said, "one of us could sit on the chair while we wait. I left it just a few paces back."

"Thank you."

"You assume that I meant you could take the chair?"

"You would sit in a lady's presence?"

"I can't really see you. For all I know, you might be sitting down."

A puff of air left her mouth. He narrowed his eyes but couldn't make out the movement. "On the floor? I am not."

"When I arrived at the office, you were doing stretches—I assume because you were tired of sitting in your chair."

"That is true."

"So, really, if I were to take the chair, it would be the gentlemanly thing to do."

"Is that how you live your life? Always a gentleman?"

"Have you ever seen me act otherwise?"

Diana made a strange choking sound in her throat. In the silence, he could hear her thoughts as she sorted through which of his ungentlemanly behaviors to list first.

"You undressed in my office."

A brilliant choice. "That is the one that came to your mind first? That I removed my coat and cravat in your presence?"

"I didn't say it came to mind first, only that it was an example of your misbehavior."

Everton took a cautious step forward. He could only just make out a shadow of his companion. He stopped at the point where he figured the base of her full skirt must rest just above the floor. Then he leaned forward. "What was the first thing that came to mind?" A sharp intake of breath. He knew what she was thinking, but he was also quite certain a mention of their previous kiss would never cross her lips. He allowed his eyes to focus on the spot where he was certain her mouth must be. There were some advantages to being in the dark. He could allow his eyes to rest wherever they pleased. "Well?"

"Do you really want to know?" Her voice was closer; she must be leaning in toward him. He adjusted his gaze.

"Yes, I do."

A delicate hand landed on his arm and gently pulled him closer to her. This time when she spoke, her voice was in his ear. Everton held his breath. They were playing a very dangerous game.

"For a gentleman . . ." she began, then stopped. He leaned in closer to her, which perhaps wasn't the best idea of his life. She inhaled, then sighed. "It just seems that for a gentleman, you have a rather unhealthy fascination with your nose."

Before he could stop himself, a laugh like a cough escaped his mouth. A sudden urge to grab Miss Barton by the waist and pull her to him overtook him. She was so proud and not a bit scared of him, not even locked in the dark with him. Didn't she know who he was?

He was the most notorious rake London had ever seen.

And a deplorable charlatan.

He held his hands stiff to his sides, determined not to take advantage of a beautiful woman in a locked room.

Diana didn't seem to recognize the danger she was in. Instead, she clapped her hands and spun around. "I win a point."

He rolled back on his heels, adjusting to the space now between them. "How is that a point?"

"Oh, don't act as if you didn't know."

Everton thought he knew, and he thought he had just garnished a point by keeping his hands to himself. "Please enlighten me."

"I just made you laugh. One point for me."

"Ah ha, and how do I earn points?"

He could just make out her head cocking to one side in the dark. "Hmm, I don't think you do."

That sounded right. He seemed to play a lot of games he couldn't win. "I'm not certain I like this game."

"Oh, you like it. I don't know you very well yet, but I can tell you like it."

In the few instances he had had the pleasure of being near Miss Barton, she had always gotten her way, and she was always right.

This was no exception. For a game where he would be awarded no points, he liked it more than he should. "I suppose since you received a point, you would like the chair," Everton said.

"Yes, I would."

Her footsteps sounded in the darkness and then stopped.

"Did you find it?" he asked.

"Yes."

"But you are still standing."

"I'm tired of sitting. It is all I do all day. I would rather stand."

Everton laughed. Diana Barton was going to be the death of him.

"Another point for me," she said.

"I think, perhaps, any points gained in this room should belong to Mrs. Oliver." If he introduced Mrs. Oliver to Mrs. Cuthbert, his social calendar would explode, although Mrs. Oliver would fill it exclusively with Miss Barton. Not that he would mind. Standing in the dark with Diana Barton was much more exciting than watching brandy. "Where has that woman been all my life?"

"For a good portion of it, married and raising children."

"Ah, that would explain it," Everton replied. Diana made a sound that was half snicker and half snort. Everton slid forward. "Is that a point for me?"

"Did you not hear me say you don't get points?"

"I am the one helping you out, young lady. Granted, Mrs. Oliver is making my task quite easy and very diverting, but it seems only fair that I should be granted points as well."

"Fine. You got one point. I shall be careful not to laugh, no matter how ridiculous you are from now on."

He stepped forward once more. If his calculations were correct, Diana would be only a few feet from him. He reached his hand out but felt only air. "I'm never ridiculous."

Diana coughed a few steps to his left. The pathway to the back of the room had widened at this spot in the room. "No, you are quite the most serious man in London."

"Thank you. I'm glad someone has finally noticed. There is only one slightly ridiculous thing about me." He took two steps in the direction he had heard her voice.

"Dare I ask?" Blast, she had moved again. She must be tiptoeing about the room, walking in silence.

"I truly am afraid of the dark," he lied.

"If you are trying to make me laugh, you are doing a brilliant job of it. You haven't done a single thing to illustrate that point up until now."

"But I'm about to . . ." Everton squinted his eyes. He could just make out the shape of her skirt against some boxes, which meant her fingers should be right . . . about . . . there. He reached forward and, with a few inches of flailing about, caught hold of Diana's fingers.

Then he waited.

He waited for her to pull away.

He waited for the thrill of her touch he had felt at his ball.

Neither came.

Until she slid her fingers through his and held them tight. "Only because you are frightened."

He held his breath and closed his eyes slowly. Had anyone ever held his hand in the dark? He didn't dare speak and break the spell. Everton had often felt there were only two types of women in the world—those who threw themselves at him because of his wealth and title and those who threw themselves at him because of his looks. Every once in a while, he would meet a woman completely indifferent or repulsed by him. He tried not to dwell on those women or every woman would morph into that type of woman. But Diana was different. She thought he was handsome—she had admitted that early on—but she didn't throw herself at him; she was simply using him. Plenty of women had used him in the past, which he didn't mind in the least, but none of them were comfortable with him. Not enough to casually hold his hand.

The urge to pull her to him returned. He would wrap his arms around her waist and simply breathe in her strange scent.

He cleared his throat. Smelling her would not exactly make her continue to be comfortable around him.

"How did you meet Lady Emily?" Diana asked. "Were your families friends?"

He found his voice. "No. Mrs. Cuthbert introduced us."

"And things are going well between the two of you?"

"Well enough, I suppose. She is quiet and doesn't talk much." He wasn't certain why Diana was interested in Lady Emily.

"I remember meeting Miss Paynter in Hyde Park. She also seemed rather timid. Are most of the women you, um . . ."

"Dally with?" It seemed wrong to say it that way while holding a woman's hand in a locked room.

"Yes, I suppose that sums it up. Are they all quiet and shy?"

Was that a hint of jealousy? Diana was a lot of things, but quiet and shy she was not. "Oh no, I do not discriminate. I have spent time with a few troublemakers. Miss Witham, Miss Thornell—now there was a lady who knew what she wanted in life. Lady Yolten . . ." He couldn't help the smile that rose on his lips. Lady Yolten had been extremely entertaining.

"I understand your meaning," Diana said with an edge to her voice. Everton held in a chuckle. It was nice to get under her skin for a change.

"Lady Emily is different, though. Like I said before, my relationship with her is a bit more complicated and delicate." Lady Emily wasn't in love with anyone. She had no real goals in life. It was much harder to help someone when he didn't even know what she wanted. Harder, but perhaps even more important—at least to him.

"Well, I'm glad Mr. Broadcreek and I didn't cause any problems."

Problems? Like holding his hand and asking him personal questions he readily answered? She was causing problems.

"Miss Barton—"

"Diana. You always call me Diana."

"Honestly, I don't know what to call you. Half the time I'm not sure what is real and what is pretend. There is no one here to see us, and yet, I'm holding your hand."

"I thought you were scared."

He closed his eyes and inhaled her strange scent of ink and paper. "I am." This time it was no lie.

The door behind them jangled loudly, and they both jumped. Diana's hand tightened in his own. "I'm back. Are you two still in there?" Mrs. Oliver had returned. "Miss Barton?"

Neither of them answered.

"Miss Barton?" Mrs. Oliver asked again.

Diana leaned into him. "It would serve her right if we hid and gave her a bit of a fright."

But the door opened before they had the chance. Not that Diana had been serious. Or at least, he didn't think she had been. With her, it was always hard to tell. But the way she immediately dropped his hand made him think she couldn't have been serious. At any rate, he was much too old to be playing hide-and-seek with a young lady and her matronly employee.

"Mrs. Oliver, you knew full well we were in here, and what's more, you left the office unattended. You, of all people, should know how important approving the payroll is. Lord Bryant and I cannot be dallying about in the storage room. One more instance like this and I'm afraid I will have to find another woman to work here with me."

Mrs. Oliver's face paled. " But I thought . . ."

"Yes, I know what you thought, but I hope you know me well enough to know that the most important thing in my life right now is this railroad. Even Lord Bryant cannot deter me from this path."

A woman who knew what she wanted. His favorite kind. "Don't take it out on Mrs. Oliver." Everton turned around, grabbed the chair that had caused all the problems in the first place, and brought it to Diana's desk. Diana had already managed to sit down and start reading whatever gobbledygook she was working on. He sat down and scooted his chair closer to hers. "How can I help?"

Diana raised a solitary eyebrow. "You want to help me?"

"Yes. I've slowed you down. It only seems fair." Diana leaned forward, grabbed a large stack of papers, and started to hand it to him. The papers were filled with numbers. Blast. "This doesn't mean I'm trying to make you fall in love with me."

"I thought that was exactly what you were trying to do." Diana still held on to the other side of the papers as if it was hard for her to release control over them.

"Yes." Everton glanced at Mrs. Oliver. She had returned to her desk, so he lowered his voice. "But that was part of our game. I want to help you, at least until you make up for the time lost while I was here, but . . ."

She dipped her head low and to his side without taking her eyes off the paper in front of her. "You aren't seriously intentioned toward me."

"Exactly. Don't take it personally."

"How could I when you aren't seriously intentioned toward anyone?"

She was right of course. But shouldn't she be at least a little regretful about that? Even Miss Thornell, who had been deeply in love with a farmer despite her father being a viscount, was a little tempted by him. Diana just raised her chin and went to work. He leaned forward and asked her a question, his breath disturbing the one dark lock that fell from her hair. He would help her, but she would pay for his labor by spending the next few hours very close to him.

It would serve her right. No woman should have the power to make him feel like he did when she was near. It was too close to hope, and he had given up on hope a long time ago.

CHAPTER 12

In the four days since Mrs. Oliver had locked Diana and Lord Bryant in the storage room together, Lord Bryant had visited on two of them. The first visit's purpose was just to remind her not to show up to the card party he was attending that evening. The next day, he had made a similarly short visit, and the day after that, he hadn't shown up at all.

She eyed the window. Dusk was already darkening the streets outside. It seemed like he wouldn't be coming, which was fine of course. He didn't need to come more than once or twice a week. He had already more than fulfilled his end of the bargain.

Diana stacked her papers neatly and stood from her desk. "Mrs. Oliver, I believe it's time to clean up and call it a day. It was another productive one." She brushed her finger over the knotted gold on the lapel of her periwinkle dress. She enjoyed the days she felt she deserved to walk home with it.

Mrs. Oliver stood. "Your Lord Bryant didn't visit, though. I thought for certain he would, seeing as he didn't come yesterday."

"He is a busy man. He doesn't have time to stop by every day."

"He is busy doing what? Parliament isn't in session yet."

She couldn't exactly tell Mrs. Oliver that he was courting Lady Emily and most likely flirting with several other women. She had never known him not to have at least one woman, if not two, with whom he was bandying about.

Lady Emily was one.

And Diana was the second.

She shook her head. No matter what she thought of Lord Bryant or how comfortable his hand had felt in hers while they were locked in the storage room together, she had to remember that none of this was novel to him. She needed to keep her heart locked and her eyes away from the door during working hours.

Mrs. Oliver lived fairly close to the Richardsons, so they walked home together most evenings. They had been leaving earlier since Lord Bryant started coming into the office. Often, Mr. Oliver would meet them at Mrs. Richardson's home and walk the rest of the way with his wife after they saw Diana off.

After gathering their things and leaving the office, Diana locked the door behind them. She turned to see a carriage pull up in front of them, a carriage she knew well by now. She kept her eye out for it every single day.

"Oh, Lord Bryant," Mrs. Oliver said, as though Diana didn't have his carriage memorized. "I knew he would come today."

"He didn't come yesterday," Diana said under her breath.

"Which is exactly why I knew he would come today." Mrs. Oliver stood proud in her correct knowledge, eyes shining as she watched Lord Bryant descend from the carriage.

His hat was askew and his cravat hastily tied. Where, exactly, had he been? That was none of her concern. Lord Bryant was entitled to do whatever he wanted to do in his free time. "Finished already?" he asked.

Diana smiled at him. It was hard not to. "Yes."

He glanced at the locked office behind them. "Seems early for you."

"Lately, I have more time to get everything done," Diana said.

"Thanks to me?" Lord Bryant raised an eyebrow and curved the edge of his mouth into the impish grin she so often wanted to wipe off his face, one way or another. His smile lifted to the other side of his mouth, as if he could read her thoughts. "It is thanks to me, isn't it?"

"You are well aware that it is." Diana stepped to the pavement. "In fact—" Diana handed her reticule to Mrs. Oliver to hold and reached under her coat. With a quick flick, she undid the pin on her dress. "I believe tonight this should belong to you."

She stepped up to Lord Bryant and reached for his lapel. He leaned back as if he were unprepared for her touch.

"It is simply a pin," she told him. "Mr. Richardson came up with the idea. Whoever works the hardest is rewarded with wearing it home."

"Work?" He raised an eyebrow. "I wouldn't call what I was doing today *work*."

She eyed his loose cravat. No, most likely it wasn't. "If you don't want it . . ." Diana turned toward Mrs. Oliver.

"I want it."

She swiftly turned and snatched his lapel before she could think better of it. He stepped forward, closing the distance between them. His coat was made of fine wool. She grazed her fingers along the back of it until she found the best place to pin the little golden knot. She patted it into place once it was fastened. It had been too long since a man had worn the pin home.

Diana surveyed her handiwork. The knot was tiny on his tall, slender frame. "It looks good on you."

Lord Bryant ran a thumb over the pin but didn't reply.

"I expect it back tomorrow," Diana said, and then took Mrs. Oliver's arm. It would be dark soon, and they needed to head toward home.

Lord Bryant cleared his throat and fell into step behind them. "Where are you going?"

"Home." Mrs. Oliver laughed. "Where else would we be going?"

"The night is still young."

Diana scoffed. "Maybe for a man of leisure, but for Mrs. Oliver and me, we must get home to eat and rest so we can be ready to work in the morning."

"Work, eat, sleep, then wake up and do it all over again. Sounds monotonous."

She eyed his haphazard cravat. "Not all of us can live exciting lives like you, Lord Bryant."

He looked down at his cravat and chuckled. Tidying it up halfheartedly, he motioned to his carriage. "Let me take the two of you home. It will give you a few more minutes of rest on this fine evening."

"Won't we be keeping you from your evening activities?"

"I have none planned. I was at home reading when I decided to rush over and pay you a visit."

At home reading? She tried to picture him with a book. If he was truly only just leaving his home, why would his cravat be untidy? The valet of a baron would never allow such slovenly ways. She glanced up at the footman on the carriage, who was, of course, keeping a straight face. Like Lord Bryant had said before, if an untidy cravat distressed his footman, he wouldn't be his footman, which meant his footman was most likely capable of not betraying any lies Lord Bryant might tell.

Mrs. Oliver was already walking toward the carriage. She was getting on in years, and it would probably be a welcome comfort not to walk home.

"Thank you, Lord Bryant," Mrs. Oliver said. "We would be delighted."

"Diana?"

She smiled. "Of course." If he could lie about being at home reading books all afternoon, she could lie about being happy to ride in his carriage. It would break Mrs. Oliver's heart for her to say otherwise.

Lord Bryant's eyebrow rose, but he didn't say anything. He simply motioned for Diana to follow Mrs. Oliver to the carriage.

Mrs. Oliver and Diana sat across from Lord Bryant. After Diana informed Lord Bryant of her address, the inside of the carriage was silent while the wheels steadily rumbled through the London streets.

Diana shuffled her feet under her skirts, but she eventually gave in to talking. "What were you reading, Lord Bryant?"

"What was I reading?"

"Yes—just now—when you were so distracted you nearly forgot to come. What book was it that you were reading?"

"Ah," Lord Bryant said, rubbing one hand on his knee. He was trying to come up with a title. He probably hadn't actually sat down with a book in ages. Of course, neither had Diana, but she had been too busy. "Nothing of note."

"I understand." And she did. Reading was obviously a lie. She would have thought he would be better at it. She went back to being silent until the carriage pulled to a stop sooner than she was expecting. Lord Bryant alighted, then helped both Mrs. Oliver and Diana descend the steps.

"There is Mr. Oliver coming to meet me." Mrs. Oliver gave Lord Bryant a bow and stepped in the direction of her home. Diana squinted her eyes. Sure enough, Mr. Oliver was shuffling toward them. She wouldn't have put it past her employee to pretend he was there to once again leave the two of them alone. But she hadn't. Mrs. Oliver paused and turned back to them. "Thank you, Lord Bryant, for the pleasant ride. Diana, invite the man in for some tea, will you?" Mrs. Oliver was already several feet away, waving farewell. "I shall, hopefully, see both of you tomorrow in the office."

Lord Bryant and Diana watched Mrs. Oliver stride to her husband, her pace picking up just before reaching him. Mr. Oliver placed a hearty kiss on her cheek before they walked away with their arms intertwined.

What would it be like to grow old with someone like that? Someone who still waited anxiously to see her, even though they saw each other every day. Someone whom she couldn't help rushing toward just before coming together.

She bit back a sigh, but Lord Bryant didn't. His wasn't obvious, but they were close enough together that she heard the rush of air leave his lungs. That puff of air, so quiet and soft, made her wish he could stay. But he was a rakish baron, and she was a working woman. When no one else was here to make them pretend, they had no relationship.

"Thank you for the ride, Lord Bryant. I won't keep you."

He turned toward her, his eyes shadowed in the fading light. "Aren't you going to invite me in for tea?"

"Surely you have more pressing matters," Diana replied, rubbing her fingers through her gloves. She eyed his bedraggled cravat. Nothing in the home behind her would tempt Lord Bryant. "Such as reading."

He smiled. She was becoming almost tired of his smile and the way it sucked in everyone around him. She wished he would be rid of it for a day and allow her to not dwell on whom else he had been smiling at. "I do plenty of reading."

She cleared her throat and willed her mind to think elsewhere. "I'm certain you do."

He stepped back and turned his head to one side. "You don't believe me."

"I haven't seen many books dishevel a cravat like that."

Lord Bryant put his hands on his hips. "I don't read in my cravat. I would have thought you'd guessed that."

"How would I have guessed that?"

"You have seen me in my home; I've made myself comfortable in your office. Do you really think I would spend an afternoon reading in my cravat?"

Diana turned on her heel and walked to the Richardsons' door. "I don't think about what you do with your afternoons. I'm much too busy. But if you were reading without one, I wouldn't have expected you to mess it up so soon if your valet had just tied it."

Lord Bryant came up behind her and gently touched her elbow. She paused and took a steadying breath. His touch was worse than his smile. He turned her toward him. "So you think I was busy with much more nefarious pursuits than reading."

"I just told you, I don't think about what you have been doing."

That wicked grin again. "You think I spend my days chasing women and playing cards."

Of course that was what she thought. Everyone thought such things of him. He never tried to be more noble than his reputation, despite the fact that, at times, she wished he would.

His striking emerald eyes scanned her face. They were the color of the new spring leaves that burst onto the trees lining the drive of Baimbury Hall. How long would it be until she saw those trees again? It was no wonder so many women fell for him with eyes like that. The corner of his lip rose. "If I were to lie about my activities, I promise you I would come up with something more exciting than reading."

"But you don't promise not to lie to me."

"No, I don't promise that. I only promise that when I lie, they will be good lies."

Good lies? As if there were such a thing. But when Lord Bryant said it, with that curl of his lip, she wanted to believe him. Spending time with Lord Bryant was corrupting her.

She took in a deep breath and shook her head. "I'll tell Mrs. Richardson you are coming to tea."

Lord Bryant's face lit up. Somehow his eyes found enough light in the dim street to reflect and shine back at her.

She opened the door, and Lord Bryant followed. She showed him to the drawing room and asked him to wait there.

On her way to the stairs, she ran into Mrs. Jenkins coming down. "I thought I heard you come in," she said. "I've set up tea in the nursery. Mrs. Richardson is in a rare mood today—a real skip in her step—and she wanted to have tea with the children tonight."

Mrs. Richardson had seemed much happier in the past few weeks. It seemed as though time was finally starting to heal her wounds. But Diana couldn't have tea in the nursery, not tonight.

"I've actually brought a guest—"

The door behind her opened, and she turned to see Lord Bryant poking his head out. "Did I hear that tea was to be served in the nursery?"

Mrs. Jenkins grasped the railing of the stairs behind her. "Merciful heavens." She let go of the railing and clasped both hands to her chest. "You've brought a man home."

"Mrs. Jenkins, this is Lord Bryant. He will be having tea with us, so I'm afraid we will have to move the tea things into the drawing room."

Lord Bryant opened the door wholly and stepped into the foyer. "Nonsense, Mrs. Jenkins. I won't allow you to do that on my account. I'd love to take tea in the nursery. I don't believe I have ever done that."

"For good reason," Diana said. "You do realize there are children in the nursery?"

"Do you think I will be frightened by a few children?"

"I don't think you will be frightened, but I'm quite certain that it wouldn't be appropriate."

Mrs. Jenkins nodded her head in agreement with Diana.

Lord Bryant cocked his head to one side and loosened his cravat. "If you wanted an *appropriate* guest, you should have invited someone else." Diana pursed her lips. That was hardly fair. She wasn't the one who'd invited him in the first place. Lord Bryant was already heading for the stairs. "The nursery is upstairs, I presume?"

Diana scrambled after him. The last thing she wanted was to have him opening doors at random upstairs. She had been experimenting with watercolors, and needless to say, he might recognize the leafy green eyes she had been trying to paint. At least a few attempts had been left on her bedside table. "I'll show you. I suppose Tommy and Drue might enjoy having a man around for the evening."

Diana skirted ahead of him and reached the top of the stairs before he did. Having tea in the nursery? With a man? And not just any man, but a baron? Charlotte was in for a shock.

"Tommy and Drue have had a hard time since their father passed away. They are very quiet. Emma is the baby, and she is quiet too. Not because of her father passing away, of course. She is simply a sweet baby."

Lord Bryant nodded and pressed onward without stopping.

"I'm only telling this so you don't despair if they don't react well to you. If they sit still, sipping their tea without interacting, please know it's because this whole family has struggled greatly for months. It has taken a toll on all of them."

As if to refute her words, a peal of laughter rolled out from behind the nursery door. Lord Bryant squinted an eye at her.

Diana didn't blame him. What exactly was going on? In the past few weeks, Charlotte had been smiling more. Mrs. Jenkins had mentioned that Charlotte was doing even better today, but it had been a long time since she had heard laughter in the home.

She opened the door to the nursery. Charlotte was down on the ground with both of her boys, crawling about on the run next to the tea table and she was . . . growling?

The boys were also on all fours, clambering around the rug, trying to get away from her. Tommy rolled to the left just as Charlotte swiped a hand out to try to grab him. "Diana, is that you?" Charlotte craned her neck to one side. "Come play with us—" She paused as her eyes caught sight of Lord Bryant behind Diana.

Tommy took the opportunity of his mother's distraction to leap upon her back. "I've got you!" he whooped. He waved his arm in the air for a split second before Charlotte sat down in a heap, causing him to slide to the floor. Charlotte scrambled to a standing position and brushed off her skirts. The few conversations Charlotte and Diana had had about Lord Bryant hadn't exactly been positive. Bringing him into the home was not her best idea.

Once Charlotte was more or less composed, Diana opened the door farther and stepped inside the nursery. "Charlotte, this is a friend of mine who insisted on having tea upstairs with us. Lord Bryant, this is my dear friend Mrs. Richardson."

Charlotte's mouth opened slightly at the mention of Lord Bryant's name. Their home had very few visitors, and none of them were either part of the peerage or notorious rakes. And certainly none of them met in the nursery. "Welcome to my home, Lord Bryant." She made a few violent gestures to her boys, reminding them to bow. They scrambled off the floor and followed her lead.

Lord Bryant bent at the waist. "You must be Tommy and Drue. Miss Barton has told me much about you."

The boys ran to their mother's skirt and hid behind it.

"They are scared of you," Diana said under her breath, "but only because they haven't had guests for quite some time. They will be begging for you to tell them stories once tea is finished. Please keep your stories appropriate. We don't need those boys' heads turned by a—" Diana stopped. What was Lord Bryant exactly? A rake? She eyed him. Surely. A scoundrel? Without a doubt. A cad? Perhaps not, but there were so many words with which she could finish that sentence, she wasn't sure which to use. "A gentleman like you."

Those other words might well describe Lord Bryant, but she couldn't actually call him any of those things.

Lord Bryant frowned. "You don't want their heads turned by a gentleman?"

"By a gentleman *like you*," Diana repeated.

Lord Bryant held both hands over his heart as if he had been wounded, but Diana knew him well enough to know that disparaging his character didn't actually wound him. If anything, he seemed to enjoy it.

With an extra adult, there weren't quite enough chairs at the table, so Charlotte pulled Drue onto her lap. Tommy and Diana both took their seats, leaving the last chair open for Lord Bryant. All the chairs in the nursery were built on the smaller side, but not so small as to make them uncomfortable for Diana and Charlotte. Lord Bryant seemed to dwarf his. He managed to get his knees under the table but only just.

Mrs. Jenkins arrived with another tea setting for Lord Bryant, then dallied about until Charlotte told her she could go.

Tommy's and Drue's eyes never left Lord Bryant. It seemed as though everyone was captivated by this new stranger.

Diana didn't blame them.

"How did you and Lord Bryant meet?" Charlotte asked.

Immediately, visions of her standing outside Lord Bryant's home in the rain flashed into Diana's mind. She couldn't tell her friend that she had rushed to his home in the late evening and demanded his help.

Lord Bryant curled his lip, as if he could read her mind. He knew exactly what she was thinking. He turned to Charlotte, and Diana held her breath. What would he tell her friend? "I first met Miss Barton at her brother's wedding."

Oh, the truth. Her back relaxed. Lord Bryant may not be on her side, exactly, but he had proven himself very capable of subterfuge. He would manage to keep the worst of Diana's behaviors to himself. She didn't need Charlotte thinking any worse about him than she already was.

"You are a friend of Mr. Barton's?" Charlotte's question was innocent enough. She was doing an excellent imitation of someone who hadn't warned Diana to stay away from Lord Bryant.

Lord Bryant placed both hands on his thighs and straightened. "Yes."

One of his *good lies*. Diana tucked her lips into her mouth, begging herself not to laugh. Nate would never call Lord Bryant a friend. Lord Bryant was one of the very few people Nate despised.

The more Lord Bryant talked, the more Tommy and Drue relaxed, until they even answered a few of his questions. Charlotte managed to smile at a few of the things he said. She wasn't charmed by him, like so many women were. Charlotte was much too intelligent for that, but her words did come out less forced.

"Where is your little sister?" Lord Bryant asked Tommy.

"She is sleeping," Tommy said, and Drue pointed to the adjacent bedroom. "She sleeps a lot."

"Ah, to be young again," Lord Bryant said.

"Young as a babe?" Diana asked. She couldn't imagine Lord Bryant as a child. He would have been handsome. He probably caused his mother all kinds of trouble. Actually, she could picture him quite well. A spoiled young Lord, given anything he ever wanted and never being punished. It was no wonder he had turned out the way he had, expecting everyone to do his bidding.

"Perhaps not a babe, although I do envy the way they sleep. But if I were younger, there are a few things I would do differently."

Diana smiled. "Cause a few more problems, if I had my guess."

Charlotte covered her mouth to prevent a laugh. Lord Bryant simply shrugged his shoulders. "Some might see it that way, but in reality, if I had caused a few more problems while I was younger, I could have saved someone a lot of heartache. I was much too inclined to listen to my parents."

Tommy scrunched his face and glanced at his mother. "But children should listen to their parents, shouldn't they?"

Diana nodded toward the two boys gazing up at Lord Bryant.

"Of course." Lord Bryant smiled. "Young boys such as yourselves should listen to your mother. It wasn't until I was much older that I realized there are times when it is better to think for yourself."

Tommy scrunched his mouth together. "So I shouldn't think for myself?"

Diana grimaced. Lord Bryant's conversation with the boys was going almost exactly as she had expected.

Lord Bryant laughed. "Of course you should think for yourself, but for now, you should also listen to your mother."

"I should think so." Charlotte reached for Tommy's hand and gave it a squeeze. "Now, boys, it is time for you to go to bed."

"But what about our story?" Tommy's eyes looked up at Diana's. For the past week, she had read them a few stories every night before bed. It was one of the benefits of getting home at a decent hour.

Charlotte clicked her tongue. "Miss Barton has a guest tonight."

Lord Bryant smiled at Charlotte, then the boys. "I don't want to interfere with the boys' routine. By all means, Miss Barton should read to them if that is what they want," he said.

Finally, he would be leaving. This had been one of the most uncomfortable nights of Diana's life. She was used to Lord Bryant in the office. She knew how to deal with people there.

Lord Bryant turned to her. "I'd quite like to hear a story myself."

Diana grabbed the edge of the table. This was not happening. Lord Bryant shouldn't be here in Charlotte's home where Diana lived. He shouldn't be having tea in the nursery, and he most certainly shouldn't listen to her read the boys a story. "Don't you need to go home? It is getting late."

Lord Bryant winked at the boys. "Not for a grown-up gentleman like myself. The night has just begun."

Diana shook her head. Bringing Lord Bryant into the nursery was a mistake. Bringing him into their home was a mistake. She needed to keep their relationship professional. His role was simply to pretend to be interested in her in order to run off would-be suitors. Nothing could be more businesslike than that.

Charlotte glanced back and forth between Lord Bryant and Diana. She seemed to be at a complete loss as to what to do. Diana didn't blame her. The right thing to do would have been to never bring Lord Bryant into the nursery in the first place, but now that he was here, how exactly did one get rid of a peer of the realm?

A small cry from the adjoining bedroom made Charlotte stand. "I'll be back in a moment. Diana, I'll allow you to show Lord Bryant out." Diana breathed a sigh of relief, but it was too soon. "Or read to him—I mean—the boys. Whatever you feel is best."

Charlotte scampered off to the bedroom, most likely pleased about not being the one to offend the baron by asking him to leave. She had left that to Diana.

Lord Bryant leaned forward and placed his elbow on the table, his face in his hand. His eyes were as wide and eager as her old puppy's. "What shall we read first?"

Diana groaned. It was impossible for her to purposely disappoint Lord Bryant. He had done so much for her. She turned in her chair and reached for a book from the bookshelf behind her. *German Popular Stories* was one of the boys' favorites. Without thinking too much about it, she jumped right into the first story: "Hans in Luck."

She took a deep breath and began. She had gotten no farther than Hans receiving his large silver coin in exchange for seven years of work when Tommy interrupted. "Why aren't you doing the voices?" She paused. With a quick glance at Lord Bryant, who was sitting with his arms crossed expectantly, she took a deep breath and continued.

The voice she used for Hans was squeaky and well-practiced. Nothing to be too ashamed of. But the first man Hans met on the way home to his mother was a man on horseback. Without taking her eyes off the book, she lowered her voice. "What do you say to changing?" she growled, using the voice she reserved for the crafty horseman, who traded his wild horse for the more valuable silver.

Lord Bryant shuffled his feet, and she thought she heard a small cough come from his direction. She plowed on. Thankfully, the horseman's part was small. She continued reading, then abruptly stopped.

She should have chosen a different story.

"Why did you stop?" Tommy asked, his eyes wide in anticipation. "You are almost to the good part."

Diana squirmed in her seat. "Why don't you say that part, Tommy?"

"Me?" Tommy pointed to his chest. "I can't read."

"But you know it. You can say it without reading."

Lord Bryant leaned forward, and Diana was reminded, once again, how large he was for the nursery table. "Oh, I think Miss Barton should say it."

Diana shook her head. “You don’t even know which part it is.”

“But you don’t want to read it,” he said, eyes sparkling, “which means it will most likely be even better than your horseman’s voice.”

Oh, it would be better, all right. If better meant complete humiliation in front of Lord Bryant. She was quite certain that was exactly what he meant. She passed the book to Lord Bryant. “You are the guest. The boys get to hear me read nearly every night. Why don’t you read it?”

Lord Bryant shrugged and took the book. Diana leaned over and pointed to the paragraph she was on. He raised his forefinger and marked the spot on the page, their hands touching briefly before she removed hers from the book. He turned to catch her gaze. Their faces were mere inches apart. She was close enough to see that his brilliant green irises were outlined by a darker ring of gray.

A soft bang on the table, made with chubby little hands, interrupted her thoughts. “Read it,” Drue demanded.

Diana sat back and shook her head tenderly at Drue. Lord Bryant coughed, glanced down at the book, settled deeper into his too-small chair, and began to read. He tried the low growling voice, which, for some reason, felt much more convincing and much less embarrassing coming from him. “When you want to go very fast, you need to smack your lips loud and cry ‘Jip.’”

“Not like that,” Tommy said.

Oh no.

Diana covered her mouth with her hands as Drue smacked his lips loudly and bounced side to side in his chair. Heavens, but what she had done over the last few weeks to bring a smile to those boys’ faces, including traipsing about the room pretending to be poor Hans as he lost his horse.

“Diana always reads that part while galloping.”

“She does, does she?” Lord Bryant’s face blossomed into a smile. Whatever he was about to do, it wasn’t going to be good for her.

Diana straightened in her chair, trying for all the world to look like the epitome of ladylike behavior. “I wouldn’t say I gallop.”

“You do.” Tommy pursed his lips. “You gallop all over the room, and you smack your lips and say ‘jip’ over and over.”

Diana had no response to that. She couldn’t deny it. It was the reason this story was the boys’ favorite. She should never have made the mistake of reading to them while Lord Bryant was in the room, especially not this story.

“Perhaps she does more of a trot?” Lord Bryant asked. “A trot is more dignified than a gallop.”

Tommy scrunched his face. "But the book says the horse gallops."

Lord Bryant stood from his chair. He smacked his lips loudly and did a skip halfway around the table. "Jip, jip," he said before smacking his lips again. "Was it like that?"

Tommy also rose and, to Diana's horror, smacked his lips before running about the room, waving his hands in the air, crying, "Jip, jip." His right leg stayed in front as he attempted to imitate Diana's galloping horse.

Lord Bryant raised that one blasted eyebrow and craned his neck slowly but deliberately in her direction.

Diana brandished her hands in front of her face. "Truthfully, Tommy is exaggerating. I don't wave my arms about in the air like that. I'm usually carrying the book."

As if to prove her wrong, Drue decided this was the perfect time to also gallop about the room, imitating his older brother as well as his three-year-old legs could handle. His arms were decidedly waving in the air.

Lord Bryant reached down and made a show of picking up the book. He held it in one hand, then proceeded to wave his hands in the air. "That seems possible, even holding a book."

A baron was in her home's nursery, cravat still askew, waving his arms about and smiling at her like she was the one being ridiculous. She shook her head and returned his guileless smile. This time it wasn't the practiced smile she usually gave him while trying to remain in control of a situation. There was no control in this situation. This was a moment of respite for two young boys who had lost their father, and it was a moment of diversion for her. She had been working much too hard lately, and she needed this. What was this for Lord Bryant? Amusement? Excitement? Was waving his hands around in the nursery something he did every day?

Definitely not.

She stood from her chair, strode to where Lord Bryant was still waving the book in the air, and grabbed it from his flailing hands.

"That is *not* how it is done." Before she could think better of it, she put her hands in front of her, the right one still holding the book, and bounced them up and down like she was holding the reins of a wild horse. "You have to gallop."

She kept her right foot forward as she galloped across the room to where Tommy and Drue were still impersonating her. Her skirts flew about her, and a few locks of her hair fell out of their pins and rested against her neck. The three of them jipped and whooped and spun and galloped, the boys laughing harder than they had in ages. She stopped to catch her breath and turned to see Lord

Bryant smiling at the three of them. His smile was different. He wasn't trying to enchant a woman or prove his devilry with his crooked grin. He was simply smiling, with his shoulders relaxed and a hand at his hip.

Diana returned to the table, sat down, and began reading, using all of her voices without hesitation. "Lucky" Hans continued to trade his possessions for things of lesser and lesser value until he was left with only a heavy grindstone on his back as he made his way home. He hadn't seen his mother in seven long years, and the stone slowed his progress. Thirsty from all the walking and carrying such a heavy burden, Hans laid the grindstone down near a pond while he knelt to get a drink. With a plop, the grindstone, the last remaining item he had to show for all his years of work, fell into the pond and sank.

Diana paused from her reading to take in the faces of those listening. Tommy and Drue were both leaning forward, anticipating what Hans would do next, even though they had heard the story dozens of times. Lord Bryant leaned forward in much the same manner. Whether he had heard the story or not, he seemed interested in its conclusion.

"For a while, he watched it sink into the deep, clear water," Diana continued. "Then he sprang up for joy, again fell upon his knees, and thanked Heaven, with tears in his eyes, for its kindness in taking away his only plague, the ugly, heavy stone. 'How happy am I!' cried he: 'no mortal was ever so lucky as I am.' Then up he got, with a light and merry heart, and walked on, free from all his troubles, till he reached his mother's house."

The table was silent for a moment. Lord Bryant let out a puff of air, then glanced at the faces of Tommy and Drue. "Hans is one of the smartest men I have ever heard of."

"Smart?" Tommy laughed. "He isn't smart. He worked all of that time for nothing."

"Well, maybe that wasn't smart," Lord Bryant agreed. "But when he dropped his burden in the pond, he became happy for what he could be happy for—that he no longer had a burden. He didn't mourn the things he couldn't change."

"He didn't drop the stone in," Diana couldn't help but add. She could see Lord Bryant's point, but telling the boys that a man who traded away all of his income of seven years for nothing was smart didn't sit right with her. "It fell in by accident. He didn't want to lose his burden. It was only after it had slipped in that he rejoiced it was gone."

"True." Lord Bryant put a hand to his chin. "But to choose happiness when the whole world tells you to be unhappy . . . I can't help but think Hans understands more about life than we give him credit for."

Diana didn't know if Lord Bryant was the right person to be lecturing the boys on happiness, but he did have a point. After the stone was gone, there truly wasn't anything Hans could have done about it.

"One more," Tommy begged. Diana gave him a sideways glance. "Please," he added. "'The Fisherman and His Wife.'"

"I think Drue is too tired," Diana said. After their wild horse-riding escapade, he had quietly listened to the rest of the story, but she had seen him yawn a few times. "Drue, are you ready for bed?"

Drue shook his head. "One more, please."

She hated to say no to the boys. Charlotte was still in the adjacent bedroom with Emma, her humming, soft and sweet, coming through the open door. "One more," she finally agreed, "if it is all right with Lord Bryant."

His lips curled into a lazy smile and he leaned back in his too-small chair, making him look . . . almost comfortable. "I could listen to stories for hours. Especially when you do the voices."

Only a few minutes earlier, Lord Bryant's compliment would have left her face burning, but after galloping about the room with him, there wasn't much more she could be embarrassed about. She took it as a true compliment and smiled her thanks in his direction. Diana flipped ahead to "The Fisherman and His Wife" and began reading. Lord Bryant was somehow different tonight. She had always pictured him spending his evenings with his arms draped around other women while they danced. Or perhaps at card tables, working on strategy with a female partner. Surely none of those ladies had read stories to him. But did he look at them the way he had just looked at Diana—with a smile and a wish to continue on for hours?

If only she knew.

Only a paragraph in, Drue's head flopped forward, halfway to the table before he caught himself. He shook his head in an effort to keep himself awake, but as soon as she started reading again, it fell forward again. This time, Lord Bryant caught Drue's head in his hand, and Drue drowsily scrambled into Lord Bryant's lap. Diana kept the words flowing from her mouth as well as she could. Lord Bryant was stiff for a moment before finally relaxing enough for Drue to settle against his chest.

"You could take him to Mama's chair," Tommy said, pointing to the rocking chair.

"He is fine. We're almost done with this story." Diana should read faster. Lord Bryant must have more pressing things to do than sit with a child in a nursery.

"You just started," Tommy said. "Drue sleeps better in the rocking chair."

Lord Bryant put an arm under Drue's legs, leaned the boy's head against his other arm, and then stood. He rolled each foot carefully while stepping over the rug and then adjusted Drue's head once he arrived at the chair. A knot formed in Diana's throat. All that strength and power cradling little Drue's head. Lord Bryant sat down awkwardly, landing hard in the seat. Drue stirred, but Lord Bryant rocked the chair slow and steady until Drue settled into a deeper sleep.

How was this the same man who rocked London with scandals every year?

"Continue with the story." Lord Bryant's voice made her start. "Drue and I will make ourselves comfortable here."

Heat rose to Diana's face. She had been watching the two of them for far too long. She would rather he watched her gallop about the room again than see that she was affected by him. She turned back to the book and Tommy. Softening her voice so she wouldn't wake Drue, she persevered. When she finally finished, after what seemed like the longest reading of a story, Tommy gave her a strange look.

"I think Lord Bryant was right."

"What do you mean?"

"Well, the fisherman and his wife traded for more and more stuff—bigger stuff—but they were never happy. Just like Hans, they had nothing, but I don't think they were happy about it. If you are going to have nothing, you might as well be happy about it."

Wise words for a five-year-old. She turned in her seat to hear Lord Bryant's thought on the subject, but his head was slumped to one side. Drue lay still on his chest, and they were both fast asleep.

"He fell asleep," Tommy said.

"I guess my reading wasn't entertaining enough for him."

Lord Bryant was completely still, and for once, she could watch him without needing to hide her thoughts. How strange that she had been so comfortable with him tonight. They had been spending more and more time together, so it made sense that he would become more familiar to her. But in this moment, she wanted to memorize his face, enough so she could draw him again, this time without any mistakes.

"Or he was really tired, like Drue."

"Perhaps." She stood from the table and returned the book to the shelf. "Why don't you go to bed? I will bring Drue in."

Tommy nodded. "Thank you, Diana. I like when men come. It makes mama happy."

Diana nodded, then paused. Lord Bryant's visit hadn't made Charlotte happy; she had been happy before they'd arrived. What did Tommy mean by that?

"Have other men been coming to the house?"

Tommy's eyes went wide, and he clapped a hand over his mouth. His eyes flew to the bedroom, where his mother's humming sounded as cheerful as Diana had ever heard it.

"Did a man come to visit your mama?"

Tommy took a deep breath. "I'm not supposed to tell." His face scrunched together, and he bit into one of his fingers.

She leaned forward and then stopped herself. She couldn't press Tommy for more information. Not when his mother had asked him to keep it a secret. But if Charlotte was meeting with someone, why wouldn't she tell Diana?

"If you aren't supposed to tell, then don't. Despite what Lord Bryant said, you really should listen to your mama. It was your mama who told you not to tell, right? Not the man?"

He nodded, eyes still wide and solemn.

"Well, then you did the right thing by not telling me. I'm proud of you."

Tommy's face brightened a little at that. She walked him over to the room where Charlotte was still humming. The tune seemed different now . . . laced with meaning. Charlotte wasn't cheering up on her own; someone had helped her. And that someone was a man. With all the men no longer coming to the office, Diana had become complacent. But if anyone had heard about her agreement with Charlotte, that would mean Diana wasn't the only woman the men could target. She would have to talk to Charlotte about this as soon as possible.

After peeking in to make certain Tommy made it to his mama, Diana pushed herself away from the doorway and inched over to the rocking chair. She tipped her head to one side. Lord Bryant looked different when he slept—younger, like when he smiled at her earlier as she galloped around the room. It was as if his mask had been removed, and here he was in reality. Not Lord Bryant, but Everton. A person, not a title. A title couldn't sleep in a rocking chair with a three-year-old boy snoring softly on his arm.

But a man could.

His dark hair was tousled, as it often seemed to be when they were together. It hadn't been tousled at the ball—it had been parted and styled as if his fortune had depended on it. Her fingers ached to push the thick portion that had flopped forward onto his forehead away from his eyes. She was a lunatic, it seemed. One simply didn't touch a man's hair when he was sleeping. If nothing else, it would be a terrible intrusion. And she had intruded upon Lord Bryant quite enough.

Now what was she to do? She hated to disturb either of them, but Drue needed to get into bed, and Lord Bryant couldn't stay.

In the end, she decided to do nothing, at least for a few moments.

Minutes ticked by, and she watched the two of them. Shadows from the candlelight flickered on Lord Bryant's face. Who was Lord Bryant exactly? Even with all the time she had spent with him—more than she had with any other man except, perhaps, Nate or Mr. Richardson—he still remained a mystery to her.

A mystery whose face she could now draw in her sleep. She knew every curve of his cheek, his flashing eyes, and his eyebrows that seemed to only settle while he slept—like now.

With a sigh, she stepped forward. She needed to put Drue to bed. She bent down to scoop Drue from Lord Bryant's arms, but somehow, her hand went to that lock of hair falling over Lord Bryant's forehead first. She brushed it aside and quickly pulled back her hand. What was she thinking? His hair flopped back down, it's downy strands—as soft as Drue's baby locks—taunting her.

With a shake of her head, she carefully put one arm under Drue's neck and the other under his little boy legs. Her left arm wedged between Drue and Lord Bryant's chest, and as she pulled away, Lord Bryant's eyes flew open, and he grabbed her wrist.

Their faces were only inches away from each other, his eyes cloudy and confused. "What happened?" he asked, his voice low and gravelly. Something stirred within Diana's chest. The two of them, so close with a child between them, whispered of long-lost desires and budding youthful dreams from a lifetime ago.

Foolish heart.

"You fell asleep. All of that reading must have tired you out." She smiled as if it were a normal part of her day to wake a gentleman.

"That has never worked before. It didn't work last night, and it most definitely didn't work this afternoon."

She scanned his eyes for deceit, but if it was there, he hid it well. Could it be that his cravat was actually only loose because he had been reading at home? Alone? The few candles they had in the room seemed to brighten. She scarcely felt the weight of Drue in her arms. "You were actually reading before you came?"

"Yes."

She tried to picture it: Lord Bryant sitting in his office with a book open before him. His hair would fall over his forehead like it just had. All the energy of those piercing green eyes would be focused on the story as it unfolded in front of him. She quickly closed her eyes in an effort to remove the image from her mind. Lord Bryant reading was much too potent a vision. She wanted him to be that man, one who didn't flit from one thing to another but who could spend hours with one topic in mind.

With one woman in mind.

"What book?"

He shrugged as if the title wasn't important. "Books," he said. "I was skimming through about twenty, trying to find one that could make me . . . forget."

Ah. She tightened her grip on Drue and pulled away from Lord Bryant. Even in his reading, he couldn't be constant. "I hope someday you find the book you are looking for."

She strode toward the bedroom where Charlotte still hummed to her children.

CHAPTER 13

SLEEP STILL CLOUDED EVERTON'S EYES, but he blinked what he could of it away so he could watch Miss Barton while she walked away. The last thing he remembered before falling asleep was her voice wrapping around him. His chest still held the warmth of the little boy he had rocked.

Drue.

In another life, this could have been his world. He closed his eyes, willing sleep to return to him. Even sitting in a wooden chair, he would take it. Something about this room stilled him.

"Lord Bryant?" Miss Barton's voice floated above him, and he dragged his eyes back open.

Miss Barton was leaning over him, her eyes wide, peering back and forth between his. "Are you feeling well?" Her hand reached for his forehead but pulled back before touching him.

Without processing what he was doing, he reached for her hand and held it to his face, just above his eyes. Her fingers were soft and warm against his skin. She pressed her palm softly against him and bit her lower lip. "You don't feel feverish." With her other hand, she pushed away his hair and pressed her hand against his forehead more firmly. He counted her breaths while she assessed his temperature. How long had it been since someone had checked on him in such a manner?

Not since he was a child.

He wasn't sick, but if he had been, what would Miss Barton do for him? Would she care for him somehow? Tuck his blankets around him like his mother had?

He placed a hand on her elbow, then slid his fingers down her arm and wrapped them around her hand, pulling her hand away from him. Miss

Barton shouldn't play nursemaid with him. The only person who would care for him if he was actually sick was Nelson, and for some reason, that didn't quite bring the desired effect. His fingers weren't so delicate. Nelson's eyes, although Everton had seen them filled with concern, didn't make him feel quite so at home and protected.

Which was ridiculous. Everton didn't need anyone to protect him. Especially not a young slip of a girl. He stood fast enough to leave the chair rocking behind him. He still wasn't quite awake, and the room tilted oddly. Only when he tightened his grip on Miss Barton's hand did he realize he hadn't dropped it yet. She tightened her grip in his and placed her other hand on his shoulder. "Are you certain you are all right?"

He wasn't. This room, the children, Miss Barton. All of it was bringing back visions of something he could never have. Something deep inside of him, buried since his third month of marriage, burst out of him. He wanted this. He wanted all of it. The children, the laughter, reading silly books. The last time he had wanted these things, nothing had gone right. And as hard as he tried to fix it, he never could. If Miss Barton had any idea what her touch felt like to him, the longing and desire it sparked in him, she would pull away. It was one thing to dally about with a baron like him. Quite another to be serious. The pull he was feeling toward her now was serious and terrifying.

He dropped her hand. He shouldn't have been holding it in the first place. "I've got to go." She slid her hand from his shoulder. He stepped away from her and found he could finally breathe again. With sheer will, he brought a smile to his face, the crooked one that really made the ladies swoon. "You know me, card parties to attend and women to flatter." Her eyes dimmed in the soft light. His crooked smile wasn't doing its duty. "Unless, of course, you find me in ill health, and then I suppose I should simply head home and read more books."

"Skim books, you mean." Her voice was soft and low, as if he had disappointed her somehow. What would he do if she said he was unfit to go out? What would it mean?

"Yes, despite the hours I spend on it, I'm not much of a reader."

"Perhaps you should read more German children's stories."

He smiled, this time sincerely. "Perhaps I should. It has been a most agreeable evening." He couldn't make himself step away from Miss Barton. "What do you think, Miss Barton? Am I well enough to socialize?"

Miss Barton's hand lifted, and for a brief moment, Everton held his breath as he waited for the flutter of fingers to graze his forehead once again. His body swayed forward, making the space between them shrink to mere inches.

But her hand dropped, and her body reeled backward.

"There is nothing wrong with you."

Her voice was soft and low, but it was also firm. He had never been more disappointed to be classified as healthy. He took a step back and curled his lip. "That isn't what most of London thinks."

"I know," Miss Baron said, shaking her head. "And I can't help feeling you like it that way."

"Of course I do." He pulled at the lapels of his perfectly tailored jacket, the little pin she had given him flashing in the darkening room. "I've worked long and hard for this reputation of mine. I cannot afford to lose it now." Another shake of her head. Usually such shakes brought him much pleasure. Disappointing people was one of his favorite pastimes. But blast it. If he didn't leave, he would be apologizing to Miss Barton for hiding behind his reputation before he knew it. "I'll show myself out."

Without waiting for an answer, he strode out of the dim nursery. It might be best if he went a few days without seeing Miss Barton again. His tentative grasp on sanity seemed to crack a bit more each time he came near her.

CHAPTER 14

Everton didn't play cards after his visit with Miss Barton. He went home and, even though it was early, found a copy of *German Popular Stories* and read half the book. It didn't help him sleep. All it did was put Miss Barton's farcical voices in his head. When his body finally collapsed well into the morning, he was plagued with dreams of Rachel crumpling in horror at his touch. But sometimes her face would change. Her hair would go from fair to dark, her eyes from blue to caramel. But the disgust was always the same. He awoke feeling more tired than when he had fallen asleep.

Everton kicked his blanket onto the floor and slid to a sitting position on his bed. He couldn't go on living like this. He wasn't even living. He gave a few women the chance to get what they wanted here and there, but other than that, he spent the rest of his waking hours trying to forget the past or figure out how to sleep.

He needed to talk to someone.

The fact that he had spent the last few years making certain no one would talk to him wouldn't help. Everton had no close friends. Nelson was the closest thing he had to a confidante. Well, he and Mrs. Cuthbert, but Mrs. Cuthbert was more like a partner in crime than a friend. If he mentioned his reaction to Miss Barton last night, she would be scheming with the young lady herself to get him in front of a priest again. Mrs. Cuthbert acted as if she was sending him ladies to help them out, but he knew at least as strong a persuasion for her was to see a love match made for himself one day.

He needed to speak to someone who didn't take life that seriously. A few of his past scandals came to mind. Lady Yolten wasn't serious. She had been one of the more entertaining ladies he'd been involved with. But her husband, Lord Yolten—reasonable as he was—wouldn't be happy to have him visit. He wouldn't want word to get out that Lord Bryant had called on his wife.

So . . . no married ladies and no gentlemen. He didn't make friends with men. Everything was always a competition with them, and frankly, he was simply too tired to deal with the crowing gentlemen of London.

There was really only one woman in London he might call a friend, and although she would certainly be surprised to see him, she would happily sit with him.

The Duchess of Harrington.

The Duchess of Harrington had visited his country estate with her husband—the duke—and their two children. It seemed like a lifetime ago. Rachel had been alive then, and he had hoped to impress his young wife with such noble friends. The duke and duchess had been a welcome respite at a time when Everton hardly dared to walk down corridors in his own house.

Once, two months into their marriage, he had come around a corner only to collide with Rachel. Her scream had echoed through the corridor and had brought a number of the staff rushing to them. She tried to laugh it off, but her hands were still shaking after explaining the matter to the housekeeper and maid. He was always careful to whistle or hum a tune when he walked in his home after that.

The Harringtons' family visit was the one bright spot of his marriage, but when they left, Rachel sank deeper into herself, rarely emerging from her room, as if the task of entertaining had taken as much toll on her as an illness.

The duchess had been kind to Rachel. Rachel had smiled more during that visit than during any other part of their marriage. The duchess would most likely be kind to Everton as well.

Besides, he had dirt on the Duchess of Harrington's daughter, a comforting fact. Everton smiled and rubbed his face. The silly chit had run away from home to become a maid and then had the audacity to fall in love with her employer.

Ridiculous story.

He sent his card to Nelson and had him see that it was delivered to the Harrington estate.

Three hours later, he was cleaned up, presentable, and standing outside the Duke of Harrington's home. He tapped his foot on the pavement as the carriage waited directly behind him. He could easily get back in and go home. Taking a deep breath, he shook his head at his cowardice.

Plenty of people in London had friends they spoke to on sunny afternoons. He had simply never seen the point of it.

After knocking, the butler ushered him into a drawing room. He didn't seem impressed or surprised to find a baron at the door, which made sense since

Her Grace's late husband had been a duke and her son had since taken up the title. Everton stood as the door opened a moment later, only to be greeted not by the duchess, but by her son.

"Harrington," Everton said with a short nod. Everton hadn't seen Harrington since his impetuous younger sister's wedding. He had looked much happier at the wedding. His brows hadn't been so dangerously low then.

"Lord Bryant," Harrington said, his back straight and eye disapproving. "May I ask the intent of your visit?"

A disapproving eye happened to be Everton's favorite type of eye. Harrington's mannerisms were more suited to a soldier than a stuffy nobleman. This visit might prove to be more entertaining than he thought. The troublesome thought of speaking to the duchess slid away, and he retreated into the much more comfortable role of agitator. Everton tipped his head to one side and gave the duke a half grin. "I'm here to see your mother."

Harrington's eyes narrowed. "What business have you with her?"

"Why, no business at all. Must a man have a reason to call on a delightful young widow?"

A muscle in the young duke's cheek clenched. "Bryant, I hope you understand we appreciate your help with Patience last year, but we see no reason to be indebted to you."

"No reason?"

"None. Patience would gladly tell anyone what happened. We aren't trying to hide it."

"That is interesting because I heard no rumors about her parading around as a maid. It seems to me someone must have hushed the whole business."

If anything, the duke's back straightened even farther. Of course Harrington would do anything to stifle any rumors about his frivolous sister. He must have spoken to everyone who had been privy to that knowledge. Everyone except Everton. He repressed a chuckle. It seemed as though the Duke of Harrington was either intimidated by Everton or, even more interestingly, trusted him.

He wasn't sure which he would prefer.

The door opened again, and Her Grace stepped into the room, looking much more like a young aunt than a mother to the stuffy duke. A smile and a light foot did wonders to keep someone spry, which meant Everton probably looked old enough to cause Harrington concern. The duchess was most likely only a dozen or so years older than Everton.

"Your Grace." Everton bypassed Harrington and, with a flourish, kissed his mother's hand. "It has been far too long."

The duchess laughed softly and struck his shoulder. "I danced with you at the ball you hosted not long ago. I did take note that you forgot to send flowers. But a visit is even better. I will allow it." Her smile spread wide across her face.

Perfect.

Everton felt, rather than heard, Harrington growl. Perhaps he imagined it, but the look on the young duke's face was priceless. He really should make home visits a more regular occasion, especially to widows with grown sons.

Harrington strode toward Everton and grabbed him by the elbow. He pulled him roughly toward the doorway of the drawing room. Everton shrugged at Her Grace as he was dragged past her. Harrington hauled him into the hall, shut the door between them and Her Grace, and then shoved him away.

"My mother is young but surely not young enough to tempt you. What is this about, Bryant? Have you come to extort money from us because of Patience? I had thought better of you. Not much better, but better."

"I don't need money."

"I find that many men who don't need money still want more of it."

"That is not what I want. I sincerely would like to speak to your mother."

Harrington scowled. "Then you won't mind if I join you."

"This is your house, and I cannot stop you from joining me, but what I have to say to your mother will be said in private, so I will be forced to come again when you are not home."

Harrington bent his head and rubbed the back of his neck. The fact that he had let his posture slip meant Bryant was getting under his skin. It also meant the day was looking better already.

"Fine." Harrington turned on his heel and made his way across the hall and down a corridor.

"Thank you, Your Grace," Everton called after him. "My intentions are honorable, I assure you." Harrington's step faltered for a moment before he shook his head and continued.

Everton could have been good friends with Harrington at some point if Harrington hadn't gone off and joined the army for two years and if Everton hadn't become—well, whatever it was that he was now.

Everton returned to the drawing room. The Duchess of Harrington was still standing, her slim figure and dark hair a stark contrast to the tall window behind her. "I won't apologize for my son. I think he is a fine, upstanding young man."

"I wouldn't expect you to. I happen to agree," Everton said. "But you must see that makes him quite easy to fluster."

"You think that was flustered?" She motioned to the door with her head. "You should see him when I sing French dancing tunes. He has to leave the house."

A knot in Everton's back loosened. He had come to the right place. "I should like to see that."

"How have you been doing these past few years? I've only seen you at a few scattered balls and, of course, at Patience's wedding, but there never seems to be a chance to really speak."

That was true enough. They had never made it past condolences on the passing of each other's spouses. "I have been . . . surviving."

"Ah, yes, I know surviving. Too well." She stepped forward and took his elbow, searching his face for what he assumed were signs of wear. "Are you sleeping?"

Everton blinked. Visions of his dreams came rushing back. His eyes clouded. He was in the correct place all right. So correct that he felt the urge to rush back out the door. The last time he had fallen asleep easily was with little Drue curled up on his chest. He cleared his throat, but he could make no words come. The duchess's hand tightened its hold on him.

"We don't have to speak of that yet." She released him and sat down on an upholstered, high-backed chair, motioning to a settee across from her. She smoothed her dress and gave him a moment to compose himself. "Now, assuming you are not here to court me, since I have it on good authority that you don't actually court women, to what do I owe the pleasure of this visit?"

Everton took the seat she had shown him. In those few moments, he was able to find his voice again. "What do you mean I don't court women? I court many women."

"Courting many women—by definition—is not courting."

Touché.

"How is your disastrous daughter doing these days?" A change in subject seemed to be the best course of action.

"She is happy as always. Nicholas and I miss having her here."

"But she visits."

"Yes, but you know how it is. She hasn't been married long. The last thing she wants to do is spend time here."

No, he didn't know how that was. His first and only year of marriage had been . . . awkward at the best of times. "Yes, well, I'm afraid my marriage wasn't quite the type to keep us happily alone at home."

The duchess turned her head to the side and raised her eyebrows. He had never talked to anyone about his marriage. Even Mrs. Cuthbert didn't completely understand what his reasons were for wanting to help her.

"You didn't care for your wife?"

Everton took a deep breath. He closed his eyes, willing himself to remain calm. He could do this.

"I hardly knew her, but I did care for her." A vision of Rachel sitting in their garden, picking an apple from one of their many fruit trees, came unbidden to his mind. Her hair was so pale it was luminescent in the sunlight. "Very much."

"You clashed, then? A war of wills can work for some marriages. I've seen people who can have a row one day and then get on swimmingly the next."

"No, it wasn't a war of wills. Rachel did whatever I asked of her." He reached for the ring on his pinkie finger and spun it madly. "She always did."

The duchess sat waiting, as if she knew he had much more to say. But he had already said more than he had ever admitted to anyone. What else did she want from him?

Ah, yes. He was the one who had come to visit her. Brandy hadn't worked. His scandals with women had helped a little. But he still wasn't sleeping at night, and it was starting to disturb him in ways he would have never guessed. Like feeling strange sensations from only the merest touch of a hand and imagining Diana Barton bending over him in concern. He paused his frantic spinning and held the ring tight between his fingers, the thin band pressing into his fingertips.

"I loved my wife."

He had never said that out loud. Not even to Rachel. Saying it now broke something inside of him. It made him feel weak, and he hated feeling weak.

The duchess's eyes scoured his face, then his hand, still holding the ring tightly on his finger. Her head jerked back to his face, and her shoulders slumped forward. "Ah." She let out a puff of air. All the muscles in her face wilted into a frown. "She didn't love you back."

Bryant dropped his hands into his lap as a flood of memories rushed him: Waking up his bride on the morning after their wedding only to have her flinch and force a smile. Months into their marriage, finding her pillow wet with tears. Bringing her plates of food only to have her take them with listless hands. She never locked the door between them, and yet she never opened her heart either.

She had been young, quiet, and completely controlled by her parents, and he didn't realize she hadn't wanted their marriage until it was too late.

He had ruined her life and any chance at happiness. And it ate at her until she finally ran away in the dead of winter.

He managed what was surely a gruesome smile. "No, she didn't love me."

"I'm so sorry, Lord Bryant. I didn't know."

"How could you know? How could anyone have known? It isn't as though these things are talked about. How well did you know your husband before marrying him?"

"Not well," Her Grace answered quietly.

"Did you choose him?"

"My parents arranged our marriage, for the most part, but I did have some say. At the very least, I was excited by the prospect of becoming a duchess. I was so young and he was so full of life that the rest fell into place over time."

So full of life. The duke had been full of life and had made his young wife fall in love with him. Blasted lucky man. "Yes, well, nothing about my marriage ever *fell into place.*" He didn't like the hard edge to his voice. His was a common story. His parents and Rachel's parents had arranged the marriage. If there had been anything in Rachel he thought he couldn't love, he would have stopped the process before it had started. But there was nothing unacceptable about Rachel. She was beautiful, soft-spoken, and shy. He had been certain he would be able to make a marriage with her work. The heady foolishness of youth.

"I'm so—"

"No, you have already said you are sorry. I didn't come here for sympathy. I wanted a marriage that was different from my parents', one that was based on love instead of silently hurting one another." Everton stopped. Having someone to talk to and scattering seeds of ill repute on his family were two different things. His parents had rarely spoken to each other, and when they did, it was only to arrange their social lives. One summer, he had caught his mother screaming out of an open window. They weren't loud screams; she wasn't hoping for someone to hear her. She had stumbled away from the window in guilt when she saw him walk into her little sitting room.

"I was scaring away some ravens in the tree," she had told him. He had nodded as if her explanation had made sense, but they both knew there were no ravens. Nothing outside their country estate was making her scream. It was the silence inside the walls that haunted her.

He vowed then that his wife would never have cause to send muffled screams outside of windows. His marriage would be based on love and respect. It wouldn't be broken like his parents' marriage had been.

Little had he known at the time, his would be even worse.

Everton blinked slowly, as if simply closing his eyes could wash away the images of both his and his parents' marriages. That he came from a long line of unhappy people was a lot he had learned to deal with. It was a line that would end with him. His eyes refocused on the duchess. Did she know how fortunate she had been to have had love in her home, even if there was emptiness now that the duke was gone? At least it had been filled at one point.

"I came in hopes that you would have some suggestions for me."

"About what?"

"You were right; I'm not sleeping well. I haven't slept well for years. For a while, I tried spirits, but it wasn't worth the blasted headache, and I began to feel like I wasn't living. Not really. My scandals with women help."

"Your scandals with women help you sleep?" Her Grace sat back in her chair and put her hand to the back of her neck, just as he had seen her son do moments ago. They seemed so different, but in little ways, he could see the resemblance.

"When they end, they do."

She nodded as if that made at least a little bit of sense to her. But it wasn't enough for him anymore. A successful scandal was a lot of work to go through for one night's sleep.

"Lord Bryant, I'm afraid as much as I would like to help you, I have no answers. Like I said, sleep is something I am still working on. Patience can't come home to sleep by me every night."

Everton gripped the edge of his seat with his hands. He hadn't known exactly what he was hoping to get out of this conversation, but it didn't seem as though he would get it.

"Have you thought of perhaps . . . ?" She paused, but he knew what she would say, and he steeled himself to hear it.

"What?" he asked. "Marrying again now that I am older, so some young girl can be even more frightened of me?" Rachel hadn't just not loved him; she had been terrified of him. The smallest touch of their hands would send hers behind her back. "Have you seen the women getting married this past season? They are barely out of the nursery."

"Not all men marry sixteen- or seventeen-year-olds."

"No, but if I let it be known that I am open to the idea, some will be thrown at me. *That* I know for certain."

"Then don't let anyone know, and look for someone older and stronger this time. Not all women are like Lady Bryant."

Everton swallowed his uncouth reply. His marriage had been a disaster. Which part of his story had the duchess misunderstood? He wouldn't put another woman through that. He took a deep breath and squinted his eyes shut. He had been the one to come here for help. It wasn't as if Her Grace had been offering her advice unsolicited. Even still, he had hoped she would have something better to offer him than marriage. Coming here had been a mistake. It was time to make an exit. Talking with someone hadn't actually helped him at all.

He took a deep breath through his nose and tipped his head to one side. Plastering a half grin on his face, he did what he always did.

Deflected.

"Older and stronger, you say? There is only one woman I can think of who matches that description, and I'm afraid your son simply doesn't approve."

Everton had never seen a duchess throw her head back and laugh before, but he found he liked the sound of it. Like bells in a country village. "Ah, Lord Bryant," she said after calming down and wiping her eyes. "I may be older, but I don't believe I am strong. No wonder you are all the ladies have to talk about in town. Frankly, I don't know how you have avoided matrimony these past few years as it is."

"At times, it has been quite the endeavor," Everton admitted. Once it had nearly meant a duel. Preposterous things, duels, as if he would have even shown up. Everton stood. He had spoken about Rachel for the first time since her parents informed him of her death. That was something, wasn't it?

Her Grace stood as soon as he did, making his lapse in courtesy less alarming. "Are you leaving already? I'm quite certain that nothing I have said has been helpful."

She was correct about that.

"I'm not convinced I am ready to be helped."

Surely she wouldn't let him leave after having admitted that. No woman of her age had ever been able to resist a wealthy young man in need of unwanted help. But to his surprise, she nodded and walked him to the door. "If you don't want matrimony, you could always try singing. That is what I often do."

"And it helps you sleep?"

"No, singing has never helped me sleep. Not really. But sometimes it exhausts me enough that I collapse for a while, so I still do it. Honestly, the only thing that has helped me, on occasion, is my family—Patience curling up with me in bed and Nicholas finally speaking to me after years of silence. My family has healed me in ways I didn't think possible."

Everton gritted his teeth. "I don't have a family."

"And that, my dear boy, is why I suggested marriage. It's one of the few ways to create one. But if you aren't ready for happiness, you aren't ready. I, for one, can understand that. No one can force you to open your eyes and see that your future can still be bright."

His future was not bright, and no amount of opening his eyes would fix that. Nor did he think a wife would help his situation. A wife had been the beginning of all his problems. “Marriage is *one* of the ways to create a family, you say.” One he wasn’t interested in. “Perhaps you could enlighten me on some of the others.”

The duchess laid a hand on his arm “You are always welcome to join ours. Come anytime.”

“Harrington would love that.”

“Oh, blast Nicholas. He loves to have his perfectly tidy world disturbed. It is what he wants. Or at least, that is what I tell myself every day.”

Everton’s heart slowed. Something about the duchess’s use of slang, or perhaps her twisted sense of what her uptight son enjoyed, had settled him, at least slightly. The butler arrived, handing him his coat and hat. He took them and gave the duchess a deep bow of respect. He walked to his carriage, mulling over the two options the duchess had given him. Join their family or find a woman stronger and more mature than Rachel had been and create a family with her.

His one year of marriage, during much of which he didn’t even live with his wife, had been the worst year of his life. And it culminated in the most horrific way possible.

He trod up the steps of his carriage. Hopefully Harrington would get used to having him around.

CHAPTER 15

DIANA HAD GONE A WEEK without her gold pin. Mrs. Oliver scratched away at some document she was working on, the sound of her pen grating through the silent room. Diana kept her head over her own document. Looking out the window had been forbidden since Wednesday.

The scratching stopped. "Perhaps today—"

Diana stood, the chair scraping the floor loudly enough to stop Mrs. Oliver from finishing her sentence. Lord Bryant might come, but if the past few days were any indication, he wouldn't, and she didn't want to field any more questions about it from Mrs. Oliver. She was the one who had locked them in the back room together, then forced him to come to tea at Charlotte's home. Diana had thought perhaps they had shared something in the nursery that night, a part of themselves not hidden by pride and false exuberance. Lord Bryant must not have entertained those same thoughts.

Each day that the bell failed to ring and announce his arrival, she became more mortified by her actions in the nursery. Galloping about? Making strange voices? Pushing his hair away from his forehead . . . She couldn't think of that last one without a deep sense of embarrassment. She had let down too many walls that night and had treated Lord Bryant as a friend. Her fingers tingled in remembrance of the cool skin of his forehead. *Friend* was too generous to herself. She had acted like a woman fixated on Lord Bryant.

No wonder he hadn't returned.

That had never been part of their bargain. Her eyes went to the window, and she clenched the pen in her hand until she heard it crack. She needed to be away from this office. "I just remembered I need to buy another copy of *Bradshaw's Railway Timetables.*"

Mrs. Oliver's forehead furrowed. "But—"

Diana shifted to the side to block Mrs. Oliver's view of the bookshelf behind her desk. Nate's copy was sitting there safe and sound. "I want my own. I shouldn't have to use Nate's all the time."

Diana strode around the desk. Mrs. Oliver stood from her chair. "Which bookstore should you like to visit?"

Blast propriety and relying on Mrs. Oliver to accompany her everywhere. She wanted away from her as much as she wanted away from the office. Why hadn't she made more friends while she was in London? She could ask Charlotte to join her, but by the time she received her note, prepared to leave the house, and arrived at the office, it could be another hour. She had been wanting to check in more with Charlotte during the day, but in the end, her impatience won that war. "Hartform's."

"Hartform's? That is across town."

Exactly. The last thing Diana wanted to do was spend the day in the office. She might miss Lord Bryant if he finally decided to show up, but then, perhaps *he* could be the one disappointed at missing *her*. She was tired of being the one who always waited on him. Diana tied the knot of her bonnet under her chin. "I know it is across town, but they are certain to have it. I don't want to waste time on one of the smaller bookstores nearby."

Mrs. Oliver furrowed her eyebrows but didn't contradict her. Hartform's was a large bookstore but not *that* much larger than the one down the street.

By the time the carriage pulled up to Hartform's, Diana had regretted her decision to ride all the way across town. As it turned out, Mrs. Oliver felt the need to converse when trapped in a confined space. At least in the office, Mrs. Oliver had her work to distract her from Diana's social life. Diana sprang from the carriage as soon as the driver opened the door. She gulped the air as she strode to the shop door and pulled it open.

Something was different.

Diana often came to Hartform's, and although she typically saw ladies there, she had never seen quite so many, nor had they ever been gathered together, speaking over one another. The store was clouded in loud, excited conversation. A few customers were browsing books quietly, but most hovered near the geology section in a muddled haze of silks and cottons.

"What in the world—?" Mrs. Oliver had come through the door behind her. Diana turned to shrug her shoulders at Mrs. Oliver when the plethora of dresses parted, and a familiar profile made her jerk her head back. Mrs. Oliver's face broke into a smile. "Is that Lord Bryant?"

Diana reached for Mrs. Oliver's hand. They had to remove themselves from the bookstore before Lord Bryant saw either of them. This was no ballroom, but it would still be a breach of her promise not to be near him in Society. She would never have considered Hartform's a place of high Society, but apparently if Lord Bryant entered any shop, it became the height of fashion. Diana's hand caught only air. Mrs. Oliver was already striding over to where Lord Bryant—cravat impeccable, without a hair out of place—stood among a gaggle of women.

Diana caught up to Mrs. Oliver and pulled her down a row of bookshelves just before they reached the crowd. Mrs. Oliver especially could not interact with him. She still thought him a faithful and gallant suitor.

"Let's not bother Lord Bryant while he is out on an errand."

"Lord Bryant has never seemed bothered by either of us, so I'm certain he won't mind."

"But those ladies might."

"Those ladies should know what they are up against. It is obvious they are all after his title. One glance at the way Lord Bryant looks at you, and they will all know they are defeated. He looks quite uncomfortable. You really ought to go put him out of his misery. What kind of man wants a pile of women stringing along after him while he tries to buy a book?"

What kind of man? Lord Bryant was exactly that type of man. He was sure to be enjoying himself. She peeked around the corner of the dark, wooden shelf to confirm her thoughts.

Lord Bryant smiled at an auburn-haired beauty, but it wasn't the charismatic one Diana had seen him use in similar circumstances. His eyes shifted to a bookshelf, not unlike the one she was hiding behind, then back to the women who had surrounded him. He didn't exactly look as though he was enjoying himself. But she couldn't do as Mrs. Oliver suggested. He wouldn't want her to interfere.

Just then, Lord Bryant's eyes slid to her hiding space. She jumped back behind the shelf, but it was too late. He had seen her. Diana grabbed Mrs. Oliver's hand. "He saw me."

"Well then, you must go to him. You can't ignore the man who is nearly your fiancé." Mrs. Oliver gave her a small nudge in the direction of Lord Bryant. Diana held her ground. She couldn't be seen with him. She most definitely couldn't be seen with him here, where Mrs. Oliver was as likely to say something about the two of them as Lord Bryant was to deny it.

But Mrs. Oliver was having none of it. "I've never known you to be timid. Yes, those women are dressed better than you, and yes, most must be far more accomplished than you. When would you have the time to work on your talents? Not to mention, all of them—excluding the mothers—are younger and fresher-faced than you. It isn't your fault you have to spend all day in an office pouring over numbers while they remain at home." Mrs. Oliver smiled as if she were giving Diana the highest of praise. "Even if your face is not quite symmetrical, he has chosen you. Don't concern yourself with them and go speak to Lord Bryant."

Not quite symmetrical? What in heaven's name did Mrs. Oliver—?

Mrs. Oliver pushed her again, and this time, Diana was too distracted to stop herself from stumbling backwards into the open area of the bookstore. Off-balanced, she reached for anything that could stop her from tumbling to the ground in front of everyone. The only thing within reach was a floor globe that stood just outside the row of books where she had secreted herself. She caught the edge of it and righted herself, but the globe stand slipped from her grasp and tipped forward. Diana scrambled, her arms flailing forward once again to stop the whole thing from crashing to the floor, but she missed.

The stand crashed to the floor.

The globe leaped from the stand and rolled directly toward Lord Bryant and the sea of muslin and silk that crowded around him.

The store went silent. The only sound was the clanking of the horizon mount each time the metal hit the floor, sending the globe hurling off in a slightly different direction.

All eyes turned to Diana.

The only woman who didn't stop what she was doing to stare was a petite young lady standing next to the shopkeeper. "I need more information on coprolites." Her voice resonated through the shop. "Are you certain you don't have a copy of *Geology and Mineralogy* by Buckland—" She stopped, finally noticing what was going on around her. The globe came to a standstill halfway between Diana and the crowd.

Diana's eyes found the shopkeeper's, who stood next to the woman looking for the geology book. "I'm so sorry," she mouthed, and without looking in Lord Bryant's direction to see if he was watching her—of course he would be—Diana tiptoed to the globe and bent down to pick it up. She lifted it just as a strong pair of arms reached for the other side.

"I can do this," Diana said, not looking up. Only one man in London had hands that looked like they had been sculpted by Michelangelo. And where were his gloves?

"Can you?" His voice held an edge of humor. Perhaps she wasn't in as much trouble as she thought.

"Of course I can. It isn't difficult to carry a globe back to its stand." As if on cue, one edge of the globe slipped from her hand, and Lord Bryant's other hand shot out to stop a second fall.

"Why don't I take it for you?"

She pushed the globe into his arms. Their eyes met for the briefest moment. Her breath caught. A week had been long enough for her to forget his eyes' intensity. Her hand shook slightly as she pulled it away from him. "Yes, why don't you?" She needed to get away from him. Why in heaven's name did he have to be in this shop at this exact moment? "I'll go apologize again to the shopkeeper and see if I need to pay for any damages."

Lord Bryant looked over the globe. "No damage done." Their eyes met again, and this time, he was first to turn away. "I'll right the globe, but you ought to leave. Lady Emily is here, and I would rather the two of you didn't meet." Lady Emily? Here? Diana's head whipped to the side as she took in the group of women watching the two of them together. Which one was Lady Emily?

"I should warn you," she said, "Mrs. Oliver is behind that bookshelf."

He pursed his lips. Diana averted her eyes. Looking at Lord Bryant's lips was even worse than looking him in the eye. He shifted the globe in his hands. There was no pin on his chest. Had he forgotten about it? Did he treat everything of value as carelessly as he treated women? "I can handle Mrs. Oliver. You just leave as quickly as possible."

She took a quick step away from him and landed awkwardly on her foot. If she wasn't careful, she would make another spectacle of herself. Diana nodded. There wasn't anything she would rather do than leave that shop. Lord Bryant's measured footsteps echoed from the floor as he made his way back to the globe stand and the bookshelf.

Diana eyed the door. She could simply slip out and leave Lord Bryant to deal with the aftermath with the shopkeeper, but that wouldn't do, would it? If she had no relationship with the dashing baron, she wouldn't expect him to clean up after her messes, and neither would any of the ladies nearby. Besides, *he* was the one who had leaned forward to whisper to her. She hadn't meant to run into him. *He* was the one who rushed over to help with the globe. Really, Diana hadn't done anything wrong.

Not on purpose anyway.

She took a deep breath. Luckily, the shopkeeper was not in the crowd of ladies; he was still speaking with the petite young woman from earlier. Diana took the long way around the room to avoid the mass of women and reached the shopkeeper's side.

He pushed his spectacles up his nose and nodded at the young woman. "I can order the book for you."

The young lady smiled. "Yes, please do so. I'm fascinated by these coprolites. We used to think they were all bezoar stones, you know. Mary Anning, though, she figured it out. And I hear they are written about in Buckland's book."

The shopkeeper was still nodding, but his eyes were set on Lord Bryant, who must have righted the globe by now. Diana waited for a moment to be certain the young woman wouldn't be disturbed by her interruption. She seemed very intent on finding this book and reading about coprolites, whatever those were. Some type of stone?

Diana stepped forward. "I must apologize for my disruption a moment ago." Diana kept her voice down, but still, some of the other women shuffled closer to where she was. Why didn't they go back to Lord Bryant? He must have been their reason for being in the bookseller's shop, or they would have been looking at actual books. It seemed the only woman, young or otherwise not interested in Lord Bryant, was the one she was interrupting. "I couldn't see any damage on the globe, but in case you find any, I would like to leave my name so I can repair it."

The shopkeeper removed the spectacles pinched between his nose. "It is Miss Diana Barton, is it not? You've been here before. If you say there was no damage, I'm certain you are correct, but I can send a runner if there are any problems."

"Thank you." Diana gave an apologetic nod to both the lady and the shopkeeper before turning to leave. Mrs. Oliver was still speaking with Lord Bryant, but there was no reason Diana couldn't wait for her outside.

"Now, Lady Emily," the shopkeeper said. "I was a bit distracted. What, exactly, were you interested in? Bezoar stones?"

Lady Emily? Diana's foot stopped mid-stride. She turned around. That young blonde woman was Lady Emily? She was a girl, not a woman at all. Her clothes were elegant and her hair meticulous, but her face was that of a child. This was the woman Lord Bryant was pursuing? She was the reason he had initially refused to help Diana, and the reason, to this day, she had been skirting anything to do with high Society? How had he described his situation with Lady Emily?

Delicate.

She would give him that. Lady Emily was, indeed, delicate.

Lord Bryant was still behind the bookshelf. A few of the ladies had made their way over to him and Mrs. Oliver. This could be a disaster. If they asked about Mrs. Oliver's and Lord Bryant's relationship, all could be ruined.

Diana's stomach turned as she pictured the young girl in front of her trying to ward off the charms of someone like Lord Bryant. Diana knew what it was like. As a girl, she had been completely enthralled with the man. Did she even know what type of trouble she was putting herself in?

She strode back to Lady Emily and the bookseller.

"She didn't say bezoar stones. She distinctly said they were, in fact, different from bezoar stones."

Lady Emily turned toward her. Pale-blue eyes questioned her. "Do you follow geology? Have you heard of the findings of Mary Anning?"

Diana had heard of her. She was rather odd but in a fascinating way. She was a fossil hunter. "I have heard of her."

"Then you know about her discovery. Can you believe it? Coprolites. So much information will be gleaned from those stones now that we know what they really are."

Diana still didn't know what they were, and more to the point, she didn't know how to go about persuading this young woman to guard her heart from Lord Bryant. He was a scoundrel and a cad, even if he was a pleasant one.

Which was perhaps the worst kind.

And he was suddenly standing beside her. "Your friend, Mrs. Oliver, said she would wait for you outside."

"Oh." Could she not think of anything better to say? She hadn't warned off Lady Emily, and she hadn't managed not to make a scene, and she most definitely hadn't been able to get the image of the two of them—Lord Bryant and Lady Emily—dancing together out of her mind. Sitting in her office, even alone with him, was not the same as dancing. Not the same as whispering together in a ballroom. Diana blinked and turned to leave. The air in the bookstore suddenly felt stifling. It was too thick and hazy, and she felt as if she were trespassing in a forbidden land.

A small hand landed on her forearm. "Wait." Lady Emily had stepped forward. "We didn't get to finish our conversation about coprolites."

Lord Bryant's eyes widened. "You were speaking of coprolites?"

"Yes, I finally found another woman as interested in geology and paleontology as I am."

One eyebrow arched above a perfect nose. "You did?"

"What are coprolites?" asked a young lady who had followed behind Lord Bryant.

"Yes, Miss Barton." Lord Bryant leaned forward. "Please explain what coprolites are."

Oh dear. She had never actually said she knew what a coprolite was. "It is a very interesting type of stone . . ." Diana fidgeted with the belt at her waist and looked to Lady Emily for help, but she had retreated slightly behind the shop owner once the other women started speaking. Lord Bryant's smile was growing by the second, his teeth practically glowing.

He cocked his head to one side. "But would you really consider it a stone?"

Lady Emily had called it a stone. What else could it be? "Mary Anning said something truly fascinating about them. Isn't that correct, Lady Emily?"

Lady Emily took a half step out from behind the lanky store owner. Her eyes scanned the crop of four or five women who had gathered around Diana and Lord Bryant. She then looked back behind the storekeeper longingly. Apparently speaking in front of these ladies was not the same as speaking alone to Diana—or to anyone holding a book.

"Well . . ." Lady Emily's voice was quiet, her head down. Lord Bryant shook his head in a short but very understandable movement. He did not want Lady Emily to continue. But once she was no longer looking at him, she was no longer looking at anyone. "It is remarkable, really. From these fossils, we will be able to understand so much more about what strange and wondrous ancient creatures ate. At first, scientists thought they were bezoar stones because, well, they were often located in the abdomen. But they weren't stones the animals had swallowed." Lady Emily finally gained the courage to look up, and her strikingly pale eyes held on to Diana's.

Lord Bryant stepped toward Lady Emily with a hand out. But Diana could see the excitement in Lady Emily's eyes. She *wanted* to speak to those gathered around her. This was a subject more important to her than her visible shyness.

Lord Bryant reached for her elbow. "Lady Em—"

Lady Emily met the eyes of all the women nearby. "They are hardened fecal matter, of course. It is a wonder no one has ever figured it out before."

An older woman behind Diana coughed. "Fe-fecal matter?" More coughs were cropping up all over the room. Lord Bryant briefly put a hand to his forehead, then straightened his shoulders and stepped closer to Lady Emily.

"It is fascinating, isn't it?" he said.

Lady Emily nodded excitedly. Lord Bryant gave Diana a look that was a clear call for help.

He wanted her to help Lady Emily? His latest conquest? Diana took a deep breath. "I must admit to being surprised when I first heard of it." Moments ago. "But yes, I do believe they are—as you say—fascinating."

"Coprolites will revolutionize our understanding of diet, vegetation, and the digestive system. Waste passes—"

Lord Bryant stepped in front of Lady Emily and turned to the women listening. "I have heard polished coprolite is going to become the next rage. Much more extravagant and expensive than bezoar stones and more informational than amber." Lord Bryant blew on his fingernails and buffed them on his vest. "Why, after hearing all about them from Lady Emily, I've ordered a ring with a coprolite center myself."

That couldn't be true. No one moved, but all the women's eyes were going back and forth between Lady Emily and Lord Bryant. Whatever excitement Lady Emily had felt at explaining coprolites to the crowd was quickly melting off under the scrutiny of the shop. A cough in the back of the room made Lady Emily jump slightly, and her eyes shifted continuously from the door to the crowd. She was in need of an escape.

Diana shook her head. There was nothing else to be done but to help the poor woman. If Diana had simply left as soon as she saw Lord Bryant, this never would have happened. "I would love to know where you ordered that ring, Lord Bryant. I was thinking of ordering a broach myself. I'd like to do it before they become overly popular. Once that happens, they will be terribly hard to find."

The tone of the women shifted. A few whispered behind her, then another lady piped up. "Yes, Lord Bryant, please tell us which jeweler is selling them."

Lord Bryant smiled, but it was too broad of a smile, too smooth of a motion, to be sincere. He was lying about the whole affair to take the attention off Lady Emily.

"If I tell you now, how am I to be sure I get all the pieces I need? No, I'm afraid you shall have to speak to your own jewelers and see if they have any to spare."

There was a communal pout, and Diana took the opportunity to usher Lady Emily toward the door. "Who is your chaperone?" she said quietly to her.

"Mama, but she left to go to the lace shop for only a few moments. She won't be happy when she hears I have been speaking of Mary Anning again. She hates when I talk of her."

"She left you here alone?"

"Mrs. Nixon is here, and she said she would keep an eye on me."

Diana had no idea who Mrs. Nixon was, but it didn't matter. As long as they remained somewhere in the store, Lady Emily's reputation was safe. "Let's see what other books on geology they have here. I know they didn't have the one you were looking for, but perhaps there is something else that would interest you."

"I've read them."

Lady Emily was not quite as quick-witted as Diana had hoped, at least not socially. Diana lowered her voice. "Even if you had, would you rather remain here with that conversation going on?"

Lady Emily's small bud of a mouth opened, and realization dawned. "No," she whispered.

The two of them walked quietly away, once again leaving Lord Bryant behind to deal with the mess they had made. Once behind a bookshelf, Lady Emily ran a slender, tapered finger along the books. "Will he be all right?"

"With all those women?" Diana peeked behind her and around the shelf that was only a few inches taller than she was. She couldn't hear what he was saying, but the way his arms waved about seemed to indicate that he was enjoying himself. "He will be all right."

Lady Emily stopped walking and turned around. "Who are you?"

"I am Miss Diana Barton."

"I heard you say that earlier." Lady Emily's eyes flicked to the center of the store. "But who are you to him?"

She didn't need to ask who Lady Emily was speaking about. This was exactly the reason she shouldn't be in the same room as Lady Emily. Now Lady Emily was suspicious of Diana's relationship with her would-be suitor. She had expected Lady Emily to be very different from this soft-spoken young girl with a fascination for fossilized—no, she couldn't even think of it, though a small smile tugged at her cheek. No, Lady Emily was not at all what Diana had pictured. Did Lady Emily know what type of man was pursuing her? Did she know how many other women he had pursued this year alone? And was it Diana's responsibility to warn her?

Diana placed a finger on the bookshelf and slid it along the smooth, wooden strip just in front of the books. She could hint a little at least. Lord Bryant's reputation wasn't exactly a secret. "Like a lot of women, I'm not really anything to him. You know what he is like."

Diana's declaration didn't seem to cause Lady Emily any concern. She didn't even blink. "He looks at you, though." Lady Emily's eyes sought hers. "Most women he looks *through*. Sometimes he looks at me when I say something unexpected or strange, but his eyes never left you. Not since you walked into the store."

He had seen her when she'd first walked in?

"That is most likely because I'm a thorn in that man's side."

Lady Emily's chest rose and fell. "Then I suppose that must be what he has been looking for."

Diana had no idea what she could mean by that. But the thought of Lord Bryant watching her was making the back of her neck itch. He couldn't see her—the bookshelf was covering both of them—but he must be wondering what they were talking about. A niggle of guilt touched the back of her mind, but she brushed it away. She hadn't said anything wrong. Not really.

Diana brushed the dust from the bookshelf off her gloved finger. "My chaperone is waiting outside for me. I should go."

"It was nice to talk to you. It isn't very often that I meet someone else who is as fascinated by fossils and stones as I am."

Diana smiled and gave a short curtsy.

She would have to read up on a few books on the off chance she met Lady Emily again. Coprolite was about the only paleontological term she knew, and it wasn't one she was ever planning on using.

She didn't look for Lord Bryant's gaze as she walked past his group. She nodded a brief goodbye to the shopkeeper and burst through the door and out onto the street.

Everton made certain the door shut behind Miss Barton. She should have left the first time he had asked her. Then again, he should have known she wouldn't.

This trip to the bookstore had been a disaster.

Miss Barton and Lady Emily had conversed, a room full of tongue-wagging socialites and their mothers had seen him engage with Miss Barton, and lapidaries all over London were going to have to figure out how to polish and shape coprolites.

All because he thought a trip to the bookstore would be a more comfortable outing for Lady Emily than a dinner or a ball. And in truth, she had been more comfortable here. Too comfortable. Coprolites and Mary Anning were not going to improve her social situation.

He turned around only to see that Lady Emily had, once again, hidden herself away behind a bookshelf. In order to find her, he would have to navigate back through the crowd. He sighed, but there was nothing to be done about it. He couldn't leave without bidding farewell to Lady Emily. Most of the young ladies in the shop were pleasant on their own or even in a group of two or three, but there were seven or eight of them here, and even for him, that was quite a lot.

It took him over half an hour to make it out of the bookshop, but eventually, he did. Instead of sending someone to fetch his carriage, he walked along the store-lined street. He was a long distance from Rochester Street and the Richardson Rail office. Miss Barton must have hired a cab, so there was no chance he would overtake her if he set out to find her. He didn't know what he would say to her if he did.

He had gotten as far as dressing to visit her twice this week, but for some reason, after his visit with the Duchess of Harrington, he couldn't make himself enter that office, not even with her little gold pin mocking from his dresser every day. Each time he stood in front of his valet, getting his cravat tied, the words *someone older and stronger* flashed through his mind. Both times, he had grabbed John's hand at his neck and stopped him.

As if Miss Barton qualified as older and stronger. Technically, she was older and stronger than Rachel, but she was still so very young. The duchess could not have meant a few scant happy years older than his wife had been. Miss Barton was still too bright of a light to snuff out. If he were to consider heeding the duchess's advice, he would need someone who had seen more cruelty, someone as hardened as he was. Someone without a full, unclouded future ahead of her. Together, perhaps he and this older, stronger, hardened woman could drudge through life. Perhaps that would be better than drudging through it alone.

He was, by no means, ready to take that step. But for the first time since Rachel died, he admitted that marriage could possibly be in his future. He still doubted it would, but the duchess had opened his mind to it a bit. Not all women had futures that lit up a room when they walked into it.

Miss Barton, however, did.

So he had stayed away.

And he would continue to stay away until he could tame that small part of him that saw her copper eyes every night when he laid his head on his pillow. When he could return to her indifferent and playful, he would visit her office again.

Another week should do it.

Everton stopped walking and glanced around himself for the first time since he had left the shop. He was three blocks closer to Rochester Street and his home was in the opposite direction. He spun on his heel.

A week might not be long enough.

CHAPTER 16

Diana closed the Society section and laid the newspaper on her desk. Lord Bryant had attended a card party and an opera, so he wasn't ill or indisposed. It had been a week since she ran into him at the bookstore and two weeks since she had truly spoken with him.

She had known from the beginning that this time would come.

Her novelty had worn off.

Or, perhaps, he was irritated with her. She had spoken to Lady Emily after he had specifically asked her not to.

Whatever the reason, she would not admit to missing him. Not even when she was giving his excuses to Mrs. Oliver every day.

The bell clanged, and Diana's eyes flew to the door.

Penetrating green eyes stared back at her. He had come.

Mrs. Oliver clapped her hands. Diana tightened her grip on the pen she was holding to prevent herself from doing the same. She controlled her smile. Lord Bryant was a business associate, and she would smile at him like she smiled at all her business associates.

His eyes were hollower than the last time she had seen him, and as was typical, his cravat was askew. "Good morning, Miss Barton."

"Good morning," she replied. Neither of them mentioned the length of time since they had last met, and his eyes only met hers for the briefest of moments. Then they scanned her desk.

"May I?" He pointed to her newspaper.

"Of course."

He reached for the paper, then picked up his chair and carried it to Mrs. Oliver's side of the room. That wasn't out of the ordinary. When he used to come regularly, he would often split his time between Diana's desk and Mrs. Oliver's.

Diana much preferred it when he sat by Mrs. Oliver. The pressure of having someone look over her shoulder while she worked was annoying at best. Of course, when he sat by Mrs. Oliver, he still managed to distract her.

Diana straightened the papers on her desk. Even with the paperwork turned in to Parliament, she still had plenty of work to do. She didn't have time for a wandering eye. He opened the newspaper and started reading. He gave her no explanation for his absence and acted as if he had never been away.

"Did you know Lady Baldwin has removed to the country?" Lord Bryant folded his newspaper forward to glance at Diana.

She pretended to stop working, even though she had been watching him for at least two minutes. "Seeing as I have had no dealings with Lady Baldwin, no, I did not. Should I know her?"

"No, I don't suppose you should." He lifted his paper back up, blocking her view of him. She picked up her pen. The office always felt empty after Nate and Mr. Richardon left, and Lord Bryant seemed to fill it again, even though all he did was dawdle about. Perhaps that was why she missed him when he was gone.

"Lord Bryant, what is it exactly that you do every day?" She wanted to hear some excuse from him. Surely they had more to say to each other than simply *good morning*. "Aside from the time you spend in my office."

The newspaper folded again, and he raised an eyebrow. "What do I do?"

"Yes, what do you do?"

He looked around the room. "I suppose I do this."

"I said *besides* sitting in my office."

"You did say that, but I'm not simply sitting in your office, am I?"

"No, he isn't," Mrs. Oliver chimed in. "He is also reading a newspaper."

"I'm not certain that is what Lord Bryant meant." Diana had watched him peek over the top of his newspaper to see what she was doing enough to know that the newspaper didn't actually rivet him. It simply gave him something to occupy his time.

"Come, Diana, we both know why I'm here, and it isn't because I needed a place to read the newspaper."

He was here because she had asked him to be here. He was helping her. Was he trying to tell her he spent his days helping women? That was preposterous. He must mean something else, but what?

Her mind flashed back to that dreadful night when she had visited him. She hadn't asked him to help her. She had asked him to ruin her. Lord Bryant didn't spend his time protecting women. He ruined them. Apparently, he saw that as his purpose in life. Her stomach soured, and a foul taste entered her mouth. Lord Bryant caught the change in her demeanor and nodded as if there was nothing wrong with his choice of pastime.

She narrowed her eyes. "It seems as though you might, at times, find something more challenging to do with your intellect."

"Who ever said I have an intellect?"

"I see how you follow my accounts. At times, you have even proudly pointed out an error or two. Those are things that took me weeks to learn, and you follow them effortlessly."

Lord Bryant clicked his tongue. "My dear, that could actually be a comment on your intellect, not mine."

She scoffed. "It could be, but it isn't."

He winked at her. "No, it isn't."

"Well then? What is it you do to exercise your intellect and . . . ?" Diana paused, but Lord Bryant didn't miss her gaze sliding to his well-fitted jacket sleeves. Most lords didn't have an athletic figure like his—especially not the ones who spent their days dawdling about.

He raised an eyebrow and gave a low chuckle, though not the type of laugh that would gain her any points. If anything, her overlong assessment of his physique should have lost her a point or two.

"I fence, I have a few business dealings of my own, and in general, my mind doesn't relax very often, so I also read, as we have discussed."

He folded the newspaper and stood. His slow stride toward her desk made it impossible not to notice that his legs were as well-formed as his arms. Fencing. Perhaps she should try it. Lord Bryant didn't take his seat on her desk but instead placed both hands on top of it and leaned forward. He often did this when he wanted to say something for her ears alone.

"I don't claim to be a genius or even much more than a mediocre scholar, but I do have a mind that I cannot seem to turn off." His eyes slid over to Mrs. Oliver, who was astutely watching the two of them. After the storage room incident, Diana had only allowed her to keep her position based on the promise that she wouldn't leave her alone with any man during work hours, including Lord Bryant. "Except when I come here."

Diana's eyes jerked away from her assistant and connected with Lord Bryant's piercing ones. "Pardon?"

"You haven't noticed?"

That traitorous part of her that always reacted to Lord Bryant's nearness fired up deep within her chest, sending sparks throughout her rib cage. She shook her head, not trusting her mouth to speak. Diana never knew exactly what kind of game Lord Bryant was playing, but this one was dangerous.

"My mind can relax here. My only purpose is to help you, and I can do it most of the time simply by sitting in a chair. For whatever reason, this office is a place of refuge for my thoughts, and I have come to appreciate the hours I spend in this room, your pen scratching away at paper while Mrs. Oliver makes eyes at both of us."

"Oh."

Lord Bryant smiled, and if he were allowed to gain points, that smile would have gotten him hundreds. He was winning more points than she was this morning, and he knew it. She needed to come up with more witty things to say than *oh.*

"Why, then, have we not seen you here for two weeks?"

He pursed his lips together. "I wasn't sure if your office would still hold the same charm."

Why? What had changed about her office? "And does it?"

"I'm still not sure."

He returned to his chair, unfolded the newspaper, and began reading again.

She bent her head back over her work, noticing each time he turned a page and wondering what made him chuckle every so often. Some poor chap's misfortune, certainly.

That was the kind of man Lord Bryant was. He probably laughed at others' misfortune, she was quite certain she had heard he was a gambler, and he had no respect for women. He was more than his charming smile or his well-formed arms.

The ink from her pen blotted, and she cursed under her breath. Another chuckle arose from Lord Bryant, and this time, she was fairly certain it wasn't because of something he'd read. His stillness of mind was the opposite of hers. When he sat in that chair, her mind couldn't settle. At the moment, she was doubting every single judgment she had just thrown at him.

"A horse just stopped in front of the office," Lord Bryant said from his chair. "What should I do to chase off this young man?"

He probably wouldn't have to do anything, as it had been weeks since someone without official business had walked through the door. Diana's eyes flashed to the window to see a fine black Friesian. Her hands slammed down on her desk. The rider had dismounted on the opposite side, so she couldn't see him clearly, but she didn't need to. She would have known that horse anywhere.

"Everton, you need to leave."

"You called me Everton." His smile was mischievous as always. He had no clue what trouble he was about to be in or she was about to be in. All of them, really.

"If you go now while he is behind his horse—"

Lord Bryant suddenly took a marked interest in the man outside. "Who is it?"

"There is only one Friesian that would be stopping in front of this office. It's Bard."

"And Bard is . . ."

She stood from her desk. "Nate's horse." Why wasn't he leaving already? "My brother."

"Mr. Barton's back?" Mrs. Oliver jumped from her seat. "That is marvelous news!"

If anything, Lord Bryant's smile grew broader. He picked his paper back up and settled deeper into his chair. "And how would you like for me to deal with this brother of yours? Like we dealt with Mr. Broadcreek?"

Diana held up her arms in front of her, waving her hands back and forth. "No. Definitely not how we dealt with Mr. Broadcreek."

"I agree with Mrs. Oliver; this is marvelous news. I haven't seen your brother since his wedding. He is such a serious fellow—I do love to rile him up."

Diana ran to the coatrack and grabbed his hat. "Please, you must go."

He folded down his newspaper. "And miss seeing you so flustered? Not a chance."

She stomped across the room and reached Lord Bryant's side just as the bell clanged behind her. She froze.

"Diana." Nate's voice was low, his tone wary. Not knowing what else to do, she squeezed her eyes shut and reminded herself of all the wonderful things she had done for Nate. She was practically running his railroad business for him so he could be in Baimbury, for heaven's sake. She had no reason to feel guilty.

"Mr. Barton," Mrs. Oliver said, her excitement making it clear she was completely unaware of the tension in the room. "It is so lovely to see you here in London."

Nate's footsteps immediately pounded across the room. He passed Diana and went straight for Lord Bryant, who was still casually reading his newspaper. His arms were lifted high enough that the paper covered his face. Nate ripped it down.

"So, it is true."

"Ah, Mr. Barton. As Mrs. Oliver said, it's lovely to see you back in London." Lord Bryant leaned to one side and peered behind Nate's body. "Did your wife return with you?"

Diana had known there was some bad blood between Lord Bryant and her brother. Just as she had guessed, it was because of Grace. Nate bent over, grabbed Lord Bryant by the lapels, and physically lifted him from his chair. Both were tall and well built, but Nate was thicker, his hands rougher, and his temper hotter.

"Get out," Nate growled, his face much too close to Lord Bryant's. Diana had to put a stop to this before it turned ugly.

"Nate, he was just here reading the newspaper. He means no harm."

"Lord Bryant always means harm, Diana. Always."

Now that was taking it too far. "No, Nate, he does not. He is pompous at times and a womanizer—"

"A conniver and a gambler," Nate continued as he physically dragged Lord Bryant toward the door. All the while, Lord Bryant nodded his head at each of the inflammatory charges.

"No wonder I like your family so well," Lord Bryant said. "You understand me perfectly."

"Then you must understand why you are leaving this office now and should never come back." Nate had arrived at the door and finally dropped Lord Bryant's lapels.

"Now, what kind of pompous, conniving gambler would I be if I left at the first sign of trouble?"

"A good one," Nate said.

Diana rushed forward. She hadn't been able to finish her statement about Lord Bryant. He was all of those terrible things, but he also, somehow, wasn't. "Nate, I asked him to be here."

"Asked is a very kind way to put it," Lord Bryant drawled.

Diana tightened her grip on Nate's arm just as he cocked it back.

"He is teasing. Lord Bryant wants to rile you up. You aren't serious, are you, Lord Bryant?" Diana shook her head from side to side slowly, willing him to agree with her and decrease the tension in the office.

"When a woman comes to a man's home, begging him to ruin her, only to demand that he merely sit in her office all day long, it begs the question: who, exactly, is the tease in this situation?"

Nate turned to her. "You did what?"

Blast Lord Bryant. And blast Nate. The vote was in less than a week. Could he not have trusted her for one more week? But first and foremost, blast Lord Bryant. How could he tell her brother what she had done? "It sounds a lot worse than it was."

If she thought her words would calm him, she was very wrong. His chest puffed out, and his hand fisted at his waist. "He speaks the truth?"

Mrs. Oliver's pen dropped, landing with a clank upon her desk. She hastily picked it up and busied herself, scratching away at her desk, her head down, pretending not to hear. Lord Bryant was still at the door, this time with a foolish grin on his face. No matter how many points Diana had won in the past, he had just outdone her. There would be no coming back from this.

"I needed help, Nate."

"Then you should have asked me, Diana!" Nate shook his head and pounded a fist on his chest. "You should have asked me. Why did I have to get a letter from Mr. Broadcreek, of all men, telling me that Lord Bryant was spending far too much time with you?"

Of course Mr. Broadcreek had written to him. She gritted her teeth. Would the man never give up? "You were in Baimbury with Grace. You should still be there now. I have everything under control."

"If this man is in our office, nothing is under control."

"It is, though. It is in much more control than it was a few weeks ago, thanks to Lord Bryant."

"Lord Bryant will never have my thanks."

Lord Bryant shrugged. "I never asked for it."

"This doesn't concern you," Diana and Nate turned and said simultaneously.

"What was so wrong that you needed Lord Bryant, of all people, to rush in and save the day?" Nate asked, his arm still tense under her hands.

"Mr. Broadcreek asked me to marry him."

Nate sucked in a tight breath at this announcement. "Then tell him no, the cad."

"I did." Diana took a deep breath. "I told him no a hundred times, but he simply couldn't believe a woman could know her own mind. And not only that, he became a huge impediment to getting any work done. He knew if he delayed Mrs. Richardson's railroad line long enough for its reputation to be ruined, Parliament wouldn't give another grant for the next railroad line. Without securing another grant, Richardson Rail is worth next to nothing. Either way, it would be a win for Mr. Broadcreek."

"Why would marrying you be a win for Mr. Broadcreek?"

Oh dear. She shouldn't have said that.

"What a thing to say to your own sister," Lord Bryant jumped in. Whether he could see her discomfort or he simply wanted to get one more dig in, Diana had no idea. "It would be a win for any man to gain her hand in marriage. She is like a tiger lily in a sea of daisies."

"And yet, if I were to ask you to marry her, after spending so much time nearly alone with her in this office, something tells me you wouldn't jump at the chance."

"Me?" Lord Bryant asked. "Well, of course, *I* wouldn't."

Mrs. Oliver gasped despite her pen scratching away. Diana pushed down the pain that came from Lord Bryant's immediate answer. She had always known he wouldn't consider marrying her, but would it have hurt to act the smallest bit tempted? Other than Nate, she had spent more time with him than any other man. Couldn't he have seemed to at least consider the prospect?

Nate smiled, as if he had won. "*This* is the man you have been inviting into our office day in and day out? He has no honor."

Diana straightened. Lord Bryant wasn't a chivalrous man by nature, but that didn't make it his fault, exactly. "I take offense to that," she said.

"I don't," Lord Bryant said softly to her side. Diana filed that away as something to discuss another time, but for now, she needed to speak with Nate. The last thing she needed was for her brother to discover she had bought Richardson Rail without telling him. If he was going to find out anyway, she would rather he found out from her. "Well, you should, Lord Bryant. You have never acted dishonorably toward me."

Lord Bryant raised his deuced eyebrow at that. His eyes went to Diana's lips, and a devilish grin spread on his face. "I'm quite certain I have."

Nate followed Lord Bryant's eyes, and understanding flared on his face. Before Diana had the chance to rein him in, his elbow cocked back, and his fist slammed into Lord Bryant's Roman godlike face.

"Nate!" Diana glared at her brother, pushed him aside, and rushed to Lord Bryant. Had Lord Bryant not been so intent on wiggling his eyebrows at her, he might have dodged Nate's blow. But as it was, he was given no time to prepare, and the full force of Nate's unwieldy punch dropped Lord Bryant flat onto the floor. She knelt to examine him, her heart pounding. A fist like her brother's could kill a man, and killing a baron was at the top of the list of irresponsible things her brother should not do while visiting London.

"Lord Bryant." Her hands went to his face to inspect the damage. His eyes were open and blinking, his nose swelling up rapidly.

"That felt even better than the first time," Nate said behind her.

One corner of Lord Bryant's mouth turned up at Nate's words. He was alive, then, and apparently well enough to find her brother's statement amusing.

Diana pivoted awkwardly on her knees to face Nate. "You could have killed him."

Nate shook out his hand. "The world is not so lucky."

Lord Bryant pushed himself up into a sitting position, and Diana let her hands fall away from his face. He blinked hard a few more times and gingerly shook his head.

"You've broken my nose," Lord Bryant said. His voice was soft and calm, as if he was surprised at the turn of events rather than angry or upset with Nate.

"Good. Perhaps it will heal crookedly," Nate spoke through his tightened jaw.

Lord Bryant gingerly touched his nose with his fingertips. "One can only hope."

Nate scoffed. "Perhaps a less-than-perfect face would control the damage you can do each Season."

"Your sister would disagree."

No blood was coming from his nose, but it was swelling more and more as they talked.

"How do you feel?" Diana pulled a handkerchief from her sleeve and handed it to him. Her arms ached to reach up and feel the bones in his face again, but with Nate watching the two of them, she didn't want to risk Lord Bryant coming to any more bodily harm.

Lord Bryant closed his eyes tightly, then opened them. His hands went to his face. "I feel as though I've been hit in the head by a pugilist."

Nate paced behind them. "Good. That is how I was hoping to make you feel. Now leave and never come back."

"Nate." Diana frowned.

"This is still my office, Diana. I can remove from it those whom I wish."

"It is not *only* your office," she said.

"I'm sure I can get Mrs. Richardson to agree with me."

Oh dear. She had to tell him. He was bound to find out at some point. "Mrs. Richardson no longer owns a portion of this office."

"She sold? To whom? You said yourself she didn't take Mr. Broadcreek's offer."

"No, it wasn't Mr. Broadcreek."

A low chuckle below alerted her to the fact that Lord Bryant had just discovered what was happening.

"Mrs. Richardson didn't sell to this bounder, surely."

Lord Bryant moved as if to stand but then apparently thought better of it and settled back to a sitting position. "What would I want with a railroad company? Do you know how much work these things take?"

It was Nate's turn to raise an eyebrow. "I do have an idea."

"Then you don't know me very well if you think I would want to own one."

Nate turned back to Diana. "Who bought Richardson Rail? And why wasn't I told?"

Diana fidgeted with the buttons that ran down the front of her dress. Why hadn't she told Nate what she had done? She wanted her turn to help someone. Nate had done everything for their family while she and Mama had stayed in Baimbury. They had teased him about how serious he had become after Father's death but had never offered to help him in any way. He had come to London alone to set up the railroad company, put his reputation at risk, and delayed any future plans for himself in order to bring their family out of the brink of ruin. It was his turn to be at home in Baimbury with his growing family. He couldn't always be the one saving everyone.

Which was exactly what he would have done had she told him.

"It wasn't Lord Bryant who bought Richardson Rail," she said, her voice calm but quiet.

"Who then?"

She stood. "I did."

Nate's shoulders dropped, and he stared at her. "You bought it?"

What she had done made sense. Perfect sense. "Anyone else would have taken advantage of Charlotte."

"I thought that was why we agreed you would help her."

"And I was helping her, but even the small amount of work she needed to do—signing papers—was too much for her. Then Mr. Broadcreek kept asking her to sell. She was so overwhelmed by it all she nearly sold it to him for a ridiculously low amount."

"Why didn't you tell me?"

"Why didn't you tell Mama and me how unhappy you were when you were building this company?"

"I wasn't. At least, I hadn't known I was. And I wasn't completely alone. I had Mr. Richardson."

"And I have Mrs. Oliver and now—Lord Bryant."

Lord Bryant shot a surprised glance Diana's way, but she ignored it. He had accepted her pin, and that made him part of her team. He wore it on his lapel even now. Fortunately, Nate hadn't noticed. Nate rubbed his face with his hand. "I'm here now, so you can send Lord Bryant home."

Lord Bryant dropped a hand to the floor. "I don't think I have ever been *sent home* in my life."

"Well, there is a first time for everything." Nate stomped over to the door and opened it. The usually cheery sound of the bell clanged too fast to sound anything like a welcome. "Get out."

"Nate, you have already injured him. You cannot also remove him from our office. Despite what you think, he has been an enormous help to me."

"And what has he gotten in return?"

The air left Diana's lungs in a rush. She turned to Lord Bryant only to find him still on the floor, looking fastidiously at his nails. What had he gotten in return? A moment ago he had received a blow to the face. And in the weeks preceding that . . .

"Nothing." The word escaped her mouth like a puff of smoke rising into the wind. A pit opened in her stomach; she was missing something. "Lord Bryant has never asked me for anything."

"Then what in heaven's name is he doing here?" Nate was practically shaking, but he couldn't have been as torn as she was right now. Why had Lord Bryant helped her? And why hadn't she been asking this question all along?

"I like it here," Lord Bryant piped up after no one else seemed to want to answer. "There is no more relaxing place for me in all of London."

Diana blinked. This is what he always did—he never answered questions properly and then deflected until she had forgotten exactly why she had asked the question in the first place. "That is because you refuse to help me with the paperwork." Diana tried to keep the conversation as light as she could, but her mind was frantically trying to put the pieces together.

"If I did paperwork, it wouldn't be relaxing. I tried it once—remember?"

She did. She remembered everything.

"There are plenty of other places for you to relax." Nate placed both hands at his waist. "For some reason, my sister believes you have helped her somehow. I will not go so far as to thank you, but I will refrain from physically throwing you out. Please leave and never come back."

Lord Bryant groaned as he turned to his side, and then rose to a standing position. "As I said, this office brings me a measure of peace. I'll stop coming only when Diana asks me to stop."

Nate made a sound like a roar, and Diana jumped in front of him before he could do Lord Bryant any more damage. Nate slammed into her, not hard enough to cause any injury, but it did cause her breath to leave her lungs. He stopped and grabbed Diana by the shoulders to steady her and then whipped his head up to scowl at Lord Bryant. "She is Miss Barton to you."

Diana reached for Nate's hand on her shoulder and clamped down on it. "He calls me Miss Barton. Truly, he does. He is trying to get under your skin. For some reason, he doesn't mind provoking another blow. But I won't have it. Not in my office."

This situation needed to end. Lord Bryant's nose was swollen, his cravat askew. In the past two months, he had spent many days helping her, asking her for nothing in return. Here in her office, he had seemed like a very different person than she had seen him anywhere else. He wasn't haggard and demeaning like he had been that first night in his study, nor was he haughty and imposing like she had seen him at the ball or the bookstore. This office did seem to relax him. And if that was the only thing she could do for him, she wasn't about to take it away. But it would be best for everyone if he came to relax another day.

Diana gently shrugged Nate away from her but stayed between the two gentlemen. Nate's chest was puffed out, and his arms were pulled back as if at ready. She stepped more firmly in front of Lord Bryant and met his eyes, placing herself between the two men. "You are always welcome in this office." Then she turned to Nate. "And Lord Bryant is welcome to call me Diana. I understand it brings no real attachment with it, and because of that, he does me no harm. You will not strike him for it, for he is my friend."

Nate huffed behind her, but she ignored it. Lord Bryant blinked and then placed a hand behind his neck. For the first time since she had seen him in their office moments ago, the nervous, bounding energy he had brought with him faded. His eyes seemed to hold a question, but he didn't ask it. Hopefully being called a friend was not an impertinent discourtesy.

Finally, Lord Bryant nodded. "Then I shall take my leave." His voice was low, and his head lowered as if he had been a chastised child. "I will see you tomorrow."

"Tomorrow?" Nate stomped around her. "Why would you come tomorrow? We don't need you here."

A spark of his energy returned. Lord Bryant touched Diana's handkerchief to his nose. And then had the impudence to give Nate a wink. "Mr. Barton, you should know better. My most favorite places are those where I am not needed."

Nate's jaw clenched, but he didn't say anything. He stepped forward, and Diana moved to stop him. "I'm not going to hit him again. At least not today." Nate reached for Lord Bryant, and for a moment Diana thought he was about to go back on his word, but instead, he wrapped his fingers around the gold knot at Lord Bryant's lapel and ripped it off. A small hole was left behind in the fabric. "This doesn't belong to you."

"It did for a while. But I suppose that will have to have been long enough." Lord Bryant picked up his hat and, with a final nod to Nate and Diana, left.

Mrs. Oliver rushed to them as soon as the door closed behind Lord Bryant. "Diana, is that true? He isn't going to marry you?" Mrs. Oliver grabbed each of her shoulders and slid her hands down her arms, as if to ascertain that Diana had no physical injuries. "All that time I thought he was so respectable."

Nate scoffed. "Lord Bryant? Mrs. Oliver, he is one of the most infamous rakes in all of London. He once lured Grace into an empty library before we married. Diana seems to believe I can't keep him out of this office, but at the very least, I will not be leaving the two of you alone with the likes of him."

"Diana?" Mrs. Oliver turned to her.

The office felt empty, even with Nate in it. Diana's limbs were heavy. She needed to sit down. "Nate is right. Lord Bryant does have quite the reputation as a scoundrel."

"But . . ." Mrs. Oliver's hand flew to her mouth. "But the candles . . ."

Nate's brow furrowed. "What candles?"

Diana ignored his question. "Lord Bryant has been a great help these past few weeks despite his reputation. I'm sorry I wasn't more clear, Mrs. Oliver, but I have been using him to run off all the men who came here to waste my time. He has only been a perfect gentleman toward me, I assure you."

Mrs. Oliver's eyes were a bit haunted. She must have been remembering locking the two of them in the storage room. Diana couldn't help but feel guilty for the poor woman, but in reality, it served her right. What had Mrs. Oliver been thinking? Even if she and Lord Bryant had been engaged, her actions were completely inexcusable. "I thought he was simply waiting for the right moment to propose marriage."

"Lord Bryant will never marry," Nate said.

Mrs. Oliver looked to Diana for confirmation, as if Diana hadn't just told her as much. "That is also true. I, myself, have heard Lord Bryant say it."

Mrs. Oliver leaned forward as if she wanted to ask more questions, but then, glancing at Nate, she stopped. She shook her head slowly and returned to her desk.

"It appears I will be staying in London for a while," Nate said. He strode toward her desk and sat down.

"Nate."

"What?"

"That is my desk. It has been mine for the past six months."

He pushed off the desk with his powerful arms. "Where am I supposed to sit?"

"As long as Lord Bryant isn't here, I suppose you could take his seat."

Nate's eyes narrowed. "His seat?" He ran his fingers through his already mussed hair. "Lord Bryant has a seat in this office, but I have none? This is my office, Diana."

"It is our office, and we will find you a place while you are here."

"I could spend a few days at home with Mr. Oliver as long as you are here, Mr. Barton," said Mrs. Oliver. "Diana doesn't need me to be here all the time."

Nate sighed. "No, Mrs. Oliver, I won't take your desk. Diana, where is your old one?"

"In the storage room." Her old one was a small secretary desk. Diana sat on her chair, her legs still shaking from dealing with Nate and Lord Bryant being in the same room. Nate shuffled around in the storage room and finally emerged carrying her old desk. He set it down in the middle of the room before moving Lord Bryant's chair to the farthest corner of the office. Nate then returned to the storage room and came out holding one more chair, which he plopped in front of her old desk.

By the time he was settled, Nate looked rather ridiculous. His knees touched the bottom of her desk unless he straightened them out. His long legs protruded out from under the desk, and the square tabletop barely seemed to have room for his formidable palms.

Diana held back a laugh. "You never did grow into those legs, I see. Grace doesn't mind?"

Nate narrowed an eye at her.

"You've been married over a year. Surely she has grown accustomed to them by now."

"Grace never had an issue with my legs."

"Didn't she call them gangly?"

"I was the one who called them gangly." He tried once again, unsuccessfully, to bend his knees so he could keep his legs under the desk but to no avail. Her little desk wasn't built to accommodate a man of his size.

"That's right." Diana bit her cheek. "To impress her." She shook her head. "It is a wonder you managed to get married at all."

Nate groaned and dropped his head on the desk. After a moment, he lifted it. "Tell me where we are on the most recent Barton line. As long as I'm here, I might as well help."

Diana bent over and retrieved a folder from inside her drawer. It would be a week before the orders were due on that line, so she hadn't gotten to them yet. She walked them to Nate and placed them on his desk. "Thank you," she said. Nate took the stack of papers and started leafing through them in the efficient manner with which he always did everything. Memories of her first months here with him and Mr. Richardson flooded her with a feeling of belonging. "It will be nice to be working together again. Just like before."

Nate's eyes slid to Mrs. Oliver's desk and back before nodding. That had been Mr. Richardson's desk for years. She knew what he was thinking: it would never be the same, not with Mr. Richardson gone. Nate rubbed the top of her old desk, sliding his hands back and forth along the smooth wood. "Perhaps when you sell Richardson Rail, we should consider selling Barton Rail as well."

"Perhaps."

He tapped the back of his pen on the papers in front of him. "It is something to think about."

"I know."

Nate wanted to spend his time in Baimbury with Grace. The estate was finally becoming more profitable, thanks to his innovations and the large influx of funds that the sale of a few railroad lines had brought the family.

Diana walked slowly back to her desk. Nate had adjusted to the life he had had before he started the company, only a happier version of it. He was ready to focus on a different future with his growing family. She could see it in the way the shadows touched his eyes whenever he looked at his friend's old desk. Her hand traced the nicks along the edges of the desk she had been using for the past six months. Diana had always known working on the railroad would be temporary. But her old life didn't await her on the other side of this. Her reputation simply wasn't what it used to be. Nor was she. Even if she could go back to Baimbury, she knew what life was like there. Could she really go back to living each day waiting for something to happen instead of making things happen?

Nate might be ready to sell the railroad company, but she wasn't certain she was.

CHAPTER 17

EVERTON DRUMMED HIS FINGERS ON his thigh as his right foot tapped a silly rhythm on the carriage floor. He had never been so impatient to reach Diana. His friend. He hadn't had a friend for years, and now that he did, he wondered why the deuce he had waited so long.

Despite Everton's declaration that he would come back to the office the very next day, he had decided to give the siblings a full twenty-four hours alone together to make up for lost time, a fact that had led to one of the dullest days of his life. Even in the two weeks prior, when he had made himself stay away from Diana, he hadn't been so anxious to leave the house. Those weeks had been filled with a different sort of dullness, a deeper and more hopeless understanding that sitting at home, alone, was always to be his lot in life. He was used to that type of monotony.

The realization that he could, at any time, disrupt Mr. Barton and his sister led to a different type of tediousness, the sort that made him itch like he was wearing woolen underthings. He had followed Nelson around the house, asking him important questions, like why the silverware needed to be placed in its exact arrangement every time they dined and whether Nelson had ever purposely dreamt of being something more than a butler, like a pastry cook or a snuffbox maker. Nelson hadn't taken well to that last one. He had sarcastically assured Everton that his highest ambition in life had always been to serve a baron who trailed along after him while he tried to work.

Nelson had never seemed happier than when Everton had taken his leave this morning.

Everton's carriage rolled to a stop in front of the Bartons' office on Rochester Street. He leapt from the carriage, smiling as he loosened his cravat. His neck was always the first place Diana's eyes landed when he stepped into her office. Her brother would most likely be bothered by it as well.

Nate Barton was one of the most fortunate men he knew. He had a graceful wife who looked at him as if the sun rose and set on him. His sister loved him. Somewhere back in Baimbury, a mother worried over him as well.

Everton couldn't look at such happy men without itching to ruffle their feathers a bit.

Or a lot.

He went over his planned topics of conversation in his mind as he strode toward the door.

Mr. Barton's wife.

Mr. Barton's sister.

Mr. Barton's lackluster kissing abilities at his own wedding.

There was a positive skip in his step as he bounded across the pavement almost as if he were galloping with Diana again. It truly was a joy to have Mr. Barton back in town.

The bell had never sounded happier at receiving him than when he opened the door that afternoon.

Mrs. Oliver sat in her usual spot. A small desk had been added to the room, but both it and Diana's desks were empty.

He let the door close behind him, all his pent-up energy suddenly gone. Did the world truly insist on conspiring against him? When he was finally about to have a bit of recreation?

Mrs. Oliver stood in surprise. "Lord Bryant, what are you doing here?" Her aged mouth was turned down in a frown, accentuating the lines surrounding it. Mr. Barton's seriousness had gotten to her, it seemed. Everton would have to fix that.

"My dear Miss Oliver—"

"Mrs."

"Mrs. Oliver. I forget of course—you don't seem old enough to be married."

Mrs. Oliver pursed her lips, her brows heavy over her eyelids. "I'm old enough to have married granddaughters, and I don't take kindly to flattery."

Everton smiled in return. She didn't take kindly to it *anymore*. "Is Diana out?"

"I believe you can see that for yourself."

Yes, he could. "Do you know when she might be returning?"

"If I did, I wouldn't be likely to tell you, now would I?"

Mrs. Oliver was much more pleasant when she had considered him an upstanding young man. He would have to go about fixing that. Rakes were perfectly respectable figures at times. At least when one required their assistance, as Diana so desperately had. "Now, Mrs. Oliver, don't let Mr. Barton persuade you to think less of me. Diana came to *me* for help, and I was happy to assist her. I have never done her any harm."

Mrs. Oliver blew a puff of air upward, lifting the curls under her cap. "You consistently tried to get her alone."

Is that how Mrs. Oliver remembered it? He raised an eyebrow. "I did have some help."

She cleared her throat and busied herself, straightening the few well-organized papers on her desk. "How was I supposed to know all those wonderful things Miss Barton had said about you were falsehoods? You should have heard the way she went on and on."

"I would like to have heard them." Everything she had said was untrue, yet the thought of Diana singing his praises to nearly every man who crossed the threshold to this office brought a warm feeling of pleasure. After all, it was only natural for friends to compliment one another. "When will they return?"

Mrs. Oliver straightened in her seat. "Not for hours." Her eyes flashed to the window behind him, and her brave, stiff back softened. Her face drooped into a frown. Not two seconds later, the bell jingled.

He didn't have to turn around to know that his favorite brother and sister duo had walked through the door. The look of disappointment on Mrs. Oliver's face made it clear that he would need to apologize to her soon but not quite yet, not while Mr. Barton was in the room. It was finally time to enjoy a little sport at the serious man's expense. He turned and said, "Ah, Mr. Barton, Diana, I'm so glad I didn't miss you."

The siblings had walked in arm in arm. Everton found Diana's eyes first. Mr. Barton pulled Diana tighter to his side. Mr. Barton's brown eyes were hooded, a darker version of his sister's coppery ones. "That makes one of us."

"You speak for your sister?" Everton frowned. "Perhaps she is of my mind, not yours."

Mr. Barton stiffened. "I highly doubt that."

Interesting. It seemed that Mr. Barton could raise his chin just as high as his lovely sister could.

"I suppose we will have to ask the lady then. Diana?" He still loved the sound of her name on his lips. His relationship with her no longer made his stomach tighten and his neck sweat. She was his friend. It was perfectly understandable to be excited to see your friend. "What is your opinion on the matter? Aren't you glad I didn't miss you and Mr. Barton?"

Diana curled one side of her ambrosial mouth. Her arm was wrapped around her brother's in a casual, light manner. There was neither clinging nor an effort to move away. She cocked her head to one side and raised an eyebrow. "I believe you *did* miss us."

Mr. Barton dropped his sister's arm and threw his hands up in the air, but Diana remained still. Watching him. Devil take that chin of hers. As if she knew he had been bored out of his mind waiting for a chance to torment the two of them again.

"Why would Lord Bryant miss us?" Mr. Barton asked. "He barely even knows us."

Everton put a hand to his heart. "I take offense to that statement. I was at your wedding."

"By no invitation of mine," Mr. Barton growled.

"And," Everton added, "Diana and I discussed you often and at great length. Enough that I had even imagined you to be a friend."

"You two spoke about me?" Mr. Barton turned toward his sister. They hadn't really. His name had come up once or twice, but he had never been a real topic of conversation. How would Diana respond to his deceit? Most women he knew would have been thrown off course and mumbling by now.

"Oh, don't you bother your head about it, Nate. It isn't as though we talked about your gangly legs. I trust you know I am capable of keeping family secrets."

Oh dear, that was brilliant. Diana was brilliant. Mr. Barton's nostrils flared as his eyes flashed back and forth between Everton and Diana.

"The two of you are incorrigible. This is as bad as dinner at home."

Dinners at Everton's home were sad, quiet affairs. After a year or two of dining alone in his cumbersomely large dining room, he had finally opted for a tray in his study each evening instead. What would dinner be like at the Bartons' home? Family members talking over each other, most likely. It wouldn't be the stiff, formal affair his family had endured, back when he'd had a family.

"Diana, how might I assist you today? Any men need chasing off?"

Mr. Barton shook his head. "I'm here now; she doesn't need your assistance."

"You will chase men off for her? As you are her brother, I can't help but think you would be less effective at getting rid of would-be suitors. After all, you haven't managed to run me off yet."

"But you aren't a suitor, are you? Not really." Mr. Barton stepped closer to his sister, a protective gleam in his eye.

"Seems to me that might be *more* of a reason to run me off, not less."

Mr. Barton took a deep breath. If Diana hadn't laid a hand on his arm, Everton might have found himself on the receiving end of his fist once again.

"Nate," Diana said, "he is simply provoking you. So was I. I'm sorry. Surely the three of us can sit in a room together for a few hours without resorting to violence."

"Hours?" Mr. Barton turned to his sister. "You think he will be here for hours?"

"He often is."

"But I'm in London now. There is no cause for it."

"He said he likes it here. I'm not about to turn out a man who helped me. You must give Lord Bryant some credit. Truthfully, if he weren't such a devil, he might be considered a saint."

"Whoa." Everton held both hands out in front of him. "I won't be staying if you continue in that vein. I'm far from a saint, and I won't have my reputation tarnished with such accusations."

Mr. Barton ignored him, instead sighing with frustration at his sister. "Fine, he can stay. But, Diana, you know what he is. I beg you to proceed with caution."

Diana patted her brother's arm. "Don't worry, Nate. I'm not a fool. No sane woman would desire an attachment to Lord Bryant. He flits from one woman to another as if they mean no more to him than his cravat. I'm not a romantic, nor am I dull-witted. Lord Bryant and I were very clear about our relationship from the beginning. Isn't that right, Lord Bryant?"

Everton nodded. He put one hand on his hip, taking a page out of the Barton family book and raising his chin in the air. "Of course."

No sane woman would desire an attachment to Lord Bryant.

A dinner at the Barton home suddenly felt a lot less appealing. There would be riveting conversation and jests thrown about, but none of it would involve him. He would be watching from the outside. The prospect sounded much lonelier than eating alone at his desk.

"You two go about your work. Feel free to pretend I'm not here." A newspaper lay on the small desk that had taken over the spot where his chair had been. "Do you mind if I read this?"

Mr. Barton shook his head. Everton snatched up the paper and strode over to his corner. He wasn't ready to go back to his empty house quite yet.

CHAPTER 18

If Lord Bryant weren't such a devil, he might be considered a saint. Had Diana really said that to her brother? Lord Bryant's newspaper rattled, marking another turning of the page. He settled deeper into his chair, the wooden legs' slight squeak giving him away. She should have gotten him a more comfortable chair, a club chair or even a small settee. He had come often enough that she should have made certain he was comfortable while he was here. A larger chair would have been more difficult to place by her side, though. Nate shifted uncomfortably beneath his little desk. Exactly how long did he plan on being in London? Did she need to think about finding him something more comfortable as well? She couldn't imagine him staying away from Grace for long. Not in her condition.

Diana shrugged her shoulders and started sorting through the mail. Nate owned the larger portion of Barton Rail. If he wanted to buy himself a desk, he could do it himself. No one talked for the course of ten minutes. That had often happened before Nate returned, but today it was a much more uncomfortable silence. She placed a pressing letter in a pile to her right.

The silence was broken by a string of curses erupting from Lord Bryant's mouth. Diana dropped her letter, and her head jerked up. Lord Bryant snarled and threw the paper he had been reading to the floor.

Mrs. Oliver sucked in a deep breath at the profanity Lord Bryant had just uttered. Nate stood so quickly from his desk that he had to grab it so it wouldn't topple over and spill his paperwork onto the floor. "Lord Bryant, there are ladies present."

Lord Bryant didn't acknowledge any of them. He strode to the coatrack and grabbed his hat and coat. Without so much as a nod or a goodbye, Lord Bryant yanked the front office door open. The bell protested angrily at being so violently disturbed, and then he was gone.

Nate ran his fingers through his hair. "Exactly what kind of man did you invite into our lives, Diana?"

Diana ignored her brother as her eyes dashed to the paper Lord Bryant had left on the floor. Diana's fingers went cold, and a sour taste engulfed her mouth. Something was wrong. Very, very wrong. What in heaven's name had Lord Bryant just read? Nate followed her line of vision.

"What was all that about?" Mrs. Oliver asked, shaking her head.

"I don't know." Diana placed both her hands on the top of the desk and rose. She approached the paper cautiously, as if it were a snake and could come to life and bite her. Nate was not so hesitant. He scooped up the paper, and a low chuckle escaped his throat. "He was reading scandal sheets. What kind of a muttonhead gets so worked up over scandal sheets?"

Mrs. Oliver stood from her desk. "Did he get involved in another scandal?"

The pit of Diana's stomach tightened. Was it her? Had her charade with Lord Bryant gone so far as to reach the scandal sheets? She wouldn't put it past the people of London. Lord Bryant was a tantalizing topic. And she was a railroad owner. It was just the type of story someone at the paper would love to tell.

She tore the paper from Nate's hands and scanned the contents. She saw nothing of railroads or the mention of their names. The page he was on dealt mostly with upcoming marriages of the elite. Lord Bryant had no family that she knew of. He was one of the wealthiest men in London, and in general, he didn't seem to care about—well—anything. What could have upset him enough to run off like that?

And then she saw it: "Lord Falburton's Daughter to Marry a Peer of the Realm."

Diana's heart stopped. "Nate, what is Lord Falburton's eldest daughter's name?"

"You know I don't really follow the peerage."

She clenched her teeth and bit back a groan. "But you did back when you were building up the company and looking for investors."

"Women don't want anything to do with the railroad. Why would I learn about them?"

Diana raised an eyebrow at him.

Nate rubbed his hands down his face. "You know what I mean. *Most* women. Everyone knows you are different."

Diana didn't have time to be offended. Besides, he was right, for the most part. "Was it Lady Emily, perhaps?"

Nate cocked his head to one side. "You know, that does sound right. I think his daughter was named Emily. I don't remember her at all, though. I think she is quite young."

Lady Emily was getting married.

Lord Bryant's Lady Emily.

Or someone was confident enough in her marriage to predict it in the paper.

If the article was the result of someone trying to force Lord Bryant into marrying Lady Emily, that would definitely lead to cursing.

She struggled to swallow as she reread the article. The marriage was supposed to take place in three weeks—almost no time at all. She sank down into Lord Bryant's chair. Lord Bryant was a rake, but he had spent hours helping her and had asked for nothing in return. She had truly come to see him as an ally and friend. He had mentioned several times how delicate his situation with Lady Emily was. For all Diana knew, his time spent with Diana could have thrown off whatever balancing act he was trying to manage and may have even contributed to this surprise attack by Lady Emily's family.

She crumpled the corner of the paper she was holding. Last week, she had met and spoken with Lady Emily, after Lord Bryant had specifically asked her not to. What sort of problems had that caused? She stood and paced in front of the chair. She needed to do something about this. But what? She couldn't exactly visit Lady Emily or her family and ask them to release Lord Bryant. She wouldn't even be admitted to the drawing room of a marquess's home.

She threw the paper down on the chair, marched to the coatrack, and grabbed her coat.

"Where do you think you are going?" Nate asked from behind her.

"I need to visit someone."

"Lord Bryant?" His footsteps sounded behind her. He would reach her any moment. "I will not have you going to him."

"I won't be visiting Lord Bryant."

"Then whom?"

Whom? That was the question. The only person she had ever heard Lord Bryant talk about, when it came to his affairs with women, was Mrs. Cuthbert. Diana had met Mrs. Cuthbert once. She would allow Diana a visit, and she might have some ideas to save Lord Bryant from a marriage he most obviously didn't want. Poor Lady Emily . . . that young girl couldn't have done anything to deserve being thrown into such a scandal. If Lord Bryant ran off, as he was sure to do, her reputation would be ruined. Diana had to find a way to protect both of them. Blast Lord Bryant and his scandals. Couldn't he behave like everyone else in London?

As soon as the thought filled her mind, she knew it was wrong. Lord Bryant was nothing like the other men in London. He was like a dragon among fish—beautiful and mysterious to the point of lore and capable of burning the hearts of anyone near him. You couldn't love a dragon, nor could you get close to one, but you wouldn't wish it to become a fish.

"I'm going to visit Mrs. Lucinda Cuthbert."

Nate scrunched his face. He obviously had no idea who that was. "Not without me, you aren't." Nate grabbed his coat as well.

"You don't trust me?"

"I don't trust Lord Bryant."

"He won't even be there."

"Not if I come with you, he won't."

Diana nodded. It wasn't as if she could go about town on her own. She could run and operate a railroad company, but she couldn't be seen out and about without someone acting as her protector or chaperone. She could ask Mrs. Oliver to accompany her, but she had disappointed Mrs. Oliver enough for a lifetime with her scandal with Lord Bryant. She didn't need to disappoint her again by having her witness what she was willing to do to help him evade a marriage he didn't want.

She did up the buttons on her coat and marched toward the door. With any luck, once they arrived at Mrs. Cuthbert's, she might be able to convince Nate to wait for her in the carriage.

CHAPTER 19

Diana was in luck. Nate had agreed to stay in the carriage. He didn't want her associating with Lord Bryant alone, but he also didn't feel the need to meddle in any of her other affairs. She was grateful she hadn't lost all of his trust.

Diana waited in Mrs. Cuthbert's drawing room. It was unlike any room she had ever been in before. Every space was covered in embroidery, framed and hanging on every wall and every surface. On each table sat at least one piece, on top of which sat vases that had also been covered in needlework.

In all the times Diana had spoken with Mrs. Cuthbert, she hadn't known about her passion for threads, yarns, and—well—color. It was as if a haberdashery volcano had erupted in her drawing room.

Mrs. Cuthbert opened the drawing room door. Diana dropped the small, framed embroidered likeness of a Great Dane back onto the table from whence it had come and stood up.

"Miss Barton, what a pleasant surprise. I haven't seen you in much too long. Is that brother of yours still controlling your time with that railroad of his?"

If she only knew. "I spend time with the railroad because I like it, not because my brother forces me."

Mrs. Cuthbert's head bounced up and down in agreement, even as her eyes said otherwise. "Of course you do, darling, of course you do. It gives you a chance to forget what you want and do your brother's bidding, all while proving to yourself that you are different from any other young woman in London. It is exciting—I will say that."

For a moment, Diana's mind went blank. She had never admitted to anyone the desires she had to be helpful to Nate. Any time she had spoken of her work there, she had always been careful to mention that it was her idea to join him in the business. And it was. It was a way to spend time with Nate while also helping him. When he immediately agreed to letting her do some of the more mundane tasks, she had realized what kind of pressure he was under and how much he truly needed her.

As for being different? Of course she enjoyed that.

She shook her head. It didn't matter that Mrs. Cuthbert understood her better than half of London; she was here with a purpose.

"Have you heard about Lord Bryant and Lady Emily's marriage?"

Mrs. Cuthbert's whole demeanor dropped, and her face went white. "They are married? That is impossible." Mrs. Cuthbert reached for the arm of a chair and shakily sat down. "Lady Emily would be the death of Lord Bryant. He as much as told me so himself."

"No, not married, but they are to marry. I read it in the paper."

"What paper?" Mrs Cuthbert frantically looked about the room as if the paper would appear from under one of her embroidered pillows. Diana should have thought to bring it, but she hadn't. "Did it specifically mention Lord Bryant?"

"No." Diana stepped forward and held out an arm. Mrs. Cuthbert was becoming pale. She hadn't thought news of Lord Bryant's marriage would be so disastrous. "Not by name, but I know he has been pursuing her. Surely there aren't two peers who are possible candidates."

Mrs. Cuthbert inhaled slowly and let it release. Her hand went to her heart. "It isn't Lord Bryant, then." She gave a shaky laugh. "I shouldn't have worried."

Diana blinked. The room went cloudy around her, like someone had let in the London haze. Lord Bryant wasn't being forced to marry Lady Emily? The haze lifted, and the brightness of the room returned in full force. Could this be true? If he wasn't, then why, exactly, had he cursed?

"He seemed very upset, though, as if someone were trying to pressure him into marriage."

"No, he has been pressured to marry before. Nothing like that would disturb him. He would leave town for a while, and it would blow over."

"Then why?"

Mrs. Cuthbert shook her head and sighed. "Because Lady Emily is marrying."

His outburst was because she was marrying? Why would that anger him? If he didn't love her, why was he so upset at her marriage? If he did love her, why not just marry her? She didn't understand Lord Bryant at all. And she didn't understand her need to understand him. Diana took a deep breath. "Why would that distress Lord Bryant?"

Mrs. Cuthbert shook her head. "That is a question you may need to ask Lord Bryant. Although, I will say that if it is Lord Silverstone—and I suspect it is—the man is three times Lady Emily's age and doesn't actually know her. Her parents are the most controlling and neglectful things I have ever had the displeasure to meet. Lady Emily isn't being married off: she is being sold to the man who would give her parents the most upward social movement."

Controlling *and* neglectful? Was that even possible? "That describes about half the marriages in London." Perhaps not the age discrepancy, but a marriage driven by social connection wasn't unique at all.

"But should it?" Mrs. Cuthbert raised an eyebrow. "I must go visit Lady Emily. I need to know how all of this was decided." She strode to where Diana stood and patted her on the arm. "I'm happy to hear that no one is trying to force Lord Bryant into a marriage. He isn't ready; he may never be ready."

Diana hated the way her stomach sank at those words. Lord Bryant wasn't a proper candidate for marriage, of course, but a small part of her didn't want to believe it. If only he weren't such a rake. If only he weren't so fickle . . . She had seen sides of him that were beautiful, and they had nothing to do with his face.

She shook her head to clear it. Lord Bryant was what he was. There was no escaping the facts, no matter what Diana wanted to believe. "Why, though? Why is he so opposed to marriage?"

"Marriage didn't suit him."

"Could he not bear to stay faithful to one woman? Didn't he love his wife?"

Mrs. Cuthbert tsked. "You think too little of my Lord Bryant. Of course he loved Rachel. He loved her fiercely. If he hadn't loved her, life would be better for him now, wouldn't it?"

Rachel.

His wife had a name—of course she did. Rachel. A name that rolled off the tongue and spoke of gentleness. Nothing like Diana, the goddess of the hunt and wild animals.

Diana had started feeling unsettled as soon as Lord Bryant stormed out of her office, but now the sickness worsened. She had thought . . . she had hoped . . . she had wondered if perhaps Lord Bryant hadn't cared for his wife. She had hoped if he could just fall in love with a woman, perhaps he would change his ways. If he had loved Rachel and still became the man he was today, where did that leave Diana?

Exactly where she had always been. One more name on an ever-growing list of women scandalized by Lord Bryant before he forgot them and left on his merry way.

Mrs. Cuthbert had been a flurry of movement since she walked into the room, but now she stilled. Her eyes narrowed as she measured Diana from top to bottom. "How well do you know Lord Bryant?"

Diana cleared her throat. Mrs. Cuthbert's stillness put her nerves on edge. "How well does anyone know Lord Bryant?" Diana asked. Mrs. Cuthbert's only response was to laugh. Diana swallowed. "But *you* know him . . ."

"Perhaps better than most."

"Why does Lady Emily's marriage bother him so much?"

"Lord Bryant doesn't trust easily, Miss Barton. I'm afraid I will not speak on this subject anymore until I understand exactly what your relationship is with him."

"I have no relationship with him. Not really."

"That is exactly what he told me."

Lord Bryant had mentioned her to Mrs. Cuthbert? Diana took a deep breath and lifted her chin. "Then it is true." She reached a side table nearby and used it to steady herself.

"You say that, but I don't quite believe you. I'm not sure I believed him either."

"Mrs. Cuthbert, I know exactly what Lord Bryant is. I would be a fool to think anything with him could be permanent."

"You are a smart woman. I see that. But I will say this: when Lord Bryant told me there was no relationship between the two of you, he said it in the exact manner that you just used." Her eyes snapped to the hand Diana was using to support herself, then back to Diana's face. "As if he were trying to convince himself."

Diana closed her eyes. The room smelled of Mrs. Cuthbert's rose perfume and yarn. Mrs. Cuthbert was an interfering old woman. That was the only explanation for it. Lord Bryant had never given her any indication that she could mean more to him than any other person he had met. "I'm sure that isn't the case."

"He assured me of that as well. I don't like to pry into Lord Bryant's business. He means a lot to me. But I also want to see him happy. And, Miss Barton, I've never seen him quite so interested in a person as he is in you. A marriage to Lady Emily would most likely end with Lord Bryant losing his mind. But if you had walked in here today and told me it was your marriage that had been announced—" Mrs. Cuthbert smiled, her eyes glistening as she took a step toward Diana and took her free hand. "I would have congratulated you."

Diana swallowed. "But you said yourself Lord Bryant will never marry again."

"No, I said *he* said that. I happen to disagree with him. But he doesn't handle my criticism well, so I try not to mention it often. The man has had a hard enough lot in life as it is."

Diana scoured Mrs. Cuthbert's face for signs of deceit, but it appeared that she was being sincere. Not many people in London would have the audacity to say that a baron's lot in life wasn't a good one. He had brought most of his troubles on himself. So, he had loved his wife and lost her. Did that give him the right to hurt so many other women? Did that give him the right to settle into Diana's heart only to slide out of it at the first sign of inconvenience? No. Diana was no fool. She would not trust her heart if her head didn't agree with it. Too many lives were ruined when decisions were made based solely on feelings. "Well, thanks to him, he is sharing that hard lot with all of the women he has scandalized."

Mrs. Cuthbert threw her head back and laughed. The colors of the room were suddenly suffocating. Diana needed to leave. What kind of company did Lord Bryant keep? She hadn't thought Mrs. Cuthbert mad, but . . .

"Is he?" Mrs. Cuthbert asked, wiping a tear from one eye and cocking her head to the side. She leaned forward with a strange, mirthful smile on her face. "Do you know any of them?"

Diana didn't. How could she? She had spent most of her life in Baimbury and most of her time in London on Rochester Street. What was Mrs. Cuthbert trying to say?

"I like you, Miss Barton, and what's more, I think Lord Bryant likes you. You have something that no other woman of his acquaintance has."

"What is that?" Diana asked. "A railroad company?"

Mrs. Cuthbert scoffed. "No, not a railroad company." Mrs. Cuthbert leaned forward, her eyes still shining from the tears of her laughter. "You know what you want. Not only that, you go after it, no matter what anyone else thinks of you. You are no shrinking violet. You are like a . . . a . . ."

Diana was starting to feel lightheaded as well as sick to her stomach. What was it Lord Bryant had called her? "A tiger lily?" She supplied the word to Mrs. Cuthbert.

Mrs. Cuthbert put her finger to the side of her nose and pointed at Diana. "Yes, exactly. Lord Bryant needs a tiger lily. And they are exotic, rare things. I'm not sure if he will be able to find another one." Mrs. Cuthbert stepped away from Diana and pulled her cap more securely down on her head, her excitement from earlier returning. "I will see what I can do about Lady Emily. Perhaps I'll talk some sense into her. At the very least, I'll lambast those poor excuses for parents she has. I don't know what went wrong. Things were running so smoothly a week ago."

A week ago? That was about the time Diana had met Lady Emily.

Mrs. Cuthbert peered at her. "Are you all right? I was about to call for tea, but under the circumstances, I should like to forgo it and seek out Lady Emily. But if you feel the need for sustenance, I can ring the bell."

Diana stepped forward. If she accompanied Mrs. Cuthbert, she could ask if something she had done had caused all of this trouble. One week. It seemed like too much of a coincidence. But a railroad owner with a damaged reputation wouldn't be admitted to the home of a marquess. "Of course not. Thank you for seeing me on such short notice."

They both strode toward the door. Mrs. Cuthbert's determined steps belied her age. When they reached the entry hall, Mrs. Cuthbert paused to bid Diana farewell. "Thank you, Miss Barton. I'm very grateful you thought to come tell me about this news. If Lord Bryant and I cannot stop this marriage, he is likely to be . . ." She sighed deeply. "In low spirits for quite some time. I hope you will find a way to call on him."

Without waiting for an answer from Diana, she turned to her butler. "Thacker, have George ready the coach. I will be making some afternoon visits."

Diana slogged to her carriage in a daze. Her meeting with Mrs. Cuthbert hadn't gone at all how she had planned. She had come here determined to help Lord Bryant avoid a forced marriage and had left more confused about him than ever. She was also fairly certain she was somehow to blame for Lady Emily's disastrous engagement.

Nothing was adding up.

"That wasn't a very long visit," Nate said as soon as she entered the carriage.

"Mrs. Cuthbert is on her way to visit someone." Diana settled into her seat.

"Back to the office, then? Or to Mrs. Richardson's?" he asked, but Diana didn't answer him. Her mind was still back in Mrs. Cuthbert's gaudy drawing room. "I don't see why you don't want to stay with me while I'm in London."

"Mrs. Richardson needs me."

"You told me she was doing better. Smiling even."

"She is, but . . ." Ever since Tommy's slip, it had been hard to trust that happiness. "What if her happiness isn't real?" If it was real, why wouldn't she talk to Diana about it?

Nate scoffed. "It is hard to pretend to be happy."

Diana narrowed one eye, her concern over Charlotte suddenly pushed aside. Sitting right across from Diana was one man whose marriage might not have happened without Lord Bryant. Mrs. Cuthbert's laughter about the unhappy state of the women with whom Lord Bryant had scandals came back to her.

"Are you and Grace happy, Nate?"

Nate leaned back in his seat and stretched his long legs out in front of him. "I don't think anyone in England is nearly as happy as we are."

Diana smiled and leaned back into her seat as well, but she couldn't relax. Having Nate happy like this was one of life's great pleasures for their whole family.

That might never have happened if Lord Bryant hadn't been involved with Grace.

That made at least one happy marriage thanks to Lord Bryant nearly ruining a woman. How many more would she find if she continued to dig?

Even without visiting Lady Emily, she could find the answer to at least one of the burning questions that had arisen since she'd entered Mrs. Cuthbert's home.

Who were these women Lord Bryant had scandalized, and were their lives truly ruined by him?

CHAPTER 20

Everton paced outside Lord Falburton's residence. In his entire existence, he had never been denied entrance to a home.

The Falburtons' behavior was outrageous.

Racing here after finding the news of Lady Emily's betrothal in the newspaper had done him no good. The butler had claimed no one was home, but after waiting in his carriage, he had seen two other callers admitted and an upstairs curtain move often enough that he was certain Lady Emily was watching him. He had spent the last half hour outside his carriage watching that blasted window.

Had her opinion been sought out before making the betrothal official? He wished he knew. He had no idea whether she sat up in her room worried that he would dash into the house and make a scene or hopeful for it.

Only because he knew Lady Emily well enough to understand that any sort of attention given to her was unlikely to help matters did he stay on the street and out of the stately home.

"Pull the carriage forward, stopping just after you cross the next street," Everton told his driver. He bounded into the carriage. It would have been preferable to walk the hundred feet or so, but he wanted the Falburton household to believe he had given up.

When the wheels stopped, he alighted and paced in front of the carriage. They may believe he left, but now what? Lady Emily wasn't likely to take a stroll at all, let alone an unaccompanied one where he could speak to her openly.

Although it would be inappropriate, he could write her a note. It had been a long time since he had allowed propriety to hinder him from getting what he wanted. Not that his lack of decorum would make a difference—even if he sent one, the note would never reach her.

He punched the side of his thigh hard enough that he was certain to see a bruise tomorrow. The whole of Great Britain's Society should rot with the devil for selling its quiet daughters to the highest bidder.

A carriage pulled to a stop in front of Lord Falburton's home. A carriage he recognized.

"Stay here," he told his footman.

A moment later, he was standing to the left of the Falburtons' stairs as Mrs. Cuthbert knocked on the door. The butler opened the door, took her card, and motioned for her to come in. Lord Bryant took the stairs two at a time until he was standing just behind Mrs. Cuthbert.

"Lord and Lady Falburton have returned, have they?"

Mrs. Cuthbert turned in a startled jump and screeched in surprise, sounding not unlike a barn owl.

Everton stifled a laugh. After an hour of grinding his teeth, frightening Mrs. Cuthbert—who, in all fairness, was the one who started this mess—made his jaw relax, at least for a moment.

"Lord Bryant, I didn't see you there." Her eyes widened farther. "What has happened to your face?"

Lord Bryant had nearly forgotten his scuffle with Mr. Barton. "It is nothing. I'm sorry. I do tend to sneak up on people when they are least expecting it, don't I?" This question he posed to the butler, who was gulping air as if he couldn't get enough of it. Despicable. Nelson would never act in such a way, and he had dealt with much more unpleasant business than an unwanted baron at his doorstep. "Now, where is Falburton receiving guests?"

Mrs. Cuthbert stepped forward. "He was just showing me to the drawing room before you pounced on us."

"Then to the drawing room we shall go." Everton gave the butler a devilish grin. The man had no recourse now that Everton knew the marquess was at home. If he hadn't so blatantly lied to him less than an hour ago, Everton would feel almost apologetic.

As it was, the man could gulp all he wanted. He would get no sympathy from Everton. A few more hard swallows, and a furtive glance to the door he suspected was the drawing room, and the butler finally succumbed to the truth he should have known an hour ago.

If the Baron Bryant wanted entrance to a home, he gained it.

Mrs. Cuthbert shot an elbow into his side as they followed the sweating butler. She bent her head in his direction. "You didn't have to come. I'm the better candidate to find out what is going on."

The two men in the drawing room—Lord Falburton and Lord Silverstone—stood as soon as Everton and Mrs. Cuthbert were admitted to the room. Lady Falburton sputtered, then covered her mouth with a handkerchief. Lord Falburton's face turned a deep purple, all while Lord Silverstone looked between them, confusion apparent on his middle-aged face. Lady Emily was not there. Blast Lord and Lady Falburton for betrothing their daughter, then not even allowing her out of her room. All the while, her lecherous fiancé plotted her future with them.

"Is Lady Emily not at home?" Everton asked.

"She is feeling unwell," Lord Falburton said, each word punctuated as if affirming there would be no more questions about it.

"I would like to speak to her."

Lord Silverstone eyed him closely now, as he should. Lady Emily deserved a lot of qualities in her future husband, including not being old enough to be her father. Lord Silverstone should know what Lady Emily could have and should have if he weren't in her way.

"An introduction, perhaps?" Lord Silverstone asked.

"Lord Silverstone," said Lord Falburton, "this is Lord Bryant." Lord Silverstone's jaw clenched upon hearing his name. Good. His reputation had preceded him. "Lord Bryant, this is Lord Silverstone, Lady Emily's newly betrothed."

"So I have heard."

Lord Silverstone's expression, which had, up until now, looked as though he had been spun in a circle and dropped in a stream, now took on a harder edge. "What do you want with Lady Emily?"

Lord Bryant smiled. That was an easy question for any respectable rake to answer. "What do you think I want?"

Lord Silverstone leapt forward and stopped just shy of grabbing Everton's lapels. "I know enough about you to know your intentions cannot be honorable. I would bid you not seek out my betrothed ever again."

"And how honorable are your intentions?"

Lord Silverstone furrowed his eyebrows. "We are engaged to be married. How much more honorable could I be?"

"From where I stand, it would be much more honorable to marry a woman who isn't less than half your age." The blood drained from Lord Silverstone's face. Everton had hit the mark. Good. "I would like to repeat my desire to see Lady Emily."

Lord Falburton's lips formed a hard line. "And I will repeat that she is feeling unwell."

"I shall be the judge of that," Everton said.

Lady Emily's room would be upstairs, most likely the room with a view of the street, for he doubted anyone else in the house would have been moving the curtain about on the upper story of the home while he had been waiting outside. He spun on his heel.

"Lord Bryant!" It was as if the whole of the household decided to call his name at once. He ignored them all, dashing out of the drawing room door and shutting it behind him. They would be behind him instantly. Even Mrs. Cuthbert would likely chase him down for his foolishness. But waiting outside on the street had stirred a restlessness inside of him, and it wouldn't settle until he had seen Lady Emily with his own two eyes.

This was a lamb he wouldn't allow Society to lead to the slaughter.

He ran to the foot of the stairs only to find the same butler standing there.

"Move aside," Everton commanded him. The drawing room door was already open. Rushed footsteps and shouts followed him out. He pushed the butler to the side but was surprised by the man's reflexes and strength as he gripped Everton's arm and twisted it behind his back. Taken aback, he shook off the butler but not fast enough. Just as he freed himself, two other arms grabbed him.

"Berta!" Lady Falburton shouted. "Lock Lady Emily in her room."

A maid shuffled quickly past them and up the stairs. Everton took the chance to throw an elbow at Lord Silverstone and twist out of Lord Falburton's grasp. The butler still stood on the bottom step, blocking his way. He was at least a foot shorter than Lord Bryant and two decades older, but his face showed no fear—only a mouth set hard with determination.

"I may have let you disturb my Lord and Ladyship, but you won't be disturbing Lady Emily."

The fierce loyalty in the man's eyes stilled Everton. He was the first person in the household to show real concern for Lady Emily's welfare. It took all the bluster out of him.

Everton was the scoundrel here.

How easily he could forget.

Mrs. Cuthbert apologized and pulled on his arm. "Lord Bryant hasn't been himself lately. You will have to forgive him."

Lord Falburton rubbed his wrist and glared at Everton. "He isn't to set foot in this household again."

"Of course," Mrs. Cuthbert said. "Of course."

Everton allowed himself to be pulled to the door. All of his limbs had lost their strength. Under her breath, Mrs. Cuthbert was cursing him, which he rightly deserved. He had been too distracted helping Diana. He had not been available to Lady Emily when he should have been. Barging into her bedroom to try to alleviate his guilt at his failure would help no one, least of all her.

The butler managed to open the door for them but gave no bow as they left. With a sudden rush of returned energy, Everton turned and put his foot in the door. The butler held firm against the door and did not open it to him. His face was as stoic as before. No matter. Everton wasn't trying to regain entrance. He only wanted to ask one question.

"How is Lady Emily faring through this?"

The butler's eyes scrunched together, and the pressure against his foot relaxed enough that had he wanted to, Everton could have pushed his way back into the house. But he had been ridiculous enough for one evening.

"Is she well?"

The butler looked behind himself before leaning forward. "Lady Emily is as she always is."

Everton closed his eyes slowly, then opened them again. "Resigned?" he asked.

The butler nodded his head once.

Everton cursed but removed his foot, and the door shut with a soft clink that defied all the noise that had just been held therein.

"What in heaven's name did you hope to accomplish by barging up to a lady's bedroom?" Mrs. Cuthbert hissed under her breath.

Everton scuffed his foot like a misbehaving schoolboy. "I *wasn't* thinking."

"That was quite obvious." Mrs. Cuthbert pulled him away from the door. He was tired of being pulled around and ripped his arm away from her as they descended the stairs.

"What was I supposed to do?"

Mrs. Cuthbert knew he couldn't sit idly by while a woman as timid as Lady Emily was taken advantage of.

"For starters, you shouldn't have used me to gain access. I wanted to speak with Lady Emily, and now there is no chance they will permit me to be anywhere near her again."

Everton groaned and rubbed his forehead. This day had gone from bad to worse. He kicked a stone into the street, only afterward realizing he should have made certain it didn't hit anyone. Thankfully, the street was mostly clear. With his luck lately, he was surprised.

"I'll write to her," Mrs. Cuthbert said.

"There is no possibility that her parents don't read her correspondence."

"I'll have one of my servants deliver a note to the butler or perhaps to a maid in the household. We have three weeks before the marriage. It isn't time to give up yet." Mrs. Cuthbert patted his arm as if he were a small child. In truth, he felt like one. "Now, where is your carriage? Or did you walk?"

He pointed with his chin to his carriage down the street. Mrs. Cuthbert nodded and gave him a slight shove in that direction. "I'll discover what I can and send word to you." He trudged toward his carriage. "And Lord Bryant," Mrs Cuthbert called after him, "don't let this get you down. We have had a good run, but you can't save every young woman."

She didn't need to tell Everton that. That fact was engraved in stone in a churchyard sixty miles from his home.

"I cannot accept Lady Emily being forced into a marriage. She is too much like—" He stopped. His wife's name never came easily to his lips.

"Rachel."

Everton took in a deep, steadying breath. "Yes," he said. "She is too much like Rachel."

"Have you gone to visit her?"

"Rachel?" He said her name again. It came easier the second time.

Mrs. Cuthbert nodded.

"I have, several times. Her parents laid her to rest near their country estate. They didn't feel that she deserved to be buried anywhere near the Bryant ancestors."

Mrs. Cutherbert's face puckered as if she had just been scalded by tea. "Whyever not?"

"She didn't give me an heir. She ran away from me and back to them because she was unhappy, and do you know what they did?"

"They sent her back to you?"

"Yes. What kind of parents do that to their child? She was young and scared. The first brave thing she had ever done was to leave me, and they tried to send her back."

"*Tried* to send her back?"

Everton nodded. He had never told anyone the full story of what had happened, but after his debacle with Lady Emily, he owed Mrs. Cuthbert an explanation for his behavior. "She never made it back. She slipped away from the groom and ran away again. This time, none of us knew where. The next news I received of her was of her death six months later."

"Where had she gone?"

"She had been living with her nurse. She had helped raise Rachel, and in the end, she was the only person who had made her feel safe."

"Have you ever been there?"

"To see the nurse?" Bile rose to his throat as he thought of it. "To see the wretched cottage where she spent her final days? No, I have not been there."

"Perhaps you should go. Let me deal with Lady Emily while you go talk to your wife's nurse."

"She lives in Alfriston."

"Alfriston? Isn't that near Brighton? You could take the train. If you catch it this evening, you could even be back tomorrow. Perhaps by then I will have more news for you about Lady Emily."

Visit Rachel's nurse? He closed his eyes. Mrs. Nora Henderson. Each letter of her signed name came back to him as if he had received the letter yesterday. He had thought about going to Alfriston many times, but what would he find there? More than anything, it seemed like an invasion of Rachel's private realm.

"I don't want to disturb her."

Mrs. Cuthbert furrowed her brow. "The nurse?"

"Rachel."

"Rachel is dead. You are still here. I've loved helping you create scandals. Society is ridiculous, and I have loved the games we have played. Together, we have made fools of so many. But more importantly, we have helped some young couples escape the burden Society has placed on them. I want you to let go of your burden as well, Lord Bryant. It is time to help yourself heal."

There was truth in what Mrs. Cuthbert said. He couldn't keep going as he was. His visit to the Duchess of Harrington hadn't helped, most likely because he hadn't listened to her advice. Perhaps he should listen to Mrs. Cuthbert. Maybe seeing where Rachel had spent her final days would be the key to finally letting them both rest.

CHAPTER 21

Diana paced back and forth in her office. She hadn't seen Lord Bryant for two days. With the way he had stormed away, she wasn't certain he would ever come again. The parliamentary vote was the next day, and once it was over, they would no longer have an agreement. Two months, that was as long as he had ever promised, and that time was speedily coming to an end.

She had managed to discover the names of several of the women he had scandalized. Charlotte had only known one of the women personally and not very well. But Charlotte described her as very happily married, even though her husband was a merchant who came from a station well below hers.

Of the other women Charlotte mentioned—and there were many—one had married a man whose name she recognized—Lord Yolten. Lord Yolten was one of her investors. She had sent a message via Mrs. Oliver stating that she would like to meet with him. Luckily, the last two days had been uneventful enough that Nate had trusted her to Mrs. Oliver's care for a few hours while he ran errands. Any minute now, she would hear the door chime, and Lord Yolten would walk in.

She dredged up, from memory, what she knew about his marriage: his wife, Lady Yolten, came from money but didn't have the advantage of a good birth. That was it. That was all she knew.

Charlotte hadn't been to the types of social activities to which Lady Yolten had been invited, not at the beginning of Lady Yolten's entrance into Society and certainly not near the end, when she had climbed the ranks enough to attend events where Lord Bryant and Lord Yolten would be present. Charlotte had married Mr. Richardson when neither of them had had much in the way of worldly possessions. However, Mr. Richardson's prowess in the railroad industry had changed all of that.

The bell clanged, and a regal man about Nate's age walked through the door, his top hat taller than any other Diana had ever seen, his collar stiff and high. Diana jumped to her feet. What had she been thinking? Requesting that a peer come see her in her office? The man must have a thousand other things to do, and she invented some trumped-up reason to speak with him. Spending so much time with Lord Bryant must have made her less aware of impropriety.

"Lord Yolten, please sit down." Diana motioned to the chair in front of her desk. "I'm sorry to interrupt your busy schedule."

Lord Yolten scoffed. "Yes, well, today I had hoped to solve the mystery of why one of my favorite novels went missing." He shrugged his slim shoulders. "But then I found it."

Or perhaps the man wasn't as busy as she had thought. "Where did you find it?"

"On my nightstand. I had set another novel on top of it, you see, and it covered up the one I had been searching for. With the book found, my schedule opened up quite conveniently, and I am happy to meet with you."

She couldn't quite tell if the man was serious. Most likely not. "I'm glad to hear it."

"What can I do for you, Miss Barton? I must admit I am quite curious about how the railroad line is doing since—" He stopped.

"Since a woman took over?"

"Well, yes." He leaned forward, his eyes filled with curiosity. "You don't find it exhausting? I find my investment meetings with my solicitor exhausting, and we only meet once a week."

Exhausting? Of course it was exhausting. "I find the business side of the railroad to be quite fascinating. I suppose that keeps me from feeling overwhelmed."

Lord Yolten's eyes widened, and he raised an eyebrow. Diana looked down at her desk. Perhaps she shouldn't have requested he come. The last thing she needed was a married man's interest on top of all the other men.

"I should have brought my wife with me."

Diana jerked her head back up and met his eyes. He was interested in her but not romantically interested. Too many merchants giving her attention for her business had gone to her head. Heat rose to her cheeks. When had she become so vain? "She's welcome to come anytime she would like. I'd be happy to show her what I am working on."

"Do you mean that?"

"Yes, of course."

"Perfect." He jumped up from his seat. "She is waiting in the carriage. When I told her who I was about to meet, she wouldn't stay at home."

"Oh," was the only thing Diana managed to say. Lady Yolten had wanted to meet her?

Lord Yolten practically skipped out the door. There went a man who enjoyed pleasing his wife.

Diana smiled and stared at the door for a moment. It wasn't often that she saw a man so openly happy in marriage. Nate was, almost disgustingly so. He and Grace lived in a world built for the two of them, and neither of them could have been happier.

"Did he just say he is bringing his wife in here?" Mrs. Oliver asked. "A lady?"

"We are both ladies, and we are here."

"You know what I mean. Do we have any tea we could offer her?" Mrs. Oliver asked.

Tea? Why hadn't she thought of that? They had tea but only three cups. They had never entertained at the office. Occasionally, she had offered tea to business contacts who had stayed for over an hour, but that happened rarely enough that they were completely unprepared for a social visit in the office.

"No, don't worry about tea. That isn't why they came."

"Why *did* they come?"

Diana fumbled with the pen at her desk. She couldn't tell Mrs. Oliver that she had invited Lord Yolten because Lady Yolten had had a scandal with Lord Bryant. Mrs. Oliver had been eyeing her warily ever since she found out Diana had been using Lord Bryant and his reputation to help her in her business. It would only get worse if Mrs. Oliver discovered she was investigating his past relationships. "I had a few questions for Lord Yolten. I didn't realize he would bring his wife."

Diana quickly moved Lord Bryant's chair next to the one in front of her desk, then stood, smoothing down her skirts, until the door chimed.

Lady Yolten was stunning. Lord Bryant certainly knew beauty when he saw it. She had dark hair like Diana, but that was where the similarities stopped. Lady Yolten was petite like a flower, one that didn't seem to belong in the harsh climate of London. Her eyes caught Diana's, then demurely looked down.

Diana stepped forward. "Lady Yolten, what a pleasure to have you here."

Those downcast eyes flashed back to Diana's, a spark she hadn't noticed before almost bursting from them. "I'm so pleased to meet you, Miss Barton." Lady Yolten dropped her husband's hand and rushed forward. "I've heard whisperings of you running this business by yourself and have wanted to meet you ever since. I hope you don't mind me coming with Yolty."

Yolty? Diana checked for Lord Yolten's reaction, but he was smiling at his wife. So . . . not quite as demure as Diana had first thought. After meeting Miss Paynter and hearing of Lady Emily, she had assumed Lord Bryant preferred quiet women. She should have known better. Lord Bryant obviously seemed to prefer a variety of women. He had made no secret about it. She should have believed him.

"I don't mind at all. As I told your husband, you are welcome anytime."

"You may not want to offer that so lightly." Lady Yolten had wandered to the table that held their maps and was flipping through them. "I'm so very fascinated by the railroad. And even more so, I'm fascinated by you."

"Me?"

"Yes, a young single woman working day in and day out in industry. You are quite the talk of the town."

Diana wrinkled her nose. "I suppose I was aware of that. I hadn't heard of any such talk being positive."

Lady Yolten's eyes glowed. "I assure you the women in my circle are positively inspired by you. The enjoyable ones, anyway."

"I can attest to that," added Lord Yolten. "You should have seen Penelope squeal when I received your invitation."

"Pshaw." Lady Yolten playfully gave her husband a push on the shoulder. "I never squeal; it is so undignified." Then, turning toward Diana, she put a hand to the side of her mouth and whispered, "I did. I definitely squealed."

Diana struggled to keep a straight face.

Lady Yolten left the map table and came to Diana's desk. She leaned forward on her arms like Lord Bryant often did. Her eyes were on fire. "I have a thousand questions."

Oh dear.

"How do you get all those rough tradesmen to listen to you?" Didn't Lady Yolten's family come from trade? Diana was used to hearing negative comments about people in trade, but she was surprised to hear it from Lady Yolten. "They never took me seriously, no matter how many ideas I had."

Ah, that would explain it. "Well, I suppose it helps that I am the one in charge of payroll."

Lady Yolten laughed, a bright sound that Diana had already become accustomed to, even though she had only been in the room a few moments. No wonder Lord Yolten was so taken with his wife. She created an almost frantic energy all around her. What would Lord Bryant have been like while he was pursuing her? Would he have smiled more? Surely he wouldn't have gone home each night and sulked in his study like the night Diana had found him at home. Not with a woman like this in his life.

"That's all I needed, then—for Papa to allow me to hand out payroll." She wiped a tear from her eye. "Can you imagine?" She slid her fingers down her husband's arm and wrapped her hand around his. "Papa didn't think I could handle reading a newspaper. He would have bled through his eyes before allowing me to do anything with the business."

Diana dipped her head to one side. "I came about it with extenuating circumstances, I assure you."

"Your family approves, though?"

Did they? Mama still didn't know what she was doing. Not completely. She knew she had been helping Nate and later Charlotte, but she didn't know the extent of it. Nate had just found out, and although he was put out that she hadn't asked for his help, he hadn't insisted she sell him the company or leave everything to him. She wasn't sure that counted as approval, but perhaps it did count as trust, which was at least as important.

"They haven't tried to stop me. But my family is a bit unconventional. When Nate started his company, it went against everything Society said he *should* be doing. But in the long run, it has been essential to saving our estate in Baimbury and has made many investors quite wealthy."

"Yes, but a man starting a business and woman owning one are two very different things," Lord Yolten said.

Diana shrugged. "I don't disagree with you. Nate had to start his business from scratch. I simply have to keep it running. My part is much easier, for certain."

Lord Yolten raised an eyebrow and chuckled. "Yes, *that* is what I meant—that it is easier to own a business than to start one." He chuckled. "You have it easy. It is a wonder more women aren't running railroad companies."

"I said easi*er*. I wouldn't exactly say it is easy. I have run into a few issues since I started." Like the fact that if she married, the business would essentially belong to her husband.

Lady Yolten curled her finger around a ringlet that had escaped her bonnet and skipped over to Mrs. Oliver's desk. "How do you like working for Miss Barton? Is she quite the taskmaster?"

Diana's stomach dropped. She and Mrs. Oliver hadn't spoken much since Mrs. Oliver had discovered Lord Bryant's true nature, or the nature he wanted everyone to think was true. Diana was less and less sure of him every day.

"Miss Barton is the best of employers," Mrs. Oliver said loudly, then motioned to Lady Yolten to come closer.

Oh dear. What would she say in private? For some inexplicable reason, Diana wanted Lady Yolten's approval, and it had nothing to do with the fact that her husband was an investor. Lady Yolten was the type of woman Diana would want as a friend, someone full of life and not seduced by societal rules. The first trait would have attracted her anyway, but the second was a prerequisite for any friend now that Diana was a businesswoman.

Fortunately, Mrs. Oliver was a bit hard of hearing and had lost the ability to understand how loudly she whispered. "Just don't lock her in the storage room. I learned that the hard way."

Lady Yolten's head jerked back in surprise, and she gave Diana a look that seemed to say, *Just what kind of employees do you have here?*

Diana laughed in return. "It was simply a misunderstanding. I'm certain it won't happen again."

"Oh, it definitely won't," Mrs. Oliver said.

"Now that my wife has introduced herself to your staff and made herself comfortable in your office, what did you want to see me about?" Lord Yolten asked.

Lady Yolten returned to Diana's desk, and both she and her husband sat down. Diana took a deep breath. How did one go about gleaning information about Lord Bryant? Had Lady Yolten loved him? Had he broken her heart? Or she his? None of those questions were appropriate, but she would stay at the office working late for weeks in return for knowing the answers to them.

"This is rather a delicate situation," Diana began.

Lady Yolten leaned forward in her chair. "Do you have a competitor you want us to pulverize? I think we could do it, couldn't we, Yolty?"

For a moment, Diana's mind went blank. She had barely met the woman, but Diana had the distinct impression that Lady Yolten would happily race off to destroy some young railroad company in Diana's name. Diana shook her head to one side, then slowly to the other.

"No, nothing quite so delicate as that." Diana's fingers were tapping a quick pattern on the desk, and she stilled them. Both Lord and Lady Yolten sat on the edges of their seats, waiting for her next word. "I simply would like some information on one of my investors." She paused as the couple leaned forward. Diana lowered her voice so Mrs. Oliver was less likely to hear. "Lord Bryant."

The change that came over the two of them was palpable. They both immediately sat back in their chairs, their faces guarded. All the brightness and excitement the two of them had brought into the office was gone.

This was a bad idea.

The couple in front of her was obviously in love, but one mention of Lord Bryant, and suddenly they were eying each other awkwardly.

Lord Yolten shifted uncomfortably in his chair. When he did speak, he followed her pattern of speaking softly. "What, exactly, are you looking to learn about him?"

How to proceed? She couldn't regret meeting Lady Yolten, and yet, if she had only one of the two here, no doubt she would get a more honest answer. Together, they were more likely to protect each other's feelings than give Diana the information she needed. "My main interest is knowing a bit about his character. I hear such conflicting reports on him."

"Conflicting?" Lady Yolten asked. "In my experience, Society has been ever consistent at painting him as a rake and a scoundrel."

Diana smiled slowly. "I suppose you are right, Lady Yolten. If Lord Bryant is anything, he is constant in the impression he makes. But I, for one, don't always trust Society as a whole, and I was hoping to get your viewpoint on the matter."

"What made you think to ask us?" Lord Yolten asked stiffly.

Diana glanced back and forth between the two of them. Should she admit she knew Lady Yolten had had a scandal with him? Wasn't that, in fact, what Lord Yolten was inferring? Up until this point, she was quite certain the couple had seen her as competent and not completely unaware of the world around her. She didn't want to lessen their opinion of her.

Nor did she want to cause them marital strife.

"I may have heard something about you and Lord Bryant both vying for Lady Yolten's hand at one point. You came off conqueror, of course."

Lady Yolten sniggered, then quickly covered her mouth with her hand. Lord Yolten simply lifted an eyebrow.

"You may have heard that?"

Now it was Diana's turn to shift uncomfortably. "I may have sought out that information."

Lady Yolten leaned forward again, her eyes dancing. "Has Lord Bryant shown an interest in you?"

"No," Diana answered before remembering their pretense. "I mean, yes." Her hair was suddenly itchy, her face exhausted from controlling her reactions to anything Lord or Lady Yolten said. "I don't know how to answer that."

"Are you, perhaps, in love with someone?" Lord Yolten asked.

Lady Yolten leaned forward again. "Does his family approve?"

Lord Yolten joined in. "Is he beneath you?"

"Or perhaps," Lady Yolten eyed her husband, "above you?"

Their questions came so quickly, Diana didn't know where to start. Gone were their uncomfortable gazes from earlier. They were eager to hear any news they could of Lord Bryant or, more specifically, of her love interests that had nothing to do with Lord Bryant at all. All their energy from previously had returned, but there was no plausible explanation as to why.

"I'm much too busy with this railroad to pursue a relationship with any man."

"Pshaw." Lady Yolten flicked her wrist in the air. "Now you are speaking like a man. You are a woman. You were made for taking on more than one interest at a time. I see no reason why you can't build railroad lines and also spend time with a suitor."

"You mean with this man you believe me to be in love with? Or with Lord Bryant?"

Lady Yolten grinned. "Both."

Yes, the woman was most definitely mad. Lord Yolten glanced at Mrs. Oliver and back, then leaned forward so he could speak softly. "Whatever Lord Bryant is offering you, I would suggest you take him up on it. I haven't known him to fail when he puts his mind to something. You can trust the man."

He sat back in his chair with a satisfied smile on his face. Lady Yolten seemed just as pleased with the turn in conversation. Why would the man who had been Lord Bryant's rival recommend him so heartily yet so secretly? Diana closed her eyes and allowed her mind a moment to think. The pieces finally fell into place.

There was only one possible explanation.

Lord Bryant hadn't been a rival at all.

Diana opened her eyes and, in an effort to not seem so overcome, straightened the papers at her desk. When she was certain her emotions were contained, she leveled her gaze at Lord Yolten. "Lord Bryant has offered me nothing," she said truthfully. "I'm not certain what you mean," she lied. Then, with a quirk of a smile, she made certain he knew she was lying. Lord and Lady Yolten glanced at each other and beamed. Diana couldn't have chosen a more perfect couple to interrogate.

Diana quickly went over Lord Yolten's account and answered a few more of Lady Yolten's questions before they left.

"Don't forget to invite us to the wedding," Lady Yolten said as she walked out the door. A pain crossed Diana's chest as she smiled and nodded. Lady Yolten had been nothing but kind to her, and Diana had repaid her with dishonesty.

"There most likely won't be one, truthfully."

Lady Yolten clicked her tongue and shook her head. "I can't believe that. Simply do what Yolty said and trust Bryant. He is a good egg." Lady Yolten nodded as if the whole thing were already settled and she could expect a wedding invitation anytime.

To what man, Diana had no idea, but that didn't seem to bother Lady Yolten.

As soon as the door closed, Mrs. Oliver rushed to her side. "That was exciting, wasn't it? To have a lady here in the office. What did they want to talk about?"

"She wanted to know about the railroad business," Diana answered truthfully.

"I thought I heard them mention Lord Bryant. What did they have to say about that scoundrel?"

Diana winced. What had she done? "He isn't a scoundrel, Mrs. Oliver."

"But Nate . . . and even you . . ."

Diana returned to her seat and slumped into her chair. How could she have been so wrong about him? Lord Bryant was supposed to be a scoundrel. He wanted everyone to believe him a rake.

It wasn't her fault that she had trusted in the facade he had so carefully constructed.

Her head fell forward onto her desk and landed with a clunk. No pain came.

She had known. Somewhere deep in the recesses of her mind, she had always believed Lord Bryant to be an honorable man. She would have never gone to his house unaccompanied and so late at night otherwise. She would have never asked him to ruin her if she had thought him actually capable of it.

Lord Bryant was decent, noble, and kind.

And she had taken advantage of him.

She put her hands in her hair and dug her fingers into her scalp. Every devastatingly handsome smile of Lord Bryant's flashed before her eyes, now painful to remember. All that time, he had been helping her. Every hour he spent in her company, he put Lady Emily at risk, and yet he did it for Diana with that devilish smile on his blasted face.

A face that was now sporting a possible broken nose due to her interference. And all because she had forced him into their little agreement. At this moment, he was sitting at home, knowing he had failed to help Lady Emily, and it was all her fault.

How could she have been such an unthinking fool?

She placed her hands beside her head and heaved her body back into a normal sitting position. "I have to go."

"But we won't be closing up shop for a few hours yet."

Diana shot up from the desk and practically ran to the coatrack. "Can you handle things here on your own? I can send a runner to have Mr. Oliver come. I hate to leave you alone."

"I won't have a problem, but what should I say when Mr. Barton returns?"

"Tell him the truth," Diana said, buttoning the last button on her coat. "You don't know where I'm going." She reached the door and yanked it open.

"He will think you have run off with that rake." Mrs. Oliver stood from her desk.

"I am *not* going to run off with him," Diana said, then shut the door behind her. She would apologize to Mrs. Oliver later and beg forgiveness from Nate. But for now, she had to see Lord Bryant, proper or no. She had bungled his plans and used him poorly. She had to release him from their ridiculous agreement and help him, in any way she could, with Lady Emily's situation.

CHAPTER 22

Everton crumpled the letter in his hand and laid his head on his desk. This was not the news he had wanted to receive upon returning from Alfriston. Lady Emily was happy with her soon-to-be marriage, was she? The letter had been addressed to Mrs. Cuthbert, but it had always been intended for him. The question was, did Lady Emily write it on her own, or did her parents force her to write it?

He smoothed out the letter and read it once again, trying to reconcile his preconceived notions with what this young girl had written to him. A few of her reasons made sense.

Lord Silverstone owned a quarry, and not just any quarry, but one that produced fossils. He read her underlined sentence once again. Her excitement was palpable and most likely not written by her mother's hand or dictated.

A blasted quarry, a pianoforte sitting neglected, and the fact that she wouldn't have to attend balls or host many callers, as Lord Silverstone's estate was far from London. Those were apparently reasons enough for her to agree to the marriage.

Her last reason, though . . .

Why was everyone foisting Diana Barton on him? Of course Lady Emily would believe Diana looked at him as though she were in love with him. It was all part of the charade. That part of his relationship with Diana was a sham—exactly like all his other relationships. She was using him, and he was happy to help. She didn't love him. She was everything vibrant and optimistic. He was darkness. They had at some point during all of this nonsense become friends, but that was it. And even that was astounding.

He stood up, strode to where his jacket hung, and pulled from his pocket the dried violets Rachel's nurse had given him. Just underneath them was a packet of seeds Rachel had collected and carefully wrapped.

She had been planning on coming home, and these seeds were the proof of it. She was the one who had gathered together and bound up those seeds. They were going to sprout violets at their country estate.

"She wasn't ready to be married," her nurse had said when she placed the package in his hands, "but she was trying. Her garden has bloomed here every spring for the past four years. You should come visit it sometime."

Everton had nodded, but he wasn't certain he ever would.

"She wanted to go back to you. She wanted to do what was right."

Everton returned to his desk and spread the violets out around his papers. A waft of springtime reached his nose, and then it was gone. The darkened petals looked back at him, waiting for him to ask his questions.

What else could he have done? What was he supposed to do now? He crunched a few of them in his hand, the spring scent returning, but this time it was bitter. She wanted to return to him because it was the right thing to do?

He had wanted her to return to him no matter what. Whether it was right or wrong. Whether her parents wanted her to or not. He had wanted to be loved for himself and not because a piece of paper handed to them in a church told them it was what they were supposed to do.

Curse Rachel and her always wanting to do what was right.

A knock on the door of his study interrupted his thoughts.

Lord Bryant closed his eyes and took in a slow, steadying breath. He had been explicit in his instructions to Nelson. Lady Emily's letter and Rachel's violets were enough to deal with for one afternoon. No one was to disturb him.

No one.

The door swung open, and Diana Barton stood on the threshold, her chin raised and a hand on her hip, as if to challenge anyone who argued that she didn't belong in a man's study without an escort. He cursed under his breath. This was the second time Nelson had disobeyed him in favor of Diana. Dash it all, what was so convincing about the woman that even Nelson couldn't say no to her? What had she come to demand now? Not that it mattered. He wouldn't agree to anything—not today.

But besides the quarry and the pianoforte and the quiet, I think Miss Barton is in love with you. And perhaps, even, you are with her.

He held tightly to the edge of his desk. Lady Emily's words meant nothing. They were ridiculous. Diana was his friend, his friend whose eyes and dark hair sometimes haunted his dreams—all the more reason she shouldn't be near him without Mrs. Oliver or her brother to protect her.

"What can I help you with, Diana?" He didn't hide the exhaustion from his voice. His trip to Alfriston had emptied him, hollowing out pieces of his soul he had thought could not be more barren.

"I didn't come for your help."

He scoffed. All this woman had done was ask for help, and all he had done was give in to her every single time. If she was here in his study, she needed his help with something. She was too clever for her own good, and she knew how to disguise her demands to make him believe he was getting his way . . . until one day, he might blink and find himself in the lace section of a mercer shop on her behalf, debating whether ecru and cream were the same color.

"You say you don't need my help, and yet, you have never come to me for anything else."

Her hand slid off her hip, and her chin lowered. Contrition? From Diana? She must be here for a large favor indeed. "I know."

"Then please go." Everton couldn't handle Diana Barton right now. He needed time to . . . *not* think. "You keep barging in at the worst possible moments."

"But—"

He rubbed his forehead. "No, Diana. Do not come up with some excuse for me to allow you to stay. Today you will not get your way. I'm tired. I need to be alone."

"But—"

"Why do you never listen to me?" He was finding it harder to breathe. Diana's eyes were soft with worry, and every time they caught his, Lady Emily's blasted letter kept repeating itself. *Miss Barton is in love with you.* "You never leave when I ask you to." Even when she was gone, she lurked around in his brain, that stubborn chin and the way those copper eyes flashed whenever he asked her to do anything. She was so alive, and he—wasn't. He envied her optimism. He envied her future, still so full of possibilities. He envied her youth. If only he still had it. His had been used up by the time he turned twenty-six.

"I warn you, Diana, today I should not be trifled with."

Instead of listening to him, she stepped the rest of the way into his study, strode across the room, and slid some of his papers forward, making room to set both of her hands on his desk. "Today I am here to help *you*."

He closed his eyes for a moment. The best way she could help would be to take that light of hers away from him. Didn't she know he could snuff it out in a moment of weakness? He couldn't bear to see disgust in Diana's eyes.

But still . . . what would it be like? To have someone help him for a change? He leaned toward her, ever so slightly, and then opened his eyes. Her head was tilted to one side, as if she had been examining him, trying to read his thoughts, his desperate, lonely, empty thoughts. Whatever Diana wanted to do to help him, it would be useless. Diana didn't have the power to change the past.

He leaned back in his chair. He should stand. He was, after all, in the presence of a lady. He was simply too tired to conform to social niceties, and honestly, he didn't think Diana cared one whit.

"You are here to help me?"

"Yes." She bent her elbows and brought her face closer to his. Close enough for him to smell fresh paper and ink. "In any way I can. I am aware—"

"Stop saying things like that."

"Like what?"

There it was again—that innocence that brought her so boldly into his study, completely unaware of the temptation she was to him. His eyes went to her lips. Kissing them again would clear his head. He would have a few seconds of peace before she ran out of the room, disgusted by him.

And then he would lose her.

His first friend.

Diana puffed out a breath of frustration. "Oh, don't go acting rakish on me. It doesn't suit you."

That bite. No one talked to him like that. It didn't strengthen his desires to be a gentleman. He raised his eyebrow and studied the little turn at her mouth. He would kiss that first, softly, and then, when she opened her mouth to complain, he would kiss the rest of it. "I've been told it does."

A trace of a smile blossomed on her lips. He had thought his comment would warrant a frown. If she knew what he was thinking . . .

"All right." She sighed. "Perhaps it does."

He found himself leaning forward again. It was impossible to fight off Diana. She plowed her way into anything she wanted. His study, his life, the railroad industry. If more women were like her, he would be out of the scandal-making business. There would be no shrinking violets. No women would need his poor reputation to clear a way for themselves.

"I'm confused, Diana. Would you like me to be rakish tonight or not?" He lifted a hand and brushed her cheek. Instead of pulling away, she rested her head upon his hand.

He froze.

"Lord Bryant." Her voice was careful and soft and pulled him closer to her. She lifted her head off his hand and looked him in the eye. "I want you to be yourself."

Himself? What the devil did she mean by that? "So . . . a rake I will be."

She shook her head in the slightest of movements. "No." She pushed herself away from the desk and started instead to pace in front of it. All tenderness was gone. She was, once again, the calculating businesswoman he saw so often in her office. He waited for his heart to stop sounding so loud in his ears, but just having her here in his domain was doing funny things to him. "You are no rake, and I'm sorry I didn't realize that." She stopped pacing and turned to him. Her head was lowered, her eyebrows furrowed. "I have taken advantage of an innocent, it seems."

An innocent? Everton blinked. Exactly what had Diana heard? Everton was a lot of things, but an innocent was definitely not one of them. "I'm sorry. Are we still speaking of me?"

Her eyebrows furrowed deeper. "Yes, of course."

"I believe it is quite well known throughout London that I am undoubtedly a rake. I kissed you after only spending a few minutes in your company."

She waved her hand in the air, as if his arguments were inconsequential. "That hardly makes you a rake."

"I'm quite certain it does exactly that."

"No, you were helping me."

"I didn't have to kiss you to help you. There are plenty of other ways I could have convinced Mr. Broadcreek to leave you alone, much more gentlemanly ways."

"I never said you were a gentleman, only that you are most definitely not a rake."

"I know a few women throughout London who would convince you otherwise."

"Women like Lady Yolten?" she asked, her head turned at an angle. "I did hear rumors about the two of you."

Lady Yolten. What a firebrand she was. "Yes, exactly like Lady Yolten."

Diana walked around his desk until she was standing directly to his side. He rose, not comfortable sitting any longer in her presence. He may not be a gentleman, but his mother had raised him as one a lifetime ago.

"Lord and Lady Yolten came by my office today." The corners of Diana's lips lifted. "They had nothing but good things to say about you."

The devil take Lord Yolten. The man was much too open and honest. How many times had he threatened the man against saying anything of Everton's involvement in Lord Yolten's marriage? His eyes narrowed. "I'm not surprised that Lady Yolten would say a few positive things about me. I did manage to give her a very exciting Season." He could bluff his way out of this. "But Lord Yolten? Surely he doesn't approve of me."

It was a gamble. Lord Yolten should have known better than to say anything about his scandal with his wife. He prayed Diana was bluffing as well.

Instead of looking uncertain, her smile deepened, and one solitary eyebrow rose in a high arc.

"You would think that, wouldn't you?" She stepped closer to him. The back of his legs pressed against his chair. "I definitely thought that before meeting with them. Why would a man speak kindly of a gentleman who had a scandal with his wife?"

"Perhaps he is a little daft. I never did understand what Lady Yolten saw in the man."

Diana's copper eyes were turning gold. He took half a step back and moved around his chair. She was like a cat about to pounce on a mouse, and feeling like a mouse was not comfortable.

"They are a positively delightful pair. And what's more . . ." She pointed a finger at him. "You know it."

His back bumped into the window behind him. The coldness of it grounded him. "I don't know what you are talking about."

"You helped all of those women. Every single scandal you have had in the last three years has led to a marriage. A happy marriage. Nate's included."

He placed a hand on the frigid window, letting the sharp chill seep into him. "What are you implying?"

She stepped so close to him he could feel her warmth as surely as he felt the cold behind him. The cold was familiar and comfortable. Her gaze was not. "You are a good man, Lord Bryant. No matter how hard you try to convince everyone otherwise."

Everton closed both of his eyes and concentrated on the unforgiving glass behind him. Diana was all softness and heat. She was life, comfort, and good old-fashioned stubbornness. Diana thought him a good man. It was sweet of her. Really it was. But she was dead wrong. And she didn't belong anywhere near him.

"With all due respect, Diana, you don't actually know me."

"I know you well enough."

"No one knows me well enough. I've worked very hard to keep it that way, and if you continue to claim that you do, well, there will be no quicker way to ensure I never visit your office again."

She narrowed her eyes. "You are bluffing."

"I assure you I am not."

Diana sighed, but she didn't back away. "All right. You are a terrible person, but my offer to help still stands."

"You can start by stepping away from me."

She smiled but leaned closer to him. "I meant help with Lady Emily."

Ah, Lady Emily. A safer topic. Everton slid to the side and brought some much-needed space between the two of them. Diana turned and looked at his desk. "Is this a letter from her?"

"No." Everton jumped around Diana and grabbed the letter. His chair slid between the two of them. He folded the letter and tucked it in his breast pocket, his traitorous hands shaking slightly.

He didn't like the way Diana's eyes followed his movements. "That was a woman's hand. You haven't started another scandal already, have you?"

This was preposterous. If he told her yes, would she want to help with that one too? He had enough meddling women in his life. He didn't need another. "No, I haven't. And there is nothing to do for Lady Emily. She is content to marry that old man as long as it means she doesn't have to attend any more balls."

Diana gasped. "She can't mean that."

"I would tend to agree with you, but Mrs. Cuthbert and I have been essentially banned from the Falburton household. And if I'm not mistaken, you don't exactly run in those circles, so we have no way to verify that this letter is true."

Diana's lips scrunched together. He could practically see the wheels turning in her head. Diana didn't like being told something was out of her depth. "What of Lord and Lady Yolten?"

"Why would they help?"

"They owe you."

"They owe me nothing." Everton pulled at the fabric of his untied cravat. It slid off silently, and he threw it on his desk. Why couldn't she understand? "I dallied about with the man's future wife, for heaven's sake."

Diana put her fingers to her temples and massaged the sides of her head. She then threw her hands to her side and grabbed the chair between them, leaning forward. "That couple couldn't say enough good things about you. Are you so accomplished at lying that you have managed to convince yourself of your devilry?"

Yes, yes he was. And he was comfortable that way. He didn't need Diana barging in here, telling him he was some kind of deserving man.

"You should get home to your brother. Does he know you are here?"

Without releasing his eyes, she shook her head. "No."

"Does anyone know you are here?"

"No."

"Blasted fool woman." His words were angry, but his voice was soft. Diana was lucky he was a gentleman. Not a proper gentleman, but a gentleman nevertheless.

"I couldn't help but come. Not when I found out . . ."

"What did you find out?" he asked with a shake of his head.

"You've been helping women." She tucked the chair into the desk and stepped forward. "All these scandals weren't improper at all. You were using your reputation to either raise or lower a woman's prospects to the point that she could marry the man *she* chose."

He was going to end up backed against the window again if he didn't stand his ground. "Don't get any ideas. I'm no saint. It was quite diverting to help those women. And, at times, I was definitely improper."

"I don't believe it."

"Do not turn into another woman who wants to save me, Diana. I have plenty of those."

"You don't need saving."

"Then what exactly are you doing here?"

"I thought I was here to help you with Lady Emily."

"Lady Emily no longer needs our help." Our. Why had he said *our*? He and Diana were not partners.

"No, she doesn't. I believe you."

"Then why are you still here?"

A soft laugh escaped her parted lips. "That is a good question." She shook her head as if surprised by something pleasant. "You were right. Of course you were right. I didn't think I needed anything from you, but it turns out that I do."

"What?" The word was like a puff of smoke. He could manage no more syllables.

"You are in the business of helping women get what they want. I've come to get what I want."

His chest expanded. "And what is that?"

Her impish smile softened into a wide, open, serious expression. "You."

This time he did step back. Not only did he step back, but he turned away and walked around the desk. He wouldn't be trapped by her. Diana didn't know who he was. She didn't know what *kind* of person he was, what kind of husband he had been.

"Why did I ask you—of all the men in London—to help me with this scandal?" Her voice was strong and insistent. It was her voice, after all.

He didn't look behind him, but he could hear her following him. Her steps were slow and steady but following nonetheless.

"Because you knew I didn't mind a scandal."

"That is true, but honestly, I wanted to see you again. I had been in London for nearly a year and only stumbled upon you once. I liked to tell myself I was no longer the young girl that was infatuated with you at Nate's wedding, but when I had an excuse—when I needed help—you were the first man to whom I ran. It wasn't an accident." Everton had reached the door, but he couldn't bring himself to open it and step out of the room. Her words were breaking something deep inside him, and he was a glutton for pain. "You are the only man who has ever fascinated me. Since the moment I saw you, I've been on a train hurtling down a track that always leads to you. I used to try to derail that train. I knew you were a cad and a terrible person, and I couldn't be as stupid as all those other women who fell for you. But today, Lord Bryant—*Everton.*" Oh, that was low of her. "I discovered that you aren't actually a terrible person. And now I'm left wondering why, exactly, I'm still trying to talk myself out of loving you."

A hesitant hand slid across his shoulder, barely brushing the fabric of his coat, but he jumped and turned around as if her fingers had burned him.

"Don't touch me."

She looked up at him, trusting. "Are you afraid of me?"

Of Diana? He could physically have her removed from his house with the snap of his fingers. It wasn't as though Nelson was his only servant. There were *some* who listened to him. It wasn't fair what she was doing to him, though. He had thought they were friends. He had enjoyed her company and even the company of her brother, despite his painful history with him.

"Diana, I am not afraid of you."

"Afraid of my touch, then?"

A disdainful laugh escaped his throat. "You ask that and yet claim to know me? All of London knows the touch of a woman means nothing to me. Those ladies we have been speaking of? I did much more than touch their cheeks, and I will not have you think otherwise."

"Not that much more, though. Not really. And they weren't thinking of you when you snuck off into the garden or got caught kissing. How long has it been since a woman who longed for you has embraced you?"

There was no possible way to answer that. He needed Diana to leave. Now. Everton caught her by both shoulders, spun her around, and pushed her toward the door. His brain wasn't settled enough to have this conversation. It might never be.

"I'm not leaving until you answer my question." She squirmed until she was able to turn partially around to face him. "If I had to hazard a guess, I would assume it has been since your wife passed away."

Everton hadn't been making much progress at removing Diana, but at her guess, he froze. The room darkened around them, and the air seemed to grow thick. Diana completed the rest of her turn slowly, and he let his arms drop to his sides. He blinked once, his eyes so heavy he barely managed to open them again. Here was the heart of it. The one truth that would finally make Diana leave.

"And you think you know me so well." She may have guessed what his scandals were about, but she still had no insights into his marriage. "I can assure you, on that account, you are wrong."

Diana stumbled back a step. "Merciful heavens." Her eyes were wide, and she covered her hand with her mouth.

"What?" Lord Bryant's voice was hard. "Whatever your scheming mind is up to, you are wrong."

Diana's hand shook as she lowered it. "She didn't love you."

And there it was. The hole that had eaten his life away in painful increments was now opening in front of Diana. She would never look at him the same again.

CHAPTER 23

Diana watched Lord Bryant's chest rise and fall after her accusation, but he didn't deny it. He spun away from her and strode toward the door. Diana couldn't follow. Her mind was still frantically trying to make sense of what she had just learned. His wife, his precious Rachel, whose ring he still wore on his finger, hadn't loved him.

He had loved her. Mrs. Cuthbert had told her as much.

All this time, she had thought he wouldn't marry again because of the sacred love he had shared with his deceased wife. But if she hadn't even loved him back? What kind of love was that?

Not a living love. Not one that breathes and demands to be fed. It was a torture device, not happiness.

Lord Bryant threw open the study door and motioned for her to get out. She ignored him. "In all of your marriage and in all of the scandals that happened after your marriage, you have never been held, never been caressed by a woman who cared for you?"

"Leave, Diana."

"I'm going to fix this."

"I'm not yours to fix, Diana." Lord Bryant's hand was gripping the door handle so fiercely his knuckles were white. If he moved, the handle might break off and fall to the floor. "Plenty of women desire me. Women practically throw themselves at me. I'm certain you have seen it yourself."

"Those women don't care about you, not like I do. They are attracted to your money, title, and good looks." Diana stepped gingerly across the study until she was within a foot of Everton.

He put his free hand on his hip and furrowed his brows in what she was certain was pretend affront. "You don't care about my good looks?"

She smiled back, but she wasn't going to allow him to scoff and return to their sparring relationship of earlier. "I care a little. But I'm here now, even though your nose is still swollen and puffy. We don't even know what it will look like after it heals."

"You said a crooked nose would improve my appearance."

"I lied. Nothing could improve your appearance. You are devilishly attractive, with or without a crooked nose."

Without taking her eyes off his, she tugged on her right glove, one finger at a time, until it was loose in her hand.

He swallowed, making the hard ridges of his neck more prominent. Everton claimed to know he was attractive, but she was certain that even he had no idea what the lines in his neck did to her.

He swallowed again. "What are you doing?"

She started removing her left glove as well. "You practically undressed in my office, yet you are concerned about me removing my gloves?"

"Why would you remove your gloves when you are on your way out?"

"Oh, that is a good question. Why would I?" She tucked her gloves into the belt on her waist.

"Don't make me call Nelson."

"Nelson is welcome to witness this."

"I mean to have him throw you out."

Diana bit back a smile. Nelson wouldn't throw her out. The look of relief on his face when she appeared on the doorstep mimicked the relief on Charlotte's face whenever she arrived home early enough to take a turn with the children. It was as good as a blessing.

"You know, Everton." His name on her lips clearly sent a jolt of energy through him. He had been using hers for so long. Why had she been denying herself the pleasure? The rise and fall of his chest as she said it made her wonder how often he heard his name. Always Lord Bryant—or Bryant to those who considered themselves his equal or were being insolent—but never Everton. Lord Bryant was the insufferable rogue. Bryant was a haughty aristocrat. But Everton was the man standing in front of her, alarmed by her uncovered hands. "When you held my hand in the storage room, I had the strangest feeling my hand belonged in yours."

She reached for his left hand, hanging limp at his side, and lifted it, cupping it in both of hers. She softly traced the narrow strip of exposed skin on the inside of his wrist with her thumb. He had threatened once to kiss her there, and she had never looked at her wrist the same since. If she could possibly affect him the same way, she would take the risk.

His hand was that of a gentleman, his long fingers smooth and uncalloused. One tiny white scar, shaped like the tip of an arrow, graced the back, just between his thumb and index finger. She ran her fingers over it. "What is that from?"

Everton released the door handle. "I don't remember."

She pulled his hand to her mouth and gently kissed the scar.

His eyes closed at her touch, but he didn't jerk away like he had earlier. Emboldened, she kissed the inside of his wrist, his pulse raced under her touch, and for a moment, she allowed herself to breathe in the bold, spicy scent of him. She lifted her head and intertwined her fingers in his. A prickle of excitement ran up her arm. She had held Lord Bryant's hand before. Heavens—she had even kissed him before, but this was different.

This was real.

And more than anything in the world, she wanted to know if he felt the same way.

His eyes flashed open, and they were on fire.

But his chest still rose and fell in a pattern that resonated fear.

"Diana."

She tightened her fingers. "Yes."

"I don't think I can do this."

"Hold my hand?"

"Yes."

"That's all right. I'll hold yours."

His face crumpled, warring emotions raging behind his eyes. His grip on her hand became uncomfortably tight, and his breathing raced.

"Everton?"

"I'm all right."

"Do you need to sit down?"

"I think I need you to stop touching me." His hand still grasped hers securely. She couldn't pull away, nor did she want to.

"I could do that." His eyes widened, and if anything, his grip tightened in hers. "Or I could touch you a bit more so you can grow accustomed to it."

His grip relaxed enough to no longer be painful, but it was still firm. He didn't drop her hand. "How do you come up with such ridiculous ideas?"

"You've loved every single one of my ideas."

"I may love this one too much, which means it is probably a bad idea."

"Let me help you decide." Not willing to untangle her fingers from his, Diana reached for his cheek with her left hand. The roughness of his stubble skimmed the tips of her fingers. She slid her palm back and forth along the hollow of his cheek. "So, this is what a man's cheek feels like."

He was still breathing a bit harder than normal and deeply. But he tried one of his familiar jaunty expressions. "You've never felt a man's cheek before?"

"My father's, I suppose, but I was quite young, and I don't remember his ever looking quite this rough."

"I wasn't expecting visitors." Her eyes went to the open neck of his shirt. That was obvious. "You always manage to come when I'm not expecting you." All she could do was nod. "So much about you is unexpected."

Everton gently released his fingers from her grasp. Her hand was empty without his there. Was he going to ask her to leave? After all this?

He leaned forward and cupped her face in his hands. His thumb stroked her skin, just inches below her eye, as if he were wiping away a tear. "So this is what a woman's cheek feels like."

Diana laughed. He wasn't asking her to leave—not yet. "I know you have touched a woman's cheek before."

"Never one who smiled at me like you are now." His thumb moved from her cheekbone to the corner of her mouth. She closed her eyes and leaned forward, waiting.

And waiting.

Cracking one eye open, she found Everton watching her with a strange half smile on his face. Devil take the man. Had he been pretending this whole time? Was this his way of winning their nonsensical game?

She stepped back, and his hands fell off her face. "Are you mocking me?"

"I wouldn't dare." Everton stepped forward. His hand brushed her elbow, then slid down her arm and claimed her hand. "But you must understand I cannot kiss you."

"Why not? We have kissed before, for heaven's sake."

"Yes, but that was as a favor." He shrugged his head to one side. "And admittedly, for a bit of fun."

They were already close, but she stepped closer. "This would be fun."

He shook his head. "You know what I mean."

"I will let you consider it a favor."

"Diana." His fingers traced her cheekbone again, sending tiny pinpricks of pleasure rushing through her. "I—quite honestly—don't know that I can give you anything. I don't think I have anything to give. I will not take advantage of you."

Diana drew in a slow, steady breath. This was not the Everton she had come to know. He didn't care about propriety. "Why not? Of all the times to live up to your reputation, please, Everton, do not become a stuffy, uptight gentleman on me now."

"Diana, we are alone . . . in my study."

"That can be easily remedied." Diana took the one step necessary to exit the study and entered the darkened corridor, pulling him along with her. "Now we are no longer in your study."

Everton closed his eyes and didn't reopen them.

"Are you still scared of me?"

His eyes slowly reopened. "Terrified."

Diana sighed. "Still?"

"You don't know me. Not really. I've sworn never to marry again, and I didn't make that promise lightly. I cannot lead you to believe I've overcome that part of me when I am only just beginning to understand it."

Diana's stomach knotted. She had thought . . . what? That she could be the woman who changed his mind? Did she really think she was that powerful? "I had thought you made that promise because you and your wife had had such a deep love you couldn't fathom marriage to anyone else. But the two of you didn't—"

"That is new to you, Diana, but not to me. I was married to Rachel for months before I knew anything was wrong. When I finally discovered what the problem was, I was powerless to fix it. I couldn't make her love me. No matter how hard I tried. I broke that woman, and I cannot trust myself not to do it again."

"She broke you." Diana's voice was soft but firm. "*She* broke *you*."

"I won't have you speaking ill of her. Her family has done enough of that to last a lifetime—one much longer than hers. She did everything everyone had ever expected of her. Her parents, Society, me. She tried. She never complained; she never even let anyone know how unhappy she was. She wanted to love me. She simply couldn't. But she was going to try." His voice broke. "She was coming back. And regardless of her feelings for me, I did love her. She was my wife. So you see, you weren't exactly wrong about your earlier assumptions."

"That's not love, Everton. Love is meant to be shared. It cannot only be given and given until you have nothing left to give."

Everton's face grew turbulent and as dark as the corridor around them. "I don't need a twenty-two-year-old woman to explain what love is." She had lost him. He was back to being defensive. "Even if she does own a railroad company."

She knew Everton loved his wife, but Diana was beginning to hate her. "Why would you break your heart and spirit over a woman who never loved you back? Everton, there is so much more to love than that. Why—?"

Everton slammed his fist into the wall beside him. His voice rose to a roar. "Because I was supposed to." Plaster scattered to the floor, and Everton pulled his hand out of the hole he had created. His face grew strange and empty like she had never seen it before. He stared at his hand like it was not a part of him.

Diana reached out toward Everton, but the broken look on his face made her pause. This was not something she was going to be able to fix. Not right now. Diana let out a long sigh. She wasn't sure what she had expected to happen tonight, but this wasn't it. If he wasn't ready, he wasn't ready. She couldn't expect him to change over the course of one conversation. It might never be, but she wouldn't give up. She could always come back tomorrow after the vote. "You win. I'll leave."

She turned and faced the line of Everton's ancestors on the wall opposite her. The portraits stretched down the length of the corridor. Opulent golden frames encased the dark, stormy men and women in each painting. But at the end of the wall, where the corridor opened into the entry hall, the large, framed portrait of Everton that she had seen on her first visit was missing. In its place was a familiar charcoal drawing in a simple wooden frame. The inaccurate nose jumped out at her. He had hung her drawing? Here, among his forefathers?

"Where is your portrait?"

"I had Nelson take it down." Everton came up behind her, his voice giving away the fact that he was only inches from her ear.

"Why?"

"It is being sent somewhere."

"To another estate?"

"No." He sighed softly before his hand came to rest on her shoulder. "One fifteen Rochester Street."

Her lips quivered, and she quickly covered them with a hand. He was sending her his portrait? When had he decided to do that?

"Why did you do that?"

He took a breath so ragged she couldn't help but hear the torment behind it. "Because I wanted to." The two of them were alone in a darkened corridor. Nelson, or any one of his servants, could come upon them at any moment. They probably would after Everton's last outburst. "I think . . ." His voice was low and close to her ear. "I think I have been looking at everything wrong. And

I want you to stay, and that suddenly means something to me. Something I should have realized all along. Nothing about you leaving would be winning for me."

Diana focused on that crooked nose in front of her. She had hoped . . . She had hoped for so much . . . "What are you trying to say?"

"Before I answer that, answer me this: if your brother knew you were here, what would he think?"

"He wouldn't think." Diana reached her right hand up, slowly, and rested it on his, still on her shoulder. She couldn't see him, but she could feel his warmth. "You would end up with a matching black eye and an even more swollen nose."

He squeezed her shoulder, and in return, she clutched his fingers and turned to face him. His eyes scanned hers. "And what of Society?"

She raised her chin. She wasn't sure what Everton was trying to say, but if he was pointing out how badly she had damaged her reputation, that was a concession she couldn't deny. "London would have my head."

"Your mother?"

Diana cocked her head to one side. What would her mother think? She would probably prefer that she didn't come to a man's house unchaperoned, but as long as she came away unscathed, she might enjoy sharing the story with her later. "Mama is a bit trickier, but even she would think I am acting rashly and tell me I was a fool to come dashing over here."

Everton nodded, and with that slow movement of his head, something seemed to settle in him. He laced his fingers in hers. "Then why did you come?"

Diana had laid all of her cards on the table earlier, in the study, but if he needed reassurance, she would not withhold it from him. "Because I couldn't stay away. I wanted to be with you. I wanted to see you so badly."

Everton's eyebrows came together, his free hand reaching up to cover his mouth as he took in a shaky breath. His striking green eyes shone in the few candles dotting the corridor, a brightness that came only with unshed tears. "Despite all of them."

Diana leaned into him. "Honestly, I never gave any of them a second thought. I was only thinking of you."

"Diana." Her name was like a prayer on his lips.

His gaze went to her lips, then back to her eyes. They blazed so brightly she could almost feel heat emanating from them. He released her shoulder and reached for his smallest finger on his left hand. "This was a ring that was worn out of duty, and foolishly I have continued to wear it because I thought I should." With one slow but smooth movement, he removed the small gold band. "I'm done loving because I should. No one wants to be loved that way. Give me one moment."

Lord Bryant returned to his desk and placed the ring on a pile of dried petals. For three breaths, he leaned forward without moving, then turned around.

She waited for him in the corridor, heart pounding. His steps quickened with every footfall, until he reached her and grabbed her by the waist. He spun her in a quick circle, and then set her back down but didn't release her. "I love you, Diana Barton, goddess of light and hope. I know I shouldn't, but frankly, I'm done dictating my feelings based on what *should* be done."

Diana lifted her chin, stood up on her toes, and wrapped her arms around his neck. Her cheek rubbed against the roughness of his, and her lips found his ear. "Does that mean you will kiss me?"

Everton groaned. "I've spent too many years as a scoundrel to turn down that offer."

She leaned back so she could see him. A small, devilish part of her wanted to goad him—to tell him his first kiss had been acceptable but that she expected more from him now. But in all honesty, that first kiss hadn't needed improvement, and she didn't dare speak for fear that he would change his mind. Still, the look in his eye was anything but wavering. Something had changed. It was as if he had finally decided to live again, and even though she hadn't thought it possible, he became even more beautiful.

"Is that smile for me?" Everton asked, wonder taming the earlier fire of his eyes.

"Am I smiling?" She couldn't stop herself.

"Your face is lit up like a gas lamp. Luminous, just like your name. I promise I won't make that light go out."

"How could you when you were the one to put it there?"

His shoulders relaxed. He traced her lower lip with his thumb and then waited, as if afraid she would run away. She bit it softly, and he hissed in surprise.

"You—Diana—never do what I expect."

"What did you think? That I would run aw—"

He lowered his head, and his mouth covered hers before she could finish the sentence. Diana—young, fanciful Diana—rose fully to the surface, only it wasn't her young, naive self. This was who she was now—old and new melded together, both surging with a blazing light.

Everton could have any woman in London, and yet, he had chosen her. His first kiss had been about show—hands everywhere, lips moving firmly against hers. This was different. His touch was soft and hesitant. He barely brushed her lips with his own, but it sent waves of longing rushing through her. Heaven help her, she needed to kiss him more forcefully. She reached for the lapel of his vest with her right hand and pulled him closer. He ignored her pull and continued the soft exploration of her lips. She inhaled his scent, expecting at least a bit of brandy after the day he had been through, but there was none. No spirits were clouding his judgment. He knew exactly what he was doing.

She pulled at him again, this time with both hands, and his response was instantaneous. His fingers made their way into her hair, disheveling it as he went.

He had remembered her request.

He stepped in closer, removing the need for her to pull him any longer. He was here. All the way here, with her. She slid her hands around his waist and traced the fabric of his vest up his back.

She would definitely want to do this again.

And again.

Everton seemed to be in agreement.

He pulled away after a few luscious moments and looked at her. If her eyes were as hazy as his, she must have looked like a wanton.

She didn't care. They were safe in the corridor where anyone could stop by at any moment. They were being as proper as they could be, all things considered.

Everton leaned forward and kissed each of her eyelids. "Those amber eyes of yours have caused me no end of torment." He then nipped the bottom of each earlobe. "And those ears. They never listen."

"So you have said."

"And your throat . . ." Everton's eyes darkened, and Diana sucked in a breath.

A forced cough echoed in the hall to their left. Everton froze.

"Shall I see the young lady out, then?"

Everton pulled away, his eyes clouded in confusion. He blinked a few times before turning his head back to her.

"In a minute, Nelson." He bent his head and pushed her softly, causing her to step back until she was pressed against the portrait-lined wall behind her. His parents' portrait tipped to one side as he made room for her against the panel. Everton's lips hovered just below her jaw. He did realize Nelson could still see them, didn't he?

"I'll wait here, then."

Everton groaned. He leaned forward to Diana's ear. "Should I relieve him of his position?" His breath tickled her neck.

"No, I like him."

"Of course you do. He does everything you ask of him." He kissed her cheek with a quick swipe. "In his defense, I have yet to see a person deny a request from you." He pulled away and turned to face his butler.

"You may see Miss Barton out."

Nelson gave a brief nod. "Thank you, sir."

Diana stepped forward, but her hand had somehow found its way back into Everton's, and he didn't follow her forward. With no choice but to stop, she turned back to him. He eyed their entwined hands as if he couldn't quite believe what he was seeing. She gave him a tug, and he followed her silently toward the door.

"I'm going to have to say something to Nate," Diana said, "to warn him."

Everton nodded. He still seemed to be in a sort of a fog.

Nelson opened the door for her, and she reluctantly dropped Everton's hand.

He watched his fingers for a moment before looking up at her. "I will see you in Parliament tomorrow. We will get your act approved once and for all."

She would finally know if her plan to save Mrs. Richardson was a success or a complete failure. "Until tomorrow, then," she said. Nelson still stood at attention by the door, waiting for her to take her leave. "Thank you, Nelson," she said.

"Thank you, miss." A brief smile transformed his otherwise serious face. "I trust this won't be the last we see of you."

"I should hope not." She flashed a brilliant smile at Everton and gave him a wink. "Lord Bryant is one of my investors. It would mean bad news, indeed, if I weren't to hear from him."

Diana took the opportunity of Nelson's stunned surprise to slip out the door and into the open air. Everton's laughter caused a spring in her step. It was a sound of joy, and that joy blossomed in her own chest as she climbed the steps into the carriage. Each step squeaked out music as she sprang off it. She could spend her whole life making that man laugh.

After what had just occurred, she was quite certain she would get the chance. She simply needed to convince Nate of that.

CHAPTER 24

Nelson had never been the type of servant to stand on ceremony, not when they were alone. So when Nelson didn't speak after Diana left, it wasn't out of respect to his employer.

If he wasn't going to ask, Everton wasn't going to explain. "I'm going to bed."

"Not to your study?"

"No."

"Should I bring your brandy to your bedroom, then?"

"No, I'm going to sleep. Tonight I'm going to dream, and I'd like to get started on those dreams as soon as possible."

Nelson eyed his bare neck and rolled-up sleeves. "Are we to expect changes here?"

"I . . ." Everton knew what he was asking. "I believe we will."

"Women like Miss Barton don't come around every day. I think it may be time to snatch happiness while it is sitting right in front of you."

"It isn't my happiness I'm worried about."

Nelson eyed the door through which Diana had just left.

Had Everton really just kissed her? In the corridor of his home? He really was a cad. And yet, he couldn't make himself feel bad about it. "She is so young. She hasn't even begun to live her life. Not really."

"With all due respect, sir, neither have you." Nelson placed a hand on his shoulder, a motion much more like a father would do to his son than a servant to master. "And you can't rob someone of their future if they willingly give it to you. I may be wrong, but she seemed quite happy before she left."

Everton couldn't help the grin that came to his lips. "She did, didn't she?" The weight of the past four years suddenly made it hard to breathe. He closed his eyes and saw Diana again, waiting to be kissed with a smile on her face.

A smile. For him.

"I think I may be on the verge of becoming a stodgy family man."

Nelson smiled and squeezed his shoulder. "That has always been my highest hope for you."

"Me too." It was hard to admit it after years of running away, but it was true. That dream had slowly been crushed over the months of his unhappy marriage. He had always thought that if he had loved Rachel enough, their marriage could have evolved into the marriage he had always hoped for. But it only got worse, and his heart only grew harder. He had loved her out of duty, and there was no possibility that Rachel hadn't known that.

Nelson cleared his throat, perchance to cover some strong emotion. "You hid it well enough."

The hope of his youth had landed on dry ground. He had always considered it dead, but it hadn't been. It lay dormant, waiting for Diana to come shower it with the giving waters of her smile. He could feel those seeds growing in his chest, even now. An opening of his world that he had been certain would remain dark and unfruitful. "I didn't think it would ever happen for me."

Nelson dropped his hand from Everton's shoulder and straightened. "I knew I was right to let her in all those months ago."

"Are you trying to claim credit for this?"

"Don't you think I should?"

Everton placed his hands on Nelson's shoulders and squeezed them. His smallest finger still felt oddly bare. But Diana didn't need that ring to protect her. She had come to him of her own free will. Despite the whole world telling her she shouldn't. He didn't know what he had done to deserve such a show of faith, but he would go to the devil before breaking her trust. "If there is good news to be had, I say we all take credit for it."

Everton made certain not to skip as he made his way to his room. How long had it been since the future ahead of him looked bright?

But he didn't fall asleep quickly. Hope had settled in, and it wouldn't allow his head to rest. A happy home life had been something he had given up on long ago. It was hours before he calmed himself enough to sleep, but he didn't begrudge those hours. Even without sleeping, his head had been filled with dreams.

CHAPTER 25

Diana's neck ached, but that didn't stop her from leaning forward one more time to get a better view of the members of Parliament discussing her would-be railroad line.

Everton hadn't come. There was still time for him to arrive before the vote took place, but she thought he would have been there for the discussion. So far, everything seemed to be going well, although it was difficult to tell what all those men in wigs were thinking. But her paperwork had held up. There were no faults found there.

"Why isn't that scoundrel here?" Nate didn't look at her as he spoke under his breath.

"What scoundrel?" Of course he meant Everton. Despite Nate trying not to show interest in him, he had spent as much time as she had leaning over the balcony in hopes of catching a glimpse of him. Still, he was no scoundrel.

"Lord Bryant, of course." Nate spoke through his teeth, turning his head only slightly toward her. "He didn't even bother to show up."

"Something must have happened." But what? Everton knew how important this was to her. She smoothed down her skirts and tried to calm herself. Everton was a grown man. He could take care of himself. He was certain to be all right.

"What could be more important than this vote?"

"I don't know. I hope he isn't injured."

Nate snorted. "You and I have far different hopes for that man."

"Nate, I wish—"

"Whatever you wish doesn't change the fact that he isn't here, and if he isn't hurt, what excuse could he have? That he overslept?"

"It is nearly five o'clock."

Nate shrugged as if the idea wouldn't surprise him.

"He didn't oversleep."

"Then either he doesn't care for you, which would be no surprise at all to me, or something bad has happened to the louse." Nate turned to face her. "Which would you prefer?"

Diana gripped the bench in front of her. She needed something to anchor her here, in the noisy parliamentary hall. "He is not a louse."

"Why do you defend him? Why does every woman defend him? Does a perfect face truly cover a multitude of sins?"

"He is not a sinner, Nate. I can't think of a single sin to lay at his feet."

"Diana." Nate ran his fingers roughly through his hair. "The man has a different woman every week. There isn't a constant bone in his body. He has ruined at least three different women this year."

Nate's voice was starting to rise, so she purposely lowered hers. "Ruined the *reputations* of three women, you mean. He didn't actually ruin anyone."

Nate shook his head, but he did respond in a lower voice. "According to London, it is the same thing."

"But it isn't the same thing, is it? When you judge someone, you try to understand his heart. Ruining a woman's reputation and actually ruining a woman are very, very different things. I asked him to ruin my reputation." She pointed to her chest with all four of her fingers. "I asked him to. Perhaps those women did the same thing."

"Why in heaven's name would they do that?"

"To get what they wanted, Nate. Do you know how hard that is for a woman? Did Grace have any avenues open to her when she was chasing after you? No. You were her only choice."

"But she loved me."

"How fortunate for the two of you," Diana hissed. "However, some women are not so fortunate. They are forced to marry men for the station in life they can provide and not by any choice of their own."

Nate narrowed his eyes and, once again, ran his hands through his hair. "Now you are exaggerating. Grace's situation was unique."

"But having a husband selected for a woman is not unique, is it?"

"What are you saying? Are you telling me Lord Bryant has multiple women a year asking him to ruin their reputations so they will be free to marry men of their choosing?"

"No."

"Good, because that would be ridiculous."

"What I'm saying is that he and Mrs. Cuthbert offer that service to women they find in need of it."

Nate put his elbows on the bench in front of him and dropped his face in his hands. "Is that what he told you?" His voice was muffled.

There was the bang of a gavel and an announcement of a ten-minute recess. People around them stood. She grabbed Nate's hand and steered him off the bench and into the aisle. The two of them climbed the stairs toward the exit.

Once out of the stifling hall, she pulled Nate to one side. People shuffled around them. She found a corner to the far side of the corridor and led him to it. "This arrangement of his with Mrs. Cuthbert . . . At first, I only suspected it, but after some investigation, one of our investors confirmed it. Nate, look at me." He turned his head slowly, as if it were the last thing he wanted to do. He looked miserable, unsurprisingly. She was consorting with a man whom most of London considered to be a rake of the worst kind. Not long ago, she believed the same thing about him. "Lord Bryant is a good man. I believe he deserves happiness, and I want to share that happiness with him."

Nate's eyes narrowed, as if doubting her motives. He glanced around to be sure no one was within hearing distance. "Diana, don't be ridiculous. Lord Bryant is not worthy of you. You are smarter than this." Nate's head fell back and rested against the wall. He ran both hands through his hair. "I never should have asked for your help in the office. I should have hired an assistant."

Diana stood in front of him and reached for his hand. She breathed in slowly for a moment. "The day you asked me to help you was one of the happiest of my life. I watched you lose yourself in this railroad business after Papa died. We all knew you would succeed, but what we didn't know was the toll it would take. And Mama and I—all we could do was watch."

Nate's head slowly lifted from the wall. Tears were pricking Diana's eyes, but that didn't matter. She didn't have to be a businesswoman in front of Nate. "I don't know what would have happened to you if Grace hadn't come along. She showed you a life beyond paying off our family's debts and bringing the estate out of the brink of ruin." Nate's face softened, as it did any time his wife's name was mentioned. "Do not regret asking me to work with you. I cannot say that I have loved every minute of it, but to accomplish something that helps our family, and now the Richardson family, has been one of the most fulfilling things I have ever done." Or, it would be, assuming the act passed.

Nate pursed his lips together. "You are so very capable. I'm glad the world will get to see your competence today when your act is passed and you can finally build a line that *you* developed and fought for. But Diana, Lord Bryant—" He shook his head. "Even if what you say is true, his reputation is thoroughly damaged, and all of London knows he has sworn to never remarry. I've heard him say it myself, and I don't believe he was bluffing."

Everton hadn't been. But she had seen him change. At his home last night, his heart had certainly been softened to the idea. More than softened. "He wasn't bluffing, but I believe he has changed his mind."

"You *believe* he has changed his mind? You have already put your reputation at risk by consorting with him. Are you willing to also risk your heart because you *believe* he has changed his mind?"

No other man had ever even interested Diana. It had always been Everton—ever since she was eighteen years old. No matter how difficult their path would be, she would always be willing to take a chance on him. "Yes."

Nate pushed himself away from the wall and walked away from her. Three steps later, he turned around and came back. With both hands out in front of him, he started to speak twice, his mouth floundering for words.

Diana took his hands in hers. "You told me I should have asked for your help at the beginning of all of this." She swallowed. "Well, I'm asking for it now. Nate, help me with Lord Bryant. If he asks for my hand, give him all the conditions you want, but tell him yes. When we go out in Society together, stand with me as my brother. Help others to see the man that he is instead of the man he has portrayed himself to be."

She squeezed his hands, and for several breaths, there was no response. Then softly, Nate clasped her hand just a little bit tighter. "He hasn't even asked to court you. This is all moving much too fast."

"How long had you and Grace known each other before you became engaged?"

Nate shook his head, not willing to answer. But Diana knew. Two weeks. She and Everton had spent four times that amount together.

Nate ran his fingers through his hair again and groaned. "I want to see you go to a better man."

"Nate, I truly don't believe there is one." At her words, Nate narrowed his eyes. He didn't believe her. "Barring yourself, of course."

Nate glanced heavenward, then to the door they had just come through. She could see what he was thinking: *If he is truly such a good man, why hasn't he come?*

"I may give him a chance, but I won't like it. And it will ultimately come down to his behavior." Nate pulled Diana back toward the door. Everyone had already returned to the hall. They had most likely missed a portion of the proceedings. "They should be voting soon. We need to go back in."

She wrapped her arms around Nate's waist, pressed her face against his back, and squeezed. "Thank you."

Nate patted her hands at his stomach, then pulled them away so he could open the door. "I haven't done anything yet. I'm still hoping I won't have to."

"Still—" The clamoring noise of the assembly hall stopped Diana.

Something was wrong. The atmosphere of the room had completely changed after the recess. Nate's eyes widened, and he motioned toward the bench they had been sitting on. They picked their way down the rows until they reached their spot and sat down.

"What is happening?" Nate asked the gentleman to his right.

The man grunted, his mouth puckered up in lines underneath a voluminous gray mustache. "It appears that a woman has been running the railroad business."

Nate and Diana exchanged a glance. Nate threw back his shoulders. "Yes, and what of it? All of her investors must have known that, and her paperwork has been declared in order."

"It has been brought up that having a woman run a company is quite a risk, perhaps not one that Parliament should take."

"Who brought that up?" Nate asked.

"Lord Rayleigh," the man said. Lord Rayleigh? Diana's teeth clenched together. He was heavily invested in Mr. Broadcreek's company. "You must admit he has a point," the man continued. "Apparently she is a young, unmarried woman. What if she married some good-for-nothing scoundrel? He would take control of the company."

Diana dug her fingernails into the palms of her hands. "Perhaps the investors trusted her enough *not* to marry a scoundrel."

The older gentleman simply shrugged and continued listening to the speaker below.

"An addendum must be added . . ." one of the lords was saying.

"Is that Lord Rayleigh?" Diana leaned over and asked Nate.

"Yes."

Lord Rayleigh paced the floor in front of the other Lords. "A woman may be counted on to do certain things in a business. It is quite obvious that she has been meticulous in her paperwork. But are we willing to grant permission to build a line—a process that could take years—to someone in such an uncertain position as this Miss Barton is in?" He glanced at someone in the balcony to his left. Diana craned her neck to see the benches on the other side of the hall. There, sitting with a smile on his face, was a man whose mustache she couldn't mistake.

Mr. Broadcreek.

Of course he would be here. "Who knows what could become of her?" Lord Rayleigh continued. "If, however, there were some way to ensure she married a responsible citizen—one who knew at least as much about the railroad industry as she did—I would happily vote to pass this act."

Whisperings rose throughout the room. An addendum that she would have to marry with an additional requirement that her husband be an established railroad businessman? Adding the addendum alone could take weeks, possibly months. There would be a huge delay on building, and her investors might seek to invest elsewhere rather than wait. Mr. Broadcreek sat back in his seat, his arms crossed over his chest. He thought she would have to marry him . . . impossible. She would bankrupt Richardson Rail first.

But she couldn't. Not with Charlotte counting on her to sell the company for a much higher profit.

A commotion on the floor caused the assembled Lords to turn toward the doorway. Diana reached for Nate's elbow and squeezed it.

Everton strode toward the middle of the room. He was here. Every eye followed him from the balcony and from the floor below. The hall around her suddenly turned brighter. The reds that adorned so much of the chamber no longer felt oppressive; instead, they were cheery. Sunshine from the windows reflected off every surface, and especially off Everton. She couldn't see his eyes from this vantage point, but she knew what expression they would hold. They would be alive with light.

"Lord Rayleigh," Everton called out, "your proposed amendment has no merit. Are we to meet each time Miss Barton begins courting someone? Are we to weigh in the balance whether or not her suitor is trustworthy enough to finish this proposed line? Is there anyone here who would like to take on that responsibility? When did it become the duty of the House of Lords to oversee a woman's personal life?"

Murmurs of assent carried through the room.

Lord Rayleigh stepped closer to Lord Bryant, his stout belly puffed out. "If you had been here for deliberations, perhaps you would understand. How can we, in good faith, give such a responsibility to a woman? More particularly, to an unmarried woman who lacks the guidance of a husband in her affairs?"

Lord Bryant scoffed. "Have you met Miss Barton?"

"No, I haven't had the pleasure."

"I had thought not."

"Whatever do you mean?"

"Only that if you had met Miss Barton, you would know she doesn't *allow* men to guide her affairs." The man on her right chuckled. Many of the other spectators, as well as some of the Lords, made similar noises. Perhaps having Lord Bryant in charge of her defense wasn't the best idea.

Lord Rayleigh cocked his head to one side. "That doesn't exactly sound like a glowing recommendation."

"Ah, but it is. You argue that if a man were to marry her, he would exercise control over her business."

Lord Rayleigh was too far below Diana for her to get a clear view of his face, but his movements started to look more agitated and less sure. "I'm not merely arguing that: it is reality. Under the law, husband and wife become one flesh, but within that flesh, it is the husband's duty to sign for documents and control the finances."

"Lord Rayleigh, from the sound of it, it almost seems like you have someone in mind for her."

Diana did not like where this was going. She did not want Parliament to start throwing out names of possible husbands for her, but she had no way to stand up and speak for herself.

"My only stipulation is that he be someone well acquainted with the industry—perhaps someone who owns a successful company himself. That way, he will be able to ensure that this line gets built as originally intended, according to these documents."

Lord Bryant turned and looked slowly around the room, as if trying to look each Lord in the eye. "If our intent is to ensure that Miss Diana Barton builds the railroad line in the manner that she documented and designed, then, Lord Rayleigh, I have a different proposal that I think you will find more rational than your own."

"What do you propose?" Lord Rayleigh's words were low, and Diana could barely make them out.

"She should marry a man with absolutely no interest in running a railroad company. Then he can simply stay out of her way."

Most of the Lords on the lower level chortled and whispered to one another at his suggestion. A few people around Diana snorted. Diana put her head in her hand. How had her personal life become a topic for Parliament?

"This is the man you trust your heart and reputation with?" Nate's voice was more of a growl than a whisper. "He should learn to keep his mouth shut." Diana lifted her head, but she had no response to give Nate.

Lord Rayleigh looked around as if to judge Parliament's reaction to Lord Bryant's suggestion. "That is an interesting proposition."

"It is more than just interesting; it is the only proposition that holds merit, and since we would all like the reassurance that such a man might be found, I would like to make a suggestion. Miss Barton is here, is she not?" Lord Bryant had seen her—she had caught his eye several times while he spoke. But being theatrical seemed to be a part of his true nature, not just a part of his façade. Her heart and Nate's accusations pounded loud in her ears. Did she trust Everton? Everton's eyes were fastened on her, and though he was too far away for her to see his expression, she could feel his intensity.

Yes. She trusted him, and she would always trust him.

She raised a hand so the other Lords could search her out.

"Ah, yes, there she is. Since she is the subject of this conversation, which has turned so personal for her, I would like to ask her a few questions."

Lord Rayleigh snorted. "I don't think—"

Lord Bryant silenced him with a look that was quite theatrical, indeed.

Diana stood. If she was going to speak before Parliament, she refused to be seen as sheepish or hesitant. Nate reached for her hand, and she squeezed it tightly. "Prepare yourself, Nate," she said under her breath.

His only response was to squeeze her hand tighter. For the first time since his return, she was extremely grateful to have him nearby.

Lord Bryant looked up at her. "Miss Barton, have you been following these proceedings?"

"Yes."

"Despite the absolutely ridiculous notion that Parliament is trying to dictate such a personal part of your life, I would like to ask whether you believe my idea has merit. Would you be willing to marry a man who is completely uninterested in running a railroad company?"

The thrumming of her heart in her ears softened as she focused solely on Everton. "I most certainly would." A murmur went through the crowd. What, exactly, were these men saying about her? Her chin went up in defiance. If she was going to be talked about, she would be in control of the conversation. "Provided he was handsome."

The murmur turned to a roar as people around her gasped, then laughed, turning to their neighbors to ascertain they had also heard what she'd said.

When the crowd quieted, Lord Bryant looked at his fellow members of Parliament. "I think we can guarantee that he'll be handsome."

Lord Rayleigh blubbered for a moment. "Lord Bryant, how can we guarantee something like that? This is the House of Lords. We don't manage such trifles as a man's looks."

Lord Bryant leveled his eyes at Lord Rayleigh. "We were managing trifles when I came in the room, so I believe we can strike that as an argument. You had already established the fact that, as a body, we can be quite ridiculous. Today I am going to see exactly how ridiculous we can be."

The murmurs turned lower, with a hint of anger. It was one thing to offer up a conflicting option to Lord Rayleigh's, but it was quite another to insult the whole body of Parliament.

"Now, Miss Barton, you would wish him to be handsome, and I would wish he didn't meddle in your business affairs. Have you any other conditions before we settle this dispute and start looking for a husband for you?"

Diana smiled. The room about her faded away, and all she could see was Everton, standing in front of the world, asking her what *she* wanted. "Yes."

"Please, do tell. Today Parliament has joined the matchmaking business. We would like to do a good job of it."

Diana glanced at Nate before dropping his hand. He was shaking his head, but not out of anger, more out of disbelief. She could accept that. Disbelief could be a stepping stone to acceptance. Diana grabbed the back of the bench in front of her and leaned forward. Lord Bryant wasn't the only one who enjoyed being theatrical now and again. "I must admit I wouldn't complain if you found me a Lord. I have always wanted to be called 'Lady.'"

More gasps at her audacity. Lord Rayleigh stepped forward again, but Lord Bryant silenced him with a movement of his hands. "What of his nose?" Lord Bryant asked. "Are you particular about his nose?"

"No, I'm certain I can live with most noses."

"How tall would you like him to be?"

"How tall are you, my lord?"

Lord Bryant turned to a scribe. "Please note that her husband-to-be should be six two."

The scribe nodded, as if in a trance, and jotted it down.

"What else, Miss Barton?"

"Green eyes that sparkle like emeralds when I walk into a room."

Lord Bryant checked on the scribe. He was still taking notes. A few of the Lords were starting to stand. They wouldn't allow such ridiculousness for much longer. If they had been in the House of Commons, the speaker would have stopped this nonsense already. Fortunately, this was the House of Lords, and the Lords were expected to govern themselves.

"I shouldn't like him to be too young either. I think thirty-one would be the perfect age."

"Why, Miss Barton—" Lord Bryant's head shot up, as if she had surprised him greatly. "That is exactly my age."

"Is it?" Diana asked in feigned incredulity.

Lord Bryant held up his fingers as he counted off her qualifications. "Six two, a lord with any type of nose, and thirty-one years of age . . ." He looked around the room as if assessing all the men there. "There is nothing more to be done, I suppose. My Lords, I would like to propose that Miss Diana Barton marry me. There isn't a man in existence, other than myself, who meets all of her qualifications."

Lords and spectators alike rose from their seats, some laughing but most shouting in surprise.

The Lord Chancellor banged his gavel to bring everyone back to order. "Lord Bryant," he said, "you have made your point. Perhaps we were being presumptuous in taking the role of choosing a husband for Miss Barton. But there are less absurd ways to argue your case."

"Lord Chancellor, I only find this absurd if you select a husband for her that is not me."

The Lord Chancellor coughed. "You were in earnest?"

"More earnest than I have been about anything in my life."

Diana clutched the seat in front of her. Tears pricked her eyes, and her chest filled with joyful light. People all over the hall, lords and spectators alike, craned their necks to get a good look at the woman who had finally trapped Lord Bryant into a marriage. Nate had yet to give his permission, but with such a public declaration, it would be difficult to refuse Everton now.

Which felt wonderful.

She simply needed to keep Everton from running off before the vows were said.

Several Lords now surrounded Lord Bryant, and she could see the concern in their faces as they talked to him.

"Lord Bryant—to marry?" she heard one spectator say at her side. "He has been opposed to marriage for so long."

"He doesn't seem to be the loyal type. I hope this Miss Barton knows what she has bargained for."

That comment had been said loudly enough that she was certain it was intended for her ears. She turned to the voice, an older gentleman who seemed genuinely concerned. She gave him a smile. "I know exactly what I have bargained for." She glanced at all the commotion going on around her. The incredulity and disbelief that London's most notorious bachelor was about to tie the knot with a woman of business had set everyone on edge. "It is London who will be surprised by who Lord Bryant really is."

The Lord Chancellor called for the bell to be rung for the vote. After the waiting period, votes were cast.

Her railroad line was granted an act of Parliament.

She had done it. She sank deeper into her seat in relief. She had actually done it.

CHAPTER 26

Everton closed his eyes for a moment and took in the sounds of a chamber filled with cheers. In his youth, he had dreamed of exactly this—passing an act that would cause members of Parliament to cheer. He never would have guessed that, long after losing his zeal for life, he would gain his childhood dream as a result of proposing to a woman in front of, in essence, the whole of England.

The Queen wasn't there, but Victoria would hear of it.

He found he didn't mind. Not one bit.

Hands grabbed his shoulders and shook him out of his reverie. He opened his eyes to find Lord Yolten beaming at him. "You've got a young lady and a scowly faced brother upstairs who seem to be waiting for you."

There was Diana, standing just in front of the seat she had claimed during the vote. She looked happy, or at least, he hoped she did. It was hard to tell from this distance. Interestingly enough, it wasn't hard to tell that Mr. Barton was put out. Something about the slope of his shoulders and the glare Everton could feel, rather than see, betrayed the man's emotion without getting a clear picture of his face.

Everton waved to him like a fool.

Lord Yolten clicked his tongue and shoved Everton toward the door. "I didn't mean from here. Go talk to them, you lubberwort."

Everton dashed to the doorway, stumbling through the other members of Parliament, until he reached the stairs. He jumped in front of a man about to climb the steps.

"Oi!" The man grabbed his arm, but when he noticed it was Everton—the fool who had borne his heart to Parliament—he stepped aside and gave Everton a friendly push.

Everton took the stairs two at a time, and when he reached the top, he was out of breath. Still not waiting, he found the door that would lead to the balcony Diana sat in. He pulled it open.

"Diana," he called.

Nate Barton stepped in front of Diana, even though they were still many feet away. Everton weaved his way through those trying to exit until he came up to the pair.

The muscles in Nate's jaw worked frantically. "Before we go any further, I will remind you I have not given my permission for—well—anything. I know Diana thinks the best of you, but I have a hard time understanding it." Mr. Barton—Nate—for why would he stand on ceremony with his soon to be brother-in-law—glared at their spectators, but continued. "Where were you today?" he demanded.

Everton carefully maneuvered his way past several overly interested bystanders to where Diana and Mr. Barton stood.

"I'm sorry. Truly I am." Everton reached into his breast pocket to pull out the note that had caused him so much trouble. "I was intercepted on my way into Parliament and given this note." Everton held out the note, looking back and forth between Diana and Nate before finally handing it to Diana. She stood, and he pointed to the scrawling script. "I thought it must be a hoax, but Diana, you have been telling me how much happier Mrs. Richardson has been of late. The more I thought about it, the more I realized I had to find out."

Diana skimmed the contents of the hastily scrawled note he had handed her. It was from someone named Daniels. "Do you know this Daniels?" he asked.

"No, I've never heard of him in my life." She didn't look up, and her brother leaned over her shoulder to read the note as well. "This says Mrs. Richardson is to marry Mr. Broadcreek today," Mr. Barton said.

Diana shook her head. "That is ridiculous. Mrs. Richardson knows Mr. Broadcreek is only after her railroad line."

Nate took the note from her hands. "But it is *your* railroad line now."

Lord Bryant pulled at his already crumpled cravat. "That was my thinking as well, but if he knew of your agreement to sell and split the profits once it had more value . . . Did Mrs. Richardson ever tell you the name of the man who was calling on her?"

Diana froze. Everton pushed down his desire to fold her into his arms. The swelling in his nose was only just beginning to come down. He couldn't risk another blow.

"No," Diana said. "She never did. She never even admitted there was such a man. Whoever it was, she didn't want to tell me."

"At first I thought perhaps this was a ruse to keep me away from the vote. But I couldn't deny that the note might actually be true." Everton reached for her hand and tightened his fingers around hers. "I don't know Mrs. Richardson very well, but I know she's the reason you have fought so hard to make this company successful. Knowing that, I couldn't wait for the vote. I had to ascertain whether there was any truth to this. First, I checked to see whether you or Mrs. Richardson were home. I supposed that if she had been home, I could quickly rule out the hoax and return to Parliament in plenty of time to vote."

"Was she there?"

"No one was home."

"Not even the children?"

"No, just the maid."

"Mrs. Jenkins?"

"Yes. She informed me that the children and Mrs. Richardson had, indeed, gone out, just after you left, and more importantly . . ." He released Diana's hand and pulled Mrs. Richardson's note from his other pocket. "She had left you this note."

"I don't understand this. It is too late in the day to get married, and no banns have been read." With shaking hands, Diana opened the letter and read out loud.

"Diana,

By the time I see you again, I should be happily married. I hadn't thought I could find someone after my dear Mr. Richardson left this earth, but I have. I know you will be nervous about him, as he has told me as much, but I am tired of living alone, and I'm tired of the melancholy. I want to live again. In time, I'm certain you will see that I have made the correct choice.

We will return on the morrow, and I will happily introduce you to my new husband. Please be happy for us.

All my love,

Charlotte"

Diana flipped the note over, but Everton had already checked; there were no other clues on the other side. "I cannot believe Charlotte would marry without confiding in me. Did Mrs. Jenkins tell you what time they left?"

"It wasn't until noon."

"Then they cannot be married yet." Nate took this note from Diana as well. "Marriages are only performed in the morning. Surely they're waiting until tomorrow."

Everton shook his head. If only that were true. "If he acquired a special license, they can be married anytime. They could have purposely planned to hold the wedding while we were distracted by the vote."

"But Mr. Broadcreek has been here the whole time." Diana rubbed her eyes. "Something about this scenario isn't lining up. How could he have gotten married?"

A tap on Everton's shoulder made him turn around. A page boy was holding out a note. Everton rushed to open it and discovered it was from Nelson.

I have found the happy couple. Mrs. Richardson is no more; she is now Mrs. Winston. She would like to convey her happiness and apologies to Miss Barton. Based on an encounter he had at the office, Mr. Winston was under the distinct impression that Diana didn't approve of him. But Mrs. Winston assures me he is a childhood friend who had heard of her loss and wanted to make her happy again. Which, apparently, he has done.

Nelson

Everton handed the note to Diana. She quickly skimmed its contents. "Mr. Winston." She shook her head. She sat down on the bench with a heavy sigh. "How frightening I must have been that day to cause him such trepidation." Diana reached for his hand. He happily took hers. "It is a wonder I have found myself a husband."

"He isn't your husband yet," Nate ground out through his teeth.

Everton took in the chaos still ensuing around them. It had been an exciting day in Parliament. Lord Rayleigh hadn't left the floor, but someone had joined him. They waved their arms agitatedly as they spoke to each other.

Mr. Broadcreek.

"Nate," Everton called his soon-to-be brother-in-law by name. The look on Nate's face was worth the breach in etiquette. "I wonder if you would join me downstairs for a moment."

Nate followed his eyes until they landed on Mr. Broadcreek. A grim smile rose to his lips. "That is the first sensible thing you have said all day. I would be glad to join you."

CHAPTER 27

With a nod to Lord Rayleigh, Everton and Nate each took hold of one of Mr. Broadcreek's elbows as if they had decided on it beforehand. Everton gave Lord Rayleigh a winning smile. "Pardon us while we have a quick word with your friend." Lord Rayleigh sputtered, but after eyeing Nate's thick shoulders, he clamped his mouth shut. Everton hadn't realized the man was that intelligent.

Mr. Broadcreek wriggled his arms and tried to backpedal with his feet. But it was no use. He was no match for the pair of them. Mr. Broadcreek had deceived the wrong man with that note of his today. Wrong *men*. Mr. Broadcreek had deceived the wrong *men*.

They propelled Mr. Broadcreek out of the room, despite his legs flailing backwards and a look of supplication to Lord Rayleigh. Once out of the hall, Everton pulled the note he had received that morning out of his pocket. "I believe this must be your handwriting, Mr. Broadcreek."

Mr. Broadcreek sputtered. "I didn't write that. I'm not sure what you are talking about."

"Should we remove him from the building before we rough him up or simply start now?" Everton asked Nate.

Nate shrugged. "I'm happy to rough up anyone, anywhere." He glanced pointedly at Everton's still-swollen face. "As you are well aware."

Mr. Broadcreek's eyes widened. "It's true—I didn't write it! Mr. Daniels did . . . upon my request."

"Sounds like we should remove ourselves from company first," Everton said, and Nate nodded his head.

They pushed Mr. Broadcreek out the nearest door and half dragged him away from the building. "I suggest we head away from Westminster Abbey,"

Nate said nonchalantly, as if discussing the weather. "This shouldn't be done in sight of a church."

Mr. Broadcreek yelped, but no one seemed interested in interrupting Everton and Nate. They made quite a striking figure together. Everton could get used to having family again.

He and Nate seemed to have the same destination in mind—an alleyway behind one of the buildings in front of them.

"Did you think Miss Barton would marry you if you could convince Parliament that she wasn't fit to run a company without a man?"

"I didn't say anything in Parliament." His voice rose an octave. "The House of Lords was concerned about her. You can't blame that on me."

"What do you think, Nate?" For the first time, Nate didn't wince when Everton used his Christian name. Apparently when two men were about to pound the living daylights out of a man, Christian names were appropriate. He would have to remember that. "Can we blame him?"

"I feel very comfortable blaming him. I saw the paperwork. There was no reason for any concerns to have been brought up."

They had crossed the street and were only a few steps away from the darkness they needed.

"Wait, wait. There has to be some way I can fix this."

"There is nothing to fix." Everton shrugged. "Everything turned out as it should have. Although, we feel a bit concerned about the prospect of you involving yourself in Miss Barton's life ever again." The man was a cur, taking advantage of women and only begging for mercy once men were involved.

Darkness enshrouded them. With a silent nod, Nate dropped Mr. Broadcreek's arm and shoved him forward. Then he proceeded to remove his jacket and gloves.

"You are removing your gloves?" Everton asked.

Nate folded them and placed them neatly on top of his jacket on a clean spot in the street. "They are new. I would hate to stain them."

Mr. Broadcreek gulped. There was no other word for it. Nate rolled up his sleeves and returned his grip to Mr. Broadcreek's arm.

Everton removed his jacket. "I'm going to leave my gloves on. They are due to be replaced, and I'd rather not sully my hands with the blood of a rat like this one."

Everton cracked the knuckles of one of his hands and shook it out a bit, dancing on his toes. It had been much too long since he had been in a back-alley scuffle. The closest he had come was when he had let Nate hit him, and that didn't really count. "This will be quite fun."

"I'll stay away from her!" Mr. Broadcreek said, squirming about in Nate's arms. "I'm a busy man; I have no reason to ever see her again."

Everton paused. He glanced up at Nate. His lips were scrunched to one side in consideration. "How much trouble has this man caused Diana in the past months?"

Mr. Broadcreek swallowed. Nate dropped his arm and balled his own substantial hands into fists. Mr. Broadcreek eyed the opening to the alleyway, but there was no way he could escape the two of them, and he knew it.

Nate cracked the bones in his neck. "I took the time to speak with Mrs. Richardson yesterday afternoon. It seems some of Diana's jewelry is missing."

"I didn't take it."

"Mrs. Richardson—I mean, Mrs. Winston believes that Diana had to sell it for some reason. Can you think of a reason Diana would have to sell off her jewelry?"

Nate didn't wait for an answer, instead plummeting his fist into Mr. Broadcreek's abdomen. Mr. Broadcreek gasped.

"Hey," Everton pouted, touching his still-sore nose. "Why did you hit me in the *face*?"

Nate turned to him. "Because your face makes me angry."

"And Mr. Broadcreek's stomach makes you angry?"

"Everything about him makes me angry." Nate cocked his fist back again.

"Now, wait a minute." Everton placed a hand on his shoulder. "I haven't even had a chance to dirty my gloves yet."

Mr. Broadcreek was still doubled over, trying to catch his breath. He held out his hand and shook his head. "I think . . ." he said, sucking in more air. "I think I may know why she had to sell that jewelry."

Everton paused. "Why?"

"She was late on an order of ballast, and although I cannot claim full responsibility for that, I may have distracted her a bit on the day her payment was due. She most likely had to pay an exorbitant sum for faster shipping."

"She most likely had to?" Nate asked.

Mr. Broadcreek's snakelike eyes slithered back and forth between the two of them. "She had to. I spoke to the ballast company owner myself. I know how much it cost. If the two of you would simply let me go without further harm, I will pay it myself. *Please*. I wasn't built for physical violence."

Everton swore under his breath. He had been looking forward to punching the man. He stepped closer to Mr. Broadcreek. "How much was it?"

"One hundred and forty pounds."

Everton cocked back his fist and slammed it just above where Nate had landed his first blow. Mr. Broadcreek doubled over, grabbing his stomach.

Everton dusted off his hands. "I'll pay it myself."

"If I so much as hear that you have been near my sister again . . ." Nate paused.

"You will be on the next boat to New South Wales," Everton finished for him. "If you are lucky."

Mr. Broadcreek hadn't excelled in the railroad business without understanding a good deal when it was presented to him. "Of course," he panted, still bent over. "Of course, I understand. I won't go within a mile of that office."

"Good," Nate said.

"Now, that wasn't so hard, was it?" Everton asked. "As long as everyone sticks to ethical business practices, I see no reason why we cannot all get along."

Nate picked up his jacket and gloves. "My gloves stayed fresh, and yours won't need to be replaced for a while yet."

"All in all, a successful day," Everton agreed.

The three of them stepped out of the alley and into the sunlight. Diana was standing not far from the Parliament building. Mr. Broadcreek—his arms curled about his stomach—took one look at her and pointedly turned the other way.

Nate chuckled. "Looks as though we have some good news to tell Diana."

"I should have taken care of him long ago."

Diana was wringing her hands but looked decidedly less concerned than she had before the two of them stepped back into the light. Mr. Broadcreek had left on his own two feet, and apparently, that was reassuring to her. Everton wasn't one hundred percent sure he agreed.

Nate looked back and forth between his sister and Everton. With a deep sigh, Nate returned the gloves to his hands. "Why don't you tell her?"

"Me?"

"Yes, you were the one who was here for her as she worked to build up her business. I was home, happily enjoying life with my wife, while Diana was struggling with the likes of Mr. Broadcreek. Go tell her she needn't worry about him anymore. I will be waiting in the carriage."

Everton didn't wait for him to change his mind. He jogged across the courtyard and took Diana's hand in his own. A small side garden bordered the churchyard, and he steered her toward it.

"You let Mr. Broadcreek go?"

"Of course we did. We are reasonable gentlemen."

"You are?"

"We are, and what's more, Nate convinced him to never interfere with your company again."

"He did? How did he do that?"

"By removing his gloves, I believe."

Diana laughed.

"But I do have some bad news." Diana's brows pinched, so he hurried on. "I owe you one hundred and forty pounds, and I am going to have to ask you to not question me about it." He flexed his hand, still sore from the punch he had landed. "I promise you, it was money well spent."

She tipped her head to one side, not missing the movement of his hand. "All right."

"You aren't going to argue with me about it?"

"Why would I? I know you are one of the wealthiest men in London. I'm guessing I don't want to know how you came to be in my debt."

"You probably don't."

"After what transpired in Parliament today, I guess we should consider ourselves engaged."

"I guess we should."

"No cold feet?"

Everton shook his head. "My feet are decidedly warm."

Diana threw her hands around his neck.

"Diana."

"Yes."

"You might need to remove your arms from about my neck. Anyone could see us."

Diana raised an eyebrow. "And . . . ?"

"I'm trying to change my ways to prove to London that I'm worthy of you."

"That might take a while. I'm not sure I am willing to wait."

"We won't be rushing to the altar. I need to give you some time to make sure you don't want to change your mind."

Diana laughed. "I don't need time. I know I won't change my mind."

Everton pushed back a lock of Diana's hair that had tumbled out of her bonnet. "I need the time. I need to be certain you will be happy with me."

"If you need time, I will be patient. But I plan on convincing you as soon as possible." Diana traced a finger over his swollen nose. "Although, it's probably a good idea to wait and see how your nose turns out after the swelling goes down."

Everton laughed. If it weren't so inappropriate, he would kiss her for that comment. But they were out on the streets of London and only possibly engaged. Nate had not officially approved yet, and Everton wanted to speak to her mother. Not to mention, her brother's very large fists would be waiting for him if he ever got out of line. "Would you prefer that it healed crooked or straight?"

"I don't very much care."

And then, before he could even think to stop her, Diana rose onto her toes and brushed a soft kiss on his lips. Her eyes sparked with mischief when her heels hit the walkway.

"Diana, nothing is officia—"

She popped up and kissed him again.

"You might change your—"

Her heels didn't even touch the ground before she kissed him one more time. This time, she wrapped her arms around his neck and gave him the chance to enjoy it. Her lips were soft against his but not hesitant. They were confident, just like she was. As if they had a mind of their own, his arms reached around her back to pull her tightly against him. She might be confident, but he still needed to be reassured that this vibrant woman was actually willing to share his life with him. She pulled away but left her arms about his neck just as he was beginning to believe it could be true.

"If your brother sees us . . ." Everton didn't need to finish that sentence.

Diana smiled at him, her head still conveniently tilted to one side. "Nothing could be more scandalous than proposing to me in the middle of Parliament. Nate will be all right. He knows what love is."

Heaven forgive him, he had never been able to deny this woman what she wanted. He pulled her to him and lowered his mouth to hers. There was no hesitancy, no fear, and no guile. Diana sighed into him, and he tucked her closer to his chest. It was scandalous really, to kiss a woman outside the halls of Parliament. And yet, nothing about this moment felt wrong. Diana—his own goddess of hope—was to be his wife. His days of brandy watching and scandalizing women were over.

He pulled away. "You know . . . I really did enjoy helping those women . . ."

Diana pursed her lips together and narrowed one eye. "We will find another way to help them."

"I thought my plan worked rather well. What are we to do now if a young lady needs to damage her reputation a bit?

"Then she can come help me in the office."

"And if she needs to have her prospects raised?"

"Then she may become our friend."

Everton laughed and pulled her back to him. His chin rested on the top of her hair, and she nestled into his chest as if she had always belonged there. His life had changed the moment this woman had come barging into his study dripping and desperate for his help. He had been bitter, broken, and determined to live out the rest of his life as a sorry shadow of a man. He wrapped his arms tighter around Diana. Thanks to her, his future lay open before him, and it was as fearless, bright, and exhilarating as the woman he was holding.

EPILOGUE

Diana opened the nursery door, careful not to make any noise. She peered into the room and found Everton and little Hope exactly where she thought they would be. Hope's head and mop of black hair were tucked directly under Everton's chin, her darling little outstretched arms rested on either side of Everton's neck. Everton's eyes were closed, and from the tilt of his head and stillness of the rocking chair, he had, once again, fallen asleep with their daughter nestled into him. Diana couldn't help but smile. Marriage had tamed his reputation some, but many of the people of London still saw him as a complete scoundrel.

They had obviously never seen him sleeping.

She set the package that had just arrived on the bookcase and silently made her way to her husband's side. She pushed the fallen lock of hair off his forehead and traced her finger along his brow and down his perfectly straight nose. His eyes opened with a blink, and the corners of his mouth curled upward at the sight of her.

"Sorry to wake you," Diana said. He shook his head slowly to let her know it was fine. "Let me put Hope to bed. You are spoiling her, you know. She needs to learn to sleep in her cradle."

"I know," Everton said with no remorse in his eyes. He may have known it, but he wasn't about to change his daily routine of rocking with Hope in the afternoon. Diana couldn't blame him. And besides, if he did stop, she wouldn't have the pleasure of watching the two of them sleep.

"We just received a parcel from Baimbury. I assumed it would be for me, but it is addressed to both of us."

Everton nodded, but his eyes started to close again. "And were you able to visit with Mrs. Cuthbert?"

"I was."

"Any news?"

"She did mention that coprolite has become a sudden rage. Apparently Lord Silverstone gave Lady Emily—Lady Silverstone now, I suppose—a ring with an enormous polished chunk of it set in a crown of diamonds. They had found it together on their estate. She seems to be quite proud of it."

Everton chuckled, sleep finally starting to leave his eyes. Diana bent over to pick up Hope. The past two months with her in their lives had opened both of their hearts in ways she hadn't realized were possible. She placed a kiss on Everton's forehead, then wrapped her arms around her daughter.

Hope stretched her arms and neck with a few soft, squeaking groans. Her green eyes, a deeper shade than Everton's, blinked open for a moment just before she settled into Diana's arms.

She crossed the room and laid Hope down in her cradle. By the time she returned, Everton was standing by the bookcase. He picked up the parcel and examined it. "What would Nate and Grace be sending us?"

"Let's open it and see." Diana took the package from him and untied the string. Inside the outer box was a smaller one. One corner of the interior box was smashed, and the top was indented. She put the packaging back on the bookcase and showed Everton the fragile box. His eyes widened as he took the box from her. It was small enough to fit into the palm of his hand. His fingers softly caressed the broken edges.

"Do you know what it is?" Diana asked, leaning forward so she could see.

Everton nodded. He opened the top of the box, but the only thing she could see was a folded piece of paper. He opened the paper and glanced at it, a quirk of his lip turning up before handing the note to her.

It was short, and it wasn't Grace's or Nate's handwriting.

For your firstborn. May you cherish every moment with the child and each other.

"Did you write this?" It was definitely Everton's bold, scrawling hand. But how had it managed to end up in a package from Nate and Grace?

"Yes," Everton said, but he didn't look up at her. He was still looking inside the box. "I never thought I would see these again." He reached inside and pulled out a pair of ornately knitted booties. "These were made by my grandmother."

"How did my brother end up with them?"

"I gave them to him as a wedding gift."

"You gave Nate baby booties as a wedding gift?"

Everton walked backwards until he found himself in front of the rocking chair once again and sat down. "I never thought—" He rubbed one hand along the bottom of his chin, then kneaded each of his eyes. "I never thought I would get the chance to use them."

Diana rushed to him. He dropped the box and booties into his lap and wrapped his arms around her waist. His head pressed into her middle. She stroked his hair as he breathed heavily into her dress.

He pulled her tighter and shook his head against her. "Thank you."

Diana knelt and laid her hands on Everton's cheeks. "You were always meant to be a father."

"I don't know if that is true, but I do feel as if I was meant to be Hope's father. And I never would have been without you."

Diana smiled and kissed each of his eyelids. "Then it's a good thing that when I needed a man to ruin me, I thought of you."

His smile tightened, and he narrowed one eye. "Were there any other candidates?"

Diana racked her brain to think of any other rake she could tease him with, but she couldn't come up with a single one. "No, you have always been the only man I thought of."

"I was a rather obvious choice, though. I did make quite a career of it."

She shook her head. "You did, didn't you?"

Everton took a deep breath and ran his fingers down the careful knitting of the cream-colored booties. "Never has a man been so happy to settle down as I."

Diana pulled Everton's face toward her, the chair rocking him forward, and kissed him on the mouth. Diana wasn't certain she would call their lives settled. They still owned Richardson Rail, and between the business and Everton's parliamentary duties, life was always throwing them surprises.

But surprises also seemed to bring the best rewards. She scooped up the booties and the box and set them on the floor, then crawled into Everton's lap. The arm of the rocking chair dug into her back, but she didn't care. Everton tightened his arms around her ribcage and found her mouth with his own. She twisted just enough to get her arms around his neck and into his hair. He placed an arm below her knees and stood. He carried her to the door of the nursery but then had to set her down to open it.

She didn't give him the chance, instead wrapping both his arms around her waist. He pressed his forehead against hers for the briefest of moments before capturing her mouth once again. Sleep—it appeared—was now far from his thoughts. His lips found the hollow of her throat. She had discovered not long after their marriage that it was a favorite spot of his. She lifted her chin and he inhaled deeply. As if breathing in her scent gave him life. He yanked open the nursery door and pulled her out of the room. His mouth returned to her lips as they clumsily made their way down the corridor.

Diana smiled against him. Even if he hadn't been as terrible as all of London had thought, Diana wouldn't have known it from his kisses. In that aspect, at least, Everton had always lived up to his reputation.

ABOUT THE AUTHOR

ESTHER HATCH GREW UP ON a cherry orchard in rural Utah. After high school, she alternated living in Russia to teach children English and attending Brigham Young University in order to get a degree in archaeology. She began writing when one of her favorite authors invited her to join a critique group. The only catch was she had to be a writer. Not one to be left out of an opportunity to socialize and try something new, she started on her first novel that week. Now she is an award-winning author—*A Proper Scandal* even won the Forward INDIES Silver Medal for Romance.

Follow Esther on social media:

Facebook: facebook.com/authorestherhatch
Instagram: instagram.com/authorestherhatch
Twitter: twitter.com/esther_hatch
Website: estherhatch.com/